KAT DUBOIS CHRONICLES

Books 1 - 3

LINDSEY FAIRLEIGH

Rubus Press

Editing by Sarah Kolb-Williams
www.kolbwilliams.com

Cover by Molly Phipps
www.wegotyoucoveredbookdesign.com

ISBN 9798609442420

ALSO BY LINDSEY FAIRLEIGH

ECHO TRILOGY

Echo in Time

Resonance

Time Anomaly

Dissonance

Ricochet Through Time

KAT DUBOIS CHRONICLES

Ink Witch

Outcast

Underground

Soul Eater

Judgement

Afterlife

THE ENDING SERIES

The Ending Series Origin Stories

After The Ending

Into The Fire

Out Of The Ashes

Before The Dawn

World Before: A Collection of Stories

ATLANTIS LEGACY

Sacrifice of the Sinners

Legacy of the Lost

Fate of the Fallen

Dreams of the Damned

For more information on Lindsey and her books:

www.lindseyfairleigh.com

To read Lindsey's books as she writes them, check her out on Patreon:

https://www.patreon.com/lindseyfairleigh

Join Lindsey's mailing list to stay up to date on releases

AND to get a FREE copy of *Sacrifice of the Sinners.*

www.lindseyfairleigh.com/sacrifice

INK WITCH

Book One

For Greg and the rest of the guys in the shop.
Thank you.

CHAPTER ONE

"Same question as last time?" I stared across a round table at my Friday night regular, Rita. She was pretty, trendy, and young enough that hanging out in a fortune-teller's studio having her cards read on what was most Seattleites' go-wild night out struck me as a little odd. Especially considering that Rita always asked the same thing: will I fall in love this week? Maybe, but she wouldn't find it in the back of my tattoo parlor, where I moonlighted with my tarot deck. I didn't even need my cards to tell her that.

If I had fifty bucks for every time somebody asked me a variation of the love question . . . well, actually, I did have a fifty for every time, and it more than paid the bills. Nine out of ten clients returned, because I'm that good. Because my cards are legit; made them myself. Because I'm a Nejeret, a god of time. Or a goddess—and I'm really more of a demigoddess, if we're getting technical, descended from the ancient Egyptian god, Re—and my soul is jacked into the time stream. Sort of.

Rita sighed, resting her chin on her palm and tapping the side of her jaw with nails polished a vibrant indigo. "I guess I'm pretty predictable," she said, laughing dryly.

"Only you and the rest of humanity . . ." A species I didn't belong to anymore—hadn't for nearly two decades. I shuffled my hand-drawn deck of tarot cards one more time, then slid it across the pentagram seared into the tabletop. The symbol was purely atmospheric, but clients appreciated the witchy vibe. "Cut," I told Rita.

She straightened and reached for the deck, picking up a little less than a third and setting it next to the larger stack of cards. "You know, Kat," she said, flashing me a sly smile, crimson lipstick stark against her straight, white teeth, "I've got a good feeling about this reading."

She leaned forward as I retrieved the cards and stacked them to shuffle a few more times. All the shuffling was really for show; the only part of my routine that actually affected the reading was Rita touching the cards. So long as they contacted her skin—her DNA—the spread would fall the same way regardless of whether I shuffled the cards five times or fifty. It's not magic, exactly. Magic doesn't exist, not really. But what I can do—what my people, the Nejerets, can do, tapping into the primal universal energies—is as close of a thing to magic as exists in the real world.

"I've got a good feeling, too," I said, tapping the edge of the cards on the table to straighten out the deck and flashing Rita a quicker, slyer smile. Not that I could actually sense anything from the deck. That wasn't my gift. But Rita didn't know that, and it wouldn't hurt her to have a little faith. My gift lies in the ink itself. Anything I draw has a tendency to take on a life of its own, revealing hidden truths about the past, present, and future, connecting dots that otherwise seemed unrelated.

I set out five cards in a cross formation, then added a column of three cards on the right and one over the center of the cross. And frowned. I'd done this layout thousands of times, but this time it was different. Not because the pattern was strange, but because the designs on the cards were. They'd changed themselves. Again. It hadn't happened in nearly a year, and with the way my life had been plodding along—the definition of predictable—I wasn't expecting the change.

"Is this a new deck?" Rita was craning her neck to look at the cards. She'd been coming to me for six months now, maybe a little longer, and she'd seen every card in the deck at least once. "They look . . ." She tilted her head to the side, eyes squinting. "I don't know . . . darker?"

I shook my head and glanced at her briefly before resuming my study of the cards. "It's the same deck. I just tweaked them a bit." It was a lie. They'd tweaked themselves.

The designs on the cards were actually a reflection of me—of *my* past, present, and future. They'd gone through three major overhauls since I first created them a couple years ago, always when something major was causing upheaval in my life, but they'd been relatively static for the past year or so. Probably because *I'd* been relatively static during that time. It didn't bode well for whatever was to come. I suddenly felt like a live wire, channeling so much sickening dread that my body practically hummed with it. Something would happen, and soon, and there was nothing I could do to stop it.

And there wasn't a single doubt in my mind that it *wouldn't* be a happy something. The cards had taken on an edgier, almost ominous aesthetic. Only heightening the effect was the fact that all of the people depicted on the cards were real people. My family and friends. I hadn't designed the cards that way, and the appearance of familiar faces disturbed me intensely, though I couldn't put my finger on why.

Lex, my half-sister, was depicted as the High Priestess, serene and wise and as unconcerned about the wisps of darkness reaching out for her from one edge of the card as she was about the wisps of light from the other. She also appeared on the Lovers card alongside her husband, Heru. The Hanged Man was my half-brother and mentor in all things lethal and dark, Dominic, all but his pale, haunting face shrouded in shadows. The only card in the spread that I appeared on was Justice—I was dressed in jeans and a leather jacket, wielding a glowing, crystalline sword in one hand and a golden set of scales in the other.

Disturbed but determined to finish the reading, I focused on the task at hand. Even though the designs on the cards were linked to my soul, the spread—this spread—was all Rita. And there was zero question in my mind that it answered her question. For once, the cards addressed Rita's love life in full.

Sitting back in my chair, the violet, velvet armchair I'd inherited from my mom along with the rest of the shop, I rested my hand on the bulbous ends of the chair's arms and studied Rita's features, trying to gauge her mood. "This is the clearest reading I've done in a long time," I told her. "The cards are split half and half—there's good news, and there's bad news. Which do you want first?"

Rita pursed her lips, then twitched that perfect crimson pucker from left to right and back. "Bad news first." She raised her hand, stopping me before I could start. "No, good news first." She nodded to herself as she leaned forward, placing her elbows on the edge of the table, fingers tangling together. "Good news first," she repeated.

I returned her nod and touched my fingertips to the Two of Cups, then to the Ten of Cups and the Lovers. "These three cards indicate that love is very nearby, and that your partner will make you happier than you ever could've hoped for. This card," I said, touching the Six of Cups, "tells us the person you're destined to be with will be someone you already know, likely someone from your past, possibly even from as far back as your childhood."

"I'm in love with you," Rita blurted before I could warn her that, according to the Three of Swords, Ten of Swords, Hanged Man, and Justice cards, this person would sweep in to mend her very recently broken heart. Which, apparently, I was about to break.

Well, this is awkward. I shut my mouth, pressing my lips together, and stared at Rita. Her hopeful expression, her flushed cheeks, her bright eyes—this, right here, is why I don't do love. Love is pain and disappointment. It's a blip of joy with a massive hangover of misery. I choose not to feel any of those things, not anymore.

I inhaled slowly, tapping the tips of my fingers in a restrained, steady rhythm on the arm's cutting. "Rita . . . I think we should call it a night. I've got a big job in the morning." A clean break was best. The last thing I wanted to do was give her mixed signals and prolong her agony.

"We could get food, order delivery . . . ?" The hopeful glint in her eyes had faded a little, but she wasn't ready to give up yet. "Or I can cook?"

"Listen, Rita—"

"Is it because I'm a woman? You're not attracted to me?" She was pressing her fingertips into the tabletop so hard that her nails were bleaching of color. "But Jeff at the Goose said he'd seen you leave with both men and women, and I thought, you know, we always have such a nice time on these Friday night dates, and—"

I stiffened. "These aren't dates, Rita." My voice was cold, hard, and Rita flinched at my words. "You make an appointment, you come here, and you pay me for a service." She wasn't the first client to read too much into our relationship—the misperception of friendship, or *more* in Rita's case, was bound to happen when clients shared so much of their personal lives with me—but Rita's profession of love had still taken me by surprise. I was irritated with myself; I was usually better at reading people. Mostly for the sole purpose of avoiding situations like this.

Tears welled in Rita's eyes, spilling over the brim of her eyelids and leaving behind a gray trail of mascara. "But the cards—you said . . ." Her chin trembled, and she covered her mouth with her hand. "Oh God, I've never been so embarrassed in my life."

I scooted my armchair back enough that I could stand. "I'm sorry for that," I said, forcing the words out. I pushed myself up using the armrests and, standing, gathered up the cards. "I'll walk you out." I cleared my throat. "No charge for tonight's reading."

Rita nodded, though she didn't look at me. It was a relief. She slid her chair back and stood.

The tarot studio was in the back of my tattoo parlor, Ninth Life Ink. Back in my mom's day, the place was a retail shop called the Goddess's Blessing selling all things mystical and witchy. But that was years ago, before a war between Nejerets claimed her life, leaving all of her worldly possessions to an eighteen-year-old—me. The Ninth Life had been open for a little over three years now, offering ink to those desiring it and fortunes to those looking for something a little bit more ethereal.

I moved through a heavy beaded curtain of quartz, amethyst, and moonstone that had been around since my mom's time and made my way into the main part of the shop, crystals clanking and Rita sniffling in the background. Rita's kitten heels clacked quietly on the hardwood floor as she followed me across the tattoo shop to the glass front door. I unlocked the deadbolt and opened it for her. She left, head hanging and feet dragging.

"Again, Rita," I said, watching her linger under the covered stoop on the sidewalk outside, "I'm really sorry for the misunderstanding, and I wish you the best. Something good *is* coming your way." *It's just not me,* I thought blandly.

Her head moved in the barest of nods, and she shuffled away.

I shut and locked the door, then wandered around the reception desk to close up shop for the night. I paused to pull out my phone and open my music app, scrolling through playlists until I found one that suited my mood—vintage alternative rock. Some Nirvana, Foo Fighters, and Third Eye Blind was exactly what the doctor ordered. I set the playlist to shuffle and, once the music started blaring over the shop's speakers, closed my eyes and tilted my head back, soaking in the manly angst.

Feeling recharged, I set to work closing out the register. I was just printing out the credit card report for the day when the shop door opened, jingling the little copper bell hanging over the door.

Had I forgotten to lock up after letting Rita out? I was usually pretty good about it when I had after-hours clients, but I'd forgotten a time or two. Except I distinctly remembered turning the deadbolt.

Not that it mattered; there wasn't a lock in the world that could've kept out the man who'd just walked into my shop. He was on the taller side, and athletic, his broad shoulders only emphasized by his long, black leather jacket. His dark brown hair was styled in an undercut, the sides buzzed and the longer top portion combed back loosely. His face belonged to an angel . . . or a fallen angel . . . or a statue of a fallen angel, with all those bold lines, chiseled angles, and that insanely strong jawline covered in a couple days' worth of stubble. A large, brushed silver belt buckle emblazoned with a black Eye of Horus drew my gaze to his trim hips. He was proclaiming his Nejeret clan affiliation pretty boldly with that buckle—Clan Heru all the way. Nobody who knows what they're looking for—and what he is—could miss it.

The intruder stopped a few feet in from the door, his pale blue eyes locked on me. "Hey, Kitty Kat." The corner of his mouth quirked, curving his lips into a confident smirk. "Been a while."

I didn't think. I reacted.

Hands on the counter, I leapt over the top, sliding on my hip until my boots landed on the floor on the other side. I crouched, bending my knees, then sprang at him. I landed one solid smack against his cheek, the force of the hit jarring my whole arm, and then it was a game of striking and blocking, then striking and blocking again. Neither of us held back, and it felt amazing. It had been ages since I'd lost myself in a fight. Too long. Not long enough.

He could've ended it at any time. His brand of "magic" would've allowed him to wrap me up in unbreakable, otherworldly bonds. But the light in his eyes, the vibrancy turning his pale blue irises into burning, gaseous flames, told me he didn't want this to end. Not yet.

He kneed me in the stomach, knocking the wind out of me, then grabbed hold of my ponytail and jerked my head back so he could see my face. "And here I thought you'd be out of practice." His tongue darted out to catch the blood seeping from his broken lip.

"Never," I said through gritted teeth, right before my hand shot out. I gripped his groin through his jeans, fingers viselike.

He grunted, releasing my hair and doubling over. My hand slid off his jeans as he moved, the friction burning the tips of my fingers. Off-balance, I stumbled to one knee.

I pulled myself up with a hand on the edge of the counter. Breathing hard, I straightened my ponytail. "Why are you here, Nik?"

Nik was someone I'd considered an ally a long time ago. Maybe I'd even considered him a friend, but that was before he'd disappeared without a word several years back and nobody had heard from him since. He'd risked his own life to save mine, and then he'd vanished.

I crossed my arms over my chest and glared at him. "Why now?"

Slowly, Nik straightened, wiping the blood from his mouth with the pad of his thumb and giving it a quick, dismissive glance. He'd be healed soon enough—relative immortality was a bonus to being a Nejeret, thanks to our regenerative abilities. It keeps us healthy and young-looking, permanently in the prime of life. In Nik's case, he appeared to be in his mid-twenties. I wasn't so lucky; I would be forever eighteen.

Nik returned my stare, breathing just as hard. "It's Dom—he's missing."

My heart stumbled a few beats at the thought that my half-brother was in some kind of trouble, but I held my head high and redoubled my glaring efforts. "Dom's a big boy," I said. "He can take care of himself." More than—Dominic l'Aragne wasn't just my half-brother; he was also the one who'd trained me. He was one of the most careful and disciplined people I'd ever met, not to mention one of the deadliest. He was also, hands-down, the person I trusted most in the world. If something had happened to him . . .

A seed of dread settled in my stomach. I could feel the roots growing, the branches spreading, the trunk thickening. I balled my hands into fists, appreciating the sting from my nails digging into my palms. Dom was too strong—too smart and skilled—for anything to have happened to him.

"He's been missing for three weeks," Nik said.

That tree of dread spread out, its sickening branches extending into every part of me. But I couldn't accept the possibility that someone could get the better of Dom. The thought disgusted me, and I refused to even consider it. "You were gone for three *years*," I deflected.

Nik shrugged, the motion lazy. "Still would be, but when my mom told me about Dom, well . . ."

My eyes narrowed. "You talked to your mom?" I scoffed and shook my head. "So she found you. Nice of her to tell me you're alive."

Nik's pierced brow arched higher. "The way she tells it, she's been trying to get ahold of you. Maybe if you answered your damn phone every once in a while."

"Well, she could've left a message." I held my glare for a second longer, but shame pushed my gaze down to the floor. I hadn't spoken to his mother, Aset, in over a year. In fact, I hadn't spoken to Dom or Lex or anyone else from our clan in at least that long, and not because they hadn't tried. Though their efforts had certainly waned. They didn't try nearly as hard to get ahold of me as they used to. But after the things I'd done . . . they were better off without me. "I've been busy," I said, fully aware of the lame excuse.

Nik laughed under his breath, then turned, wandering to the nearest open doorway to get a look at the tattoo chair, stool, and desk within the semiprivate room. There were four such "offices" in the shop, each rented out by a different artist, aside from my own private room. This one belonged to a guy named Sampson.

"Yeah," Nik said, walking all the way into the room. "Me too. I've been real busy."

I rolled my eyes and shook my head. "Fine, whatever," I said, leaning against the counter. "So what's the deal? Why are you here, now? Why are *you* the one telling me about Dom?" So far as I knew, the two had never been close.

"Everybody else is too busy searching for him," he said from within the office. "Which they should've come to you about earlier, except I'm pretty sure they don't know about your little moonlighting gig." He was quiet for a moment. "And I'm not talking about fortune-telling."

My eyebrows rose, and I made my way to Sampson's office. "But *you* do?"

"You find people, Kat. You find people nobody else can."

I stood in the doorway, leaning my shoulder against the doorframe. "How perceptive of you," I said dryly. "How long have you been spying on me?" I was both irritated and flattered at the prospect. But mostly irritated.

"What I can't figure out," Nik said, ignoring my question, "is how you do it."

I wasn't really sure how it worked, either—the magic, so to speak, was in the ink; that was about all I knew. So I gave Nik a dose of his own medicine and ignored his question. "Why hasn't Heru gone after him? Or Mei?" Both were Nejerets with the innate ability to make spatial shifts, and it wasn't beyond their power to focus on a person rather than a place and jump to their target's side in the blink of an eye. Theoretically, either of them should have been able to find Dom by simply thinking about him, then shifting.

Nik glanced at me, elbows folded behind his head. The light from the streetlamps and traffic lights on Broadway shone through the slits of the blinds, making an eerie pattern across Nik's face. "Don't you think they've tried? Dom's not the first Nejeret to go missing. The Senate sent him and a few others out on a mission to find the missing Nejerets—ones even Heru and Mei couldn't find. Mari's among the missing." Mari, my old partner in crime, was as tough as they come. And as powerful.

I swallowed sudden nausea. "Doesn't that mean—" I licked my

lips and took a deep breath. "If Heru and Mei can't find them, wouldn't that suggest that they're dead?"

"Most likely," Nik said. "That's what the Senate thinks, at least. But I've been around longer than most of them . . . long enough to know there are limits to our powers. There's always a chance that something is blocking them. I figured it couldn't hurt for you to try, especially since it's Dom . . ."

I crossed my arms once more. "Yeah, okay," I said, nodding. "I'll do it."

CHAPTER TWO

"You fascinate me, Kitty Kat." Nik gave the shop a quick scan. "When did you become so interesting?"

Those words were funny, coming from him. Real name Nekure, Nik is one of the ancients of our kind. He's I-don't-have-a-clue-how-many thousands of years old and easily the most interesting person *I've* ever met. His mother is Aset, the real-life woman the ancient Egyptian goddess Isis was based on—twin sister to Heru, the real-life man behind the god Horus. Nik's father was some now-dead Nejeret who abducted and raped his mom. I've never heard him given a name.

Nik was the first ever of our kind to be born of two Nejerets—the females of our species are infertile once their immortal traits manifest—and as such, he was born with an additional piece to his soul, a *sheut*, which made him not quite a god, but not just a Nejeret, either. At the time of his birth, he was something new, something more.

All Nejerets are born with a *ba*, the part of our soul that enables us to live forever—so long as we don't get ourselves killed. But not Nik. He was different, the first to be born with a *sheut*, the rare part of a soul that gives its bearer seemingly magical powers. Others came after him—even I had a *sheut* now, a gift from the new gods, who've since abandoned us—but Nik has had the most practice with his, not to mention he played host to one of the old gods in his body for several thousand years.

I have no idea all that he can do with his *sheut*, but I imagine it must be more than he's ever let on. But then, he's never been very open, always hiding behind a wall of sarcasm and smirks. Even when we were close, or close-ish, he'd wielded his attitude like a sword, keeping me at a distance. I was just a young, cursed Nejeret. He was the closest thing left on this earth to a god. I was hardly worth his time, as he'd made so abundantly clear over the years. So how the hell could *I* fascinate *him*?

I stared at the shop's glass door a moment longer, then turned away—from the door and from Nik—and retreated behind the counter to finish the evening tasks. I left the music on as I closed out the register, counting the cash and checks and stashing it all in a zippered bank deposit bag. Somehow, I managed to do it all without looking at Nik despite him watching me from the other side of the counter.

"You grew up," he said.

My heartbeat picked up for a few beats, and I paused in folding up the long credit card report. I couldn't help a quick glance at him. He was just standing there, arms crossed over his chest and pale eyes scrutinizing. I continued folding the receipt tape. "You and I both know *that's* not possible." Thanks to a hasty decision made two decades ago, I was stuck in an eighteen-year-old's body. It was *my* body, always had been and always would be. Teenage hormones and all.

Nik tutted me. "Literal *and* bitter . . . what trick will she do next?"

Closing my eyes, I took a deep breath. While I would never grow into a fully mature adult physically, I was fairly certain Nik's growth was stunted in a much less tangible way. For as long as I'd known him, he'd had the emotional maturity of a frog—and that was probably being harsh. To the frog.

I placed the folded-up credit card receipt into the deposit bag, tucked it under my arm, and picked up my tarot deck and phone, turning off the music with a tap of my finger. "So . . ." I looked at Nik across the counter. "You delivered your message."

"I did."

I rounded the end of the counter and headed toward the beaded curtain. "Isn't it time for you to disappear?" It was what he was best at.

"I was thinking I'd stick around for a bit," he said. "Maybe help you with the Dom situation."

I clenched my jaw. The last time we'd worked together, it hadn't ended well. "I work alone," I said as I passed through the curtain with a clacking of stone beads and turned to the right, angling toward the door to the stairway that led up to the second-floor apartment.

"Fine." He was following me, practically walking on my heels. "Can I at least crash here tonight? The trip wasn't exactly planned."

I yanked the door to the stairs open. "It's not too late to catch the last ferry. Go stay with your mom on Bainbridge."

"Yeah . . . no."

I stomped up the stairs. "There are hundreds of hotels in this city."

"I'm afraid of bed bugs."

I chuckled without meaning to and caught myself as soon as I noticed I was doing it.

"Kitty Kat . . ."

"Fine," I snapped. "One night. You can sleep on the couch." I twisted the knob of the door at the top of the stairs and pushed it open a few inches, then hesitated. "I, um, don't usually bring people up here." And by usually, I meant *ever*.

Nik leaned in, and when he spoke, his breath tickled the hairs at the back of my neck. "Lucky me." His voice was low, vibrating with a deep thrum that resonated through me.

My breath caught, and I shivered. "Can you *not* do that?" I said, glancing at him over my shoulder.

"Do what?" he asked, eyes opened wide, innocent as a preacher's daughter.

"Be yourself. Can you just *not*?"

A Cheshire grin spread across his face.

Rolling my eyes, I pushed the door open the rest of the way and walked into the barren living room, noticing things that hadn't stood out to me in years. The only furniture in the room was a couch pushed up against one wall so I had room to move through my daily routine of mixed martial arts poses . . . which had been taught to me by Dom. Several cardboard boxes were piled up against the opposite wall. They'd been there unopened for so long that I no longer had any idea what they contained.

I placed my tarot deck on the kitchen table as I passed it on my way to the hallway. "I'll be right back."

My bedroom was the second doorway on the right—a corner room that had once belonged to my mom. My old bedroom was behind the first door; now it functioned as my personal office, my sanctuary where I experimented with my *sheut* power as well as stored everything relating to the missing persons cases I worked on for private clients. I pulled the door shut all the way as I passed. I didn't want Nik to go in there. I didn't want him in the apartment at all, but I wanted him in *there* least of all.

I stored the deposit bag in the safe in my bedroom closet, swapped my tank top for one not smeared with drying blood from our impromptu scuffle, then headed back out to the living area. Nik was in the kitchen, scoping out the contents of my fridge.

"Eat whatever you want."

"That's easy to say when there's nothing to eat." Nik pulled out a Chinese takeout carton, sniffed it through the closed lid, and gagged. "I'd throw this in the garbage, but I think the smell would stink us out of here," he said, replacing the carton in the fridge.

I pursed my lips, trying to think back to when I'd last had Chinese takeout. Or *any* takeout. I shrugged one shoulder. "There's some frozen pizzas in the freezer. Pick out a couple." I replenished my stock every few days. It was what I lived off of—

that and Dick's Drive-In, just a short walk down Broadway. Oftentimes, my trips to grab greasy fast food were the only times I left the shop. All of the teens who worked there knew me by name.

"Maybe you should convert the fridge into a freezer," Nik suggested, head in the actual freezer. "Monthly trip to Costco, and you'd be set . . ."

Fists on hips, I watched him. Or, at least, what I could see of him from behind the freezer door. He'd slung his long, black leather jacket onto the back of one of the kitchen chairs, revealing his array of tattoos in black and varying shades of gray. Our kind healed preternaturally quickly, and as a result, ink didn't stick quite so well in our skin.

Much as I wanted to take full ownership for my own love of the inked needle, I wasn't delusional. Nik had been there when my world fell apart all those years ago. He, and even more so Dom, were the ones who picked up my broken pieces and fitted them back together as best they could. Nik had left an impression. One only needed to look at my choice of business and the ink in my own skin to see that.

"Yeah, maybe." I pulled out a chair and started shuffling my cards. Habit. "So where've you been, anyway?" Shuffle. "And let me offer up a preemptive *fuck you* for saying, 'Around . . .'"

Nik barked a laugh, pulling his head from the freezer to look at me, those icy eyes glittering with mirth. "Like I said, you grew up, Kitty Kat." The top quarter of him disappeared for another second or two, and then he emerged with two pizza boxes. "Hawaiian and Supreme—two of my favorites."

"Adventurous . . ."

He turned on the oven. "You're the one who bought the pizzas."

I gave him a side nod. "Touché." Was it weird that it felt so *not weird* for him to be there? "So where've you been—really?"

"Everywhere." He tore into one of the boxes. "Nowhere long enough to matter."

"You know, I hated you for leaving like that. After everything . . ." In many ways, I still did.

"I know." That was it, that simple agreement. No apologies, no explanations. Not that I'd expected any. I learned a long time ago that expecting anything from other people was the quickest pathway to disappointment. So I stopped expecting things. No more disappointment.

I huffed a laugh. If only I could do the same with myself.

Nik glanced my way but remained quiet. Good. I wasn't up for sharing my feelings, and I had work to do.

After one last shuffle, I laid out a simple three-card spread—past, present, and future. I didn't need more than that, not with my cards, and not while finding Dom was preeminent in my thoughts. I wasn't surprised to find that the deck had redesigned itself further after the events of the past hour. The illustrations were even more realistic than before, the colors even starker.

The leftmost card represented the past with a row of five crystal tumblers lined up on a barren surface, an ouroboros—a snake eating its own tail—burned into the surface, encircling the cups. Two were shattered, one was broken in half, and the other two remained half filled, one with a clear liquid, the other with something bloodred. Disappointment. Inability to let go. Bitterness. Refusal to give up, to move on. A sliver of hope. The Three of Cups was a depressing card to represent Dom's past. Especially when I knew, deep in my bones, that it was about his past with me.

My eyes burned, but I jutted out my jaw and moved on. The past was the past. I couldn't do anything about it now.

The middle card, representing the present situation, was the King of Swords, reversed. The king sat in his upside-down throne, his massive black claymore planted in the floor at his feet and his head bowed over the pommel, concealing his face. Tyranny. An abuse of power. Deceit. Manipulation. Relentless drive toward a goal. An at-any-cost mentality.

I squinted and picked up the card to get a closer look. There was something engraved into the steel of the sword blade, just above the hilt. "What the hell?" It was another ouroboros, much smaller this time.

"Everything alright?" Nik asked from the kitchen. He was sitting on the counter opposite the oven, watching me. I could see him in my peripheral vision.

"Yeah," I said with barely a glance his way. The self-cannibalizing snake was one of the many ancient symbols my people had used over the years, representing eternity and the cyclical nature of time, but I'd never drawn it on my cards. Why the hell was it showing up now? "Just a . . ." Frowning, I shook my head. "Nothing. It's probably nothing."

"Is this how you do it—tarot cards?"

"Be quiet," I said absently, then moved on to the third card.

The Hanged Man. Again. Goosebumps rose on my skin, starting on my arms and moving inward. The illustration showed Dom dressed all in black and hanging upside down by his ankle. A bright light glowed behind him, illuminating the dark, inky tendrils creeping in all around him, and a snake coiled around his calf, suspended from a branch, holding him in midair. Indecision. Sacrifice. Waiting. Letting go. Surrender. But who—me, or Dom? And why the hell did the snake's tail, once again, disappear into its mouth?

I gathered up the cards and shuffled twice more, then drew three, laying them on the table in a neat row. It was the same cards. One more time—the same spread, the same cards—and I accepted that it was locked in. The universe had spoken.

I settled into a pattern of drawing a single card, a single, specific question in mind.

Where is Dom now?

Did someone capture him?

Is he in pain?

Is he alone?

Who could help me find him?

Is he alive?

Eventually, no matter what I asked, I pulled the same card—

the Hanged Man. *Wait,* it seemed to be telling me. *Not yet. You'll understand soon enough.*

Frustrated, I flipped the entire deck over and fanned out the cards. They all had one thing in common—the ouroboros. Sometimes it was hidden, and sometimes it was blatant, but it was always there. I settled into the kitchen chair and started going through the cards one by one. There had to be more they could tell me. There *had* to be.

CHAPTER THREE

"Why'd you do it?" I ask a bulking Nejeret who calls himself Shank. He's down on his knees, his hate-filled eyes locked on my face, the point of my sword, Mercy, digging into his neck hard enough to draw blood. "Why'd you make him kill himself?"

"Why not?" Shank says. "He was just a human."

I feel my eye twitch, and I'm having a hard time not shoving Mercy's blade forward. That human *was my friend. He was helping me. And for that reason alone, this asshat decided to use him as a warning. I grit my teeth. "Give me the names of two others, and I'll let you live." I'm literally lying through my teeth, shame-free. This Nejeret is going to die, regardless of anything he tells me.*

Shank smirks, his eyes still locked on mine, and jerks forward. His eyes bulge and his body stiffens as Mercy's blade slides through his neck with almost no resistance.

I raise my right foot and plant the bottom of my boot against his chest, pushing him off the blade. He slumps to the floor, twitching and gurgling as he dies. Preemptive, but no matter. I was going to kill him anyway.

I drop to one knee to wipe the blade off on the side of his sweatshirt.

Shank's eyes are wild now. Scared. Good.

I lean over him and bring my mouth close to his ear. "Don't think this is over." Nejeret souls live forever. If there's a way to make the rest of his exis-

tence one of never-ending agony, I'll find it. He's on the top of my shitlist, dead or not, just under the Nejeret who killed my mom.

BANG. BANG. BANG.

I snorted awake, jerking upright in my chair and reflexively wiping the lower half of my face with the back of my hand. It came away wet. Of course.

I could still smell the tangy, metallic scent of blood. I could still hear Shank's final, gurgling breaths. No matter how deserving my victims were of death, they still haunted my dreams.

BANG. BANG. BANG. It was the door downstairs, the one from the street to the shop.

"You should probably get that," Nik said from the couch behind me. "Sounds like a cop knock."

"Oh joy of joys," I grumbled. I pushed my chair back with a screech of wood on wood and stood, blinking gritty eyelids. My cards were still on the table, though not in the neat stack I'd left them in, thanks to my flailing arms. I combed my hair back with my fingers, running my tongue over my teeth in an attempt to decide how terrible my morning breath might be. Pretty bad, I gathered. I felt my chest. At least I was wearing a bra.

I trudged past Nik and the couch, slogged down the stairs, and rubbed my eyes with my left hand as I pushed through the beaded curtain. It was bright, but not full-morning bright. Early-dawn bright. Like, five-in-the-freaking-morning bright. I don't do five in the morning. At least, not from this end.

A large man stood on the other side of the glass door, his physique disturbingly similar to Shank's and his dark blue uniform looking almost black in the pale morning light. Nik, that sneaky charlatan, had been right. Cop knock, indeed.

I unlocked the door and pulled it open a few inches, keeping the toe of my boot wedged behind the door so the guy couldn't shove his way in. I don't have anything against the po-po—they're great, I'm sure. Do-gooders and all that. But I'm not, and that makes us potential adversaries. I have a past that would incite this fresh-faced officer to try to take me in and throw me behind bars without hesitation. Then things would get ugly and he would get dead, and I would feel bad. And really, I wasn't looking to murder one of Seattle's finest at five in the damn morning.

"Is there a problem?" I asked, then cleared my froggy throat. I could hear footsteps on the stairs in the back. Relative immortality, crazy-fast healing, and the occasional "magical" power aren't my kind's only gifts; our senses are extra keen and our reflexes unnaturally quick. I had no doubt that Nik was eavesdropping from the back room. Just in case.

The cop, a Native guy in his mid- to late twenties, nodded to me in greeting. He was quite a bit taller than me and twice as wide—all muscle, from the looks of it. "Morning, miss." He did a quick scan of me, his eyes lingering on the tribal orca tail tattooed on my exposed abdomen, the flock of seagulls flying along my collarbone and over my shoulder, and on the two tiny studs in the snakebite piercings on my lower lip. He glanced over his shoulder, then back at me. "Can I come in?"

I narrowed my eyes. "Why?"

He frowned. "I have an important matter to discuss with, uh . . ." He glanced down at his hand, where my name was scrawled across the palm. "Katarina Dubois. She owns this business, doesn't she?"

I raised one eyebrow. "She does."

"Well, can you get her?" Again, he looked over his shoulder. "Please?" He didn't know enough about me to know that *I* was Katarina Dubois, which told me he wasn't after me for an arrest or anything like that. But he definitely wanted something from me. My help in finding someone, probably. Too bad for him—I only worked for private clients, never for the police. Too many strings.

I flashed him a bright smile. "Sure. Be right back." I shut the door, locking it before turning around to head to the back. I was fully intending to return to the apartment upstairs to continue my investigation into Dom's and the other Nejerets' disappearances.

The cards had been stubborn last night, not revealing anything new, no matter how long I studied them. For all intents and purposes, I was in a universe-ordained holding pattern, and it pissed me the hell off.

Nik stepped away from the wall, blocking my passage through the beaded curtain. His eyebrows were drawn together, and the corners of his mouth were turned down. He wanted me to listen to the cop, and he was judging me for planning to ignore the guy. His feelings on the matter were plain as day. Damn it, if Nik was functioning as my moral compass, my own personal Jiminy Cricket, then the world was seriously screwed up.

My shoulders slumped, and I let my head fall back, a groan rumbling up my throat. "Fine."

"Good girl," Nik said, placing his hands on my shoulders and turning me around.

Feet dragging, I headed for the door. I unlocked it and yanked it open. "Come on in." Once the cop was inside, I twisted the lock again and turned to face him, leaning my back against the glass. "Officer . . . ?"

"Smith," he said, pointing to the name tag on his right breast pocket: G. Smith. He craned his neck to peek into the nearest tattooing office. "Officer Garth Smith. Will Ms. Dubois be joining us soon?"

"You're looking at her," Nik said, pushing through the curtain. I glanced past the cop, and my eyes locked with Nik's for the briefest moment. It was like he was allergic to minding his own business.

To Officer Garth Smith, I was sure it looked like Nik was there to intimidate him—it was what Nik did best, after all. But I knew better. He was there for the cop's safety. He probably still thought of me as the loose cannon I'd been two decades ago—the one who'd nearly killed herself in a suicide mission attempting misplaced vengeance for her mother's death. But he didn't know that girl was long gone, killed by an assassin of rogue Nejerets.

Killed by me. He didn't know any of that, because he hadn't been around.

"You're Katarina Dubois?" Officer Smith said, spinning around to face me.

I crossed my arms over my chest. "Last I checked."

He did another scan of me, longer than before, from my black combat boots up until, finally, he reached my face. I imagined what he saw—a troubled girl who'd been out partying all night, if the mussed hair, disheveled clothes, and smudged and crusted dark makeup around my eyes were anything to go by.

"You own this place?" he asked dubiously.

"Yep."

"And *you've* been helping people find their missing loved ones for the past two years?"

"Yep."

"But you can't be more than nineteen—"

"I'm older than I look," I said dryly.

His head quirked to the side, his keen eyes narrowed. He thought I was yanking his chain. "How old *are* you?"

"Twenty-five," I lied. I'm thirty-eight, but experience has taught me that telling people anything beyond twenty-five is pushing it. Now, here's to hoping Officer Garth Smith here didn't go look up my actual records . . . then he'd learn the impossible truth. It was probably time for me to start posing as someone new —my own daughter or niece, maybe. But damn that sounded like a lot of work.

"Call it a hunch," I said, "but I'm betting my remarkably good genes aren't the reason you're here."

"Oh, no, of course not, um . . ." Officer Smith shook his head, a surprisingly adorable smile curving his lips. "I've heard rumors—well, more than rumors, really—that you can find people . . . people nobody else has been able to find. I looked back over a few of the cold cases that were solved this past year—always assisted by an anonymous tip." His gaze became hawklike and focused. "It was you, wasn't it?"

Looking to the side, I shrugged.

"The guys whisper about you . . . they say you're a psychic. A real one. Word is you track people through sketches." He inhaled, hesitating with a held breath.

Don't say it. Don't say it. Don't say it.

"They call you the Ink Witch."

I looked past him, to Nik. The ancient Nejeret burst into laughter, almost doubling over.

I glared at him, my hand balling into a fist. "I hate that name," I said under my breath.

Officer Smith looked from me to Nik and back, missing the joke. *I* was the joke.

"You still haven't told me why you're here. I have other things to do . . ." *Other people to find . . .*

"There's a case," Smith said. "Homeless folks have been going missing for a couple months now, but the department can't afford to commit any resources to it."

I cocked a hip and examined my nails. "So, what—you want *me* to solve your missing bums case, pro bono?" We locked gazes. "Out of the goodness of my heart?"

"Well, um . . ." His shoulders drooped; his whole body seemed to deflate. "Yeah."

"Well, um . . . no." I smiled at him, lips pressed together and fake as hell. "Sorry, bud, but I don't work for free." I pushed off from the door, unlocked it, and pulled it open, holding it for Officer Smith.

He headed for the door, pausing when he reached me. His rich, coffee-brown eyes searched mine, his face filled with pleas. "They're kids, mostly. Dozens of them."

My resolve wilted.

"Dom . . ." Nik's voice was barely a whisper, too quiet for Smith's human ears to pick up. I couldn't afford to waste a single ounce of concentration on anything other than finding my half-brother. Not even on missing kids. I had to be ready for the moment the universe decided to throw me a bone and feed me some useful information. If I let myself become distracted by another case, if I let my concentration split, I might miss whatever signal the universe sent my way. Not even poor, missing kids could lure me away from what I had to do.

I hardened my heart and met Smith's desperate eyes. "Best of luck."

CHAPTER FOUR

"So, when you say 'dragon,' are you thinking more *Lord of the Rings* or more traditional Chinese?" I watched my client's puzzled face. "Or something else entirely?" We were sitting in my tattoo office, the one nearest to the back room. I'd chosen it purposefully—anyone who approached the beaded curtain leading to my personal space had to pass by this doorway.

My client looked at his girlfriend for help.

I sat with my sketch pad propped against my upraised knees, pen poised. I just needed some sort of direction for this piece . . . some sort of *anything*. I was down here, working, because there wasn't much else I could do for Dom at the moment. Nik reached out to his mom shortly after Officer Smith left, asking her for a list of all the names of the Nejerets who were missing. With that, I might be able to do some psychic triangulation and finally make some progress. Until then, I had to do *something* to prevent me from losing it completely.

"Well, I mean," the girlfriend started, "we definitely want it to look, you know . . . totally unique."

"Of course," I said, suppressing an eye roll. Maybe working had been a bad idea. I hardly had the patience for this kind of thing right now.

"We were thinking, like, *real*, maybe," the girlfriend said. "Does that make sense? Like, what a dragon *really* looks like."

I was quiet for a few seconds, eyeing them. When neither of their faces gave me any clarity, I said, "But dragons *aren't* real . . ."

The girlfriend waved a manicured hand, her dark green polish contrasting with her almost colorless skin. "You know what I mean."

I stared at her for a moment, not sure I had the slightest idea what she meant. "Right, so . . ." I looked at my sketch pad and started to draw. "I'm going to sketch out a few possible styles of dragons, and we can go from there." The last thing I wanted was a bad Yelp review simply because this couple couldn't describe what they wanted.

The first sketch of a dragon was a pretty crappy attempt, even I could admit that. It was generic and blah. I didn't even bother showing it to my clients. I flipped the page and started again. The result was something that looked an awful lot like an iguana with tucked-in wings and visible fangs. Pretty damn realistic, if you asked me.

"What about something like this?" I asked, showing them the sketch. "Realistic . . . unique . . ."

The girlfriend bit her lip. "I don't know . . . I mean, maybe if the wings were open and it had more spiney things?"

I watched the dude's face as his lady weighed in. "What do *you* think?" He was the one actually getting inked, after all.

He nodded, frowning, just a little. "You know, I'm thinking that maybe it should be bigger—more like something that would be in a world with elves and dwarves and shit like that."

I bit back a snide re-mentioning of *Lord of the Rings*. "Alright . . ." I sketched out a rough idea. A monstrous, scaly beast with a long, snakelike tail covered in enough spikes to skewer a whole herd's worth of lamb kabobs, soaring across the page, its enormous wings extended to either side. "So how's this look to you?" I turned the sketchbook to them.

"Dude, that's badass," the guy said.

Smile cautious, I looked at the girlfriend.

"I like it, I guess, but . . ." She scrunched her nose. "Why is its tail in its mouth?"

My eyes opened wide, my eyebrows shooting upwards. I turned the sketchbook my way again, my feet sliding off the edge of the chair. My rubber soles landed on the wood floor with a thump.

The dragon, the sneaky, snakey bastard, had moved. Its back was now curved, its clawed feed tucked in, its wings extended behind it, visible only in profile, and its tail sweeping up to its mouth. Its body, from nose to tail, made a perfect circle. Just like an ouroboros.

I licked my lips, sparing only the briefest glance for my clients before flipping to the previous page. That dragon, the glorified iguana, had twisted itself into an awkward position, its forked tongue extended to reach the tip of its stubbier tail. A quick peek at the first attempt showed me that the lame-o dragon, too, was imitating an ouroboros.

I stood abruptly, hugging the sketch pad to my chest, and muttered a breathy "Excuse me." I hurried to the next office over. Sampson, the only male artist in the shop, sat beside his rented chair, his coil tattoo machine buzzing merrily as he worked on his client's upper back. His coil went quiet, and he looked at me.

"Big piece?" I asked him. I felt hollow, my voice reverberating throughout my entire body.

Sampson nodded. "My whole morning's blocked out for this one." So he wouldn't be able to take over with my clients. "Why?"

"No reason." I forced a smile. "Looks good," I said, barely having glanced at whatever he was working on.

I made a beeline for the counter, where the shop's receptionist was seated on a stool, marking up passages in a textbook with a pink highlighter. "Hey, Kimi, who's got the least busy schedule today?"

She closed her book, marking her page with her highlighter, and tapped her tablet's screen, chewing on the inside of her cheek.

"Nobody," she said, looking at me. "We're booked solid through to close."

I closed my eyes and took a deep breath. This shop was my life, my livelihood. I *needed* to work. But I needed to find Dom more. I'd been begging the universe for a sign, for a clue of any kind. Maybe it had already responded, and I simply hadn't been listening. That damn tail-eating snake was important. I just had to figure out why.

"Everything okay?"

I opened my eyes and looked at Kimi. "No, it's not." Even I could hear the resignation in my voice. "I need you to call everyone on my calendar today—I have to cancel."

"Oh, no." She pouted her bottom lip. "Are you feeling alright? You do look a little pale."

"I, um . . ." I took a step backward. "I just can't do this today."

"I can," Nik said, pushing through the beaded curtain.

Both Kimi and I looked at him, eyebrows raised in surprise—Kimi, because she hadn't even known he was there, and me, because I had no clue that Nik knew the first thing about giving tattoos; I thought he was just an expert at receiving them. Kimi's eyes lit with interest as she scanned Nik, and I could hardly blame her. The guy oozed more bad-boy sex appeal than all of Cap Hill combined.

"Hi." Nik strolled to the counter and held his hand out to Kimi. "I'm Kat's cousin, Nik."

"We're not related," I said.

"We grew up together."

I snorted. Nik and I couldn't have grown up further apart—his childhood ended thousands of years ago in an oasis in the heart of the Sahara. Mine ended here, some twenty years ago, the day my mom died to save my life. The day Nik dragged me off of her murderer's dead body. The day he watched me come absolutely unhinged.

"I've got years of experience with inking people," Nik said, and my eyes narrowed. People, or just one person—namely, himself?

"I'd be more than happy to cover for you if you're not feeling up to it." In other words, *You should be searching for Dom. Why are you even down here trying to work in the first place?*

Because this is the only sane thing in my life, I wanted to scream at him, and I needed a bit of normal to balance out our crazy world. And yet, part of me knew he was right. I'd rather lose this place than lose Dom.

"I just got off the phone with my mom," Nik added. "That information you've been waiting for is upstairs." The list of names of the other missing Nejerets. Finally!

"Yeah? Awesome." I shot a quick glance over my shoulder to where my client and his girlfriend were sitting, heads together as they argued about the style of dragon. "My morning appointments are all consults, but I've got a couple cover-ups this afternoon." I looked at Nik. "Sure you can handle that?"

He grinned. From the spark of mischief in his eyes, I wasn't sure if this was a great idea or a terrible one. It was my business, after all, and I should've cared one way or the other. But I didn't. The hunt for Dom was calling to me through the ink. I had no choice but to answer.

Nejeret is French, technically, derived from a set of ancient Egyptian hieroglyphs—*Netjer-At*—that translate roughly to "god of time." A remnant of where we came from, originally. The universe was dying, and Re, one of the two original old gods, or Netjers, and the co-creator of our universe, along with his partner, Apep, possessed a human just a few moments before birth in the hopes that he could restore universal balance, known as *ma'at* to my people. That human's name was Nuin, and he became the first Nejeret, the father of our species.

Lucky for us all, Re succeeded, and thousands of years after he first came to earth, two new gods were born. And they just happen to be my niece and nephew, Susie and Syris. That's right, my half-sister, Lex, is the mother of the gods . . . but that's another story entirely. The point is, I wouldn't have my special gift, my *sheut*, without those rascally new gods. Of course, I'd probably have a much better idea of what all I could do with my *sheut* if they hadn't gone off to another universe completely to learn how to use their own, much more substantial *sheuts*. So, the new gods and I, we were sort of in the same boat. Or, at least, in the same marina. The one where you go when you don't have any clue about what you're doing. It's a shitty marina. Lots of shipwrecks and flipped boats.

I knelt on the floor of the second, bed-less bedroom in the apartment, surrounded by a ring of sketches. They were all unique, each focusing on a different missing Nejeret, but for one thing—the tail-eating snake. The ouroboros. I couldn't get away from it, not even in my sanctuary.

This room was the only one I actually cared about, the only place I felt at home. At peace. The only place I could be *me*. The only furniture in here was a built-in bookcase covering the entirety of the wall behind me, and I'm not even sure it counted as furniture. Its shelves were filled with a mishmash of trinkets and doodads, of toys and rocks and other little mementos that each had meant enough to someone once that they'd allowed me to forge a connection with that person strong enough that I could find them through the cards and my art. I kept them all, reminders that I could be good. That I didn't always hurt people, that I could help them, too.

One wall, the smallest by the door, was taken up entirely by a closet. That was where I stored my less-savory possessions, the equipment and gear I'd used during my previous, darker career as one of the Senate's deadly hounds alongside Mari. As one of their assassins. It had been more than three years since I'd stowed those tools of death away in there, three years since I'd opened the doors. Had it only been three years? Had it *already* been three years? It felt like yesterday. Like yesterday, and like a lifetime ago.

The other two walls were far from bare. They were covered in black paint as permanent as a mountain, as changeable as a volcano. Like the designs on my tarot cards, the paint on these walls had a tendency to take on a life of its own. It's basically magic, so I don't know why I don't just call it that.

I remembered the way the dragon sketches had changed on their own and felt a flit of panic in my chest. Usually it was only these walls and the tarot cards that reacted so autonomously, along with the odd sketch or tattoo here and there—all things I'd created with intent. With purpose beyond simply existing. All things I'd poured a bit of myself into.

I glanced down at my left arm. The tattoo of the Strength card from the traditional Rider-Waite tarot deck was still there on the inside of my forearm, the lion and the white-robed woman with my mom's face faded almost to obscurity by years of regeneration but otherwise unchanged. There was no sign of a serpent. There was nothing but the tarot card, a reminder of my mom. A reminder of what happens when I care about someone . . . and when I let someone care about me. A reminder to avoid that at any cost.

I blew out a breath. Thankfully, the ink was staying put.

I stared at my latest drawing of Dom. The perspective was strange, as though I was looking down at him from the ceiling. He was standing, looking up at me, and screaming. In pain? In warning? I couldn't tell. I also couldn't tell if I'd drawn something that had already happened, was happening right now, or would happen sometime soon. My gift didn't work like that. I just thought of the person I was trying to find, and if the connection between us was strong enough, my hand started to move.

The ouroboros was in this picture, just like all of the others. It wound around him multiple times before its mouth reached its tail.

"What does it mean?" I whispered. My fingertips traced the sketched lines of Dom's face.

With a splat, a wet spot appeared on the paper, barely missing the snake. I blinked several times and felt my cheek with the fingertips of one hand. It was wet. Because I was crying.

I almost couldn't believe it. I hadn't shed a tear in at least a decade.

Dom's faced changed suddenly. For a few seconds, he wasn't screaming. For those few seconds, it was as though he was actually looking at me through the paper, could actually see me.

"I'm alive," he mouthed. "Find me." I blinked, and he went back to screaming.

"How?" I asked the sketch, voice raised. "Where are you?" I sat up on my knees. Leaned forward, hunching over the drawing. "Dom! Where are you?" I was yelling at a creation of ink and paper, and I didn't care one bit how insane that made me. "How am I supposed to find you?"

I heard the slap of a hand against a wall behind me, then another, and another. Out of the corner of my eye, I could see the paint on the wall bleeding away, pooling near the floor. And still, behind me, the slapping continued.

Until it stopped.

Hand shaking, I set the sheet of paper down on the hardwood floor and climbed to my feet. I turned around and gasped, my fingers migrating up to cover my mouth.

Black hand prints covered the wall in a strip maybe three or four feet off the ground. Small hand prints. *Children's* hand prints.

Eyes wide, I backed out of the room and slammed the door shut. The last thing I wanted was for Nik to stumble across *that* little horror show. I ran into the kitchen and grabbed the tarot cards off the table, stacking them roughly and more or less shoving them into their little drawstring carrying bag.

It was time to pay Officer Garth Smith a little visit and talk about his missing street kids. I was ready to help. Pro fucking bono.

CHAPTER FIVE

According to Officer Smith's card, he was stationed at the Seattle Police Department's East Precinct, right here on Capitol Hill, just a half-dozen blocks southeast of my shop. I didn't even have to take my bike. Not that I ever minded riding the Ducati. But still, how convenient and thoughtful of Officer Smith.

I haven't been in many police stations before, and I'd certainly never been in this one. The building is two stories of whitewashed brick, broad-paned windows, and Tardis-blue trim. I passed under a stoic steel sign proclaiming this the right place and pulled a glass door open. There was a small waiting area to my right—very doctor's office-esque—and a reception window straight ahead. Through the window, I could see several rows of cluttered utilitarian desks, each with a laptop and a phone and a stack of files higher than I thought any one person could get to in a week, let alone a day. Most of the desks were vacant, but a couple were occupied by officers in their blues, neither of which was Officer Smith. The doughy, middle-aged officer watching me peer through the window wasn't him, either.

I spotted Smith standing in the back corner, a coffee cup in one hand and a sugar dispenser in the other, an endless stream of the sweet stuff pouring into his cup of coffee. The man was a damn hummingbird.

I approached the reception window, aware of the stares of the few other people seated in the waiting area. My fitted black leather motorcycle jacket covered the tattoos on my arms, but those peeking out from the top and bottom of my tank top were visible enough. I could practically hear the thoughts whispering through their minds—*troublemaker . . . bad kid . . . keep an eye on her . . .*

I shook my head, laughing under my breath. If only they knew. A quick recount of my personal and professional history could clear a room faster than teargas.

"Fill this out," the heavy, mustached officer at the counter said. The one who'd been watching me. There was the sense of a walrus about him. *C. Henderson*, the name badge on his right breast pocket read. Not knowing what the "C" stood for, I named him Charles in my head, Chuck to those of us who know him especially well.

I glanced down at the form and frowned, then raised my gaze back up to Officer Henderson's face. "Why would I fill that out?"

He coughed, ruffling his mustache. "Aren't you here to report another missing homeless kid?"

"Why would I be doing that?"

Henderson lifted a hand and sort of pointed my way. "You just look the type."

I raised my eyebrows. Homeless kid—that was a new one for me. I slid the form back across the counter to him. "I'm here to see Officer Smith, Garth Smith." Remembering that Garth hadn't seemed too keen on being seen standing outside of my shop, I batted my eyelashes and added, "We have a date." I flashed Henderson a cheeky grin. Maybe I could lend the youthful Officer Smith a little street cred in the process. "So if you could just skedaddle on over to him there, Chuckster, and let him know I'm here, that'd be swell." I sighed. "Isn't he so dreamy?"

Officer Henderson did that coughing, mustache-ruffling thing again, watching me like I'd sprouted two new heads.

I rolled my eyes and leaned to the side to see around Henderson. "Garth," I called out, "I changed my mind about that thing you wanted me to do." I glanced at Henderson and winked.

In the very back of the room, Officer Smith choked on a big gulp of ultra-sweet coffee, his eyes bugging out as he stared at me through the reception window.

I pointed to myself, then to the door beside the reception window, then to myself again, asking without words if I could enter his worktime abode.

Officer Smith, seeming to collect himself a bit, nodded and waved me through. "You can let her in, Charles," he said to Henderson.

I gave a tiny fist pump at my predictive powers. Charles indeed.

Once Henderson opened the door for me, I tucked my hands into my coat pockets and strode into the room. I didn't want anyone mistakenly accusing me of having sticky fingers. I can't count the number of times I've been called a shoplifter—mostly because I don't care enough to keep track—despite that I've never actually stolen anything. I mean, what kind of monster do they think I am? Stealing—how mundane.

"Can I get you some coffee?" Officer Smith said as I drew near.

I gave his mug a pointed look. "Thanks, but no. I'd like to leave this place with all my teeth intact."

The faintest rosy blush crept up Officer Smith's tan neck.

"Nice place," I said, looking around.

Officer Smith set his mug down on a desk. It had "CHIEF" written on its side in big, bold, black letters. "You're acting like you've never been in a police station before."

I adjusted the strap of my leather messenger bag on my shoulder. "You say that like you assume I have." I tilted my head to the side and smiled sweetly. "I haven't, just FYI. At least, not beyond the waiting area." I pointed to the mug. "You're a little young to be the police chief, aren't you?"

Smith shifted in his chair. "It's a nickname."

"Oh," I said. "Right. It's nice to see that the PD is so PC."

Garth chuckled. "They mean well."

I leaned in and lowered my voice. "So, talk to me about these kids."

Officer Smith exhaled a relieved breath. "I was hoping you'd come around." A hand on my back, he guided me toward the door to the reception area, grabbing a midnight-blue coat off the back of a chair as we passed by. "Let's talk somewhere a little more private."

As we left the station, I gave it an over-the-shoulder scan. All eyes were on us. Either the other cops were super interested in Smith's love life or they hadn't bought my act. Inconceivable, I know.

Smith pointed to a coffee shop across the street from the station, and I nodded. We paused at the corner and waited in awkward silence for the crosswalk signal to change.

Officer Smith seemed a little nervous and fidgety, so I took pity on him. "So . . . how about that local sports team?"

He blew out a breath of laughter, and shallow dimples appeared on his cheeks. "Sorry. I just really wasn't expecting you to come by." He looked at me sidelong. "The guys are going to give me a hard time about that little show you put on in there for weeks."

I flashed him a cheeky smile a moment before the signal changed. I nodded to the other side of the road. "Our turn."

We crossed the street and slipped into the coffee shop just as it started to drizzle outside. I headed for a small two-person table tucked away in the back corner and sat with my back to the wall so I could see everything in the shop. Old habit.

Officer Smith sat in the chair opposite me and leaned forward, resting his elbows on the table. "So, what changed your mind about helping?"

"I'm a bleeding heart." I pulled back the flap on my bag to dig out my cards. I paused, the deck's drawstring bag partially exposed. The bag was made of a midnight crushed velvet, an Eye of Horus embroidered in silver thread on one side, an Egyptian-style cat on the other. The first was a symbol of my Nejeret clan, changed from my clan of birth—the Set clan—to the Heru clan via an oath. The other I thought pretty obvious: cat . . . Kat.

I looked from the cards' bag to Officer Smith and back, squinting thoughtfully while I tugged on the inside of one of my lip piercings with my teeth. I returned to looking at Smith. "Would you consider yourself a superstitious man? Like, on a scale of one to ten, how open would you say you are to things like, say, *magic*?"

"Which end is which?"

"Ten is 'I wish I could do that,' and one is 'burn them all.'"

"I don't know . . ." Smith scratched his jaw. "I was raised in Seattle, but I spent summers back on the Suquamish reservation with my people, learning our traditions and whatnot. I think a lot of folks would say there's some magic in that."

"Well, alright," I said, mildly impressed. It didn't happen often.

I pulled the tarot cards out of their little drawstring bag and started shuffling. "So, officially, I'm a tattoo artist and a fortune-teller. Finding people"—I tapped the two halves of the deck on the tabletop, then shuffled once more—"that's just an extension of the fortune-telling gig. I'll do a reading for you here, but the rest of what I do . . . that happens behind locked doors. I'm going to need everything you have on the missing kids. The more accurate your information is, the more accurate mine'll be." I paused, glancing at Smith. "I don't suppose you have anything that belongs to any of these kids?"

He shook his head. "Do you need that to make this work? Because I know where some of the kids were bunking down. We can go by in a little bit and—"

I raised a hand, cutting him off. "Thanks—I appreciate it, really—but no. I work alone." I gave the cards one last shuffle, then slid the deck across the table to him. "Just give me the info and I'll take it from there." When Smith didn't do anything, just sat there, I glanced down at the deck pointedly. "Cut it, please.

And while you do, think about this case, these kids . . . how much it means to you to find them."

Smith's brow furrowed as he concentrated. He was actually taking this seriously, which was both a pleasant surprise and a welcome relief. He looked at the deck like he was trying to set it on fire with his stare alone, then finally cut it, dividing it almost perfectly in half. "Just the once?" he asked, eyes on me.

I nodded and reached across the table to retrieve the deck. I opted for a simple three-card spread to start off, wanting to ease Smith into my brand of divination.

Once the cards were laid, there was no ignoring the fact that the deck had altered itself once more. I wasn't surprised this time. Of the three cards—the Five of Pentacles, a card representing poverty and insecurity, the Eight of Swords, representing isolation or even imprisonment, and the Tower, representing disaster, upheaval, and sudden change—two displayed a person, and each was a child. Both children displayed were strikingly different. It didn't slip past me that Dom was the man tumbling out of the crumbling tower, but for the briefest moment, all I could think about was the children.

"How many kids have gone missing?" I asked. "That you know of, at least?"

"Seventeen have been reported missing by their friends, all in the last two months."

I flipped the deck over and skimmed through the rest of the cards, double-checking what I felt in my gut—the major arcana cards like the Tower all still depicted Nejerets, but each and every figure of a person on the minor arcana cards, like the trio of girls on the Three of Cups, had transformed into a child, and each one was unique. Instinct told me I was looking at the faces of the missing kids.

"Seventeen," I said quietly, shaking my head as I counted the children. "That's not all of them." *Thirty-two . . . thirty-three . . . thirty-four . . .* "There are thirty-five kids missing, total," I said, finally setting the deck down.

Smith leaned forward, craning his neck to get a better look at the cards. "And the cards told you that?"

"Sort of." I didn't explain how it worked, partly because I didn't understand it fully myself, but mostly because he wouldn't understand *at all*. Smith was open-minded, and that was almost more dangerous than a skeptic. If I shared with him how I knew there were thirty-five missing kids, he'd want me to explain how it worked. He'd want me to explain everything. And then I would have to get rid of him, because, in the case of my people, sharing is *not* caring. The Senate had a strict policy on not telling humans about our existence. It used to be allowable to share with parents, spouses, and children, but the Senate had tightened up the policy of the past few years to be explicitly "No humans allowed."

When Smith opened his mouth and inhaled, preparing to dig further, I cut him off with a raised hand. "I won't tell you more. I'm sorry, but I can't." I met his rich brown eyes. "It's for your own good, trust me."

He shut his mouth. Smart man.

"Officer Smith—"

"Garth, please."

I nodded. "Garth, does this symbol mean anything to you?" I asked, tapping one of the snakes on the Five of Pentacles card. The external circle of each pentacle was an ouroboros.

Garth leaned over the table to get a better look at the card and the symbol I was pointing to. "Can't say it means anything to me, personally."

I huffed out a breath and drummed my nails on the tabletop, staring at the tail-eating snake. Why did the damn thing keep showing up?

"But," Garth continued, "I'd guess there isn't a person in this country who wouldn't recognize it these days."

My eyes snapped to his. "Why?"

"That's the logo for that company that's making Amrita. I swear their commercial is on between every show on TV."

"I don't have a TV," I told him. "What's 'Amrita'?"

Garth's eyes rounded, like he just couldn't believe I didn't turn into a couch zombie along with the rest of America every evening. "Amrita—the elixir of life. You know, the one that claims it can add another fifty years to your life." His eyebrows climbed up his forehead. "You've really never heard of it? It's on billboards and the sides of buses . . . in magazines . . ."

I shook my head. "Not ringing any bells, but then, I don't get out much. So what's this drug company called?" I pulled out my phone and opened the Internet app. "And how do you spell 'Amrita'?"

Garth told me, then shook his head slowly, his eyes squinted in thought. "I can't remember the company's name. It's something strange . . . definitely not an English word. Might be Latin."

My phone was working at a slug's pace, but I didn't need it anymore anyway. I set it down and looked at Garth, a strong hunch perching on my tongue.

He frowned. "I think it starts with an *O*."

"Ouroboros," I said, letting that hunch fly free.

Garth snapped his fingers. "That's it. The Ouroboros Corporation."

I bolted up out of my chair, adrenaline coursing through my veins. I stuffed my cards back into their little drawstring purse and tucked them away in my messenger bag, then slung the strap over my shoulder, a genuine smile curving my lips for the first time since Nik arrived. Dom was alive, his disappearance was linked to the missing kids, and it all had something to do with this Ouroboros Corporation.

Finally, I had something to go on. A sleazy pharmaceuticals company that specialized in life-extension drugs; it was about as solid of a lead as I could've asked for.

"Thanks, Garth," I said, standing beside the table and looking down at him. "This has been insanely helpful."

"What—where are you going?"

I turned away and started across the coffee shop toward the door. "To track down your missing kids." I glanced back at him. "I hope you're not a fan of that corporation. They're involved in this somehow, and I *will* burn them to the ground."

Garth blanched.

I winked at him. "Figuratively, of course."

Once I was out of the room, I uncrossed my fingers. If Dom was hurt in any way, I would stop at nothing to destroy them.

CHAPTER SIX

I tossed back the remaining bourbon and thunked my glass down on the kitchen table beside my laptop, already reaching for the bottle. My eyes never left the computer screen. The rest of the apartment was a dark cavern compared to the glow from the screen. Afternoon had come and gone in the blink of an eye and the click of a mouse, and evening had fallen. Nik was still downstairs, working in my place, and I'd been alone in the apartment, barely having moved since getting back hours ago. I couldn't, not when my eyes were glued to the screen.

I checked my inbox for the bazillionth time—I'd emailed Garth as soon as I got home, reminding him to send me the info on the missing kids—before maximizing the browser window again. I now knew pretty much all there was to know about the Ouroboros Corporation. At least, everything available to the public.

Ouroboros is the pharmaceutical arm of a multibillion-dollar global conglomerate called Initiative Industries, which owns subsidiaries in all branches of industry and commerce. Ouroboros focuses on what they call "life-extension technology and therapy." In other words, they're looking for the fountain of youth—eternal life—something they can cram into a pill and bottle up.

Funny. Nejerets *have* eternal life. At least, so long as we don't get ourselves killed. There was zero chance that those two facts weren't linked, and that left little doubt in my mind that the missing Nejerets hadn't just been abducted for shits and giggles, they were being experimented on. Apparently, right alongside the missing street kids. These Ouroboros people were their own special brand of sick fucks.

I took a sip from the fresh glass of bourbon, thoughts of grim reapers dancing through my mind. I would find them, and I would hurt them. It's what I did best, even if I was retired. This was worth getting back in the game for.

I'd moved on to reading reviews of some of their products. The most elite was Amrita, a series of injections given weekly for one year, but there wasn't much information about what the injections actually did, other than "rejuvenate the body and soul," let alone a price tag. The most popular product seemed to be Amrita Oral, a pill taken twice daily for some undisclosed period of time that was purported to slow the aging process through metabolic and adrenal regulations. It was pricey, though they offered the first month free for anyone who visited one of their many nationwide open houses. They held them weekly in New York City, Boston, Chicago, Dallas, Los Angeles, San Francisco, and—what do you know—Seattle.

Their Seattle open house was every Sunday morning at ten thirty at their corporate headquarters downtown. It was Saturday night. The next one was tomorrow.

I clicked back to the official website and started filling out the registration form, a requirement to attend. First and last name—I went with Katherine Derby. Date of birth—I shaved off a decade and a half there. Email—easy enough to create a new account for Ms. Katherine Derby. Phone—I hesitated here, not willing to enter the numbers for my cell or the shop phone.

I stood and went into the kitchen, opening the drawer where I used to keep a stash of unopened burner phones back during my former, illicit career. Although, technically, I *had* been licensed to kill by the Senate, it still felt like my sixteen years as one of their leashed assassins was about as wrong as a thing could be. All of the old burners were gone, leaving just one antiquated cell phone in the drawer—my mom's old phone.

I picked it up and pressed the power button, knowing full well the battery had died eons ago. Nothing happened. But even though the phone was kaput, the line wasn't. I'd purchased the rights to both her and my cell phone numbers seventeen years ago, just after the bill legalizing the universal privatization of all forms of "intangible property" passed in Congress. I grinned. When I'd purchased her line, I'd registered it to her—Genevieve Dubois—not to me. It was perfect.

I swapped out her name for my hastily created pseudonym, signed her up for a brand-spanking-new email address, and typed in her phone number. My pointer hovered over the *REGISTER* button. I'd made it this far at least a dozen times so far, using a dozen different identities. *Don't be a moron,* my brain screamed. *It's too risky—I'm a Nejeret; they're abducting Nejerets . . .*

The apartment door opened, and Nik walked in.

I clicked the register button reflexively, then closed out the window. Decision made. I was going.

I gulped down half the glass of bourbon and slid the bottle toward Nik as he neared the table. "Drink?"

Stopping to stand at the end of table, he spun the bottle around and whistled. "You might be a culinary prude, but your taste in booze doesn't suck."

I snorted a laugh, my gaze trailing down the length of his body. He looked damn good right now. It was the alcohol, I knew it, but I couldn't stop myself from appreciating his appearance. Tall and lean. Athletic, but not bulky. His thin, faded black T-shirt just snug enough to show some muscle definition across his chest and shoulders. The front hem of his shirt tucked precariously into his jeans, showing off his silver Eye of Horus belt buckle. The black and graying ink staining his arms and neck. I thought his neck piece—a tattoo of the goddess Isis, kneeling, her extended wings wrapping around to the back of his neck—just might be my favorite. At least, of the ones I could see. Who knew what was under his shirt—my eyes traveled lower—and elsewhere. But that Isis tattoo was similar to something I'd been planning for my forearm for a damn long time.

And then there was his face, all pristine, hard lines and sharp edges. It was perfectly symmetrical except for a slight bend in his nose where he must've broken it and been too slow to reset it before it healed. He could still fix it easily, if a little painfully. But then, Nik had never shied away from pain. Rather, so far as I remembered, he reveled in it.

His dark eyelashes and brows contrasted with his eyes, making his pale blue irises stand out even more, icy and calculating. There was nothing soft or warm about Nik. Especially not the way he was watching me study him.

"See something you like?" he asked, his striking gaze locking with mine. There was heat in his stare. Heat, and a challenge. I wondered what would happen if I told him, "Yes." Something, I felt certain. But what? It was impossible to predict.

I cleared my throat and took another sip of bourbon. "Professional admiration," I lied. "I like the neck piece. Who did that one?"

"Someone in Anchorage," he said, his expression blank, his eyes anything but.

"A woman?" I asked without thinking.

The corner of his mouth quirked, hinting at his usual smirk. "Why?"

I shrugged. "How long did you have to sit for it?"

"Six hours," he said, a knowing glint in his eyes.

I licked my lips. "Just, um, one session?"

He nodded and turned to head into the kitchen.

"How much did she charge?"

Nik grabbed a glass from the nearest cupboard and returned to the table to pour himself a drink. "I didn't pay her in money," he said, glancing at me, more than a hint of a smirk now.

I tried my hardest not to react, but damn it, I could feel the traitorous blood heating my neck and cheeks. I lowered my gaze to stare at the bottle across the table and cleared my throat. "Where are you staying tonight?"

Nik chuckled, low and quiet, and my stomach did a little flip-flop that wasn't entirely unpleasant.

I spluttered my bourbon. "I didn't mean—" I stood partway and reached for the bottle. "You know what I meant," I said, not quite sure that *I* knew what I meant.

Nik's stare burned into me for a moment longer. "Sure, Kitty Kat. I know what you meant." He turned and walked back into the kitchen. "I was hoping to crash here again—payment for a day's work." He opened the fridge, shook his head, then opened the freezer. "Pizza?"

I watched him for a moment, gathering my scattered wits. "You don't want to go back to Bainbridge, do you?"

Bainbridge Island was the current territorial base of Clan Heru. Heru ruled over the entire Pacific Northwest, including Northern California from San Francisco up, extending all the way to Alaska. He owned the entire northern quarter of Bainbridge, where he, Lex, and their daughter, Reny, lived with several dozen other Nejerets. Nik's mother, Aset, was among them. Hundreds of others passed through each year, as it was required for Nejerets from other clans to request permission and receive a license of passage *or* residency, depending on their intended length of stay in his territory.

Nik was quiet for a few seconds, his head in the freezer and the rest of him unmoving. I took it as an opportunity to ogle a bit longer. "They don't know I'm here," he finally said.

I blinked, surprised. "But you talked to your mom and—"

"I didn't tell her I was actually coming back here to help with the search." He pulled two frozen pizzas from the freezer. "Just that I'd look into it."

"So nobody knows you've involved me, either?"

He shrugged one shoulder, then turned on the oven. "Who's to say the Senate's not involved in the disappearances?" He tore into one of the boxes. "It's better for us both if nobody knows I'm here."

"Except for me," I said quietly.

Nik looked at me, the tiniest smile curving his lips.

My heartrate picked up, and I broke our stare, focusing instead on my empty glass. "You can stay." I lifted one shoulder. "It's only fair, with you filling in downstairs . . ."

He grunted a thanks. "So what've you found?"

"Hmmm?" About Dom. Right. "Oh, um, it looks like the missing Nejerets are linked to other disappearances. A bunch of homeless kids have vanished from the area as well."

"What that cop came to you about this morning?"

"Garth, yeah." I nodded and refreshed my inbox, using the computer screen as a way to avoid eye contact with Nik. "I'm just waiting for some files from him right now. Until I get those, I'm in a holding pattern . . ." I purposely didn't tell Nik about Ouroboros. He was barely involved in this as is, aside from playing messenger, and I didn't want to suck him in further. He still had people who would be devastated if he died, his mother, first and foremost. I respected Aset too much to get her only son killed. And then there was me . . .

"No plans for the night, then?"

I raised my eyebrows. "None that I'm aware of." I laughed to myself. Really, did I *ever* have plans for the night? For *any* night?

Nik hoisted himself up onto the counter, where he sat, boots dangling. "I could use a few touch-ups. We could trade . . ."

Frowning, I nodded. As far as ideas went, it didn't suck. Besides, I relished the chance to get a peek under his shirt—professional curiosity, of course. "Let's eat," I said, "then head down to my office." I was already thinking about what I'd have him work on. I always had a gang of tattoos in the lineup. Unlike Nik, I didn't just trace over my already-existing pieces, refreshing a static pattern. I liked to change it up. When one piece was faded enough, I just inked something new over the top.

I laid off the bourbon while we ate, and by the time we'd polished off the pizza, I was sober as a stone. Some might see it as a perk, but the metabolism that comes hand in hand with Nejeret healing can be the most annoying of burdens. When we need to eat, we *need* to eat. If we don't, our regenerative ability will turn off until it has enough energy to fuel it, and we start aging or losing weight—rapidly. It's the only way I'll ever look any older than my physical eighteen years, however temporarily. On the plus side, our metabolisms also enable us to process alcohol insanely quickly. I could be ass drunk one hour, dead sober the next.

"Alright," I asked Nik as he followed me into my private tattooing office. I flicked on the light switch on the wall, then turned on a secondary lamp. "What am I touching up first?"

He tugged his shirt off over his head, and I stared without blinking. His entire torso was a mass of black and graying ink over taut skin and hard muscles. It was chaotic and beautiful and impossible to take in completely in just a few seconds. I licked my lips, swallowing roughly as my heart rate escalated once more. So maybe it hadn't been the alcohol fueling my attraction to him upstairs. Clearly, I needed to get laid.

Nik seemed oblivious to this round of gawking. "My left rib piece is probably the worst," he said, lifting his arm and craning his neck to get a better look. "It's nothing complicated—just a list of names."

"I can see that," I said, leaning in close and breathing softly. He smelled amazing—clean and fresh, with just a hint of something spicy and ancient that reminded me of the incense my mom used to peddle in this very shop. Aroused didn't even come close to how I was feeling. "Only, um, a few of the names are in English."

Nik laid on his back on the narrow, padded bed. "Well, since English didn't exist for most of my life . . ."

"Right. That makes sense." I turned away from him and started gathering up my tools, impressed by how tidily he'd worked in my space. "So, who are they? Or *were* they? People you cared about? Or people you killed?" I asked, projecting with that last guess.

That was the list of names I'd ink into my own skin. It was a long list.

"Something like that." Nik's voice sounded distant.

"Sorry." I set the ink and tattoo machine on a rolling table, along with a fresh needle and a few sanitizing wipes. "Didn't mean to pry. So, why only black ink?" I'd never seen him with anything else.

Nik laughed under his breath. "I tried color once, back in the forties—didn't like the look of it as it faded."

I could relate. I only rarely incorporated color into my own tattoos, and even then, only as accents.

"But I do have one piece that isn't done in black ink," Nik said, rolling onto his side.

I sucked in a breath. "Holy shit . . ."

Nearly his entire back, from his broad shoulders down to his trim waist, was a cascade of hieroglyphs done in some impossible iridescent ink. It shimmered in the light, making his skin look like it had been inlaid with mother-of-pearl.

"Is that—"

"*At*?" he said. "Yeah. Made the ink myself."

At was one of the two energies that made up everything in the universe. All of space and time was held together by *At* and its counterpart, what I'd dubbed *anti-At*. The closest human science has come to capturing the truth of things is through particle physics, with matter and antimatter. That's the closest humans have come to understanding the universe—and it's not very close at all.

For thousands of years, my people were gifted with the ability to leave our bodies and enter a higher plane of existence, one where those primal forces are visible as a swirling, rainbow miasma of the fabric of time and space. There, we'd been able to view almost any time, any place, from that other plane in what we'd called echoes. The echoes were closed to us now, had been for over three years, ever since the new gods abandoned us.

Nik had the unique innate ability to pull one of those otherworldly forces, *At*, into our physical plane of existence, courtesy of his *sheut*, his internal, magical power source. He was the only person alive who could do it, and there was just one person in the world who could do the same with *anti-At*—Mari, my old partner in crime—though her abilities were far more limited. And way more dangerous. A single touch of obsidian-like *anti-At* could unmake a Nejeret from the *ba* out, erasing their poor, dwindling soul from the timeline completely until it was as though they'd never existed at all.

At, however, was different. Touching it wouldn't harm a person, and Nik's control over it was mind-blowing. He could make virtually anything out of the otherworldly material, including the sword stashed away upstairs in my closet with the rest of my forgotten assassin's gear. He could create whole buildings out of *At* or restrain someone in seemingly living vines of *At* or turn an entire person into *At*, either to preserve or punish. Apparently he could make tattoo ink, as well.

"It's the only way I've found to make a permanent tattoo," he explained. "For us, I mean."

I licked my lips. "Would you make me some of that ink?"

"Yeah, sure, Kitty Kat." He extended his arm over his head in preparation for me to begin working. "Whatever you want. All you have to do is ask."

CHAPTER SEVEN

The Ouroboros corporate headquarters were housed in the tallest building in Seattle, the Columbia Center. The skyscraper was intimidating for more than its height—it was a dark giant, an immense structure with an exterior as black and reflective as fresh-cut obsidian that took up an entire city block. The ground floor consisted of an expansive and varied food court, the second by a mall's worth of shops. I may have stopped at the coffee shop near the entrance for a couple of donuts—a maple bar and an old fashioned—and a black coffee on my way in. Aaaaand I may have scarfed down both pastries by the time the escalator carried me up to the second floor, the lowest level reached by the elevator.

There was a sign at the top of the escalator advertising the Ouroboros open house, proclaiming that it was today, on the sixtieth floor. And would you look at that—they *hope to see me there!* So friendly, these evil, kidnapping, child-torturing corporate scientists . . .

I rode the elevator up with a handful of people of various ages. A man and a woman in their thirties stepped off on floor eighteen, chatting about people in their office, and an older, dignified woman in a tailored skirt suit left on floor forty-one, leaving me with a middle-aged man and a younger couple. We all rode to the sixtieth floor.

When the elevator dinged and the doors slid open, I hung back, scoping out the scene. A couple of greeters waited a dozen or so steps out of the elevator. Both were attractive men in the prime of youth, wearing identical gray slacks and navy blue button-down shirts. Nice subliminal advertising, these handsome, youthful fellas. They latched onto my elevator companions, leaving me to slink out unnoticed.

I'd like to point out that I even dressed for the occasion. I was wearing my nicest jeans—dark and totally hole-free—the one and only turtleneck I owned, and a charcoal-gray hooded trench coat, tied at the waist. I'd swapped out my usual combat boots for some black leather riding-style boots, and I'd even removed my lip piercings. By the time I returned home, the damn holes will probably have closed up already, which was a pain in the ass. I looked downright respectable . . . at least, to these kinds of people. But I *felt* ridiculous. Anybody from the shop would've spit out their coffee if they'd seen me like this. Which was precisely why I'd slipped out the back door.

The shimmering tip of my brand-new tattoo—an image of the goddess Isis very similar to the one on Nik's neck, with the exception that *this* goddess bore a striking resemblance to my mom—peeked out from the end of my sleeve onto the back of my hand. All other tattoo ideas had gone out the window as soon as I'd seen the *At* ink piece on Nik's back. I tugged at my sleeve as I walked across the lobby, hoping nobody noticed. It didn't really strike me as the tattoo kind of place.

"Miss!" someone called after me. "Excuse me!" Fast footsteps carried the voice closer, and a third young man dressed just like the other greeters in gray slacks and a blue button-down shirt jogged my way. "Are you here for the open house?"

"Yes," I said, splashing on a broad smile and airhead eyes. I blinked several times and pretended to scan my surroundings. "Am I going the wrong way?"

"No, but you do have to check in." His brow furrowed. "Did you register online?"

"Of course I did," I said, touching my fingertips to his forearm and meeting his eyes. "I *can* follow instructions . . . when I want to." I gave him a wink. Too much?

"Great!" He pulled a sleek little smartphone from his pocket and traced a circle on the screen. "Name?" he asked, looking at me.

"Gen," I said. "Genevieve Dubois. I just registered last night—it was sort of last minute." I put on a worried expression. "I hope that's okay . . ."

"Yep," he said cheerily. "I see your registration right here." He held his arm out, telling me to head toward the single open door on the left side of the lobby, where a table was set up with name badges and a fanned-out stack of navy blue folders with the tail-eating snake emblazoned on the front in metallic silver. Two women manned the table, one in the increasingly familiar dark gray and blue—I was sensing a color scheme—the other wearing a smart black pencil skirt and a cream blouse.

"Candace will finish checking you in," my greeter said, handing me off to the uniformed woman. "And lucky you, Ms. Dubois, you can meet one of the Amrita leads, Dr. Marie Jones."

I glanced at the non-uniformed woman and froze. She was no "Marie Jones"; her name was Mari. She was *my* Mari—my ex-partner in assassinating the Senate's enemies. The same one whose name had been counted among the missing Nejerets. Things hadn't ended well between us, what with her calling me a coward the last time I'd seen her and me flipping her the bird. But we'd had some good times . . . and some dark times. Regardless of our past, or maybe because of it, I was genuinely glad to see her. At least I now knew that she wasn't one of the victims.

Then, dread sprouted in my belly. If she wasn't one of the victims, why was she here?

"Ms. Dubois," Mari said, extending her hand. She looked awesome. Her sleek, short inverted bob offset her Japanese features beautifully, and her brilliant jade-green eyes had never been more striking. "A pleasure to meet you." She grinned woodenly. "What brings you to our open house today? You couldn't be a day over eighteen."

I shook her hand, narrowing my eyes minutely. What game was she playing? "Twenty-five, actually. And it's never too early to start planning for the future, at least that's what my mom's best friend Mei always said." Mei was a Senate member and the leader of her own clan, occupying the Great Plains territory. But more importantly, she was Mari's adoptive mother.

Mari's cheek twitched. "How fascinating. Please"—she gestured for me to step off to the side with her—"chat with me for a moment. Yours is a demographic we've yet to really reach, and I'd love to get your input on a few ideas."

I matched her, wooden grin for wooden grin. "Love to."

Mari led me to a cluster of chairs in a corner of the lobby about as far as we could get from the check-in table and the elevator. "Just keep smiling pleasantly," she said through clenched teeth as she smoothed down the back of her skirt and sat.

I did as requested, sitting in the chair beside hers and angling my knees her way. "What the fuck are you doing here, Mars?" I asked through gritted teeth.

Her jade eyes flashed with irritation. "I should be the one asking you that. Did the Senate send you?"

I shook my head, stupid smile plastered in place. "Nik showed up and told me that a bunch of Nejerets are missing. It's looking like this place—you guys—are involved. But no, the Senate didn't send me." I laughed under my breath. "I'm sure the Senators would shit their collective pants if they knew I was here."

Mari leaned in a little. "Nik's back? I thought nobody had seen or heard from him for years."

"They hadn't," I said, not bothering to tell her that he'd been in contact with his mom. "Mari, what are you doing here?"

"The Senate sent me in undercover about six months ago because they thought the corporation's research was suspicious. I was just supposed to blend in . . . to monitor. But a couple months ago, when I heard about some of our people going missing, I started to actively investigate."

It was my turn to lean in, elbows on my knees. "What did you find? Do you know where Dom is? Is he still alive?"

Mari's eyes widened, her smile faltering. "Dom's missing, too?" She shook her head, a crease forming between her eyebrows.

"You didn't know?"

"Smile," she reminded me. "And no, I had no clue about Dom. The most I've been able to find out is that there's some sort of a shipment that goes out every couple nights—one that's off the books. It *might* have something to do with all of this, but . . ." She shrugged. "It's weak, at best. I tell you what—one of those shipments is going out tonight. Why don't I text you the address and you and Nik can check it out? I'll snoop around here to see what else I can find out and contact you in the morning."

I nodded absently, chewing on my lip where my piercing had been. It itched like crazy. It was already closing up.

Mari glanced around, then reached out to give my knee a squeeze. "We'll find him, Kat. I promise."

CHAPTER EIGHT

After my mom was killed, I went into a bit of a tailspin. It's a little embarrassing, really, but I was devastated, naïve, and pissed off—and in combination, those three things created a monster. I became a rash, unstable creature driven by a single thing: vengeance. It was my air and water and food. It was the blood pumping through my veins and the dreams disturbing my sleep. It was my everything.

And then Dom came in and gave me focus. He taught me discipline and how to fight. He gave me the skills and tools I needed to make vengeance a reality.

And then there was Nik, helping me understand the enemy. Helping me plan. Driving me ever onward and cautioning me when I exhibited too much recklessness. Until, one day, he pushed a few too many buttons, and I snapped. I almost died that day. On Mari's *anti-At* blade.

Maybe I'd still bear a closer resemblance to the Kat I used to be—the Kat who still had a mother and hopes for the future and a sparkle in her eye—if not for Dom and Nik and Mari. Maybe, but I also never would've avenged my mom. I didn't regret leaving the girl I used to be behind one bit. My heart was cold, my memory of the taste of vengeance crisp and clear. It had been delicious. Until it soured. Until those the Senate had me hunting no longer bore any resemblance to those responsible for my mother's death. Until it became bitter ash on my tongue.

But by then it was too late. By then, the girl I'd been was dead, a hard, empty shell left in her place.

Maybe that was why I felt such excitement about having seen Mari. She'd known me way back when. It was by Mari's side that I'd spent sixteen years hunting down those even remotely responsible for my mother's death. She'd seen the transformation. Hell, she'd been a part of the transformation. In a way, she reminded me of who I used to be. And I couldn't ignore the sense of grief I felt when thinking of that sad, lost girl.

I pulled my phone from my coat pocket as soon as I was out of the elevator and called the shop, figuring Nik was still lurking around. AKA covering for me. I was right. Kimi answered, but she retrieved Nik as soon as I asked for him. Good thing, because I didn't have his number, and I was going to explode if I didn't share what had just happened with someone.

"Hey, Kat—"

"You're *never* going to believe who I just saw," I told him.

"Who?" he asked. "And where are you? It's loud as fuck on your end."

"Oh . . ." I glanced around me, taking in the hustle and bustle of business professionals sneaking in an early lunch. There were so many of them, I doubted there were many people left up in their offices. "I'm in a food court," I told Nik. "Sorry. Hang on . . ." I weaved my way through the crowd of lunch-goers and made it to the glass doors to Fourth Avenue a good thirty seconds later.

I pushed through the rightmost door, only to be greeted by a blast of cold air and a crowd of people huddling on the covered stairs to stay out of the pouring rain. "Excuse me," I mumbled to one woman.

She shifted an inch. Unfortunately, I wasn't quite that thin.

"Excuse me," I repeated.

A few glances were cast my way, but nobody really put any effort into moving.

So I did what any reasonable person would do—I raised my voice and broke out the big-kid words. "Oh for fuck's sake, *move*, people!"

I received shocked looks and grumbles from the crowd this time. But hey—they made a path that was just my size. What peaches.

I pulled up my hood and hunched my shoulders as I trudged up to the bus stop at the next block. I'd have taken my bike, but the outfit didn't really work on a motorcycle, especially not if I wanted to keep it looking nice. Not that *that* mattered now. My stupid "nice" boots had shitty traction on the wet cement, and I longed for my heavy-treaded combat boots.

"Sorry," I told Nik, again. I'd been holding the phone against my lapel when I'd shouted, but Nejeret ears were sensitive. "Anyway, I was at this open house thing at Ouroboros—that's the pharmaceutical company that—"

"I know who they are, Kat; I'm not a moron. Why were *you* there?"

I stopped walking, pressed my lips together, and inhaled and exhaled deeply. There was no reason for him to get all snippy with me just because I wasn't a slave to the idiot box like everybody else. "They're connected to all this somehow," I finally admitted.

Nik was quiet for a few seconds. "You knew they were connected to the disappearances and you went there anyway?"

My eyes bugged out. Sometimes he *was* a moron, whatever he said. "Why else would I go there?" I gave a derisive snort and continued up the hill. "It's not like *I* need to drink from the fountain of youth." Though a sip from the fountain of *un*youth might do the trick. Especially if it would wrangle my pesky lingering teenage hormones. They could be a real bitch sometimes.

"Kat—"

"Mari was there," I said, flinging out the one thing that might waylay him from laying into me for being reckless, then held my breath.

"*What?*"

"Yeah, she's working for them. But really, she's undercover for the Senate. Did you know?"

"I didn't," he said. "But then, I haven't really been keeping up with things . . ."

"Right, well . . . that's crazy, right?" I reached the street corner at the top of the hill. "She's going to do some digging and see what she can find out about Dom. And—" I caught myself before I let it spill about the fishy shipment. I could check it out without him. No need to put anyone else in danger. Besides, I worked better on my own. Let's just say I have trust issues. I don't trust others not to do stupid shit and get themselves killed—like my mom—and I don't trust myself not to stop them.

"And *what?*" Nik asked.

"And . . . it was good to see her."

"Jesus, Kat." Disappointment was a loud, clear bell tolling in his voice.

"What?" I stopped some ways from the crowded bus stop and ducked under the ledge of another skyscraper.

"What the fuck were you thinking, going there alone—and without even letting me know?"

I reared back as though he'd slapped me. "Excuse me?" Since when was he my self-appointed keeper?

"They're the ones taking people—taking *us*—and you walked right into their house. They caught Dom, for fuck's sake. *Dom.* You think you're better than him? Really?"

"No, I just—"

"Then get your head out of your ass. A reckless move like that's what almost killed you last time." I shook my head as he spoke. How dare he? "This time, I might not be around to—"

"You know what," I cut in, voice raised. A few people turned their heads my way. I gave them the finger. "You can just fuck off, Nik. Just fuck the fuck off. Just walk away. Just disappear." I pulled the phone from my ear and stared at his name. "That's what you're best at," I said and hung up, fuming.

My phone started vibrating with an incoming call almost immediately. It was Nik. I rejected it. I did it twice more before I turned the damn thing on silent and stuffed it back into my pocket, grumbling "Asshole" under my breath.

I strolled into the East Precinct station with a chip on my shoulder and a bone to pick. I couldn't go back to the shop until I'd cooled off, but I also couldn't stand being unproductive. I marched straight to the unmanned reception window and dinged the little bell with equal parts purpose and ferocity. And just kept on dinging. It was their own damn fault for putting the thing out in the open in the first place.

Garth sprang up from behind his desk near the back of the room and hustled to the window, slamming his hand over mine to stop the dinging.

He looked at me and blinked several times, then his lips spread into an unsure grin. "I almost didn't recognize you like that."

I rolled my eyes. "Are you going to let me in, or what?" I asked, gesturing to the locked door with my chin.

Garth released my hand and let me in. I followed him back to his desk.

"Gah . . ." I dragged a rolly chair over from the desk in front of his and plopped down. "I hate every single thing that I'm wearing."

"You look nice," Garth said, sitting at his desk and typing on his laptop. He clicked his mouse a few times, then settled back in his chair with his arms crossed over his broad chest. "So to what do I owe this visit?"

Resting my forearm across the corner of his desk, I leaned in and locked eyes with him. "Where are the files?" I sat back. "I can't do my part until you do yours . . ."

He frowned and reached for his mouse, pulling up a new

window on his computer. "I sent them to you an hour ago." He looked at me. "You didn't get them?" He went back to scanning the screen. "The combined file size was pretty large, but it doesn't look like it bounced back."

I exhaled heavily and pulled my phone from my coat pocket. Sure enough, there was an email from the SPD. There was also a string of texts from Nik and one from Mari telling me the supposed location of her off-the-books shipment—Harbor Island. "No, no," I told Garth, pocketing my phone. "It's my fault. I just haven't checked my phone in a bit." I started combing my fingers through my hair, forgetting I'd pulled it back in a rare bun, and ended up pulling a few chunks free. "Damn it," I grumbled, taking down the whole thing.

"Everything alright?" Garth asked, a little wary.

"Yes," I snapped, then sighed. "No." I shook my head, laughing under my breath. *Damn you, Nik . . .* "Everything's really not alright." For whatever reason, he'd always been able to get under my skin, and his admonitions had cut pretty deep.

"Well . . ." Garth turned his wrist over to check his watch. "I had an early shift today. I was technically done thirty minutes ago, so if you want to head down to the Goose and grab a beer . . . ?"

I perked up. "Dear God, yes." I stood and looked down at him, still seated in his desk chair. "Are you ready?"

He chuckled. "Just give me a minute, alright?" He glanced over his shoulder. "Feel free to grab a coffee while you wait."

"No, I'm good."

"I think there might still be a few donuts back there, too."

I was already on my way.

Again, he chuckled. That deep, softly rumbling sound—and the fact that *I'd* caused it—eased my chip, just a bit.

As I took a bite of apple fritter, I realized something truly terrifying. I *liked* Garth. Like, he was a cool dude. He was interesting, and he cared about missing street kids—the kind most people considered pests and *wanted* to get rid of. He was a genuine good guy. And he was a fragile, short-lived human. A surefire path to heartbreak and devastation.

But I still wanted to grab a beer with him, despite knowing I shouldn't. Knowing I was asking for trouble. Nik was being an overprotective dick, I was sad and pissed, and Garth was being nice to me. It was a rare thing for me. A dangerous thing.

"Ready?" Garth asked, hand on my shoulder.

I jumped and turned around, half-eaten fritter to my chest.

"Sorry, didn't mean to scare you." He smiled, causing little crinkles at the corners of his coffee-brown eyes.

"S'okay," I said around a mouthful of donut.

He chuckled *again*, and I wanted to punch myself for thinking it was cute. I mean, this guy was at least ten years my junior. But then, I was getting to the age where hooking up with anyone my own age was pretty creepy, considering that *I* looked like I'd barely graduated from high school. It was getting harder and harder to shake the pedophile ick factor with anyone who didn't make me feel like Mrs. Robinson.

"You swear you're over twenty-one?" Garth asked me, eyes narrowed. "I don't want to get suspended for drinking with a minor using a fake ID."

I snorted, amused that his train of thought hadn't been far off from mine. "Trust me, bud. I'm good."

CHAPTER NINE

I drink too much. I know it, but it's hard to say no to the blissful numbness the bottle provides when I'm guaranteed to have zero side effects, at least health-wise. It's my favorite medicine, and for a good long while, it's been the only way I'm able to let my guard down enough to sleep with someone. Sometimes, it's the only way I can fall asleep. If only the dreams didn't kick in when the booze wore off. I'd probably smoke cigarettes, too, if they didn't make my hair smell like an ashtray and inspire me to spend half my day in the shower or brushing my teeth. Trust me, I'd tried.

"So," Garth said, watching me knock back my fourth shot of tequila, "bad day?" We'd been at the bar for maybe ten minutes. From the look on Garth's face, I was impressing the hell out of him with my gusto. Or was that shock? We'd grabbed street tacos from the food truck out front, and the Mexican food had inspired me to stick with a theme—tequila and Coronas. Oh yeah, did I mention I was sipping on a beer as well? Garth was being a smart human and sticking to beer alone.

I laughed bitterly, then took a bite of one of my tacos—shredded pork belly with cilantro-lime slaw, hot-hot salsa, and extra guac. Better than a frozen pizza, that's for damn sure. "I'd tell you just how bad," I said after swallowing. I glanced at him sidelong. "But then I'd have to kill you."

Garth laughed.

I eyed him as I took another bite. He thought I was joking. That's adorable.

"I'm going to hit the head," Garth said, standing from his stool. "Be right back."

As he made his way to the back of the room, I caught the bartender's eye at the far end of the bar—it was a different one from the chick who'd been serving us—and pointed to my empty shot glass. I watched him refill it, grabbing the bottle before he could take it away. "Just leave it," I said, looking into his Caribbean-blue eyes. His *Nejeret* eyes.

Not even an ounce of shock shone on his ageless face. A handsome face, even with that cruel twist to his mouth and the challenge glinting in his aqua eyes. Or maybe *because* of those things. Regardless, it was an unfamiliar face as well. This Nejeret wasn't part of Clan Heru.

"I haven't seen you around before." My lips spread into a slow grin. "Does Heru know you're working in his territory?"

He released the bottle but didn't answer.

"Do you know who I am?"

With a blink, he was looking at me again. He nodded. "Rogue Hunter." It had been my title back when I'd been working as one of the Senate's pet assassins, chowing down on revenge with a side of hefty paycheck.

My smile widened to a grin. "Does Heru know you're here?" I repeated. "Show me your papers." Though the Senate's way of tracking and regulating Nejerets was easily forgeable, at least it would give me this one's name. Of course, even if he had residency papers granting him permission to work and live here, there was no way for me to verify their authenticity without calling up Heru himself. And *that* wasn't going to happen. I was out. Done. He was still involved in Senate shit, and I wanted no part of that.

Besides, they were all better off without me.

"Don't have any," the bartending Nejeret said.

My eyes narrowed.

"Don't need them. I work for the Senate."

I scoffed. "Why would they station anyone on Cap Hill? I'm the only one who lives—" My eyes widened, and my lips parted as realization struck. He was here to keep an eye on me, the wild card. The loose cannon. The ex-assassin with too much time on her hands.

That cruel twist to his mouth broadened to a sly grin, and damn my neglected libido to hell if I wasn't equal parts turned on and pissed. How long had he been spying on me? And why? Just to make sure I didn't turn on the Senate themselves? Did he know I was investigating Ouroboros? Or the missing Nejerets? What about the street kids? Did he know that Nik was in town, staying with me? Nik hadn't wanted the Senate to know either of us were involved in the case—because he didn't trust that they weren't involved on the other end.

What if Nik was right? What would that mean for Mari? What if the Senators who'd sent her to Ouroboros were really involved in some sort of a hidden faction—a shadow Senate?

My blood chilled as I continued to stare into the Nejeret's eyes. Without warning, he plucked the bottle from my loose grip and replaced it on the counter behind him, swapping it out for a two-thirds-full bottle of Grand Centenario from the second-to-top shelf. He set the new bottle on the bar, met my eyes, and said, "On the house."

I uncorked the bottle, filled two shot glasses, and offered one to him, my not-so-sneaky way of checking if he'd spiked it with something. He clinked his glass against mine and tossed back the shot. I did the same. "Don't think this gets me off your back," I said, throat burning. I took a swig of my beer. "We *will* have a little chat. I want answers." I flicked the bottle with a fingernail. "But this'll buy you an hour or two."

He picked up my empty shot glasses, leaving only one behind, locked eyes with me, and licked his lips, that wicked grin returning. "I look forward to it."

My belly gave a little tingly flutter, and I crossed my legs on the stool. Now I was looking forward to our chat, too, and not for the words that would be exchanged. I cleared my throat, averted my gaze, and nodded to Garth, who was just returning from the bathroom. "Grab my friend another beer." As an afterthought, I added, "Please."

"You got it," the Nejeret bartender said and turned to fill a pint glass at the tap. He set it on the counter, then retreated to the other end of the bar.

"So . . ." Garth sat and took a swig of beer, draining his first pint glass and sliding it out of the way. "What was that all about?"

I held my finger up to my lips. "Shhh . . ." Reaching for the tequila bottle, I leaned closer to Garth and whispered. "He's got really good hearing, you know, because he's like me." I filled the shot glass, emptied it, and filled it again, then met Garth's dubious gaze. "A *witch*."

His eyes didn't widen, and he didn't laugh. Instead, he leaned in a little and spoke so quietly that I wouldn't have been able to hear him over the classic rock blaring throughout the bar without my Nejeret senses. "I know what you are . . . Nejeret."

Shit. Balls. If he shared even that name with the wrong person—if the wrong person overheard him and reported it to the Senate—they wouldn't hesitate in issuing a kill order, and whoever had taken my and Mari's places would hunt down Garth and silence him, for good.

"I have to go," I said, hopping off my barstool. I couldn't ever see him again; it would only put him in danger. I slapped a wad of cash on the bar and made a beeline for the door.

Garth's hand closed around my arm. "Kat, wait . . ."

I twisted my arm, yanking it free. "Stay away from me, Garth, and keep that word to yourself. Trust me, it's better for your health," I said, before turning and stalking out of the bar.

CHAPTER TEN

"Hey! Ink Witch!"

I stopped in my tracks, barely a dozen steps out of the bar, and spun around to glare at the Nejeret bartender. "What?" I snapped. I *really* hated that nickname.

The Nejeret's wicked grin was back, as was the challenging glint in his cerulean eyes. "What about our chat?" he said as he strode my way.

Frustrated and irritated after that little scene with Garth, I turned and continued down the sidewalk.

His quick footsteps told me he was jogging to catch up. He planted his hand on the brick wall in front of me just before the corner of the building, intending to block my retreat, but I ducked under his arm, barely missing a step. His next move was to grab my arm, just as Garth had, and pull me a few steps into the alley between the bar and the salon in the next building over.

I froze, giving his hand a pointed look, then raising my gaze to meet his. "I'm not in the mood to chat anymore."

He stepped closer and stared down at me, interest lighting his eyes. "Then what *are* you in the mood for?"

With the adrenaline pumping through my veins, making my heart race and exaggerating the rise and fall of my chest, I was itching for a fight. Or a fuck. Either would do. I stood on tiptoes and brought my lips nearer to his ear. "I don't think you can handle what I'm in the mood for." I dropped my heels, locking eyes with his.

The corner of his mouth lifted, exaggerating that cruel twist to his lips. "Try me."

I tilted up my chin just a fraction of an inch, and in the next heartbeat, his lips were on mine and my back was against the brick wall. His lips were soft, but his tongue was greedy and his rough stubble scratched my face. He tasted like tequila, mint, and just a hint of cigarettes. There was nothing gentle about him or his kiss—it was rough, cruel, and just a little painful when he bit my lip. It was exactly what I'd needed.

One of his hands tangled in my loose hair, yanking my head back even as he deepened the kiss. His other hand glided up my rib cage under my shirt, shoving my bra up and out of the way. He palmed my right breast, pinching the nipple between two fingers. When he twisted it just a tad too far, I arched my back and whimpered from the intoxicating mixture of pleasure and pain.

His leg slipped between mine, and my hips rocked against him, creating a blissful friction.

Someone gasped, a kid giggled, and a woman said, "Disgusting!"

The bartender—I still didn't know his name—broke the kiss, leaving me breathless and blocking my view of the alley mouth and whoever we'd disturbed with our little show. "I'm renting a place upstairs," he said into my hair. "Want to—"

I nodded.

He grabbed my hand and practically dragged me to a metal door further down the alleyway. He fished a key out of his pocket and unlocked the door, then pulled me in through the doorway to a dingy stairwell that smelled faintly of mildew. We never made it any further than that.

He unbuttoned my jeans and yanked them down without bothering with the zipper, then spun me around and, hands on my wrists, placed my palms on the smudged wall. His fingers slipped into the front of my underwear, and I dropped my head as he deftly found my most sensitive place. Damn, but this was exactly what I needed. No frills. No strings. No emotions. I craved a momentary reprieve from the insanity dragging me back into a world I'd extricated myself from years ago.

I could hear the clink-clink of metal on metal, then the sound of a zipper. A second later, the bartender pushed down my underwear, his other hand moving from between my legs to curl around the front of my neck, and the hard length of him slid between my thighs. He kicked my feet apart, spreading my legs as wide as my jeans would allow, and I arched my back, offering him a better angle. It did the trick. He slid into me in one rough motion.

"Oh fuck," he breathed.

I gasped at the pressure, at the relief, and rested my forehead against the wall.

"Do you know what it's like?" he asked, pulling out and slamming back into me. "Watching you on the nights you go home with someone?"

"Pervert," I said, grunting when he moved his hips in that jerky motion again. A slow burn thrummed to life in my belly, stoking hotter with each of his thrusts.

He leaned into me, pressing his chest against my back and curling his arm around my middle. His hand dipped lower, and I gasped when he pinched that swollen bundle of nerve endings. "I wondered . . . what it would feel like . . . to be them . . . to be inside you . . . fucking you."

"Well now"—an inferno roared low in my belly, seeking a way out—"you know." I ground against his fingers as the pressure built to blissful heights within me.

"You're a little whore . . . aren't you?" His breath was hot against my cheek. "A dangerous little whore."

I squeezed my eyes shut, trying to block out his words even as I reached for sweet release.

His fingers stilled, and his thrusting slowed.

"No," I whispered. I was so close. So very close.

"Open your eyes, Kat," he said. "Look at me. Look at me and tell me you're a little whore, and I'll let you come."

I gritted my teeth, reaching for that glittering bliss, but he knew exactly what he was doing. He moved just slow enough to keep me on the edge—to hold me on the cusp of orgasm without letting me topple over the edge.

"Look at me, Kat. Tell me what you are."

I opened my eyes and glared at him. I was desperate for that moment of ecstasy. But my pride was non-negotiable. "Fuck you."

"I think you're already doing that, sweetheart." His breath was hot and sticky against my cheek, and I wanted nothing more than to have his hands off me. His mouth away from me. His dick anywhere but where it was right now.

"Not anymore," I said a moment before I jerked my head back, enjoying the crunch of his nose smashing against the back of my skull. It was almost as satisfying as sexual release. Almost, and maybe just a little bit more.

His hands flew to his face and I yanked up my jeans as I spun around, kneeing him in the groin, then raising my boot to kick him against the other side of the stairwell. "Fucking bitch," he said through a groan, blood seeping down his chin beneath his hands.

"Maybe," I said, pushing the stairwell door open. I stood in the doorway and glared at him. "But I'm nobody's whore." I walked out into the alleyway, donkey-kicking the door shut behind me. Guess it was a fight I was looking for after all.

I jogged the five blocks to my shop, disgust and regret a lump of lead in my stomach. I never should've let that shithead Senate Nejeret put his hands on me in the first place. I slowed to a walk when my boot touched my native curb. I couldn't wait to get out of my clothes and back into something normal. Something clean. Something that didn't smell like *him*.

I pulled the shop door open and paused six steps in to glare at the man working in my office. Nik was leaning over a woman getting her tramp stamp covered up. I rushed past the door, not wanting to give him a chance to take in my all-too-recognizable scent. With his sensitive nose, there was no way he'd miss the smell of sex if I lingered.

The door's little bell chimed, and I glanced over my shoulder. "Oh, you've got to be kidding me," I said under my breath as Garth strode in. I stalked toward him. "What did I just tell you?" I said, seething. I really didn't want to get him killed, and that was exactly what would happen if the wrong Nejeret discovered that he, a lowly human, knew about us. Protecting ourselves, our people, was our number-one priority. We might be more powerful and live longer than humans, but they outnumbered us a million to one. Probably more. "Stay away from me, Garth."

His eyes shifted to the right, then to the left. Kimi was watching us from behind the counter, but the artists and clients in the offices seemed oblivious enough. Except for Nik, I'm sure. He was probably soaking up every single word. "I still need your help with the missing kids . . ."

Nope. Not happening. With his knowledge, if I got him involved with this Ouroboros situation and the missing Nejerets . . . his days were numbered, probably in the single digits. I shook my head and rolled my eyes, putting on an air of annoyance, which wasn't all that difficult. "Fine, whatever." My mind churned a mile a minute. "Meet me at the Fremont Troll at nine, tonight." Waiting for me there would keep him distracted while I searched the containers in Mari's mysterious shipment. "You can help me go through the missing kids' shit."

His brows knitted together. "Why not now?"

Because I need to know that you're somewhere else when I go to Harbor Island. "I have to prep some stuff," I told him, which wasn't exactly a lie. "Ask the cards for guidance . . ."

His eyes scrutinized my face, but finally, he nodded. "Alright. Nine o'clock tonight—the troll."

I nodded, then turned away from him and strode toward the beaded curtain, glancing sidelong at Nik as I passed by.

He was studiously not looking at me. Until his nostrils flared and his entire body stiffened. His jaw tensed, but he remained focused on his client. *My* client. There was no doubt in my mind that he'd been eavesdropping, but at the moment I was more concerned with what his nose was picking up than what his ears had.

I paused before the beaded curtain, like I might offer an explanation or an excuse. But there were none that didn't make me sound like the degenerate I'd become. So I continued on. I passed through the curtain, shame bubbling in my belly and disgust poisoning my heart. Because Nik knew. And if I wasn't mistaken by his reaction, he *cared*.

Even more disturbing—so did I. And that scared the shit out of me.

CHAPTER ELEVEN

I emerged from the shower with skin raw and rosy from excessive scrubbing. By the time I was lacing up my combat boots, my head was clear of the slosh and slog of too much tequila and my regrettable sexual encounter. I still didn't know the Senate Nejeret's name, but it didn't change the fact that I felt immeasurably better once the scent of him was off my body and I was comfy in my favorite pair of jeans and a tank top. Though it was the boots that really sealed the deal. Feeling like me again made everything else that was going wrong seem a little less vomit-worthy.

I grabbed a leftover slice of pizza from the fridge and headed into my office. The paint on the walls had changed again, becoming a dark, swirling miasma. I studied the designs, searching for meaning in the chaos while I ate the cold pizza. The only definite shape I could make out was a pitch-black orb that seemed to bob along throughout the midnight current.

Maybe, eventually it would make sense, but right now it was meaningless to me. I brushed the crumbs on my fingers off on my jeans and walked to the closet. I stared at the door for a solid minute. Was I really going to do this? After three full years of relative normalcy, was I really considering jumping back into this life

—one where I needed a sword at my back and a half-dozen other blades stowed about my person? Once I opened this door, once I came face-to-face with the darkness within—with my past—I wasn't sure I'd be able to shut it away again.

But for Dom . . .

To find him, to save him, I needed the darkness. Wasn't that why Nik had come to me in the first place? Not only because my *sheut* might make me the only one who could find him, but because I, personally, might be the only one willing to do what needs to be done to save him.

"You better not already be dead," I grumbled, sliding the closet door open and ignoring the lead sinking into the pit of my stomach.

The closet was empty, for the most part. Two identical small wood and iron chests sat on the closet floor, and a few items hung on hangers. I dragged the chests out into the room, then reached up to the overhead shelf, fingers searching for the only thing up there. For a moment, I thought it wasn't there. My heart skipped a few beats. But my fingertips grazed a strip of leather, then touched cold metal, and my worry eased.

I closed my hand around the old, familiar hilt of my sword, Mercy, and pulled it down from the shelf. "Hello, old friend," I murmured. I'd named the sword a long time ago, and it seemed wrong to ignore what she'd been to me. She was what had finally brought an end to the suffering left over from my human life. She was my right hand. My salvation.

Overall, Mercy was very katana-like. Her blade was long, slender, and slightly curved, with only one sharp edge, and the hilt was wrapped in worn black leather cording, leaving the shiny steel underneath peeking through in a diamond pattern. The butt of the hilt was solid silver, a Horus falcon molded into the metal, tarnished from the years of disuse. But however much it seemed like a katana, this sword was different. Mercy was ancient beyond any katana, and so very *other*. She'd been created by Nik, her *At* blade formed by his hands nearly two thousand years ago.

I unsheathed Mercy in one slow, smooth motion. The sound of her indestructible, crystalline *At* blade sliding against steel broke a dam in my mind, and memories flooded in. So many memories. So many lives. So many names crossed off a list with the slice of this blade through flesh and bone. My heart rate increased as adrenaline spiked my blood. I was ready. To fight. To kill. And if it came down to it, to avenge.

"Soon," I said to the bloodthirsty creature I'd just reawakened within me. Depending on what I found at Harbor Island, it could be *very* soon. I sheathed the sword. Soon, but not yet.

Kneeling, I set Mercy on the floor and opened the first of the chests. It had been so long since I'd stowed them in the closet, I couldn't remember which was which. One contained my stash of weapons and gear, the other, what would probably convince a criminal profiler that I was a serial killer. To some, maybe I was. But I hadn't killed for pleasure or for the thrill, even if, for a time, it had provided temporary relief from the grief. I'd killed with purpose. I'd killed for a cause. My cause, and the Senate's.

As soon as I lifted the lid, I closed my eyes and bowed my head. This chest didn't contain any weapons. Instead, it was filled with mementos—reminders—of the thirty-nine lives I'd taken during Mari's and my sanctioned reign of terror. As the Senate's assassins hunting rogues, rebel Nejerets, we'd taken out fifty-one targets total. I'd finished off most, not because I enjoyed taking lives, but because I enjoyed watching Mari torment our targets—our victims—less. We'd both lost our mothers to those rogues, and the hunger for vengeance could twist even the purest soul into a monster willing to do unthinkable things in the quest to sate the insatiable.

I opened my eyes and made myself peer into the chest. I reached in and pulled out the first thing my gaze landed on—a small, black leather-bound notebook. It had belonged to a Nejeret named Gerald, the last Nejeret I ever killed for the Senate. The last life I took. He'd been a deserter, running for his life, but he hadn't been a true rogue—the proof was in that little black book—

and he'd been the furthest thing from dangerous. He'd been terrified. He'd begged me not to kill him. He'd cried, in the end, when I'd freed his *ba* with one slice of Mercy's ever-sharp blade.

Groping blindly behind me, I found my sketch pad and the pen I'd left in here last time, among the droves of sketches of the missing Nejerets. I wrote down Gerald's first and last name. My victim's name. Sure, his *ba*—his everlasting soul—was out there, somewhere, maybe on this plane, maybe another, but his physical life had been ended by me. That mattered. I'd killed, and as with all the others, I'd also killed a part of me. Taking his life had been a breaking point for me, tipping me over the edge. The moment his heart stopped, I knew I was done. I'd felt it deep in my bones.

It was past time I acknowledged all that I'd done. It was time for me to accept it—finally—and, if I could, move on.

I pulled the next item out of the chest. A flyer advertising an animal adoption fair. It had been stuck to Bree Coolridge's fridge. She'd been hiding from us for six years and had amassed a small army of rescue animals. She'd had no less than seven cats, three dogs, and a turtle when Mari and I finally tracked her down. She'd been instrumental in orchestrating the events that led up to my mother's murder. I hadn't felt an ounce of pity for her when my blade pierced her heart, but I had felt bad for her animals. I hoped they found new homes afterward.

I added Bree's name below Gerald's, the act cathartic.

I moved through the chest, cataloguing and recording names until I had a list of thirty-nine. I tore the page free from my sketch pad and folded it up, tucking it into my back pocket, then returned everything to the chest and shut it once more. I shoved the chest back into the closet, vowing to never open it again. The next time I pulled it out would be to destroy it and everything within. I would honor my victims another way from now on.

Going through the second chest was a far less draining experience. I gathered the items I needed—two knives and their matching boot sheaths, a bracelet that doubled as a garrote, two four-inch needle daggers, and a leather belt that concealed a stubby push dagger in the buckle. I set everything on the floor beside me and returned that chest to the closet as well.

Once the closet doors were closed, I pushed everything to the side of the room, clearing a large space. I drew the sword and set the sheath and shoulder harness on the floor by the wall with the rest of my gear. It had been years since I'd wielded Mercy, and though I kept in fighting shape, I was out of practice with a weapon.

I spent the next few hours reconnecting with my sword. Her balance, the way she cut through the air, the way she worked as an extension of me—it all felt both familiar and foreign at the same time. I practiced with Mercy, spinning, thrusting, parrying, and rolling, until only familiarity remained.

When I emerged from my office, sweaty but oddly energized, the oven clock said it was five in the afternoon. I was planning to leave for the shipyard at eight. I had three more hours to kill.

I pulled a frozen pizza—BBQ chicken—from the freezer and turned on the oven. Too hungry to wait a half hour for the pie to be done, I peeked into the cupboard to the right of the stove, fingers crossed that it wouldn't be empty.

"Score," I sang quietly, pulling down an unopened bag of Hot Cheetos. They're terrible for me, I know, but that knowledge never stops me from inhaling a whole bag in a single sitting. And I'm not talking about one of the little bags. Think: family size. I tore the Cheetos open and shoved a handful into my mouth, then grabbed a Cherry Coke from the fridge. Leaning back against the counter, I alternated between scarfing down Cheetos and swigging Coke. I wholeheartedly accept that I'm the poster child for what not to eat. But then, I'm the poster child for what not to *fill-in-the-blank*, so why hold back?

I chomped on a few Cheetos.

How to kill the time?

I drank from the can of Coke. I ate a few more Cheetos. I looked around the fairly barren apartment, utterly uninspired.

An idea tiptoed into my mind, and I tilted my head from side to side, considering it. I set the pop can down on the counter behind me and pulled the list of names from my back pocket. I unfolded the paper, reading over the list as I sucked the spicy fake-cheese dust from my fingertips, scraping the stubbornest bits with my teeth.

I checked the clock on the stove. The oven was almost heated, and I was down to two hours and fifty-four minutes. I had a tattoo in mind for my left forearm, a piece to replace the fading tarot card, and I'd been playing with the idea of something else that would test the extent of my innate *sheut* power. I'd be cutting it close, time-wise, but if I wasn't done by the time I had to leave, I could always finish inking myself later.

The oven beeped, and I tossed the pizza on the rack, setting the timer before I headed for the door to the stairs. The shop closed early on Sundays, so there was a good chance that everybody had already left. Kimi might still be here, closing out the register and doing the final clean-up, but everyone else *should* be gone for the day. I crossed my fingers. Hopefully that included Nik. The idea of facing him right now, after everything that happened earlier . . . I couldn't handle it.

Thankfully, everyone, Kimi included, was gone. Even Nik. I didn't know where he'd gone or for how long, and at the moment, I didn't really care. I *didn't*. The shop was empty, and I was alone. Which was exactly what I'd been hoping for.

I paused at the beaded curtain.

So why was disappointment taking root in my chest?

Hands in fists and nails digging into my palms, I ignored the troublesome emotion and pushed through the curtain. I gathered up my tattoo machine, a fresh needle, and a bottle of black ink, then paused, staring into the ink drawer. Tucked in the very back was a bottle that almost seemed to be glowing, ethereal and iridescent.

I grinned, swapping out the black ink for Nik's *At* ink, and retreated back upstairs.

I stared at my left palm wondering what exactly I'd just created. A shimmery Eye of Horus stared back at me, taking up nearly my entire palm, reflecting colors from another dimension every time I shifted my hand and the light hit my skin differently. It was my clan's symbol, proclaiming my permanent obedience to Heru better than any papers or oath ever could. But it was more than that, too.

The Eye of Horus was an ancient symbol, steeped with so much meaning—thousands of years' worth. A civilization's worth. An entire mythology's worth. It was a symbol of protection from evil, from deceivers . . . from so many things. I didn't know how it would work, or if it would even do anything beyond being decorative, but I figured a symbol as potent as the Eye of Horus would have as good of a chance as anything of doing *something*. And gods knew I could use some protection right about now.

Learning how to use the powers afforded me by my *sheut* was a game of trial and error. I never really knew what would work and what wouldn't. I'd barely had the damn thing for three years. It had been a gift from the two new true gods—the Netjer, the inheritors of our universe—who'd been born just twenty years ago to Lex and Heru. And—laugh—*I* was their aunt. On the same day they'd gifted me my *sheut*, they'd left our universe and had yet to return. Sometimes it felt like they never would.

I closed my fist, then opened it again, somewhat surprised I couldn't feel the tattoo. It had healed almost as soon as I'd inked it, as usual, but I still thought I should be able to feel a stiffness or *something*. The depiction of the goddess Isis in *At* ink on my right arm had been the same way. It just looked like something that I should feel. But I didn't.

I glanced at the clock. Six-thirty. An hour and a half until it was go-time.

Cracking my neck, I re-inked the needle in the bottle of shimmering, liquid *At* and looked at the sheet of paper listing the names of everyone I'd killed. It was time to get to work on my next piece, on my memorial to every life I'd ended . . . and to every piece of myself I'd killed along the way. I brought the needle to my wrist and pressed it against my skin, starting with a *G*.

CHAPTER TWELVE

The rumble of the Ducati echoed off buildings as I rode through downtown Seattle. As usual, an accident had jammed up I-5, turning the southbound lanes into a glorified parking lot. It wasn't a major loss; I'd only have been on the freeway for a couple miles anyway, and by avoiding it, I didn't have to deal with the high stress of lane-splitting. I was already anxious enough.

Garth would realize I'd sent him on a wild goose chase soon enough, but at least this would keep him from being able to follow me. And just maybe, after getting stood up tonight, he'd get the hint; our partnership was over. And then there was Nik. I didn't know where he'd gone after filling in for me at the shop today, but I had a pretty damn good guess. I'd eat my boots if he wasn't heading to the Fremont Troll to spy on me. After all, he'd overheard my exchange with Garth. I hoped my instincts were correct. I wanted both of them as far away from this Ouroboros mess as possible. I was expendable; they weren't.

Is it weird that I was also a little giddy? It had been ages—*years*—since I'd seen any real action. The violent kind, not the sexy kind. My little scuffle with Nik two nights back had awakened something within me, almost like him showing up had started a domino effect that would drag me back into this world, kicking and screaming, if need be. Except I was going willingly.

I zigzagged through the streets of SoDo, the Industrial District south of downtown Seattle, and parked my bike on the east side of the Spokane Street Bridge, not wanting to alert whatever late-night workers or security personnel were lingering around on Harbor Island of my presence. Kickstand lowered, I hopped off the bike and hung my helmet on the upraised handlebar, then jogged to the West Seattle Bridge Trail, which crossed the Duwamish Waterway and carried pedestrians and bicyclists across man-made Harbor Island at ground level. It was dark out and cold at just past nine at night—nobody was on the trail.

Harbor Island was a funny place—I'd been here once on a field trip for my high school economics class. We were supposed to see international commerce at work on the enormous man-made island, but we really just ended up watching an hour-long safety movie about container ships and shipyard hazards, listening to a rep from the company that runs Terminal 18—the shipping container facility taking up the northeast quadrant of Harbor Island—explain pretty much everything there was to know about containers. It was disappointing, especially since many of us had been fantasizing about climbing all over the neat stacks of thousands of containers we were only allowed to view through a razor wire–topped chain-link fence.

I reached said chain-link fence, specifically the portion blocking off the south side of the industrial part of Harbor Island, and drew my sword. One of my favorite things about Mercy was that her *At* blade could cut through pretty much anything, and the wire making up a chain-link fence was about as resistant to my sword as chilled butter to a table knife; cutting through wasn't effortless, but it didn't make me sweat, either. Within five minutes, I'd cut an opening about four feet high—tall enough for me to squeeze through without resorting to crawling.

I'd taken three cautious steps onto the parking lot of Harley Marine Services when a motion-activated floodlight winked on.

"Shit," I hissed, slinking another dozen steps to crouch between two large white service trucks. I waited for a minute or two, listening for footsteps and engines. Hearing none, I straightened a little and made my way across the lot, moving in the shadows between vehicles whenever possible.

The next lot had to belong to an auto shipping company, because it basically looked like the lot of a car dealership. And a damn fancy one. It worked perfectly for my purposes. I managed to cross to the north end of the lot without tripping any more motion sensors.

After that, the east half of the man-made island was all Terminal 18. I stood at the edge of the packed car lot between two sedans, their black paint gleaming like oil in the dim moonlight. There was a fairly large open stretch of asphalt before the never-ending rows of red, blue, green, and orange shipping containers started, some stacked four or five high. On the far right, following the island's artificial shoreline, clusters of cranes in twos and threes stood sentinel, burnt-orange behemoths watching over everything.

I snuck to the water's edge, hoping any motion sensors for floodlights or cameras wouldn't reach that far since the movement of the water would be constantly setting them off. Keeping low and moving slowly, I made my way further into Terminal 18.

Mari's text from that morning had mentioned that the Ouroboros containers belonging to the illicit shipment would be stored between slots A-27 and A-30. According to the satellite maps I'd scoured online, row A was nearest to the water. Meaning it should be just straight ahead.

I squinted as I neared the first stack of containers—a stack of two, both green and both painted with the John Deere logo on the side. They were in spot A-13. The next stack, three containers in spot A-17—two orange, one red—were unlabeled, so far as I could see, besides a series of nonsensical numbers and letters on the door side.

I scanned the white numbers painted on the asphalt ahead. Sure enough, ten spots down, I found A-27. A stack of three containers piled one atop the other, all blue, called me onward, followed immediately by a stack of four. I jogged ahead, heart pounding and blood a raging river in my ears.

"Alright, you shitstains," I said under my breath as I reached the supposed Ouroboros containers. "What are you hiding?" I stopped beside the stack of three, surveilling the long sides facing me. There was nothing to identify them as actually belonging to Ouroboros, so I moved around to the water side, where the container's doors might give me some hint that I was in the right spot.

They didn't—like so many of the containers filling the yard, they were labeled only with a series of letters and numbers, none of which made sense to me.

I took a step backward, peering at all four stacks of solid blue containers. I placed my hands on my hips and chewed on my bottom lip. They were right where Mari had said they would be, but there was only one way to find out if these were the right containers—the same way I would find out what the hell Ouroboros was up to. I had to break into them.

Drawing my sword slowly enough that the ring of *At* on steel was minimal, I approached the first stack. The lock on the bottom container looked complex and heavy duty, and there was no way for me to tell whether or not it was rigged with some kind of an alarm. But who says I have to go through the lock to get into the container? It would take some time and a fair amount of elbow grease, but Mercy was more than capable of cutting through the thick sheet of steel.

The tip of my sword was inches from the container's door when I heard the creak of metal on metal. I froze, sword gripped in both hands and breath held, and scanned the containers around me.

The door of the second container in a stack of five in slot A-30 inched open.

I pulled back Mercy and raised my elbows, settling into a ready stance.

Something tumbled out of the container, falling at least eight feet to the pavement. It landed with an oomph and a groan. Not a some*thing*; a some*one*.

"Kat? Is that you?" It was Mari—the someone. She pushed herself off the ground a few inches and raised her head. There was barely a crescent of a moon high overhead, and across the water, Seattle far outshone the stars, but my eyes were good enough to see the lab coat she was wearing. And the bloodstains marring the fabric and the dark bruises on her face and neck. She looked like hell beaten over.

My palm itched, and I rubbed it against my jeans. "What the hell are you doing here, Mars?"

Mari coughed a laugh, spitting up something that looked suspiciously like blood. "Your concern is underwhelming, as usual."

Hesitantly, I sheathed my sword and approached, offering her a hand up. Someone must've caught her poking around, but that didn't explain how she'd ended up *in* one of the containers she'd all but sent me here to find.

She accepted my outstretched hand, pulling herself up to a sitting position but not even attempting to stand. She coughed weakly and clutched one side like the action hurt her ribs. "I need a minute . . ."

I nodded, still rubbing my palm against my jeans. "Is anything broken?" Because if she had any broken bones, I had no doubt she'd prefer for me to set them now rather than wait until they'd healed so much that they'd have to be re-broken to heal properly.

She shook her head, her dark bob matted in chunks. "Not for me. I don't know about Dom . . ."

"What do you mean—Dom?" I scanned the area, searching for his lanky form but finding no sign of him. "Is he here? Where? What happened?"

"We snuck out together." She pointed up to the partially open container with her chin. "He's up there. He's in pretty bad shape, though."

Before she'd finished speaking, I'd launched myself at the

container, grabbing hold of the lip. My feet scrabbled for purchase on the vertically ribbed face of the bottom container. The toe of my boot found the boxed lock, and I used that to leverage myself the rest of the way up.

It was even darker inside the container, the sliver of light spilling in through the opening barely enough to allow even my heightened Nejeret vision to make out the interior.

But I could see Dom, lying on the floor a couple yards in. Pallets laden with boxes filled the space beyond him, their shrink-wrap gleaming dully in the barely there light.

"Dom," I said, rushing forward and dropping to my knees beside him. I turned his head so I could see his face. "Dom, are you alright?"

No response.

My heart turned to lead.

I pressed my fingers to his neck in search of a pulse, letting out a relieved breath when I found it, faint but steady enough for now. So long as his heart was beating, propelling his Nejeret blood through his body, and so long as his injuries weren't immediately fatal, he'd be able to regenerate.

I shook him by the shoulder. "Dom, can you hear me?"

But still, he said nothing. He did nothing. He was out cold. But I could see him; I could touch him. It was a far cry from the position I'd been in an hour ago, and I couldn't ignore the burst of euphoria that sprouted in my chest. The hard part was over. I'd found him. It would all be downhill from here.

CHAPTER THIRTEEN

The first time I met Mari, she almost killed me. In her defense, I was trying to kill her. She's the opposite of Nik, able to pull a far more dangerous and volatile universal energy into this realm, give it form, and shape it to her will. It was with that energy that she nearly killed not only my body, but also my eternal soul.

The universe was created by the old gods, Re and Apep, around a principle of absolute, ultimate balance known as *ma'at*. If *At* is the principle element of creation, then *anti-At* is its inverse—destruction. It binds to *At*, binds to every aspect of creation, moving it, changing it, keeping the universe from growing stagnant. We are, all of us, objects of creation, of *At*. Nejerets carry a little piece of *At* within us, in the form of our *ba*—our soul. Should we come into physical contact with *anti-At*, we'll change. The *anti-At* particles, torn from their usual plane of existence, become ravenous in their need to destroy, binding with anything and everything. Binding with us, consuming our *ba*, until we no longer exist. Until we *never* existed at all. If we come into contact with anti-At, we'll be *unmade*.

Which is precisely what almost happened to me, a long time ago, when Mari nearly killed me. Nik and I had fought, much like this morning, and I'd run off, dead set on avenging my mother's death. I'd attacked Mari, mistakenly believing she was responsible, and she'd stabbed me. With a gleaming black dagger made of pure *anti-At*. Only Nik arriving seconds later and extracting all of the otherworldly poison from my body by binding every molecule of *anti-At* with its one true mate, *At*, had allowed me to survive. Not unscathed—my *ba* had been damaged and would forever bear the scars—but I hadn't been unmade, either.

Mari had gone from my enemy to my ally in a matter of minutes. We'd been through hell together, and she was like a sister to me, even if we hadn't spoken in years. There weren't many people I'd trust with my life, but if push came to shove, I'd trust Mari.

"Mars," I called through the container door. "Can you give me a hand?" I dragged Dom to the door by his armpits. "We need to get him out of here." He wasn't wearing anything substantial, just a pair of sweatpants and a white T-shirt—both torn and covered with bloodstains that looked black in the dim light—and he felt far too cold for my liking.

"I'm still too weak," Mari said from outside. "I'll just end up dropping him. Where's Nik? He could help you."

I frowned, my hand burning. "He's not here." I set Dom down a half-dozen inches from the edge and poked my head out through the opening. "How long until you're strong enough? We need to get him out of here before anyone notices we're here." A thought struck me, and I realized we might be under a far greater time crunch than I'd previously thought. "Do they know this is how you escaped? Will they come looking for you here?"

Mari was still sitting on the ground, legs folded beneath her, back hunched, and hands in her lap. She shook her head. "I should be mostly recovered in fifteen minutes or so. They worked me over pretty good. Do you have anything to eat? That'd speed it up . . ."

I reached into the right zippered pocket of my leather jacket and pulled out the protein bar I'd stashed there before leaving my apartment. Never leave home without one. "What happened, anyway?" I asked, tossing the bar to Mari.

She tore into the wrapper with gusto. "They caught me nosing around in a restricted lab over there," she said, nodding back toward the rest of SoDo sprawling behind her. "I found the missing Nejerets, but I was only able to get Dom out. He didn't look too hot when I found him, but he was still able to help me fight our way out." She stuffed the last piece of the protein bar into her mouth, balled up the wrapper, and threw it on the ground a few feet away. "We should find Nik and go back for the others."

I glanced down at my palm. It burned something fierce now, like I held a handful of stinging nettles. My eyebrows drew together. Despite the very real and very uncomfortable sensation, there didn't seem to be anything wrong with the skin of my palm. It wasn't red or swollen, and the Eye of Horus looked the same, gleaming in the subdued evening light.

"Where is Nik, anyway?" Mari asked. "I thought he'd be with you."

"Don't know," I said, shrugging. "Don't care." Why was she obsessing about him all of a sudden? They'd never been close, and her fixation on him was setting off alarm bells in my mind.

"Damn it, Kat. You couldn't make this easy for once, could you?" Mari reached into the pocket of her bloodied lab coat and pulled out a black sphere about the size of a baseball. "I can't go back there without him, and I really didn't want to have to resort to this, but I swear I don't have a choice." She lobbed the black orb up to me, saying, "Catch!"

I reacted instinctively, reaching out to catch the thing with my right hand even as my mind screamed, *NO!* Because the orb was made of *anti-At*.

"No . . ." I gaped down at my hand, paralyzed by mind-numbing horror. Any second now, the *anti-At* would start soaking into my skin with a sickening tingling sensation.

Fuck. I'd gone and done it again. I just killed myself with my own stupidity and caught the damn orb of death. And thanks to me, Nik was nowhere in sight. This time, death—unmaking—would stick. And the damage to the timeline would be astronomical, because I'd been involved, however accidental or unwilling, in a lot of important, world-forming shit. If I disappeared from existence, everything I'd done since the day I was born would be undone.

"Where's Nik?" Mari asked, on her feet now, fists on her hips and stare intense. "Call him. He'll drop whatever he's doing and come running to save you."

"What?" I stared at the black orb, horrified and disgusted with myself, then gaped at Mari. "Why, Mars?" I looked at her, eyes stinging. "*Why?*" We hadn't been close in years, but we'd been inseparable once. She was like a sister to me. I'd *trusted* her.

"Please, Kat." She wrung her hands. "Call Nik. He'll fix this."

I blinked away tears, the chaos that had clouded my mind finally clearing enough that coherency returned, at least a little. "You need him." I cleared my throat, eyes narrowing. "That's what this has all been about. Your questions about me and him and the Senate . . . you telling me—*us*—to come check out this shipment . . ." I shook my head slowly. "God, I really am an idiot."

"Your words . . ."

I glanced down at my hand. Why wasn't it tingling? Last time, when her *anti-At* blade had been buried deep in my side, I'd felt the particles working through me like tiny, soul-consuming insects. But this time, I felt nothing but the slightly warm surface of the orb against my shimmering skin.

My eyes widened as I registered what I was seeing. The ancient goddess tattoo in my skin—she'd extended one of her wings, the iridescent feathers extending onto my palm, an unbroken barrier of *At* between myself and the *anti-At* orb. She was protecting me.

I looked at Mari, my lips curving into a grin. A low, deep laugh spilled forth. "Would you look at that . . ."

Mari stared at my hand, disbelief written all over her face.

"Not today, bitch," I hissed, then chucked the orb into the water. It was relatively harmless out there, and I hoped the Puget

Sound's current would carry it away to unknown depths where, in all likelihood, it would never have the chance to unmake anyone's soul again.

A slow, wicked smile spread across Mari's face. She looked better now, like she'd healed some—or maybe she just hadn't been that injured to begin with. Dom was still unconscious . . . still badly wounded. I frowned. He should've been regenerating. He should look better, too. But he didn't.

"Do you have any idea what you just—"

"Oh, shut up already," I spat, cutting Mari off as I drew my sword. Mercy sang out, a clear, pristine sound as her solidified *At* blade slid free of its steel sheath. It glimmered, almost glowing in the faint moonlight. I jumped down from the container, rolling on my landing and immediately settling into a defensive crouch a dozen feet from Mari. I didn't know why she'd betrayed me, but I knew how she would pay.

Mari stood with her feet shoulder width apart, twin black daggers as long as her forearms gripped in either hand. They appeared out of nowhere. "I don't want to fight you, Kat."

"Then don't," I said, lunging at her.

She raised her daggers, crossing them to block my sword. Her shorter blades met mine in a shower of glittering sparks of every conceivable color. The only thing as strong as *At* was *anti-At.* Our blades were evenly matched, even if *we* weren't. I'd always been the better fighter.

"I said I didn't *want* to fight you," Mari said through gritted teeth. "Not that I won't."

CHAPTER FOURTEEN

I was beating her. With every strike and parry, Mari weakened, and I drew closer to landing a lethal blow. She had to have known that if it came down to the two of us fighting, this was how it would end. So why set up some elaborate trap—and a shoddy one, at that—just to get to Nik? What did she need from him?

I blocked both of Mari's blades with my sword, twisting my own blade so hers tangled. She cried out, dropping one. I kicked her in the abdomen, launching her back a solid six feet. She skidded on her ass and dropped her other dagger, freeing up both hands to catch herself.

I stalked toward her, stopping just beyond her feet. I wasn't dumb enough to stand over her—not when she could materialize a new *anti-At* weapon in the blink of an eye. "Tell me why you're doing this," I said, staring down at her, sword at the ready should she try to lash out. "Why are you helping *them*? Did you really get caught, or was that all a lie, too?" For all I knew, she was the one responsible for Dom's current condition.

Mari laughed bitterly but said nothing.

"Tell me!"

"I bet you can't guess what's in that little sphere."

"I don't give two shits what's in the—"

"Dom's *ba*." She brought her hand up to her mouth, gasping dramatically. "But—oh, no! You threw it into the Sound! Now how will he ever be whole again?" She blinked, eyes wide and innocent. Mocking. "He won't be able to regenerate without it, that's for sure. And with his injuries . . ."

I shot the quickest glance at the open shipping container, suddenly more terrified for Dom's life than I'd ever been before.

Not quick enough. Mari struck, knocking my sword to the side and stabbing something into my belly.

I looked down, shocked to see her hand around the glistening black handle of a brand-new *anti-At* dagger, plunged to the hilt into my abdomen. It hurt like a bitch, stealing my breath even as the pain made me gasp. But even worse than the pain was the tingling. I could feel the miniscule *anti-At* particles separating from the blade and soaking into me, binding with my *ba*—my soul. I could feel myself being *unmade*.

"I'm sorry, Kat," Mari said, face twisted and eyes pleading. She seemed absolutely genuine, all mocking nonchalance from a moment earlier gone. Had it been an act? Or was *this* the act? "I didn't want this, I swear, but you didn't give me a choice. Call Nik and tell him to come here. He can save you." Gingerly, she pulled the dagger free and tossed it away, then eased me down to the ground with an arm around my waist.

Why? Why was getting Nik to come here so important to her that she'd risk changing the world as we knew it by unmaking me? The possible reasons were too slippery, and I could focus only on one thing. Nik. I needed him. He could save me.

I sucked in a shuttering breath. "I—I don't have—" I squeezed my eyes shut and clenched my jaw to fend off the pain. "—his number."

Mari knelt on the ground beside me. "Well, where is he? You said he reached out to you—I know he wouldn't just let you run off on your own."

Lying on my back, right hand covering my stab wound, I stared at her. Now that the end was in sight, I was just glad that I wasn't alone. Her presence was oddly comforting, even though she was responsible for my impending death. "W—what makes you say th—that?"

"Because he knows you too well. You're rash, especially when your heart's actually in the fight." She shook her head, her eyes filled with sadness. "You let your emotions get in the way. You always have." She squeezed my shoulder. "Where do you think he is? I'll track him down. We can still save you."

Tears welled in my eyes. I tried to blame the pain, but they'd only started after I'd heard the genuine concern in Mari's voice . . . seen it in her shadowed jade eyes. "You're th—the one who d—did this." I inhaled shakily. "Why do you c—care?"

"Because I love you, idiot." She combed matted hair out of her face with dirty fingers. "God, you're such a moron sometimes."

I stared at her, wide-eyed and dumbstruck. And dying. Worse. Being unmade.

"Where's Nik, Kat? Please, you must have some idea."

I narrowed my eyes, not trusting that this wasn't all another act. "How do I know y—you'll come back?" I tried to shift my body into a more comfortable position, but it only served to sharpen the twisting pain in my gut. "You know I'll c—come after you."

She shrugged. "I'll chance it. But what I can't risk is letting you get unmade. You've played too big of a part in shaping our world into what it is today. Who knows what it would've become without you?"

I coughed a laugh. "One w—way to find out . . ."

"That's not going to happen." Mari loomed over me. "Where is he?"

I stared into her green eyes for long seconds, weighing my options. There weren't many. "The troll," I finally said. I wasn't positive, but it was my best guess. "In Fremont." I switched hands, my right so coated in blood it wasn't doing any good anymore. "He's probably there." *With Garth* . . . The thought felt important, but my sluggish, blood-deprived brain couldn't figure out why. "If not—maybe my apartment."

"Alright, it's a start." She stood and started jogging away. "Don't go anywhere," she called over her shoulder, a cell phone already at her ear. "I *will* come back for you." I never even had a chance to find out why all of this was happening.

Mari was out of sight by the time I realized my palm was burning even worse than before. The searing pain became so intense it muted the stab wound to a dull ache. I pulled my hand away from the wound and held it over my face. The tattoo of the Eye of Horus had changed; it still shimmered with that otherworldly iridescence of *At*, but now shining onyx streaks spread throughout the symbol like veins in marble.

"What the hell?"

And then it hit me—the tingling caused by the poisonous *anti-At* had stopped. It was gone.

The obsidian streaks in the tattoo had to be the *anti-At*, pulled from me, body and soul, by the Eye of Horus. I stared in awe at the thing that had just saved my life. That had just saved my whole damn existence. Protection amulet indeed.

The burning in my palm subsided and the streaks settled, the *anti-At* particles bound to the *At* in the ink, and I was left lying there with an ordinary stab wound. It was the kind of injury I could easily heal from. The kind I could deal with later. There were more urgent matters to attend to.

Gingerly, I pushed myself up to a sitting position and unzipped my left jacket pocket. I fished out my phone with fingers slimy with blood and dialed 9-1-1.

The phone rang twice before an emergency dispatcher picked up. "Nine-one-one, what's your emergency?"

"I need an ambulance." I clutched my side, gritting my teeth. "My friend—"

"State your name, please."

"My friend's dying," I snapped. "He needs help, *now*!"

"Where are you, ma'am?"

"Harbor Island—Terminal 18. There's a man in a shipping container—slot A-27. It's the second container up, so they'll need a ladder." I brushed my hair back from my face, cringing when strands pulled from sticking in the drying blood on my hand. "Just hurry, please!"

"Alright, ma'am, we're on our way. I need you to stay with your friend until—"

I hung up the phone and shoved it back into my pocket. Gritting my teeth, I pulled my legs in and, ever so carefully, stood. I lifted my sword, hilt-first, with the toe of my boot, then bent down part of the way to pick it up. I strained against the pain to sheath it over my shoulder and hobbled to the edge of the shore of the artificial island to search the smooth, black and silver surface of the water for the *anti-At* orb.

It took me nearly ten minutes to find it, and by the time I spotted Dom's *ba* bobbing along on the water's surface, I could hear the approaching sirens. I dove into the water and swam to the orb, my heavy boots becoming leaden in the water and doing their damnedest to drag me down. I grabbed it with my left hand, trusting the Eye of Horus would protect me again, and crawl-stroked to the dock on the opposite side of the waterway, muscles fatigued, lungs straining, and side burning with pain. Staying afloat became so difficult that for a minute there, I doubted I would make it.

It took an insane amount of effort, but I managed to pull myself up onto the dock behind a massive container ship. I flopped onto my back, giving myself a chance to catch my breath before the police and paramedics arrived. I needed to be gone before they had a chance to spot me and drag me in for questioning. There was somewhere else I needed to be. I had to find a way to get to Nik before Mari found him. I had no idea why she was so desperate to get her hands on him, but if it had anything to do with Ouroboros and whatever they were up to, it couldn't be anything good.

Garth's at the troll, too. Again, I had the nagging sense that *that* piece of information was important, but I couldn't quite put my thumb on the reason why.

I stared up at the stars, realization a bright burst in my mind, and I suddenly understood. I may not have had Nik's number, but I had Garth's. Or, at least, I had a way to contact Garth. I'd just used it.

I fumbled with my left pocket, pulling out my phone once more. It was dead, killed by the dip in the water.

"Oh, for fuck's sake," I grumbled, sitting up. The searing pain in my side was lessening—probably not because it was already healing, but because my brain was normalizing the sensation. I was getting used to it. Worked for me.

I climbed to my feet using one of the ship's thick dock lines, took a deep breath, and stumble-jogged back to the Ducati. It was the fastest I could go.

CHAPTER FIFTEEN

The nearest pay phone I could find was four blocks east in the Industrial District outside of a twenty-four-hour convenience store. The clerk working the graveyard shift watched me through the front windows. I guess a drowned-rat motorcycle chick dripping blood on the pavement is quite the sight to see. I turned my back to him as I dialed 9-1-1.

Three rings this time before the dispatcher picked up. "9-1-1, what's your emergency?" I was fairly certain it was the same woman I'd spoken to earlier.

I cleared my throat and made an effort to deepen my voice. "I have reason to believe one of your officers is in trouble. I need you to connect me to—"

"What is your name?"

"You've got to be fucking kidding me." I leaned my forehead against the inside of the phone's metal privacy alcove. "Officer Garth Smith is in trouble, and I need to talk to him *right now*."

"Officer Smith has already called for backup. What is your name and how did you know he would be in trouble?"

"He already called for backup?" I went cold all over. Had Mari called in some Ouroboros goons to help her capture Nik? Would they hurt Garth? Would they go so far as to kill him? "Then it's too late," I said numbly, and hung up.

I stood there for a moment, feeling slightly nauseated, then took a deep breath and fished my sodden wallet out of my jacket's interior pocket before going into the 7-Eleven. Standing there being worried and afraid and feeling sorry for myself wouldn't help anyone. I headed straight for the refrigerated case of energy drinks in the back of the store, pulled two oversized cans out, and brought them up to the checkout counter. "No change," I said, dropping a soggy five on the counter before walking out through the door.

If there was one thing I'd learned during my years as one of the Senate's assassins, it's that carrying cash is one of the best ways to keep a low profile. I always have some on me. And since many of my current clients paid in cash, I almost never had to go to the bank.

I chugged the first can of sugar and caffeine in thirty seconds flat. I tossed it into the garbage can by the door, then cracked open the second and downed it in five big gulps. They should sustain me for at least an hour, even with the untended stab wound. When I crashed, I would land hard, but this bought me some time.

I hopped back onto my bike and kicked the engine on, zooming away from the convenience store. I made it to Fremont in barely ten minutes—record time—only slowing once I was within two blocks of the troll. I couldn't hear any sirens, but I could see the emergency vehicle's lights flashing off trees and the sides of houses up ahead.

I rode around a corner and pulled the Ducati up onto the sidewalk, killing the engine and backing it into the driveway of a dumpy-looking house with an overgrown yard. I left the bike tucked between a broken-down pickup raised up on cinder blocks and a rusted boat trailer and snuck out to the sidewalk, sticking to the shadows by the bushes and trees.

I had a good vantage point from behind the trunk of a massive pine about halfway up the block. I could see the five police cruisers pulled up haphazardly around the underpass the Fremont Troll called home. An ambulance was just being loaded with a gurney, and if my eyes were right—and they almost always were—Garth was the injured guy strapped in, face covered by an oxygen mask. My heart sank.

I didn't know why Mari'd attacked him, but I was just relieved she hadn't killed him outright. But don't get me wrong, the relief didn't come close to surpassing the fury burning through my veins. Garth was innocent in all this, and he was, in a sense, my friend. Or the closest thing I had to a friend right now. He didn't deserve this. I'd pay Mari back for what she'd done to him.

I scanned the rest of the people milling around, looking for Nik's lanky silhouette. But all I saw were cops and paramedics and about a dozen lookie-loos. More civilians were trickling in from around the neighborhood. I searched the streets and yards around the underpass but saw no retreating figure. Which meant Mari must've found Nik. But had she taken him by force, or had he gone willingly once he'd heard I was in danger? Or was Nik injured, too?

My anger spiked. Hands in fists, I closed my eyes and took several long, deep breaths. Mari had said I had a tendency to act rashly and let my emotions take over. She viewed that as a weakness; I never had. She was about to bear the brunt of that rashness firsthand.

Hearing a person walk up the sidewalk just a few yards away, I opened my eyes and slunk deeper into the shadows. I couldn't stay here.

I supposed I knew where Mari and Nik would be headed—back to Harbor Island to "save" me—and I played with the idea of following them back there. But there were bound to be police crawling all over the place by now, thanks to my 9-1-1 call. Mari wouldn't risk it, and she would assume I'd ducked out as soon as the cops arrived.

Head hanging and hands in my coat pockets, I headed back to my bike. There was no real reason for me to track Nik and Mari down right away. She needed Nik for something—not that I knew what—and I figured he was safe enough for now. Besides, they'd be too preoccupied searching for me to get started on whatever plans she had for him. Dom was the one most urgently in need of help.

Back on the motorcycle, I pulled out of the little hideaway and wound around the block until I was merging onto Aurora Avenue to head back downtown to Harborview Medical Center. It was the city's most renowned trauma hospital, and there was no doubt in my mind that the paramedics would've taken Dom there.

By the time I turned off the bike in the hospital's parking garage, the glowing green digits on my little dashboard clock said it was just after ten at night. I parked the bike near the skybridge and hopped off. I shed my visible weapons, stashing them in a nearby garbage can that was nearly empty—under the bag, of course—and followed the signs to the skybridge. Visiting hours must've ended a while ago, because the garage was nearly empty.

I stopped in the third-floor bathroom near the elevators to clean up. My clothes were still soaked through, the *anti-At* orb containing Dom's *ba* bulging in my left coat pocket, and my hair was a tangled mess. Whatever scrapes or bruises I'd acquired during the fight were all but healed by now, though the wound in my abdomen still throbbed in time with my pulse and seeped blood with every intake of breath.

I folded up a wad of paper towels and pressed them against the wound, wrapping my belt around my torso to hold the bundle in place. At least Mari'd had the decency to stab me below the hem of my tank top, leaving my shirt intact.

I zipped up my leather coat and stared at my reflection in the mirror. There was nothing I could do about the wet clothes, or about the eau de harbor water wafting off me, a delightful scent that would only get better. "Well, I think this is as good as it's going to get," I told my reflection. The girl in the mirror was a sorry copy of me, and I stuck my tongue out at her.

It was easy enough to find the emergency room—they're always on the ground floor, at least in every hospital I've ever been to.

Convincing the intake nurse to share any information with me about Dom was more on the difficult side.

"Listen . . ." I let the sorrow and fear and dread I'd been feeling since first finding out about Dom's disappearance well up in the form of tears. My chin trembled, and when I spoke again, the quaver in my voice wasn't on purpose. "He's my brother. I just want to be here for him when he wakes up." I wiped a tear from my cheek with my knuckle. "*If* he wakes up . . ."

Finally—*finally*—the nurse took pity on me. Her entire demeanor softened and a warm, motherly glow shone in her eyes. "Alright, hon." She turned in her chair and stood, coming around the partition. "He's in surgery right now, but you can go back to the family waiting area." She held out an arm toward a doorway leading to a bustling emergency room filled with bay after curtained bay of patients in various stages of checking in and being treated.

She guided me through that chaotic room to another area beyond, where chairs, large potted plants, and an enormous fish tank had been arranged to delineate a "waiting area" within a larger open space at the convergence of several hallways. There were magazines on little end tables and arranged in a wooden display stand and not much else.

"There are vending machines around that corner, there," the nurse said, pointing across the open space. "And I'm not sure how long he'll be in surgery, but the cafeteria opens again at six in the morning."

"Is there a phone? I need to call my family," I said, voice catching. God, Heru was going to be pissed when he found out about all of this, specifically that I'd gotten involved in Nejeret matters without talking to him first. And Lex—she was, quite possibly, even closer with Dom than I was. She was going to kill me.

"Of course," the nurse said, pointing to a plant at one corner of the waiting area. "It's just on that table, there, hidden by the plant. You go ahead." She bustled away. "I'm going to check in with the doctors working on your brother . . . tell them he has family waiting so they know to update you if there's any news."

I nodded, feet dragging as I walked into the waiting area. The boost from the two energy drinks was depleting quickly, and I could feel the pull of regenerative sleep. It was tempting to give in —my wound would heal much faster then—but I'd be knocked out until my body determined it was recovered enough and ready for sustenance. I couldn't shake the feeling that if I gave in to the pull, something would happen to Dom, but if I could hold on to consciousness with my much lesser wound, then he could hold on to life.

I plopped down in the chair by the phone and picked up the receiver. It was one of the old corded phones with real buttons you could actually push. I dialed the only number I could think of that would get me to my family back on Bainbridge. The line rang several times before anyone picked up. She probably wouldn't answer; it was an unrecognized number, after all, and it was late, especially for the mother of a three-year-old. I thought the call was going to go to voice mail, so I reached out my other hand to press the phone's hang-up mechanism.

"Hello?" Lex said after the fifth ring.

My voice stuck in my throat.

"Hello? Is anyone there?"

I licked my lips and swallowed roughly. "Lex?" My eyes stung, tears breaking free almost immediately. This was why I stayed away from the people I loved. This stupid, overwhelming vulnerability.

The line was quiet for a few seconds. "Kat? What's wrong?" Because for me to call her now, after nearly three years of radio silence, it had to be something bad.

Well, damn it, it was.

"You guys need to come to Harborview . . . Aset and Neffe need to come here." I cleared my throat, hoping Heru's twin sister and daughter, the two oldest, most skilled doctors I knew, would be able to do something for Dom even if the surgeons here couldn't. They had over ten thousand years of combined experience going for them, so the odds were in their favor. "It's Dom . . ."

Lex didn't respond for several more seconds, but I could hear her voice, muffled as though she'd pressed the phone to her shirt. And then she was back, clear as day. "We're on our way."

CHAPTER SIXTEEN

The hours passed in that waiting area in a blur, my mind trying its hardest to float away to the land of dreams while I did my damnedest to make sure that didn't happen. I guzzled far more vending machine coffee in a couple-hour period than was safe. Add to that the packaged cookies and little brownie bites I kept scarfing down, and I was feeling increasingly nauseated, my heart jackhammering against my sternum and my hands shaking even as my eyelids drooped.

Eventually, the call of regenerative sleep was too much for the battalion of sugar and caffeine or the discomfort of the belt pressing into my injury and pinching the skin of my waist. I passed out, curled up on the chair by the phone, and was, for some unknown period of time, dead to the world.

The scent of grease and fried potatoes filled my nose, luring me out of a dreamless sleep. I groaned, not understanding how I'd come to be lying down or why my belt wasn't pinching my skin.

"I knew that would work." The voice was feminine and more than a little smug. I recognized it immediately.

"Lex?" I cracked my eyelids open to see a pair of white fast-food bags with the familiar orange and blue Dick's Drive-In logo across the side, stuffed so full of glorious fast food that the paper bags were bulging. Lex's face was beside them, her head tilted to the side, her strange, crimson eyes mere inches from mine.

"Hey, Kit-Kat." Her lips curved into a hesitant smile. "How are you feeling?" She brushed a strand of hair from my eyes with gentle fingertips. She still treated me like her kid sister, even though I was technically about twenty years older than her due to a ridiculously complicated time travel situation. I didn't really mind, though. It was actually kind of nice that she remembered me the way I used to be.

I pushed myself up from the string of chairs I'd stretched out on while asleep, moving the warm bags of greasy burgers and fries to the seat next to me, and rubbed my eyes. "Better," I told her.

Peering down at myself, I pulled up my tank top a few inches to get a look at the stab wound. My belt was gone—coiled up on the floor nearby—and a neat gauze bandage had replaced the blood-crusted wad of paper towels.

"Aset cleaned you up when we first got here, while Neffe was in conferring with Dom's doctors," Lex explained. She moved the fast-food bags closer to me. "You should eat. You're too thin." It wasn't a judgment, just a statement of the aftereffects of Nejeret regeneration. My body had diverted all possible resources to healing me, including drawing from any stored energy, namely fat.

I huffed out a breath. "And here I was hoping to pick up a few years for a couple days . . . see what it's like to be a real-life grown-up." I dug into the first paper bag, pulling out a cheeseburger wrapped in foil paper and tearing it open, stomach rumbling. I was ravenous.

Lex laughed softly, but no hint of mirth touched her eyes. "I got you a strawberry milkshake, too," she said, her gaze flicking to the table with the phone, where two Dick's cups awaited me. "And a Cherry Coke."

I grabbed the latter, taking a deep pull from the straw. The sweet, fizzy liquid helped me get the burger down in three bites. I unwrapped a second as soon as the first was nothing but crumbs. "Thanks," I said around a mouthful.

She nodded and stood, not the least bit disturbed by my pig-out session. She knew my hunger as well as any Nejeret who'd been injured enough to go through regeneration cycles. She crossed the waiting area to sit in a chair beside her husband, Heru. I was studiously avoiding looking at him. I knew what I'd find if I did—that haughty, hawkish stare, his burnished gold eyes focused on me, and his expression a cold, emotionless mask. Painfully beautiful, just like his sister's and his nephew's faces, but giving nothing away.

"So, what happened?" It was Lex who asked first, despite Heru's eyes searing the question into my skin. "To Dom," she said. "And to you."

I could only stand to look at her for a few seconds. I didn't see blame in her garnet eyes, but that didn't stop me from feeling it. My gaze quickly diverted to the floor, seeking out the pale stains no amount of carpet cleaner could remove from the mutely patterned ivory and blue rug.

"Explain," Heru said, the one word an iron-clad command. It was the first time I'd heard his voice in years, but his faint, slightly Middle Eastern accent was exactly as I remembered it. As was the power he could wield with his voice alone.

He was a Senate member, elected by our people along with Aset and Lex. But he was more than that, too—the leader of my clan and the general to our people. He'd been the former for more than twenty years, since I swore an oath forsaking my clan of birth for his, and the latter for over four thousand years. Power wafted off him in waves, and he had more charisma and charm than anyone I'd ever met, though he could turn it off like flipping a switch. I never understood how Lex could do it, *be* with him. But somehow she managed, and not as a doormat, but as his equal. His partner.

I locked eyes with Heru. It was a mistake, because once he had me, I couldn't look away. My hands stilled, a half-unwrapped cheeseburger sitting on my lap.

I considered lying to him about everything that had happened over the last few days. For all of two seconds. "Nik came to me," I confessed. "He told me Dom was missing and asked me to look into it because, you know . . ." Actually, I realized that maybe they *didn't* know; I'd been keeping my distance for so long. Which then made me wonder how Nik had known in the first place. I made a mental note to pry the truth out of him later before starting my explanation. "My *sheut*," I said, "the way it's developed—well, it makes it so the things I draw have power." I continued unwrapping the burger, hands shaking a little. How could they not be, when Heru was staring at me so . . . stare-y. "In some ways, it's like they're *alive*."

I took a bite of the burger, considering the quickest and easiest way to explain what I could do and how and why Nik thought I'd be able to find Dom and the other missing Nejerets when nobody else could. "There was this case about a year and a half ago—a missing sixteen-year-old girl. The cops weren't having any luck, and the older sister came into the shop, wanting to get the girl's name tattooed on her wrist." I took another bite, washing it down with a sip of Cherry Coke. "She got to talking, and one thing led to another, and my sketches of the girl's name started taking on a life of their own, changing and spelling out different things."

I set down the cup by the phone on the end table. "I called in an anonymous tip as soon as the girl's sister left, and they found the girl later that day. She was a little worse for wear, but she was alive. Some sick fuck had abducted her and was 'training' her to be sold as a sex slave." I glanced down at the burger, momentarily too disgusted for even my ravenous post-regeneration hunger. "That's how my side business of finding people started."

"So, you're a PI?" Lex asked.

I shrugged, shaking my head. "I don't have a license or anything, and I don't advertise, but people still come to me. Word of mouth, I guess." I thought of Garth and the missing street kids. "Some of the cops have even heard about me now." I hoped Garth was all right, but my fear for Dom's life far surpassed my concern for Garth. Even so, I thought I might get up and wander the hospital in search of him in a bit. It would be nice to stretch my legs, and seeing that he was really all right—*if* he was all right—would set at least part of my mind at ease.

Heru exchanged a quick glance with Lex. "And Nik knew about this?" he asked. *How?* was unspoken, but implied.

I swallowed and nodded, just as in the dark about the *how* of that reality as he was. "He came to me a few nights ago," I said. "Told me about Dom and the others. I did some readings and sketches, and I have this wall—" I waved a hand to the side dismissively. "It doesn't matter." After a deep inhale, I continued, "I kept seeing the same symbol over and over. And then this cop got involved, and I realized the missing Nejerets are linked to a bunch of street kids who've gone missing over the past couple months."

"A cop?" Lex asked, at the same time as Heru said, "What symbol?"

I couldn't ignore Heru's question. He was a man whose passive greatness was so stifling that if you told some random human that he was a god, nine times out of ten they'd shrug and nod, admitting it was a possibility. "A snake eating its own tail," I told him. "It helped me link the disappearances to the Ouroboros Corporation."

Heru's golden tiger eyes narrowed.

"Mari's working with them," I said. "Did you know that?"

Lex's mouth fell open, and Heru shook his head ever so faintly.

"So, yeah . . . she's not 'missing.'" I gripped the side of my abdomen, still aching dully from the stab wound. "She's the one who did this. I'm pretty sure she has Nik . . . and she managed to get me with an *anti-At* dagger."

"*What?*" Lex was standing before the word was out of her mouth.

"I'm fine," I said, holding out my left hand, emblazoned with the black-veined Eye of Horus. "Turns out my sheut's good for more than just drawing pictures, reading fortunes, and finding people . . ."

Lex moved closer, crouching and eyes squinting as she studied my palm. "What *is* that?"

"*At* ink," I told her. "Nik made it." I shrugged out of my jacket and set it on the chair beside me. "It's what these are, too. The only permanent ink there is for a Nejeret."

"And it protected you?" Lex asked, looking from my hand to my face and back.

I nodded vehemently. "And that's not all it did." I remembered the way it had itched, then burned, when Mari had first emerged from the container. "I think it tried to warn me that I was in danger—I just didn't know it." I stared hard at Lex. "You guys should seriously consider letting me ink you with one of these bad boys. Could save your life . . ."

"I'll think about it," she said with a frown.

I looked at Heru. God or not, it was my turn to spear him with a hard stare. "How'd this all happen? How did you *let* it? And how the hell did the Senate *not* know what Ouroboros was up to?" Not that I really had any clue what exactly they were up to, just that it involved abducting Nejerets and human kids and apparently tearing the *bas* out of their Nejeret captives. "Even Nik's been paying attention to them. He said their 'life extension' products seemed fishy."

"For some time," Heru said, "it has been my belief that there is corruption within the Senate." Irritation tensed his exotic features. It was the most emotion I'd seen in him in years. Then again, this was the first time I'd seen him in years.

I scoffed. "You think?" I'd sensed that vein of corruption the day they tasked me, a nineteen-year-old freshly manifested Nejeret who just happened to be invisible in the echoes thanks to the *first* time Mari stabbed me with an *anti-At* dagger, with hunting down and eliminating their enemies.

Heru's responding stare put mine to shame. "All of this stays between us."

"I literally talk to *no one*." At least, no one who mattered to them. "Who do you think I'll tell? My receptionist?"

The corner of Heru's mouth twitched like he was holding in his amusement, but Lex frowned.

At the sound of footsteps coming from the hallway leading to Dom's operating room, all three of us swiveled our heads. Neffe approached, scrubs smudged with crimson bloodstains, dark hair held back by a blue cap tied behind her head, and a surgeon's mask pulled down below her chin to reveal her striking face.

Born during the most famous ancient Egyptian period, the New Kingdom's Eighteenth Dynasty, to Queen Hatshepsut and the great god Heru—the very same Heru sitting in the waiting area with me—Neffe was a stunning vision of a woman. And her brain was even better; her intellect and skill as a healer was nearly unmatched. Though her personality left something to be desired.

"How is he?" Lex asked, taking a step toward Neffe, hands wringing. Lex, Dom, and I shared a father, and she and Dom had always had a special bond.

Neffe took hold of Lex's hands, showing more compassion than I'd have thought her capable of. "It is not good, I'm afraid. Aset is still in there, leading the team, but . . ." She shook her head, her honey eyes filled with sorrow. She and Dom had been a part of each other's lives for centuries, so I don't know why it surprised me so much that she actually gave a shit about him. But it did. "He's not healing. No matter what we do, it's like working on a patient with a severe autoimmune disease—the exact opposite of what should be happening."

I opened my mouth, then snapped it shut again. Surely I hadn't skipped over the part about Dom's *ba* having been torn out of his body, had I? I quickly reviewed our conversation so far in my mind, and much to my shame, I had. "It's his *ba*," I said, standing and retrieving the *anti-At* orb out of my left pocket, then holding it out for the others to see. Neffe reached for the shimmering black orb, and I quickly drew it back to me. "Don't touch it!"

Neffe pulled her hand back. "Is that—"

"*Anti-At?*" I said. "Yes."

Her eyes rounded. "But how are you—"

"It's a long story," I said with a huff. "The point is, Dom's *ba* is in here, courtesy of Mari. Is there any way you can get it out of here and back into him?"

"Short of a needle made of *anti-At* . . ." Neffe shook her head. "No, I don't believe so. Not even Nik would be able to break through it." She turned and started back toward the hallway. "This changes things. I'll return shortly with a new assessment of the situation."

I went to stuff the orb back into my pocket, but Lex grabbed my wrist. "Is that really him in there?" she asked, bringing her face close to its poisonous surface.

I pulled free from her gentle hold. "So Mari claims . . ."

"Can he hear us?" Lex asked, straightening as her eyes moved from the orb to my face and back.

I lifted one shoulder and shook my head. "I honestly don't know."

"Mari did this?" From the hard glint in Lex's eyes, I wagered that Mari—whatever reasoning she'd had behind splintering Dom's body and soul—was about to get far more than she'd bargained for. Heru was shit-scary when he wanted to be. But if there was one person I didn't ever want to piss off, it was Lex. She'd been through hell traveling through time across millennia to get back to us, and she knew what it meant to lose everything. I mean, come on—the woman birthed the two new, true gods of our universe.

And she loved Dom as much as anyone. Maybe more. If there was anyone I pitied right now, it was Mari. She was in for a universe of hurt.

CHAPTER SEVENTEEN

I'm not used to sitting still without having something to do. I've always got a pen in hand, a tattoo machine, or my tarot cards. I had none of those things in the hospital waiting area, and once the food was gone, it was painfully dull, which only increased my anxiety about Dom. If only I had my cards . . . but then they'd have taken a dip with me in the waterway, and I doubted even their magic ink would've survived that.

The minutes felt like hours, the hours like days. Not that I'd made it even a half hour sitting down there, doing nothing, but still . . .

I pushed up out of my chair maybe an hour after I woke to the scent of cheap burgers and fries. "I need to move," I said, reaching my hands over my head and arching my back in a stretch. Now was as good of a time as any to search for Garth. "I'm gonna walk around." I picked up my leather jacket off the chair. It wasn't cold in the hospital, but it wasn't toasty, either.

Lex's eyes moved to the jacket in my hands, then back to my face. "Oh, um, alright." Did she think I was ducking out? Not that I could blame her if she did. My track record was less than stellar in the slinking-away department.

I set the coat down, hoping doing so would do enough to reassure her that I really would come back. I did pull the *anti-At* orb from the pocket, though; I wasn't willing to leave that behind with a bunch of Nejerets. To a human, it would be relatively safe—erasing them from the echoes, but nothing more, since no *ba* connected them to that higher plane. But to a Nejeret with a *ba*, it would unmake them, body and soul. Only I had immunity, thanks to the Eye of Horus inked in *At* on my hand.

Once the orb was out in the open again, Heru's eyes locked onto it.

"I'll be back in a bit." I checked the clock on the wall. It was nearly five in the morning. "The cafeteria opens soon. Maybe we can grab breakfast when I get back?"

Lex nodded. "That sounds good."

I found the stairs and headed up a floor, wandering its hallways and corridors while I tossed and caught the orb, over and over. I passed someone in scrubs every now and again, but there weren't too many people around. Certainly not many visitors at this hour of the morning, and none of them cops, which I figured would be the first sign that my hunt for Garth was bearing fruit. Nobody seemed concerned about my presence, at least not once they caught sight of the bandage on my abdomen. I supposed they thought I was a patient, even if I wasn't wearing a hospital gown.

Harborview Medical Center is an enormous facility made up of at least a dozen buildings, some connected, others standing on their own small block. I mostly just stuck to the main cluster of five interconnected buildings. After I'd done a full circuit of the second floor, I moved up to the third using the same stairwell as before.

It spat me out into a waiting room filled with cops. I froze in the doorway, heavy fire door propped open against my shoulder. All eyes were on me.

Their scrutiny was so intense that I started to ease back into the stairwell, but when my brain finally put two and two together and I realized this must be where Garth was being treated, I changed my trajectory. Slowly, I pushed through the door and into the waiting room. I spotted walrusy Officer Henderson sitting in the corner in jeans and a wrinkled blue polo. He was easy to recognize, even out of his uniform.

Henderson stood and I planted my feet, head held high, bolstering myself for the inevitable ejection from this apparently cop-only shindig. "I suppose you're looking for Garth?" he said as he drew near.

I nodded, my gaze flicking to the side at a whispered "Ink Witch." I ground my teeth together.

"Come on." Henderson waved me onward. "He's been asking for you."

My eyes widened, stinging as shame welled within me. It had taken me hours to come looking for Garth, I'd been so focused on Dom. Sure, I'd been passed out most of that time, but I certainly hadn't come as soon as I could've.

Henderson led me through the wide entrance into the intensive care unit. Lead settled in my stomach. It was my fault that Garth was here. The space was bustling with activity, and the incessant cacophony of arrhythmic beeping was enough to drive a Nejeret nuts.

We made a right, then a left, and Henderson stopped at the third doorway on the right. He reached into the room and knocked on the open door. "You decent, kid?"

"Why?" Garth said. "You looking for a show?"

My lips curved into a small smile at hearing his voice. He was alright.

Henderson laughed, a low, rough sound that came from his belly. "You've got a lady visitor."

"I said no strippers!"

Henderson gave me a questioning look.

I crossed my arms and raised one eyebrow. "I'm not a stripper."

"Kat?" Garth asked from within the room. "Is that you?"

After a deep breath—and another—I walked into the hospital room. Garth was propped up to a reclined sitting position, an entourage of beeping machines and IV bags on racks surrounding the upper half of his bed. His distinctive, noble features were mottled with bruises and cuts, and his hospital gown looked flimsy on his large frame.

"Hey," I said, forcing a lame smile.

He scanned me. "You look like crap."

I laughed. It only sounded slightly nervous. "Right back at you," I said with a halfhearted wink. I sat in the chair some visitor before me had left at his bedside.

"What happened?" he asked, his eyes searching my face. "When you didn't show up, I thought you'd pulled a fast one on me, but then your friend was there, and then we were jumped by that guy from—" He cleared his throat, then succumbed to a pretty painful-looking coughing fit.

I reached for the plastic cup and pitcher on his wheely tray and poured him a glass of water.

"Thanks," he said when he'd regained his voice. "I was afraid . . . I thought he must've gotten to you first."

I narrowed my eyes. "*He* who?" Maybe someone else who worked with Mari?

"The guy from the bar—you remember him, don't you? The bartender . . . ?"

The blood drained from my face, and I went cold all over. That fucking shitstain—I still didn't know his name—must've overheard Garth say "Nejeret" in the bar. I pressed my lips together and focused on breathing through the sudden spike of adrenaline. I would kill that fucker. It would be the first time I'd killed someone I'd had any kind of sexual involvement with, but that wouldn't stop me. My gaze strayed from Garth's as memories from that stairwell flashed through my mind, and silence stretched between us.

"Kat?"

I refocused on Garth. "How do you know what I am?" I asked, shooting a quick glance at the door. I had to know just how much he knew, just how dangerous he was—to my people, and to himself.

He was quiet for a moment, then cleared his throat. "Do you

know anything of my people's history?" he said, so softly that I wouldn't have been able to hear him if I'd been human. His gaze met mine like he was waiting for an answer. Like he knew I'd heard him.

My eyes narrowed, just a little. "The Squamish? Some . . ." I knew what most kids who grow up in Seattle know: that the Squamish had been moved onto a reservation in the mid-1800s, and that their chief had been the famous Chief Sealth that Seattle was named for. I also knew a smidgen more—over a century ago, the Squamish helped a Nejeret who was lost in time: my half-sister, Lex.

"I changed my last name to Smith when I was in middle school," Garth said. "Kids can be cruel, and they thought I was trying to claim that I was the prince of Seattle because of my last name."

"Which is . . . ?"

"Seattle."

My eyebrows rose, and I leaned forward, resting my elbows on my knees. "So Chief Sealth was your—"

"Great-great-great-great-great-grandfather, yes," Garth said with a nod. He stared past me at the broad window. "And my family has passed down a certain secret history, one that belongs only to us." He sipped his water. "My people believe that everything has a spirit—the eagles and crows, the trees, the Puget Sound . . . even the land itself. One day, two centuries ago, the spirit of a doe took human form and tasked Sealth's grandfather with a sacred duty. He was to teach his children of this duty so they might be prepared when the day came."

I licked my lips, already guessing where this was going. "What was the duty?"

"A woman would arrive one day, another spirit, and she would need my family's help." He looked at me, *saw* me, and ever so quietly whispered, "Her name was Alexandra, and she was a Nejeret."

I stared at him, stunned into silence. He was so much more

entangled in our history than I'd feared, and I was suddenly terrified that our burgeoning friendship would be the thing that brought the rage of the Senate crashing down on him and his family. I had to put some emotional distance between us, and I had to do it now.

"I did," I blurted, eyes locked with his. "Pull a fast one on you." I glanced down at my hands, fingers knotted together. "But I swear it was only to keep you *out* of danger, not to put you in it, and I'm *so* sorry."

"Oh." He sounded hurt. Good. Now I just had to make him see. Make him understand.

I forced myself to look at him. "I mean it, Garth. This thing that I'm investigating—it's bad. It's so much worse than anything you could've imagined, and I didn't want you to get drawn in any deeper. My world's not safe for people like—"

"Just stop," he said. Now it was his turn to purposely not look at me. "You should probably go."

"Garth—" Maybe I'd hurt him too much. If he wasn't willing to listen to me, he might be more of a danger to himself than he was before.

He turned his face further away from me. He wouldn't listen to me. Not right now. I'd have to find another way to make him listen. To make him understand just how important his silence was.

I nodded and stood, swallowing roughly. "Do you know what happened to Nik?" I asked.

Garth shook his head. "He was there when I blacked out, gone when I came to."

My nostrils flared. This was on me; I accepted that. But it was also on that damned bartender. And he would answer for it—just as soon as I'd dealt with Mari.

CHAPTER EIGHTEEN

After leaving Garth's room, I headed back down to the waiting area. The moment I saw Lex, sitting there, looking generally miserable, I realized there was maybe one way I could get Garth to listen to me *and* lift my half-sister's spirits a bit.

"Hey, Lex," I said as I drew nearer. "There's something I want to show you."

She glanced at Heru, her hand settling on his knee. An unspoken conversation passed between them, and he nodded. She leaned in, kissing him on the cheek, then stood and smoothed down the front of her sweater and jeans.

"Come on," I said, leading her back the way I'd just come. "It's not far . . . just up a couple floors."

Lex looked over her shoulder, her lip pulled between her teeth and her brow furrowed.

"It won't take long," I promised. "Just trust me." I couldn't help the lilt of a question. I didn't know if she trusted me at all anymore. And if she did, I wasn't sure whether she should.

We emerged from the third floor stairwell into the waiting room packed full of police officers a couple minutes later. Lex looked around, eyebrows raised. I waved to Henderson, and he gave me a slight nod.

"Where are you taking me?" Lex asked, laughing nervously.

I grinned at her over my shoulder. "There's someone I want you to meet. Someone *you'll* want to meet."

We reached Garth's room, and I peeked around the doorframe. He was just as I'd left him, gaze focused on the window and the rain pouring down in sheets outside.

"Garth, there's—"

"I told you to—" His dismissal died out when he looked at me. Or rather, looked past me, no doubt at Lex. His focus returned to me, confusion lighting his brown eyes.

"Garth," I said, stepping into the room. I reached behind me, finding Lex's arm, and pulled her in after me. "This is my sister, Lex—Alexandra." It was the name his people had known her by when she'd passed through their land—and time—over a century and a half ago.

Garth's eyes bugged out.

I turned to Lex. "This is Officer Garth Smith, who changed his last name when he was in middle school . . . from *Seattle*. He's descended from Chief Sealth."

Lex's eyes narrowed, and a second later, her lips spread into a broad grin, her gaze sliding past me and landing on Garth. "You—" She moved further into the room to stand behind the chair at Garth's bedside. "How?" She looked from Garth to me and back.

"Chief Sealth's daughter, Kikisoblu, was my great-great-great-great-grandmother. I grew up hearing stories of you and your people, but I never really believed any of them until I met Kat." His eyes shifted to me. "I did some digging after our first meeting. I found your birth certificate." The corner of his mouth lifted, and he scanned me from head to toe, giving me an appreciative nod. "You look good for a thirty-eight-year-old."

Heat suffused my cheeks.

"I—" Lex shot me a questioning glance, and I nodded, letting her know that he knew exactly who she was—and *what* we were. "I knew Kikisoblu . . . not well, but she saved my life once when I was in a bit of a sticky situation. She was a remarkable woman.

And Sealth . . ." She shook her head, laughing under her breath. "He was something else."

"This is unreal," Garth said.

"Truly incredible," Lex agreed. "Can I ask you—how many of your people know of us?"

"Just my family," Garth told her. "We've kept your secret, just as we promised all those years ago."

"Then you know how important it is that you continue to keep that secret a, well, *secret*," Lex said.

"Which means not telling every Nejeret you cross paths with that you know what they are," I added.

Alarm flashed across Lex's crimson eyes. "I can propose his name be added to the protected humans list, but there are no guarantees . . ."

Garth's expression turned quizzical.

"I'm pretty sure that's why you were attacked," I explained. "You know too much, and the wrong person found out. To the rest of the world, you have to pretend that we don't exist." I snorted out a breath. "It's probably best if you just forget about us."

"Kat!" Lex said, giving me a look of scandalized disbelief. She shook her head, her eyes narrowed, and laughed under her breath. When her attention shifted back to Garth, her features smoothed over. "I'd like to speak with you more, I really would," she said, "but I should get back downstairs. Our brother was the victim of a —well, he's in bad shape down in the ER. They're not sure if he'll . . ." Lex's voice seemed to catch in her throat. "We should get back."

Garth looked at me, some measure of forgiveness in his gaze.

I risked the tiniest of apologetic smiles.

"You should go," he said. Though the words were the same ones he'd spoken earlier, they felt entirely different. "I'm not going anywhere for a while, so you know where to find me."

Lex started back across the room, but she stopped halfway and turned back to Garth. "Kat's right, though. This secret—what we are—it's dangerous . . ."

Garth's eyes shifted to Lex, then back to me. "So the Ink Witch keeps telling me."

I bristled. "You know, I really hate that name."

Garth chuckled. "I know."

Lex and I were halfway down the stairwell by the time she spoke again. "Ink Witch?"

I groaned. "It's a stupid nickname."

"Oh." She was quiet for a few seconds, but I could feel her sidelong stare on my face. "I think he likes you. But he's upset with you, too."

"He's in here because of me," I said. "Because of all this . . ." I shook my head as we started down the final flight of stairs. "I tried to keep him out of it, but it just made things worse." I considered telling her about the bartender, but I wanted to deal with him on my own, Senate agent or not. "I never should've visited him at the station. It would've have been best for him if he'd never met me at all."

Lex grabbed my wrist, pulling me to a halt halfway down the stairs. "Do you really think that?"

I eyed her. "It *would* have been best for him if he'd never met me. It's safer that way."

Lex shook her head, her brow furrowed. "You don't get to choose what's best for people, Kit-Kat. There's one person in this world that you're responsible for—*you*." She gave my wrist a tug, then let it go. "It's not your job—your *right*—to decide what's good or bad for other people." Her carmine eyes searched mine. "Don't you get that?"

I looked away, focusing on the wall.

"Like with your mom . . ." With those four words, it felt like she'd rammed me in the chest with a wrecking ball. "She made the choice that was best for her—trading her life for yours."

A tear leaked from the corner of my eye, and I jutted out my jaw to keep my chin from trembling. "If it weren't for me, she'd still be here."

"She chose your life over hers, Kat. *She* chose that, not you.

You have to let her take ownership of that choice." Steel seeped into Lex's voice. "Stop making decisions for the people around you. We're all responsible for ourselves, for our choices. *We* love you, and you don't get to take that away just because it scares you. Because that love is *ours*, not yours."

I closed my eyes in a long blink, then looked at her. I had no words, just a shit-ton of long-dormant emotions all unfurling at once.

"Stop punishing yourself for your mom's choice. You've twisted it into something shameful in your head, but what she did was selfless; it was beautiful. Give her a little credit, for once in your life. Be proud that she was your mom . . . that you're *her* daughter. Be the legacy she deserves."

I looked up at the shiny, whitewashed cement ceiling. Tears streamed from the corners of my eyes.

"I'll give you a moment," Lex said, continuing down the stairs. "Come join us when you're ready."

"Yeah," I said, voice raspy. "Sure." I sunk down to sit on a stair and rested the side of my head against the metal railing.

"I'm sorry," I whispered. Because Lex was right. About everything. I'd been an ass for the last two decades. Ever since my mom shoved me out of the way of the gun and took the bullet meant for me, I'd made it all about me—about my loss. But it wasn't. It was about her—her choice. Her sacrifice. Her gift.

As I sat in that stairwell, facing the things I'd been hiding from for all these years, it felt like the whole world shifted around me. Everything I'd believed was based on faulty logic. On a foundation of cardboard and Styrofoam. I'd been wrong—blind—and I was finally ready to accept it. I'd been in hiding from myself for twenty years, but not anymore. Never again.

CHAPTER NINETEEN

When I emerged from the stairwell, Aset was standing near where Lex and Heru were sitting in the waiting area. As soon as I stepped onto the sitting area's rug, Aset stomped over to me, raised her hand, and slapped me. Hard.

I pressed my hand against my cheek and worked my jaw from side to side. While she might have been petite and pretty as all hell, Aset was ancient and had spent millennia training to be nearly as fierce and lethal as her twin brother. Who, at the moment, was watching from a chair, Lex's hand in his and the faintest smirk twisting his lips.

"I'm sorry about Nik," I said, assuming her anger was because her son seemed to be the latest Ouroboros victim. "I knew Mari wanted him for something, and I told her where he was to save my own life." And to keep this timeline from unraveling as the thread of my life disappeared, or so I'd thought at the time. I hadn't known there was another way.

"You're a foolish child," Aset said with a huff. Her rich, ancient accent was more pronounced than usual. "Nekure is more than capable of dealing with Mari."

My eyes narrowed. "Then why did you hit me?"

"Because I missed you." Her amber eyes shone. "For three years, you couldn't even be bothered to answer my calls, and you made it clear I was not welcome in your life. What was I to think? I had to resort to hiring a private investigator to check up on you."

My lips parted. "You did *what?*"

"Even Nekure checked in with me time and again, letting me know he was alive."

"Thanks for letting the rest of us know," Lex muttered under her breath.

I sniffed. So Aset hadn't shared her periodic phone calls with Nik with the rest of our unconventional family. Now who was the inconsiderate one? I opened my mouth to make that very point when the sound of footsteps came from the hallway leading to Dom's operating room.

Neffe appeared, crossing to the waiting area, shoulders slumped. "He went into cardiac arrest." She held up a hand to cut off our questions. "We managed to bring him back, and he's stable enough for the moment, but there's no way to predict how long that will last." She was quiet for a moment, her eyes locked with her father's. "I thought we could stabilize him, even without his *ba*, but . . ." She shook her head. "His organs are starting to shut down. There's nothing more we can do for him, and life support will keep him going for only so long. If we don't reunite him with his *ba* soon, he will die."

"Mari's the only one who can release his *ba* from that thing," Heru said, pointing to the inky black orb in my hand.

"But how can we find her, Father?" Neffe asked. "The Senate's been searching for Mari and the others for months . . ."

Heru's hawkish stare locked onto me. "She'll be looking for you if she truly believes you're infected with *anti-At*."

I nodded. "There's no way for her to know about this mark," I said, rolling the orb to my fingertips and flashing the black-streaked iridescent Eye of Horus on my palm. "So far as she knows, she *needs* to find me before this world changes into the wild unknown." I looked at Aset. "If Nik's with her, can't you just call him?"

She shook her head. "I tried that hours ago. His phone's either off or dead."

"If you made your whereabouts known to her," Heru said, "Mari would come to you."

I shook my head. "Not if she thinks you guys are around. She might prefer to preserve this timeline, but not at the expense of her own life." I frowned, considering another angle. "I think she's kind of a big shot at Ouroboros. If I walked in there alone, asked for her, and told them who I was, they'd be able to get the message to her."

"But that still doesn't get her *here*," Neffe said. "And there's no guarantee that she'll be willing to help." Neffe hesitated. "What about Mei? We could use her to coerce—"

"Out of the question," Aset said. Mei was Mari's adoptive mother. She was also Nik's only child—that I knew of—and Aset's only grandchild. She was technically dead, having been murdered during all the hoopla a couple decades ago, but being a time traveler—however grounded she currently was by the new gods' ban on time travel—she'd found a loophole to extend her life by jumping forward in time. Eventually, the day would come when she'd have to return and allow her own murder. But not yet.

"If I talk to Mari . . ." I licked my lips. She'd said she loved me; if that was true, she'd have to listen. "I don't know why she's doing all of this, but she's not a bad person. She'll help Dom. She'll make the right choice." I exchanged a look with Lex. Her red-rimmed eyes made her look a little shell-shocked. "I have to trust that she'll make the right choice."

Everyone looked at Heru, our people's general, an uncrowned king. Finally, he nodded solemnly. "If she chooses wrong—if she resists—I authorize you to use whatever force necessary to capture her and bring her here. This isn't how Dom ends. He's a warrior. He deserves better."

"I understand." I turned away from Heru and set the orb down on a chair, then picked up my leather jacket and put it on. I stuffed the orb back into my pocket and met Heru's fierce golden eyes. "This isn't how he ends," I agreed, meaning it with every fiber of my being.

This isn't how he ends.

CHAPTER TWENTY

I hurried back to the parking garage and found the trash can near my bike, where I'd stowed my weapons. The trash bag was still mostly empty, and it was easy enough to retrieve my things. Within minutes of reaching the garage, I was suited up once more and kicking my leg over the Ducati's high seat.

It was still early enough that the streets of downtown Seattle weren't crowded, only a single overnight road construction crew attempting to slow me down. Fourth Avenue was closed off, and instead of following the detour down to Third so I could swing back around on Fifth—damn one-way streets—I flipped a bitch and rode down Fifth going the wrong way. It was only a block and a half, and Dom's life was on the line.

A couple cars honked at me, and someone in a white BMW sedan rolled down their window to inform me none too politely that I was going the wrong way. I ignored them all and parked the bike on the sidewalk just a few feet from the Fifth Avenue entrance into the Columbia Center, not caring that the parking job was about as illegal as they get. I jumped off the bike, practically ripping my helmet off and dropping it on the cement, and ran to the door.

I entered the posh building on the second floor, all the mall shops still closed, doors shut and security gates pulled down. I could hear people down in the food court, though, early birds at the several cafes grabbing their morning coffee fixes.

A single woman was waiting at the elevator. I stopped a couple feet from her, crossed my arms over my chest, and met her eyes, forcing a half-assed smile. Her gaze slid to the sword strapped to my back, and her eyes rounded. She backed away slowly, then turned and jogged to the escalator. No doubt she was going in search of security or, even better, police. I sniffed and turned my back to the escalators. Some people are so jumpy.

Widening my stance, I rolled my head from side to side to crack my neck as I watched the digital counter over the elevator. *Eleven. Ten. Nine. Eight. Seven . . .*

The metallic clang of boots tromping up the escalator caught my attention, and I glanced over my shoulder. Two of Seattle's finest in their starched midnight-blue uniforms barreled up the moving stairway, one a chick, the other a dude.

I peered up at the counter. *Three. Two . . .*

Ding. The elevator doors whooshed open, and I stepped inside, hitting the "close" button immediately.

"Hey!" the lady cop shouted. "Hold the elevator!"

I raised my hand and blew them a kiss as the doors slid shut. Too slow, Joes. I heard the cop shout "Stop!" just before the elevator car started its speedy ascent.

The building was on the newer side, and the elevator was fast, but the ride up to the sixtieth floor seemed to take forever. I counted my pounding heartbeats, hoping the exercise might provide some sense of calm. It was one Dom used to make me do when my temper or frustration would get the better of me, and it always helped. Not this time. Though this time I thought giving in to my emotions might actually be beneficial, especially when it came to pleading with Mari.

On floor sixty, the elevator dinged and the doors slid open once more, revealing the medical-chic lobby. It was just past six in the morning, late enough for a receptionist to be sitting at the curved desk a dozen or so yards across the polished composite floor. She looked up as I stepped out of the elevator, and a second later, her arm moved.

"Security to reception *immediately*," she said in a voice that should have been too quiet for me to hear. If I were human. I'm not.

She watched me cross the lobby, my bootfalls echoing off the walls. I stopped a few yards from the reception desk, hands in my coat pockets. "My name is Kat Dubois. Tell Dr. Marie Jones I'm here," I said, using Mari's pseudonym. "She's looking for me."

The receptionist offered me an icy smile. "She isn't currently in her office."

I withdrew my hands from my pockets ever so slowly. "I'm sure you have a way to get ahold of her. All you have to do is let her know I'm here." I sniffed a laugh. "What could be the harm in that?"

I heard the sound of multiple pairs of boots pounding against the hard floor. Security was on its way. Dealing with them would be annoying, but hardly much of a hindrance. So long as I could convince the receptionist to get a message to Mari, the plan was still on track.

I backed away from the desk and lowered myself to my knees, raising my hands and lacing my fingers together behind my head. "Call her," I said just as a cadre of well-armed security guards emerged from the hallway to the right of the lobby.

The black-clad men and women were in the process of surrounding me when the elevator dinged and the doors opened once more.

"Seattle PD!" a man shouted. "Drop your weapons!"

The security personnel backed away from me but didn't disarm.

"We'll take it from here," the female cop said. I could hear her striding across the lobby, one shoe squeaking with each step. She came to a stop behind me. "Hands behind your back, ma'am."

I did as ordered, lowering my arms and pressing my wrists together behind my back, my eyes locked with the receptionist's.

I could just make out the sound of a phone ringing in her headset.

"Make it quick," Mari said through the earpiece, her voice faint but clear. "The helicopter's waiting."

I raised a single eyebrow. She was pulling out all the stops to find me. I felt the corners of my lips draw up even as cold steel ratcheted around my wrists. This would work.

"There's a woman here to see you. The police are about to take her away, but—"

"Is it Kat?" Mari asked. "Does she have a sword?"

The receptionist frowned. "She does, yes."

"Do not let them take her!" Mari all but shouted. "Do anything, Janelle—anything! I don't care if you have to lock the police officers in a closet yourself, do *not* let them take her. I'll be on the roof in ten minutes. I want Kat there, waiting for me."

"I understand," Janelle said, then pressed a button on the side of her headset and stood. "I'm sorry." She flashed that ice-queen smile at the officers. "But we actually need her."

"This woman is under arrest for carrying illegal weapons," the female cop said, wrapping the fingers of one hand around my arm and pulling me up to my feet.

"I'm so sorry," the receptionist said. She came around the end of the desk, her movements graceful. "That's our fault. We asked her to come in looking like a threat to test our security protocols. It was a drill." She held her hands out before her. "Perhaps a poorly thought-out drill, but nothing more." When her eyes slid over me, her cheek twitched, but her smile didn't falter one bit. I couldn't imagine why anyone had given this woman the job of receptionist; she was about as warm and welcoming as Neptune.

"Do you have documentation of this 'drill'?" the policewoman asked. "We can't release her on your word alone."

"Of course." The receptionist extended her arm to the side, gesturing toward the hallway to the right of the lobby. "If you'll both follow me, I can show you."

"Forbes," the cop said to her partner. "Stay here."

Her partner nodded.

The receptionist's chilly smile became razor sharp. She was none too pleased. "Perhaps your partner would like to oversee the remainder of the drill?"

When her stare landed on me, I winked at her. She was a clever one, this Janelle. An ice queen, perhaps, but a clever ice queen.

Janelle looked past me, focusing on one of the security guards. "I believe they were just about to escort the 'intruder' to the helipad on the roof—it's a transport scenario." She flashed the lady cop a gracious smile. "Of course, they won't actually be flying anywhere. It's just—we're on a bit of a tight schedule, and we'd like the drill to be completed before business hours."

"Fine," the officer said. She headed for the receptionist. "Let's see this documentation."

CHAPTER TWENTY-ONE

Walking up a stairwell with your hands cuffed behind your back is awkward as hell. You're hyperconscious of foot placement and you don't want to look up, because if you trip, you will fall on your face. Literally. And faces and cement stairs don't play well together. Not ever. So yeah, walking up four flights of stairs in the middle of a long train of mercenary security guards was plain torture. Especially because the guards weren't moving nearly fast enough for me.

The counter on Dom's life was ticking down, only I had no idea how much time he had left. Maybe days. Maybe hours. Maybe only minutes.

The seven guards tromping up the stairwell ahead of me passed through a metal fire door and onto a terraced portion of the multi-tiered skyscraper's roof, one of the guards standing with his back to the door to hold it open. Cold air tunneled in through the doorway, carrying with it misty raindrops and the thwomp-thwomp-thwomp of helicopter blades chopping through the morning fog. As soon as I stepped through the doorway, wind whipped my hair around, the rain making strands stick to my face. Supremely annoying when I couldn't do anything about it. Damn handcuffs.

A helicopter touched down on the helipad near the jutting-out corner of the terrace. A few seconds later, Mari jumped out. She appeared to be wearing the same bloodied and torn skirt and blouse from the previous day. At least she'd lost the tattered lab coat. She held her hair down as she jogged away from the helicopter, running in heels like it was no big deal.

Nik followed her out onto the helipad, his long, black leather coat flapping around his legs as he took lengthy strides to catch up to Mari. He ducked slightly, the helicopter blades slicing through the air over his head.

Seeing Nik whole and healthy eliminated one link in a whole chain of fear and dread. All Garth had been able to tell me was that Nik had been there when he'd blacked out. I felt a burst of appreciation for Nik as I realized he must've fought off the other Nejeret. He was likely the only reason Garth was still alive. Nik didn't pull punches, and it dawned on me that the Nejeret might already be dead. I supposed it all depended on when exactly Mari had arrived.

My eyes locked on Mari's, and I took a couple steps forward, putting a negligible distance between me and the line of guards behind me, and jerked my cuffed hands upwards behind my back. I gritted my teeth against the pain as my right shoulder slipped out of its socket, but I pushed through the pain, pulling my hands over my head. The discomfort of the temporary shoulder dislocation was sharp, but brief. A bargain price to have my hands in front of me. I rolled my shoulder, making sure everything had settled back where it belonged. The joint ached, but the pain would fade quickly as it healed.

The corner of Nik's mouth lifted, just for a second. The movement caught my eye, and our stares met. His pale blue gaze was burning with worry. For me, I realized. Damn it, but seeing his concern for me warmed my shriveled little heart.

"I'm fine," I mouthed, flashing him my palm with the marbled Eye of Horus.

His eyes widened, relief washing over his face, and a true smirk twisted his lips. He winked, his expression going blank a moment later.

"I've been looking everywhere for you," Mari said, voice raised to compete with the sound of the helicopter behind her. "You should've come straight here." She waved Nik forward. "Why haven't you been answering your phone? What if it's already too late?"

"It's not," I said, uncurling my fingers and showing them both my palm. The Eye of Horus glimmered in the pale dawn light, iridescent and inky. I didn't bother telling her my phone had been collateral damage during my dip in the Sound. "I'm fine, but Dom's not."

I looked into her eyes, searching for the woman I'd worked with so closely all those years we'd hunted rogue Nejerets together. For the woman who'd been like a sister to me. I just hoped some fragment of her remained. "He's going to die if we don't stick his *ba* back into him, and soon. Mars, there's no reason for Dom to suffer any longer. Nik's here, and I'm sure he'll agree to work with you, just like you wanted."

My gaze flicked to Nik. He shrugged one shoulder, the movement barely perceptible.

"All you have to do is save Dom. You're the only one who can reunite his *ba* with his body." I reached for her hand, gripping it tightly with both of mine. "Please. You have to come to the hospital with me."

Mari blinked, and it seemed like that was all it took for her mind to catch up and process what I was saying. She nodded once and gave my hands a squeeze. "Of course I'll help. We can take the helicopter." She pulled her hand free of mine and turned, jogging back to the helipad. "Fire it up!" she shouted to the pilot, waving one hand over her head in mimicry of the helicopter's blades in motion.

I followed her. When I reached the helicopter, I raised my arms to grip the overhead handle with both hands and lifted my right boot. Half in the helicopter's cabin, I glanced over my shoulder.

Nik stood a dozen paces back, his phone in his hand and his face angled downward.

"Nik!" I yelled. "Let's go!"

He lifted his face to me, his expression stricken. Slowly, he shook his head. "Kat . . ."

I dropped back down to the helipad and made my way to him, heart thumping and ears filled with the sound of the helicopter blades chopping through the air combined with my rushing blood. I could no longer feel the roof under my boots or the wind and rain swirling around me. All I felt was dread.

"My mom . . ." His pale blue eyes locked with mine. "I didn't see it earlier—my phone was dead, but I charged it as we flew. I'm so sorry, Kat. We're too late."

I stared at him, heart a misshapen lump of lead. *Don't say it. Don't say it. Don't say it.*

"Dom's dead."

CHAPTER TWENTY-TWO

Dom's dead.

My head was shaking all on its own. "I don't understand." My voice sounded hollow, the vibrations echoing around inside my skull. I was empty. Nik's words didn't make any sense.

Dom's dead.

Nik rested a hand on my shoulder, his pale eyes filled with sorrow. With pity. With grief.

"But . . ." Awkwardly, I withdrew the *anti-At* orb from my jacket pocket. Through the barely translucent, obsidian-like material, I could see Dom's soul twisting and swirling lazily. "But he's right here." I showed the orb to Nik, unable to take my eyes off it. "This was the plan. I—I did everything right."

I shook my head again, my heart beating in rhythm with the helicopter's blades. "We all agreed. It was supposed to work. I was supposed to save him." I looked at Nik, not understanding why we weren't flying back to the hospital right now. "We all agreed . . ."

Nik pressed his lips together into a thin, flat line, letting me work through this impossible reality.

Dom's dead.

"This isn't supposed to happen," I said, steel bleeding into my voice. "This was *never* supposed to happen." I clenched my jaw, breathing deeply through my nose. "He didn't do anything wrong. He was just trying to find our people . . . trying to help, and . . ." My fingers curled around the orb containing all that was left of my best friend and mentor. Of my brother. I stuffed it back into my pocket, eyes narrowing to slits.

This was Mari's fault. She was the one who'd trapped Dom's *ba* in the *anti-At* orb in the first place. Without her, he'd have healed like a normal Nejeret. Without her, he'd still be alive.

"Kat . . ." Nik's hand on my shoulder transformed from comforting to a warning grip. "Not here," he said, shooting a sideways glance over his shoulder. Nearly a dozen Ouroboros security guards still stood back there in a line with the police officer.

"If not here, then where?" I asked, a glare not meant for him cutting through his reticence. "He's dead, Nik. Dom's dead, and I have to know why—now. Here."

Nik returned my glare with a hard, measuring stare. After several seconds, he nodded. "Get your answers. I'll keep them off your back." Vines of crystalline *At* burst out of Nik's hands, reaching the guards between one heartbeat and the next, wrapping around each man and woman, the cop included, holding them and their weapons immobile. They wouldn't be going anywhere until he released them.

At the same time, I spun around, facing Mari and drawing my sword in one smooth motion. My hands were still cuffed together, but it wasn't too much of a hindrance. It just meant I'd be limited to two-handed sword moves. Power moves. Fine with me.

Mari had just dropped down to the helipad. She took a backward step, her rear flush against the helicopter, and held her hands out to me in placation. "Kat—"

I stalked across the helipad toward her. "You killed him!" I yelled.

Confusion filled her jade eyes.

"Dom's dead," I told her, stopping just out of sword's reach.

Mari's lips parted, but she didn't say anything. She just shook her head.

"Why? Why did he die? For what?" I pointed my sword at her, the tip of the katana's blade mere inches from her throat. "Tell me!" I screamed.

She licked her lips. "He was never meant to die." Her eyelids fluttered, tears gathering on her long lashes. "I just wanted Nik—I *need* him. I truly didn't know we'd captured Dom until you told me, but once I knew, I saw it for the opportunity it was—a way to coerce you into bringing Nik to me. A way to get you to convince Nik to work with me. He'd do anything for you. But then everything went wrong. If you'd just stayed put." A tear broke free, gliding down her perfect, pale cheek. "If you'd waited by that container like you were supposed to . . ."

"Don't turn this around on me. You're the one who tore out Dom's *ba*."

She shook her head vehemently. "No, Kat—"

"*You're* the one who trapped it in *anti-At* . . . the one who dragged him into that container and left him there to suffer without his *ba*. For all I know, you're the one who beat the shit out of him in the first place."

She didn't deny it.

"Why?"

She licked her lips, hair flying in her face. "Like I said, I needed to get to Nik, and the only way to do it was through you. He'd do *anything* for you."

It was my turn to shake my head. She was delusional if she thought that.

"You were supposed to bring him to the container yard. It was supposed to be a trade—Dom's life for Nik's cooperation. I'd have saved Dom if you'd given me the chance. Just like I'm trying to save our people."

"Our people don't need saving," I spat back at her.

"Oh, please. What would you know?" Green fire burned in her eyes. "You've been living with your head in the sand for years. You have no idea what's been going on . . . what's coming."

I moved the tip of the sword a fraction of an inch closer to her, forcing her to lean backwards into the helicopter's cabin. "What are you talking about?"

"They *know*, Kat." Her stare was hard, challenging. "About us—about our people. Ouroboros has hard proof. If I didn't help them by luring in Nejeret test subjects to use as lab rats, they'd have gone public. They'd have exposed us."

"I don't—" I shook my head. "That doesn't make any sense. Why not come forward? The Senate—"

"Is in on it," she snapped, cutting me off. "Where do you think Ouroboros got the proof in the first place? And the Nejerets I've been collecting—have you even seen the list? They're all loyalists and supporters of Heru and my mom. The Senate cut a deal with Ouroboros." Her jade eyes narrowed. "I was one of the first of our people they trapped; I *let* them take me so I could get on the inside. I'm walking on a tightrope here. If I misstep . . . if I even breathe wrong . . ." Her hands balled into fists. "I've found a way to save our people, but I need more time."

I inched closer until Mercy's razor-sharp tip was flush with Mari's skin. "Explain."

Mari swallowed, and the movement caused the *At* blade to cut into her skin. A droplet of blood snaked down her neck, leaving behind a crimson trail. "They think I'm helping them create some sort of a wonder drug based on our unique physiology." She grinned, lips closed and eyes hard. "I *have* found a way to make humans live forever, but it has nothing to do with science and everything to do with souls."

My eyes narrowed. "What do you mean?"

"A Nejeret *ba*—it's like a starfish. If you tear off a piece, it grows back. And if you extract a large enough piece, it grows back *twice*. The only problem is, encasing those fragments in *anti-At* taints them, and they become inviable. They kill their new hosts, even as they transform them. That's why I need Nik. Don't you see, Kat?" The feverish light of fanaticism glowed in her eyes, turning her irises radioactive. "I haven't found a way to make humans live forever. I've found a way to turn them into Nejerets.

And if I turn enough of them into *us*, it won't matter when they go public with their exposé. We won't have to fear their fear, because *they'll be us*."

Slowly, I shook my head. "You're insane."

Mari laughed, the sound too high and tight, and the tip of my sword cut deeper. "Maybe, but that doesn't change the fact that our people need me . . . or that *I* need Nik." Her eyes searched mine. "Let me prove to you that you can trust me. The bargain still stands—Dom for Nik." She held out her hand. "Give me the orb. I'll put Dom's *ba* in a new body. He'll look different, but he'll still be *him*." Her chin trembled. "Please, Kat. This is for the good of our people."

I stared at her for so long that the strain of not blinking in the face of all that wind made my eyes burn. "Fine," I said, sheathing Mercy, and reached into my pocket. Hesitating for only a moment, I offered the orb containing Dom's soul to Mari.

Her fingers closed around it.

"No." Nik's voice was harsh behind me.

I peered back at him out of the corner of my eye.

"If you let her do this, Kat, it'll be murder. The human—"

"Would've only lived for a few more decades," Mari said. "Now he could live for millennia."

"His human soul will die." Nik strode closer, bringing himself into my line of sight. "Dom has lived for hundreds of years already, and his *ba* will continue on . . . somewhere. But whatever human she stuffs him into—Dom's *ba* will overtake that person completely. This life is the only shot a human soul has. Who are you to take that away?"

I felt torn, paralyzed by indecision.

Nik glanced at my left forearm, where the list of names of my dead were etched in *At* ink, shielded by my leather sleeve. Nik couldn't see it, but this close, I had no doubt that he could sense it. "Do you really want to add another name? A human life . . . with such a fleeting, fragile soul. It'll be your first true murder. The first time you'll end someone's existence, absolutely and completely."

I shook my head slowly as his words sunk in, each a dagger twisting into my gut.

"If you think you're ready for that guilt, Kitty Kat, by all means . . ."

I bowed my head, my eyes drifting shut. Every single person I'd killed up until now had been a Nejeret—traitorous to some degree, but a Nejeret containing an immortal soul in the form of a *ba* all the same. Each of my victims had continued on in that other form after I'd ended their earthly life. I couldn't say the same would happen for the soul of any human Dom's *ba* took over. Just as I couldn't say the same for my mom. Much as I wanted to see Dom again, I couldn't do it. Not like this. I wouldn't be able to face him, knowing the price some poor human had paid in order for him to live again.

"I'm sorry," I told Dom, voice soft as I reached for the orb containing his everlasting soul.

"So am I," Mari said. As she spoke, my fingers passed through the orb's no-longer-solid surface. She reached up and behind her, pulling herself into the helicopter's cabin.

My eyes widened, locked on the place where the orb had been. The inky *anti-At* had evaporated, giving way to a shimmering silver mist that scattered in the wind. It was Dom's soul. And it was floating away.

Panic surged, making my heartbeat trip over itself as it sped up. "Nik!" I shouted. "Can you capture him?"

The helicopter's blades picked up speed, sending the silver mist this way and that, scattering it further and further.

"I'll try!" he yelled.

I glanced at Mari. She was watching us with sad eyes from the back of the helicopter as it lifted off. "I'm sorry," she mouthed, tears streaming down her cheeks.

I considered leaping off the edge of the building in an attempt to latch onto one of the helicopter's landing skids, but it would be suicide with the handcuffs still in place.

"He's too scattered!" Nik called, bubbles of crystalline *At* pocking the air above the roof like three-dimensional polka dots containing pieces of Dom's soul.

I stood on the empty helipad, watching the last remnants of Dom blow away like so much dust in the wind, my heart shattering. I'd failed him.

He was gone. Really gone.

CHAPTER TWENTY-THREE

"Can you call him back somehow?" Nik shouted to me. His hair was matted to his scalp, and his cheeks were high with color. He was pushing his *sheut* to the max, juggling all of those little bubbles of *At*, even while creating new ones to trap this or that little tendril of Dom's soul. He wasn't giving up.

His determination soaked into me, and I shed my suffocating cloak of surrender. "Call him back *how*?"

"I don't know. Maybe write his name or draw a picture of him? *Something*?"

"I don't have a pen or paper or—"

"You have skin!"

My eyes widened, and a moment later, I dropped to my knees. I drew a dainty needle dagger from the sheath sewn into my left sleeve and didn't hesitate to scrape the sharp tip across my wrist. The blade bit into my skin, the sharp sting no match for my resolve.

D—O—

"Is it working?" I yelled to Nik as I began the *M*. It was awkward with the handcuffs still on.

"I think so, but—"

Halfway through the *M*, I glanced up at him. He was maybe

ten yards from me, halfway between the helipad and the cluster of restrained security guards. And between us, a glittering silver mist was gathering, condensing into a mystical fog. It was working. It was *really* working.

"Dom?" My chin trembled, and I let out a shaky laugh, tears streaming down my cheeks. Setting down the knife, I reached out with one hand. My fingers sifted through his ethereal form like he was no more substantial than the air. The essence of him—his soul—tangled around my fingers in thin, ghostly filaments. "Stay with me?" I asked. I begged. "Please."

But even as I spoke, the shimmering mist that was *him* thinned.

"Hurry, Nik! Before he's too far away again!"

The mist parted as Nik pushed through. He crouched before me, elbows on his knees, and squinted around. "I've surrounded all three of us by a dome of *At*, but Kat, I can't let you out without losing some of him in the process. Bits of his *ba* are clinging to you . . ."

I hunched over and renewed the efforts on my arm with the knife. Maybe if I could just finish writing his name, I could coax him into me. Then, I could carry him with me forever.

"Kat." Nik's fingers wrapped around my knife wrist. "Stop. You have to stop."

"No, I don't."

"It's time to let him go." Nik brought his hand to my face like he was going to make me look at him, but I slapped it away. "Even if I captured him in *At*, then what? Are you really willing to hold him prisoner like that? For how long?"

I screamed, slamming the knife down on the cement tile so hard that the thin steel blade snapped in two. I glared at Nik, eyes burning with fury caused by the truth in his words—a truth I wasn't ready to face. "I'll find a way to bring him back."

"Let him have peace."

"I can't," I said, eyes on fire with something else entirely. Tears streamed down my cheeks. "Two days ago, I drew a picture of him, and he raised his head and looked at me and told me he was alive, and *it was him*, Nik. For a few seconds, it was really Dom in that picture. He looked me in the eye and told me to find him, and I promised him I would." I cleared my throat and leveled my voice. "I'm not giving up on him yet. I'll share my own body with him if I have to."

"You don't know what you're saying, Kitty Kat." Nik's voice held a fierce warning. "You have no idea what it's like to never be alone in your body." But he knew. He'd done it for thousands of years, sharing his body with the soul of the god, Re. He might've been alone in his skin now, but the haunting pain shadowing his eyes was enough to give me pause.

"But I promised him . . ."

The rising sun peeked over a nearby building, brilliant sunlight streaming in through the *At* surrounding us and setting Dom's *ba* aglow. Realization dawned just as suddenly.

In that drawing, it was *him*. With that single sketch, ink on paper, just for a blip of time, I'd captured Dom's soul—when it had still been inside him. Now, here his *ba* was, homeless. What if I gave it a home? Not another body, exactly, but something else. Something like the sketch, but better. Something to tide him over until I could figure out a way to give him a body that didn't include murdering a human.

"I think there's another way . . ." I fished my drowned phone from my coat pocket and set it on the helipad. "Do you mind?" I asked Nik, holding my cuffed wrists out to him.

Without a word, he touched the chain connecting the handcuffs. The metal turned opalescent one second as Nik transformed it into *At*, then seemed to evaporate the next, leaving my wrists naked of all but ink and blood.

"Thanks." I hunched over on my knees and drew the second needle dagger stowed in my other sleeve, holding it by the blade like it was a harmless pencil. With the tip of the blade, I started etching Dom's face into the phone's reflective surface.

Dom. I focused every ounce of brainpower on thinking about my half-brother. On remembering the way his dark eyes could pin me in place the same way, whether they were filled with disappointment or with pride. On remembering the way his severe features softened on those rare occasions that he smiled. On remembering how he would slick back his black, chin-length hair whenever he had something to say but was holding his tongue. On remembering how he listened. How he'd chosen to spend time training me when there were a million better things for him to be doing. On how he'd given a shit about me, even when I hadn't.

I wiped a raindrop off the phone's surface with the side of my hand. An electric charge seemed to pass through me and into the phone.

"Kat, look . . ."

I shushed Nik, adding shadows to Dom's face in the form of faintly etched lines. I wiped away another raindrop. "Do you mind?" I said, glancing at Nik, then up at the cloudy sky.

Except the sky was an iridescent color. Because it wasn't the sky, but Nik's dome of *At*. And the those weren't raindrops; they were tears. *My* tears. There was no wind or rain in here. No sound but our own.

It took me a moment to realize I could see the dome of *At* clearly, not through a shimmering, unearthly silver mist.

"Where'd Dom go?"

Nik's face was ghostly pale. "I'm pretty sure he's in there," he said, reaching out and tapping the side of the dead phone.

I stared at the image etched on the surface. At first I thought it was a trick of the eye, but ever so slowly, I watched the image of Dom's face move. His lips parted. His mouth opened. And he let out a silent scream.

"He doesn't look too comfortable," Nik said dryly.

"I did it." I looked from the phone—from Dom—to Nik and back. "I really did it." I held up the phone like I was taking a selfie. "Can you hear me, Dom?"

Ever so slowly, the etched likeness of him shut his mouth. The rough copies of his eyes seemed to be seeking without seeing.

"I promise I'll make you more comfortable soon, and I swear to all the gods who've ever existed, I will make you whole again." I tucked him back into my pocket, then met Nik's eyes. "Don't tell anyone about this yet," I whispered. "I don't want them to get their hopes up."

Nik said nothing for long seconds, just looked at me with those pale, guarded eyes. Finally, he nodded. "I'll keep your secret," he said. "For now."

CHAPTER TWENTY-FOUR

Nik and I burst out of the Columbia Center to the sidewalk on Fifth Avenue. My helmet was gone, likely stolen by some enterprising passerby, but the Ducati was still parked there, illegal as ever. I'd feared it would already have been towed. But, after everything, I'd only been in the building for *maybe* twenty minutes. I'd have bet a tow truck was already on its way. But it wasn't here yet.

"Can you ride?" I asked Nik as we sprinted to the bike.

He looked at me, *You're kidding, right?* in his eyes.

I snorted. "Good, because you're too tall to ride behind me." I handed him the key and waited for him to mount before kicking my leg over the seat behind him.

The Ducati Monster is not a bike designed with multiple riders in mind. Sure, it's got a narrow little extension behind the main portion of the saddle for a passenger and two tiny little kick-down pegs on either side, but the crunched-up position isn't comfortable for the passenger, and the rider has to deal with the annoyance of being top-heavy and having the passenger leaning on them, due to the passenger's raised seat. But damn, in all black with just a hint of candy-apple red, the bike is sexy as hell. And it can *move*. To say I loved my motorcycle was putting it lightly.

"And Nik, if you crash this bike . . ."

Nik kicked the bike to life like he owned it and, fingers gripping the handlebars, waited for me to wrap my arms around his waist from behind before putting it in gear and turning the throttle. We'd never sat this close together before—not ever. I was pressed up against the back of him, our bodies touching from knees to shoulders. I'd ridden with other people a few times, but it had never felt this intimate.

"Relax," Nik said over his shoulder. "I know what I'm doing."

But the tension coiling through my body had nothing to do with the bike or his riding ability and everything to do with him. With his body, snug between my legs.

Once upon a time, a long, *long* time ago, Nik and I shared a kiss. It was back during his possessed-by-a-god days, and the god, Re, had flipped out almost the moment our lips touched. It had been a breaking point for Re, forcing him to wrest back control from his host. It had had the feel of a last-straw moment. A shattering of a pact between the two beings sharing his body.

We'd never talked about it, about any of it—the kiss, the explosion, Nik's increasingly tenuous relationship between himself and his now-former resident god. Considering Nik's arm's-length attitude, I doubted we ever would. But sitting there, my legs straddling his, I couldn't help but wonder *what if?*

Nik braked at a stop sign, placing his feet on the pavement on either side of the bike, and turned his head so he could see me. "Where to?" We were at a literal fork in the road—right would take us to the hospital, left back to my shop. But there was nothing left for us at the hospital. At least, nothing urgent.

"Back to the shop?" I said, resting my chin on Nik's shoulder. After the events at the Columbia Center, I had no doubt that the police would eventually find their way there, but I figured we had at least an hour or two. I was planning to head back to Bainbridge—finally—where I would give the Dom situation my full attention, but there were things I needed to grab from my place. Things I didn't want the cops or anyone else to find, my tarot cards and the *At* ink chief among them.

Plus, I stank. I reeked of mildew and seaweed, thanks to my dip in the waterway and the slow dry that had followed. The smell was strong enough that I couldn't ignore it; it had to be overwhelming to Nik. "I could really use a shower."

"You said it . . ." Nik turned the throttle, launching the bike forward before I could smack him.

We arrived at the shop less than ten minutes later, parking in the back alleyway, right near the shop's back door. It felt like weeks since I'd been home, though it had been less than a day. So much had happened. Too much. I didn't want to think about it all.

The shop would be opening in a couple hours, and I needed to be far from there when it did. I had to clean up and clear out—or clear out as much as I could as the place's owner. It was too risky to hang out there, and the cops paying me a visit was the least of my worries. Mari was a loose cannon, and I was a loose thread. I didn't know if anything she'd said was the truth, or if had all been a lie to ease her getaway. Would she come after Nik again? How badly did she need him? What kind of bargain might she try to strike next—either Nik helps her or she kills me? Lex? His mom? None of those were acceptable possibilities.

I unbuckled my sword's shoulder harness as I tromped up the stairs to the apartment ahead of Nik. I unlocked the door and shouldered it open, already shrugging out of my stinky leather coat. "I'll be quick," I told Nik as I crossed the living room to the kitchen. I set the coat and sword on the table, then pulled out a chair and sat with a groan, bending over to untie my combat boots. Salt had crusted into the laces, making the knots insanely stubborn.

"Looks like you had to go through a regeneration cycle," Nik said from just behind my chair.

I froze while untying my boot, peering at him out of the corner of my eye. I hadn't noticed him draw so close. He was looming over me, his gaze scrutinizing, eating a piece of cold pepperoni pizza.

I finished untying the right boot and moved on to the left. "Will you grab me a piece? Or just pull out the whole thing?"

His shadow moved away from me. "Mari wasn't sure how bad she got you with that knife." I heard the fridge open, then close, and Nik set a ziplock bag of cold pizza slices on the table near the edge. "Bad enough for you to look like you just escaped from a prison camp."

I tugged my left boot off. "Gee, thanks." I pulled off the other boot, then straightened and grabbed a piece of pizza. "So what happened to you, anyway? Garth barely survived . . ."

"But he did?" Nik pulled out the chair opposite mine. It wasn't a large table, so it didn't put him more than four feet from me. "I wasn't sure he would."

Chewing, I nodded. "He's in ICU at Harborview. I visited him while we were waiting for Dom—" The words caught in my throat. I took another bite of pizza, then set the half-eaten piece on the plastic bag and dug around in my coat until I found my phone. Dom's eyes were closed, but at least he was still there. *I'll fix this,* I promised him silently. I retrieved the piece of pizza. "Garth said a Nejeret attacked you guys and knocked him out, and when he came to, you were gone."

Nik nodded slowly, nibbling on pizza crust. "The fucker jumped us. Hopped right off the overpass and landed on my shoulders, knocking me out cold for a few seconds. I came to my senses and managed to shove him off the cop before, well . . ." Nik laughed under his breath. "Not soon enough. I'm just glad the guy's alright."

I leveled a steady stare across the table on Nik. "And the Nejeret—what happened to him?"

Nik met my eyes, then looked away, a wry grin on his face as he shook his head. "I don't know. Mari showed up before I could finish him. She would only agree to take me to you if I let the little shit live." His pale eyes returned to mine, shining unexpected emotion. He smirked, ruining the moment, and said, "I couldn't let you fade into nonexistence, now could I, Kitty Kat?"

I'd have been flattered that he cared if I didn't know that he was even more attached to this world as it was now than Mari was. If I were to be erased from the timeline, millennia of Nik's life would be altered, thanks to the complicated tangle of time travel. I'd never considered that the ramifications of my life might be so far-reaching. But they were.

I looked at the Eye of Horus tattooed on my palm. Maybe Nik and Mari would've returned in time, before the *anti-At* infecting my body erased me completely, and maybe Mari would've released Dom's *ba*, allowing it to return to his body. Maybe Nik would've listened to Mari, agreed with her logic about saving our people, and gone to work with her at Ouroboros of his own free will. Maybe. But maybe not. We'd never know.

I pulled another slice of pizza from the Ziploc bag, then tossed the bag across the table to Nik. "Do you think she's right?"

Nik raised his eyebrows.

"Mari. Do you think she's doing the right thing?" I rolled my eyes. "Trying to 'save our people'?"

Nik took a big bite of pizza, inhaling and exhaling slowly through his nose while he chewed. The way his squared jaw worked, defining the contours of his face that much more, made him almost irresistible. Finally, he swallowed, then spoke. "I think Mari thinks she's doing the right thing."

"Nice non-answer."

Nik shrugged one shoulder.

"Do you think it would really be so bad . . ." . . . *if the world knew about us?* It sounded so ridiculous in my head that I shoved the thought away, shook my head, and stood. "Never mind." I didn't have the energy for what-ifs right now. I headed into the hallway. "I'm showering. I'll be out in a few."

"Yes," Nik said. "It would be so bad."

I paused, my back to him and a hand against the hallway wall. "But if they see that we're not evil . . ." *They* being the humans.

"It's never about good and evil, Kitty Kat. I've seen countless civilizations rise and fall, and in the end, it always comes down to two things—us versus them, and power."

"In this case, are we 'us' or 'them'?"

"We're 'them'—the other—and we have power. The humans can't help but want to take it from us. It's in their nature."

Hanging my head, I trudged into the bathroom. But I wasn't convinced he was right. I wasn't convinced the humans were our enemies—or that *we* were *theirs*. I wasn't convinced we couldn't all live together, peacefully, out in the open.

One day, maybe . . .

But not today. Today was for the enemy within. The Senate. Or the *shadow* Senate. We had to eliminate that threat before we could even think about a world filled with hand-holding and kumbayas.

After I no longer smelled like a dried-up seal carcass.

CHAPTER TWENTY-FIVE

By the time I emerged from my bedroom, clean and in fresh jeans and a black tank top, Nik was gone. It hadn't even been ten minutes, but I wasn't surprised, exactly. At least, not by his absence. I hadn't really expected him to stick around, not when he'd been in the wind for years. But I was surprised by the disappointment I felt at finding the apartment empty. Specifically, empty of *him*.

As I stuffed clothes into a duffel bag, I wondered where he'd gone. Off to return to his lifestyle as a wandering nomad? Or was he joining up with Mari's mission to save the world, one human-turned-Nejeret at a time? My motions became jerkier and jerkier as I crammed only the essentials into the bag—underwear, socks, jeans, tank tops and T-shirts, a zip-up hoodie. The bastard could've at least said goodbye.

I hooked my arm through the bag's handles and carried it into the kitchen by my elbow. Setting it on the table, I added my sword, knives, and other weapons and gear, then zipped it up. A quick trip into the office and I carried out a sturdy leather messenger bag packed full of sketching supplies and cash from the safe, the red leather jacket I used to wear on hunts slung over my arm. It had been in the weapons closet, and I hadn't worn it in ages. Donning it was like stepping back in time.

I could feel myself becoming *her*, the girl-assassin I'd been desperate to become at the start and had, by the end, loathed being. As the jacket settled on my shoulders, hugging my back and fitting perfectly around my arms, I realized I would always be her —just like I would always be the girl my mom raised, and the woman I'd become during my years of self-inflicted isolation from my people. Whatever else happened to me, those three personas would always be a part of me.

Jacket on, I tucked my tarot deck into the front pocket, grabbed the last piece of pizza from the ziplock bag, and put it in my mouth, holding it by the crust with my teeth. I picked up both bags, settling the messenger bag across my body and hoisting the duffel onto one shoulder.

I headed downstairs as I chomped on the piece of pizza, dropping my duffel on the table in the back room and going into the shop to grab my tattoo machine, a handful of sealed needles, a couple bottles of black ink, and Nik's *At* ink. I placed everything in the padded carrying case I used for off-site jobs. The case looks a lot like an old-fashioned doctor's kit and was actually my mom's old apothecary case. She'd never been a fan of tattoos, but I doubted she'd have minded me using it, even for this.

I set the case down by my duffel bag on the table and stopped by the counter to scrawl a quick note to Kimi on a sticky note.

Kimi—I have a family emergency and will be out of town for a while. I'm not sure how long. I'll call later today to check in, but please alert any clients I (or Nik) have this week. Thx!—K

I stuck the note to the face of the register, where I knew Kimi couldn't miss it, then crouched down to retrieve the spare key to the upstairs apartment that I kept duct-taped to the underside of the counter in a tiny manila envelope. On the not-so-off chance that Mari or Ouroboros came after me here and ransacked the place, I didn't want them gaining easy access to my apartment. The door was reinforced and quadruple-locked, and I'd slowly renovated the windows and walls over the years, replacing and reinforcing for the highest security I could afford.

Someone knocked on the shop's glass door.

Fingers still searching the rough surface for the key, I peeked over the top of the counter. "Shit," I hissed, ducking back down immediately. The police had come sooner than I'd expected.

Two cops stood at the door, one peering in, hands to the glass over his eyes, the other leaning back, scoping out the storefront. I didn't recognize either of them from Garth's station or the ICU waiting room, so I assumed they weren't here to bring me news about Garth—not that I really thought I'd have warranted such a visit, but still. It was a possibility. But not the most likely one.

No, these cops were here because of what happened less than an hour ago downtown. Back at Ouroboros, Nik and I had left the male cop locked on the roof terrace with the Ouroboros guards, and we'd made it down to the bike without encountering his partner. It would've been a breeze for them to ID me—either by security cameras or by taking down the plates on my illegally parked motorcycle. However they'd done it, they'd tracked me back here. I'd expected as much, just not this quickly.

I stuck my whole head under the counter to find the damn key and tore the damn thing free of the underside of the counter, then crawled into the backroom, sliding under the beaded curtain to avoid creating movement that would draw the officers' attention. The longest strings of beads ended not quite a foot off the ground, giving me just enough room to wiggle underneath.

The cops rapped on the door again. "Police! Open up!"

I grabbed my duffel bag and the carrying case and rushed down the short hallway to the back door. It led to the alley driveway, where some of the other shops and the single cafe on my block received deliveries. I fully intended to make a quick getaway on the Ducati, bags and all, then ditch it in some other neighborhood to catch a bus to the ferry. Reprehensible as the thought was, the bike was too recognizable to take with me for farther than a few miles.

I yanked open the door and sucked in a breath to let out a startled scream.

Nik's hand clapped over my mouth, and he stepped in through the doorway, shoving me back against the hallway wall. "You've got visitors," he said, his face inches from mine, and I nodded.

This close, I could see the whitish, almost iridescent flecks interspersed throughout his blue irises, giving them that eerie, pale hue. I'd never seen them so up close, and I wondered if the iridescence had grown over time, evidence of the increasing power of his *sheut*. He was the oldest of our subspecies, Nejerets with *sheuts*, and he'd had the most time to develop his otherworldly power, to hone his skills. Had his irises been bluer, once upon a time? One day, would the blue fade away completely?

Nik's hand fell away, and he took a step backward. His other hand held up a tray with two coffee cups, and a grease-stained paper bag lay on its side on the asphalt in the alley behind him. "Now might be a good time to make like a tree and get the fuck out of here."

Again, I nodded.

Nik backed through the doorway, doing a quick scan of either direction, and held out his hand. "Give me your bag."

There was no question that he meant the duffel, and I didn't argue. He was bigger and stronger, and me carrying so much would just slow us down. I dropped the bag to the floor and kicked it to him while I readjusted the messenger bag's strap on my shoulder.

Nik picked up the duffel bag, slinging the strap over his shoulder, then bent over to retrieve the discarded paper bag.

One whiff of sugary, fried dough told me it was filled with donuts. "You left to get breakfast?" Astonishment knocked me momentarily senseless.

Nik scoffed and waved me out into the alleyway. "Tick-tock,

Kitty Kat. I'd rather not have to break your ass out of jail. Let's go."

I didn't argue. A rush of giddiness surged through me as I followed him out through the doorway. We ran up the alley and hopped on the first bus we saw, not caring where it would take us.

To the University District, it turned out. Four stops later, we were off that bus and waiting at the main bus stop at the University of Washington on Fifteenth Avenue. In minutes, we'd be on our way to the ferry terminal downtown, and in hours we'd be stepping onto Bainbridge Island. There, I would be able to figure out some way to make Dom's afterlife more comfortable. *There*, Nik and I would be able to reconvene with our people—the non-traitorous ones—and figure out what the hell to do. Our world was a ticking time bomb crafted by our own people. Evidence of our species was out there, in human hands.

I didn't think it wasn't a matter of *if* the bomb would explode, but *when*. I just hoped we'd be ready.

CHAPTER TWENTY-SIX

I sat on the floor in my old room on the second floor of Heru's house in the Nejeret complex on Bainbridge Island, surrounded by my old things. Now, even more so than before, I felt the convergence of who I used to be and who I was now. I was at a crossroads. I could drop everything—my sword, my shop, my name—and go on the run, be a lonely woman on the lam. I'd be running from myself as much as from anything else. Or I could give in. Accept who and what I was, both to myself and to my Nejeret clan.

The desire to run was strong. After all, it was essentially what I'd been doing for the last three years—running from the past while staying put, anchored to it. Running was safe. It was simple. It was lonesome but devoid of the complications and utter devastation that come with strong bonds.

But as I etched Dom's full name, Dominic l'Aragne, into the wood frame of the standing mirror laid down on the floor before me, over and over, Lex's words in that hospital stairwell—her plea—reverberated within me. *Be the legacy she deserves.* I couldn't shake the nagging feeling that she was right, that my mom would be disappointed in the woman I'd become. Not the killer, but the recluse. The one who chose to hide from her past mistakes rather than learn from them.

I'd distanced myself from my people, from Dom, and now he was gone . . . or gone-*ish*. And just like when my mom died, I was inundated with regret about time lost. Time *wasted*. I'd unwittingly thrown away the chance to see Dom a thousand more times, to share hundreds of philosophical conversations with him, to know him better. To let him know *me* better.

It's a funny thing, being a supposed immortal being. I'm only into my fourth decade, but even I have the deep-seeded belief that I and all of my Nejeret friends and family will be around forever. I'd been going through life the past few years thinking that someday, a good ways down the road, when I've got my shit together, I'd come back to them. But I'd been waiting until I'd become someone worthy of the love they're so willing to throw my way. I'd been waiting for a day that would never come.

I shook my head and started the thirteenth iteration of Dom's name around the mirror's wooden frame. I'd figured Dom and I would reunite someday, the dynamic duo, kicking ass and taking names side by side. And now that someday would never come. I was holding onto what little remained of him, my fingernails digging into his soul in a desperate attempt to regain what could've been. Possibilities that I'd thrown away so carelessly.

"I'll make this right," I told the phone sitting on the floor beside my knee.

Dom's etched eyes were open, his sharp, rough-hewn features arranged in a pattern that I thought might, just maybe, be curiosity. I was fairly sure he could hear me, though that etched image of him moved so slowly that any responses he gave may have just been coincidental movements. I blamed his hindered mobility on the medium. Etched glass was too permanent, too hard for his *ba* to manipulate. This time I'd used ink—Sharpie, to be exact. And I'd given him a full body, taking up the entire mirror when I drew him in painstaking detail, right down to his favorite loafers with the little leather tassel things. I'd always teased him about those.

There was a knock at the bedroom door.

"Yeah?" I called over my shoulder. I wasn't ready to share Dom with the others yet, not until I knew there was a way for us to communicate with him—for him to communicate with us. Not until I knew I wasn't torturing him by keeping him here. I wanted his permission, his blessing, before I let the others know just how desperate I was to hold onto him.

"It's me," Nik said. He turned the locked door handle. "Can I come in?"

"Sure." I didn't bother getting up to unlock the door. He could do it himself by magicking up a key out of thin air. "Lock it again, though," I said, once he was in the room. Lex, Heru, and the others were still on the west side of the Puget Sound, but there were plenty of other Nejerets who lived in the Heru compound and had keys to this house. Nobody could know about Dom until I was certain. Until I—*we*—were ready.

Nik locked the door, just like I requested, and his footsteps were quiet as he crossed the room to stand behind me. He whistled. "That's Dom, alright. Nicely done."

I finished the "e" in Dom's surname, then started carving the final rendition of his name around the wooden frame. "Thanks." I was quiet for a moment. "Nik . . . am I doing the right thing?"

Nik stepped over the mirror and sat in the cushy armchair by the window. "Honestly, Kitty Kat, I'm the last person you should be asking about right and wrong."

I frowned but continued carving.

"What would Dom say?"

"That's what I'm trying to find out," I grumbled.

Silence settled between us while I finished that final carving of Dom's name. My hand ached, and my fingers were cramping, but I pushed through. Finally, I sat back on my heels and set the wood-handled carving knife on the floor, trading it for my dead phone. I held up the phone so I could look at Dom face to face, my lips pursing in thought. My focus shifted from Dom's face to Nik's. "Any idea how to get him out of here and into the mirror?"

Nik shrugged. "You're the Ink Witch."

I scowled. "Don't call me that. I hate that nickname."

"You used to say that about 'Kitty Kat,'" Nik said with a smirk. "Maybe it'll grow on you."

"I hate that nickname, too," I lied.

Nik's smirk widened knowingly. "Of course you do."

Heat creeped up my neck and cheeks, and I bowed my head, letting my dark hair fall around my face, a curtain hiding the unexpected blush. "I still hate you," I told him.

"Of course you do," he repeated, his voice even more mocking than before.

I closed my eyes and took slow, deep breaths, focusing on Dom's dark, secretive eyes. In seconds the mental image replaced Nik's pale stare, and I felt myself become centered within. Nik had a tendency to make my thoughts and emotions flail wildly, while Dom had always been able to ground me. Maybe it was why I was so desperate to hang onto him.

"Touch."

My eyes snapped open, and I looked at Nik. "What did you say?"

Frowning, Nik shook his head. "Nothing." He was sitting on the edge of the chair, his elbows on his knees and his keen gaze locked on me, watching me do my magic. He was probably hoping to learn something, to understand, to figure out *how* I do what I do so he can train to do it himself. Everyone with a *sheut* could learn to do new things, train themselves to access more facets of their otherworldly powers . . . to some degree. I was still trying to master my own damn innate power. It was like trying to leash a kraken.

Eyebrows drawing together, I stared down at the phone. Dom returned my stare with so much intensity I had no doubt that he could truly see me.

"Touch . . . mirror . . ." There was no mistaking it this time—it was Dom's voice whispering through my mind.

"Did you hear that?" I asked Nik, eyes flicking his way.

Again, he shook his head.

I licked my lips and, hands shaking, lowered the phone to the mirror. I set it down on the drawn-on glass and held my breath.

Nothing happened.

For nearly a minute, I watched, waiting. But nothing happened. Dom just stared back at me from the phone's screen, blinking every ten or fifteen seconds.

"Maybe turn it over?" Nik suggested.

"Oh, right." I gently flipped the phone over so it was facedown against the mirror.

Almost immediately, silver poured into the mirror, billowing out below the surface like ink in water. Strands of it shot up from the mirror's surface, diving back down almost immediately as the silvery filaments coiled around the lines of the drawing until the ink from the permanent marker was no longer black, but solid, gleaming silver.

My hands covered my mouth, my eyes bulging. Tears streamed down my cheeks as I watched the impossible happen.

The now-silver drawing deepened, gaining shadow and depth, becoming three-dimensional right before my eyes. Dom seemed to gain weight even as he gained substance, and his feet fell away, as though drawn by some other-dimensional form of gravity, until he was standing on an unseen surface below, face upraised. He stared up at me through the mirror.

"Help me," I said to Nik, reaching for the mirror's edges. I gripped either side and lifted it a few inches off the ground, intending to stand it upright.

"Little sister—"

I dropped the mirror back to the floor, hands clutching my chest. Dom's voice had been clear as day in my mind. There was no mistaking it. I looked from Dom in the mirror to Nik and back. Dom's mouth was still moving, but his voice was gone.

Without hesitation, I pressed my palm against the frame of the mirror.

"Can you truly hear me?" Dom asked, his faint French accent more comforting than any hug had ever been.

"Yes," I said, chin trembling. Let's be real, my whole body was trembling. I nodded, my free hand covering my mouth. "Are you alright?"

Dom nodded sedately. *"I am well enough. Though this position is not the most comfortable . . ."*

"Oh, right." Once again, I gripped either side of the tall standing mirror and lifted it up off the ground. Nik helped, and we moved the armchair aside and arranged Dom in the corner of the room, where he would have a good view of the entire space.

"Thank you," Dom said. *"That is much better."*

Nik's eyes opened wide, and a moment later, his lips spread into a broad grin. "Welcome back."

Dom's dark eyes locked on Nik. *"Should I say the same to you?"*

Nik chuckled. "We'll see." He looked at me. "Let go for a minute." The moment I did, the mirror and its frame were taken over by a sheet of *At*, spreading out like ice freezing over a lake. Within seconds, the entire mirror had been transformed into *At*. "Wouldn't want him to break," he said as he pulled his hand back.

Remotely, I could feel myself nodding, hear myself saying thank you. But I couldn't tear my eyes away from my half-brother's face.

"I'll give the two of you a minute," Nik said, backing away. Out of the corner of my eye, I watched him turn and leave the room, shutting the door on his way out.

I touched the mirror's unbreakable *At* frame with trembling fingertips so I could once again hear Dom's voice. "Dom, I—I'm so sorry . . . for everything. I tried so hard to save you, but I just wasn't good enough."

His silvery reflection clasped his fingers together, almost like he was preparing to pray. *"Answer me one thing, little sister, and all will be forgiven."*

"Anything," I said, meaning it with every fiber of my being.

"Are you done running?" His eyes, somehow just as dark and penetrating in silver as they'd been in flesh, bore into me. *"Are you back, for good?"*

I nodded vehemently. "Yes, Dom. I swear it. I'm back."

CHAPTER TWENTY-SEVEN

"And that's how you ended up in the phone," I told Dom, arching my back and stretching my arms over my head. I'd been sitting in front of the mirror—*his* mirror, now—legs folded under me and elbows on my knees, for nearly an hour. Dom's silvery non-reflection mirrored my position, if not the stretching.

I dropped my hands into my lap, flicking a few fingers at the mirror. "So what's it like in there, anyway?" I touched my fingertips to the base of the frame so I could hear his response.

"It is . . ." His eyes narrowed, and he looked around. *"It is strange. But also quite familiar."* His thin lips twisted into a wry smile. *"I'll let you know more once I've had a chance to explore."*

I nodded slowly.

"Kat . . . "

Uh-oh. I knew that tone—it was Dom's do-as-I-say tone. His I'm-disappointed-in-you tone. Especially when he actually used my name. Usually he called me "little sister." I held my breath.

"You need food," he said. *"And rest. You must allow your body to heal—another regeneration cycle, at least. You will continue to weaken until you do."*

"I know," I said, shaking my head. "I can't, though. Once Lex and Heru and the others get here with . . ." . . . *your body*. I cleared my throat, the words sticking, unspoken. "Once they get here, you need to tell them everything you can remember about Ouroboros, what they're up to, and where they kept you and the others. Now that we know some of the Senators are involved . . . I just have a feeling it's all going to blow up. I want to get those Nejerets—and those kids"—*especially* the kids—"somewhere safe before the Senate and Ouroboros figure out that we know what they're up to. We can't give them the chance to burn the evidence." It was a figure of speech, but in this case, I feared the reality would be far too literal. Those poor kids . . .

"Personally, I am more interested in why.*"*

I cocked my head to the side.

"Why did the Senate feed a human-owned and -run company the documentation proving our existence?" Dom said. *"Why are they funding Ouroboros? Why are they handing over Nejerets allied with Heru and Mei? Why have they deemed them the opposing faction?"*

I stared off into the background of the reflection, searching for answers where there were none. "And what's their endgame?" I said, adding to his list of questions.

It didn't make sense to me why any Senators would be involved in Ouroboros's plan to prolong human life indefinitely—it would only crowd the earth, especially if, unlike the females of our species, human women retained their ability to reproduce, even when relatively immortal. And why give them the proof of our existence, unless they *wanted* Ouroboros to share it with the world? It would create curiosity at first, closely followed by hostility, paranoia, and panic. Then, if Nik's fears proved true, all-out war.

"We can only speculate the reason behind their actions at this point," Dom said. *"And in your state, speculate poorly. Heru and the others have yet to return home, and there is little you can do without them. Rest, little sister."*

I rubbed a hand over my eyes. They felt gritty and dry, and my body ached with fatigue. I knew, in my bones, that Dom was right, but I wasn't ready to leave him just yet. Part of me feared he wouldn't be there when I woke up, like the magic would fade, and he would disappear from my life for good.

My mouth opened wide in a jaw-cracking yawn.

Dom stared at me through the mirror, his expression set.

"Fine," I said, giving in. "I'll take a damn nap." When I stood, I was surprised by how unsteady I felt. I touched the edge of the mirror so I could still hear him. "What will you do?"

Dom turned his head, looking over his shoulder. *"Why, explore my new realm, of course. I'm sensing that there's more to it than either of us might think."*

"Like what?" I asked, yawning once more.

"I am unsure, but there are . . ." He frowned. *"Sounds. And there are doors that do not exist on your side of the glass."* His frown faded. *"'There are more things in heaven and earth . . .'"*

It was my turn to frown. "Just don't get lost, alright? We need you." *I need you.*

Dom nodded. *"I won't go far."*

I held his reflected, silvery gaze for a moment, then nodded. Turning away from the tall mirror, I dragged my feet across the room to the bed and collapsed on it face-first. I was out within seconds.

"Just watch . . . one day, they'll know us." The rogue Nejeret, a slender guy with the innate sheut *power to camouflage himself like a chameleon, laughs bitterly.*

I'm standing over him, the tip of my sword perched on his chest, just over his heart.

"Killing me won't make one fucking difference." He coughs, blood spraying out of his mouth. I've worked him over pretty good already. He deserved it; he used those color-changing cells of his to rob several dozen banks, resulting in thirteen human deaths. "Just you watch—one day they'll know us. They'll see us for what we are: the cure sent to wipe the scourge

that they are off the face of the earth. One day, they'll know us, and the next day, they'll die."

I put pressure on the sword, shoving the blade straight through his heart.

His whole body tenses, his eyes bulging. A moment later, he goes limp.

"Self-righteous prick," I mumble, yanking the blade free.

"Tell me about it." Mari leans against the wall on the far side of the garage, cleaning her nails with the tip of an inky black nail file. "Maybe the world'll know about us one day"—her eyes met mine, almost highlighter green in the florescent lighting—"but only when we want them to. Only when we're ready . . ."

I sucked in a sharp breath and opened my eyes. Mari's words from my dream of a memory of something that happened sixteen years ago echoed through my mind.

. . . only when we want them to . . . only when we're ready . . .

Pushing myself up, I scooted to the edge of the bed, wiping the smear of drool from my cheek and chin with the back of my hand.

"Dom," I said, rushing across the room to the standing mirror. He wasn't there, at least, not that I could see. "Dom!" I pressed both hands against the frame on either side of the mirror and moved my head from side to side, searching for him in the murky reflection of the room.

"I am here," he said, coming into view. He smoothed back his hair and studied my face. *"What is it, little sister? Has something happened?"*

I shook my head. "Not exactly, but . . ." I thought back to the dream. "What if the shadow Senate *wants* the info about us to leak out? What if they want the humans to learn about us? What if they *want* war?" My thoughts sped up, spinning around my mind like race cars around a track, faster and faster. "What if they want to wipe humans off the face of the earth?"

Dom's sharp features pinched. *"It would be suicide. Without a way to reproduce, eventually, our kind would die out as well. Besides, if that is their goal, why not simply release the information themselves?"*

I chewed on my thumbnail, seeking out a phantom hangnail. Nejerets' natural regenerative abilities effectively rendered us a doomed species, since it locked the females of our kind in a constant state of infertility. Our bodies rejected any fertilized eggs almost as soon as they implanted in our uterine walls. Without human women, we would die out. It would take a while, since violent deaths were pretty much the only way to kill us, but in time, we *would* go extinct. Whatever the shadow Senate's plans, they needed to keep some human women alive, specifically the ones who carried the latent recessive Nejeret genes.

"Oh my God." I lowered my hand, my mouth hanging open. "What if that's the whole point of funding the research—to create *some* immortal humans, a select, chosen few women who are Nejeret carriers? Maybe they want to give them prolonged lives, then use them as premier breeding stock. They could commoditize the right to reproduce . . . control who has access to the women. They would have absolute control over the future of our people."

"A truly terrifying thought."

I heard the distant sound of the front door opening downstairs, followed by several pairs of footsteps entering the house.

I looked at the bedroom door, then glanced at Dom. "They're back. Are you ready for them?"

He nodded.

"Nik!" I shouted in the general direction of the door. "Can you bring everyone up here?"

"On it," he said, tapping the door with his knuckles as he passed by.

I grabbed the throw off the back of the armchair and tossed it over the mirror. "Just for a sec," I whispered to Dom. "I want to prepare them first."

Less than a minute later, Nik pushed the door to my bedroom open and let the others file in ahead of him, first Lex, then Heru, then Neffe and Aset. They looked like hell, eyes red-rimmed and puffy and shoulders slumped. Nik followed them in, crossing the room to sit in the armchair.

"Nik tells us you have news," Heru said, his voice weary. He sidestepped closer to Lex and curled an arm around her waist. She leaned her cheek on his shoulder, letting out a heavy sigh.

"I know you all must think I failed, but I didn't." I took a step toward them, wringing my hands. "I found Mari . . . and she released Dom's *ba*."

Lex's head lifted, and her listless gaze wandered my way.

"It was too late," I said. "He was already—*his body* was already dead." I took a deep breath. "But we managed to recapture his *ba*."

Aset looked at her son.

Nik raised his hands in front of himself. "Not me," he said, shaking his head. "This soul capture was all Kat's doing."

All five sets of eyes fixed on me, curiosity muting the grief, just a little.

"I, um, well . . ." I cleared my throat and took a couple small backward steps, moving closer to the covered mirror. "He's not gone—not dead, exactly." I reached out my right hand and pinched the fuzzy blanket. "He's right here." With one quick tug, the blanket slid off the mirror and fell to the floor.

Dom, the only clear thing in the murky reflection, lifted one hand and waved.

All four newcomers gasped. Neffe and Aset covered their mouths with their hands, and Lex took a couple steps forward, hand outstretched toward the mirror. Heru simply stood where he was and stared, golden eyes glassy.

"It's really him?" Lex asked, slowly moving closer.

"It is," I assured her.

"Can I talk to him? Can he hear me?"

I nodded. "He can hear you now, but you have to be touching the mirror to hear him."

She rushed forward, pressing her palm against the mirror. "Dom?"

A gentle smiled curved his lips and he raised his hand, pressing it against the other side of the mirror's surface. His lips moved, but lipreading was a skill I didn't have.

Lex rested her forehead against the mirror, shoulders shaking as soft sobs tumbled free.

Not a moment later, Heru was behind her. He settled an arm around her shoulders, the other on the mirror beside hers. "Welcome back, my old friend."

CHAPTER TWENTY-EIGHT

"So you can't say for sure where the warehouse was?" Heru paced across my old room, from the hallway door to the wardrobe and back. He'd been at it for at least an hour now, mobility seeming to help him process the information Dom relayed through me.

For the past hour or so, Dom had been explaining what had happened to him—how he'd been captured in a trap that resulted in the release of a knockout gas and what Ouroboros had done to him and the others while he was in their hands. Or rather, in their holding cells. According to Dom, the captive Nejerets were divided into two subject groups—those who were abused and brought to the brink of death, then allowed to regenerate, and those who'd had their *bas* extracted and *then* were abused and brought to the brink of death. Dom had been in the latter group.

He wasn't sure how the *ba*-extraction worked, science-wise, only that he'd been strapped down in a chair and that electricity had coursed through his body for what felt like an eternity. Once his soul was removed from his body, he had a brief moment of what felt like astral projection before he was encased in absolute darkness—the *anti-At* sphere closing in around him, we all assumed. His *ba* had been returned to his body several times during his several-week stay in the warehouse laboratory, allowing him to heal, but as a result, his moments of consciousness and lucidity were few and far between.

"I could hear the roar of the freeway, the frequent rumble of a foghorn in the distance, and, on occasion, the sound of a large crowd cheering—those are the only identifying sounds I can recall," Dom said, and I repeated his words to the others. Lex was sitting on the floor near me, Nik in the armchair in the corner, and Aset and Neffe on the foot of the bed. "Sounds like SoDo to me," I added. Not only was the industrial area packed with warehouses *and* near I-5 and the water, but it was also the location of Seattle's two professional sports stadiums—Safeco and Century Link Fields, where the Mariners and Seahawks played, respectively.

Heru nodded. "I agree, but there are hundreds of warehouses there, and I highly doubt Ouroboros would be reckless enough to leave any kind of paper trail linking them to their illicit research branch. We need more information."

"Mari," Dom said, voicing the option I was unwilling to suggest. *"She was there each time my ba was extracted. If you can find her, I am certain you could convince her to tell you the exact location."*

"We can't trust her," I told him. "She lied to me about knowing you were even there—said she didn't know until I told her. She's clearly got her own agenda. She's fanatical about 'saving our people.' It's the most important thing in the world to her."

"Is it truly?" He stared at me with those dark eyes. *"Is there not anything else you can think of that might be of paramount importance to her? Perhaps a person . . . ?"*

"Well, yeah—her mom, but . . ."

"Might Mari's priorities shift if she were to find out that her mother is just another test subject?"

My eyes widened. "Are you saying Ouroboros has Mei? That they're experimenting on her—*torturing* her?"

Dom shrugged. *"Truly, I do not know what they are doing with her, only that they have her. I watched them bring her in a few days ago during one of my recovery periods. They took her to a separate wing of holding cells."*

"Mari'd never allow that," I said.

"Then she must not know."

I shook my head. "But that doesn't make sense. Mei could just shift out of there." It was her innate *sheut* gift, along with a number of others she'd attained proficiency in through years of rigorous dedication and training. She was old, centuries beyond me in understanding and developing her *sheut*. I was still figuring out how my own innate powers worked. But her . . . I couldn't imagine anyone, especially not humans, figuring out a way to contain her.

"My holding cell was surrounded by an electromagnetic field that would keep those like Mei and Heru from being able to locate us—Mari explained it to me herself. It seems logical to me that the same field used to keep Mei out could be used to keep her in."

"Oh, shit . . ."

"Care to share?" Heru said, his tone bland. He'd finally stopped moving and was standing in the center of the room, staring at me.

I returned his stare. "How long since anyone's talked to Mei?"

Heru looked at his sister, who immediately pulled out a sleek cell phone and started tapping the screen. "You believe Ouroboros has captured her?" he asked, returning his attention to me.

I nodded. "Dom saw them bring her in." I relayed what he'd said about the electromagnetic field, then added, "If we tell Mari, she'll flip out." I shifted my legs so I was kneeling instead of sitting on the floor. My heart rate picked up, and I rubbed slightly sweaty palms on my jeans. "She'll abandon her 'save our people' crusade in a heartbeat and tear that place apart to get to Mei." I licked my lips and inhaled deeply. "If we tell her about this, she'll have no reason not to share the location."

Heru crossed his arms over his chest. "But what incentive will she have to help us? What's to stop her from simply going in there and breaking Mei out, and leaving us sitting on our thumbs?"

"Nothing." In all likelihood, I thought that was exactly what she would do. "But, her going in and breaking out Mei brings down all of the barriers. She'll disable all security measures in the process. And this is the only way I can see that she *might* tell us the location." I stared at each of them for a moment, settling on Heru's intense, golden eyes. "Back on that roof, she agreed to help Dom. She was going to come to the hospital and release his *ba*. She was going to help us save him." I had to believe that part hadn't been a lie. "She's not a bad person. Misguided, maybe, but not *bad*."

Heru rubbed his jaw with one hand.

"We can't wait to come up with something better," I persisted. "The shadow Senate will know that *we* know by now, thanks to our little show on the roof. Don't you think they'll try to cover their tracks by destroying all of the evidence—including the people?" I took a deep breath and barreled onward. "There are kids there, too, Heru. *Children* who didn't do anything wrong besides being unlucky enough to be homeless. They don't deserve this." My fingers gripped my jeans. "Besides, what's the worst that can happen? She leaves chaos in her wake? Ouroboros will send in extra security once they realize she's broken Mei out. You own companies that have satellites, don't you? If we have to, can't we just use them to monitor the whole Industrial District? Their own people will lead us right to the warehouse where they're holding ours."

Lex stood gracefully and approached her husband. She placed her hand on Heru's arm and looked up into his face. "She's right. You can see that, can't you?"

Heru's stare shifted from Lex to the mirror. Out of the corner of my eye, I saw Dom nod once. "Alright," Heru said. He looked at me. "Make the call."

I glanced at the scratched-up phone lying discarded on the floor. Her text from the previous day was the only place I had her number, and thanks to my dip in the sound, the phone would never turn on again. I bit my lower lip. Banging my head against the wall would be about as effective as this whole plan, because none of us had her damn phone number.

"Here," Nik said, fishing his phone from his pocket. He tossed it to me.

I raised an eyebrow.

"Her number's in there," he said, pointing to the phone in my hand with his chin. "She gave me her card . . . you know, because I 'agreed' to work with her."

A slow grin spread across my face. "Maybe I don't quite hate you."

Nik snorted. "Don't get soft on me now." His lips twisted into a sly smirk. "I'll blush."

I didn't know how to respond to that, so I stuck out my tongue. What can I say? I'm forever eighteen, with all the hormones and maturity that come with that oh-so-special age.

A slight tremor ran through my hands as I searched Nik's contacts for Mari's name. He had an enormous phone book, filled mostly with entries using distinctly female names. I ignored that little tidbit—for the most part—and found Mari's name. I pulled up her contact profile, tapped the call button, and brought the phone up to my ear.

She answered during the second ring. "Hello, Nikolas."

I responded without thinking. "His full name is Nekure, not Nikolas, numb-nuts."

"Kat?" From the way Mari said my name, she sounded wary.

"The one and only."

"You sound . . . chipper."

I sneered. "You know, I *feel* chipper."

"Really?"

"I just can't help but feel all tingly inside when I know something you don't know."

"Kat," Heru's voice held a warning, his eyes a dark promise.

I held up a finger, silencing him. I knew Mari better than him; I knew just how to play her like a concert pianist.

"And what might that be?" Mari asked over the phone.

"How about we trade—I'll tell you what *I* know, if you tell me where the warehouse containing your secret, evil lab is?"

"It's not my lab," she said blandly.

"Semantics," I said. "How about this—I'll go first. You don't have to tell me the location right away. You don't even have to tell me over the phone. You can text it to me, for all I care. But just remember one thing—you already owe me a debt for Dom's death. Now you'll be doubly indebted to me, and I'm not feeling too happy about you right now. The next time I see you, my sword might just slip out of my scabbard and accidentally pierce your heart. And trust me when I say I *will* see you again."

Mari was quiet for a few seconds. "Fine," she said. "I'll bite. Share."

I looked straight into Heru's eyes as I spoke. "Ouroboros has Mei, Mari. They have your mom."

Another few seconds of silence, just the sound of her breathing on the other side of the line. And then the line went dead.

Got her.

I lowered the phone, setting it on the floor by my knee.

Heru stalked toward me and crouched down, bringing his face to my level. Damn, but it was hard to look into those glorious black-rimmed gold eyes when he was so close and so very pissed off. "You're reckless," he said, his voice cold and controlled. And terrifying.

I leaned back a few inches. I couldn't help it.

"You've always been reckless," he continued. "If that causes our people their lives . . ."

Lex touched his shoulder with gentle fingertips, like doing so might help tame his rabid inner beast.

The phone buzzed, and I risked a glance downward. One new message. From Mari.

I opened it with a tap of my thumb. Straight-faced, I held the phone up for Heru to see. "If I'm not mistaken, that's an address." I suppressed a grin. "In SoDo."

CHAPTER TWENTY-NINE

8:57 PM

All bas have been released and returned to their respective bodies, security systems are disarmed, and personal are detained. Do what you want with this place . . . burn the whole damn warehouse to the ground if you want. I don't care.

8:58 PM

Just don't come looking for me. Don't look for my mom. You won't find us.

8:58 PM

This makes us even.

Mari's texts had come in quick succession while we were navigating the streets of SoDo. I'd smiled to myself after reading them. She'd always been reactionary. Once she cooled down and her more calculating, logical side took over, she would come to me, icy anger a frigid torch burning within her. Vengeance was a dish best served cold, in her case. And she made good chilled vengeance. The best, in fact.

We kept our rescue party small—Heru, Lex, Aset, Neffe, Nik, and me. We were the only people outside of the shadow Senate fully aware of the situation. This core group was the trusted few, for now. Once the rescue mission was over and the warehouse lab was destroyed, we could start incorporating others into our circle —especially those we'd rescued—but for now, we were operating small, lips zipped. Loose lips and sinking ships, and all that . . .

Once we knew where to attack, getting people and the kids out was easy enough—knocking out anything electronic is simple when you have nearly unlimited funds and resources, which Heru does. It's good to be an ancient god of time—an 'old one,' as the more ancient of our kind were called. It helped that Mari had already swept through the place, disabling all of the alarm systems and security cameras and locking the few evening employees in holding cells that had apparently been empty.

We arrived just minutes after her texts, unleashing a localized electromagnetic pulse generator that would wipe out everything for as long as it remained on, giving us enough time to get in, release all of the captured Nejerets and kids, and get out. We rushed the former captives out to the three buses we'd rented to transport them back to the Heru compound on Bainbridge. We weren't sure what had been done to the kids. They didn't appear to be roughed up, but some seemed ill, and others were out cold. Neffe and Aset were determined to use every cell of their scientific brains to figure out what Ouroboros had done to them.

Not everyone could walk. Some of the Nejerets were unconscious, having slipped into regenerative comas as soon as Mari reunited their *bas* with their bodies. Those relative few were carried out, one by one, by Nik and Heru while Neffe, Aset, and Lex remained with those already loaded onto the buses, waiting to drive them to the ferry as soon as everyone was out. Reinforcements would arrive soon—Ouroboros had probably dispatched them as soon as Mari disabled all of the security systems—so we had to move as quickly as possible.

I remained within the heart of the lightless laboratory, keeping watch on the new captives while Nik and Heru ushered the wounded out. I paced from one end of the large, sterile room to the other, following the line of glass viewing panes giving me a window into the cells. There were eight cells in this portion of the warehouse, each holding two or three people—seven scientists and nine security guards.

"You can't hold us in here!" one of the scientists shouted, pounding a fist against the thick, tempered glass of the third cell from the end. "We were just doing our jobs!"

I rolled my eyes, blowing him a kiss as I passed the viewing window to his cell. He shared it with two other scientists—one male and one female. All three looked too pale, like they hadn't seen the sun in weeks. Then again, this was Seattle. None of us had seen the sun in weeks.

The rest of the room was filled with long, freestanding counters laden with high-tech and top-of-the-line equipment, all white or black or silver or glass. I didn't know what any of it was for, beyond the microscopes, but it didn't really matter. That was more Neffe's thing.

I watched Nik's back as he carried the last unconscious Nejeret out of the lab. Heru had left just a moment earlier, meaning I had a moment alone with the Ouroboros personnel.

Finally. This was why I'd volunteered to stand guard. This was what I'd been waiting for.

I stopped at the far end of the lab and reached into my coat pocket, pulling out a vintage silver compact mirror. It had been my mom's, and her mother's before her. I opened the compact, revealing the mirror that wasn't a mirror. DOMINIC L'ARAGNE was etched around the outer edge of the glass in tiny, precise letters, and his silvery visage stared out at me, eyes squinting. My fingers trembled under the force of my adrenaline. I was starving for vengeance.

"Can you see?" I asked Dom, voice tight with the excitement of a potential righteous kill. "Or is it too dark?" There were no lights on in the warehouse, thanks to the steadily pulsing electromagnetic field generator we'd set up in the center of the cavernous building, but it wasn't too dim for keen Nejeret eyesight to see clearly enough.

"I cannot see much," Dom said, *"but I do not require sight to identify the one who tore out my soul."*

"Those people aren't even human!" the loudmouthed asshat scientist yelled. "They're not protected by any human rights laws!"

I quirked an eyebrow and started toward the third holding cell, picking up on Dom's meaning. He didn't need to see the guy who'd helped tear out his soul, because he could hear him, loud and clear. My bloodlust spiked, and my heartbeat quickened.

"We're well within our rights to do whatever the hell we want with them!"

"This one?" I asked Dom, stopping in front of the viewing window.

Dom nodded once. *"His is a voice I shall never forget."*

"Alright." I closed the compact and tucked Dom back into my pocket, then fixed my eyes on the irate scientist within. I cocked my head to the side, eyes scouring the lines of his face, memorizing his features. Fury lit my blood on fire when I looked at him.

His eyes searched what had to be absolute darkness from his perspective, looking for me.

"What's your name?" I asked.

"Dr. Bergman," he said, puffing up under his lab coat.

"Got a first name?"

He crossed his arms over his chest. "Eric."

I flashed him a humorless grin, not that he could see it. "Well, Dr. Eric Bergman, today's your lucky day. I'm going to let you out of that cell. You, and only you."

His eyes narrowed. "Why?"

"I need someone to send a message to your bosses. You're the most outspoken, so . . ." I nodded to the door, then remembered that he couldn't see the motion. "Step on over to the door." When he didn't move, I added, "You want to get out of there, don't you? Isn't that what you've been going on about for the past ten minutes?"

After a few more seconds, he moved to the door. I unlocked it, and he took a cautious step out into the lab. A moment later, he lunged to the side, attempting to make a run for it.

I grabbed the back collar of his lab coat and he jerked to a stop, falling back onto his ass. With my free hand, I pulled the door to the holding cell shut, then focused all of my attention on Dr. Dumbass.

"You, Dr. Eric Bergman, made a very big mistake," I said, taking hold of his thick mop of hair and pulling him up to a kneeling position.

He sucked in halting breaths. "I—I'm sorry. Your message—I'll pass it on. J—just tell me what it is."

I let out a bitter laugh, reaching into my back pocket with my free hand to retrieve a Sharpie. I pulled the cap off with my teeth and spit it to the side. "My brother's name is Dominic l'Aragne. He's one of the non-humans you so blithely experimented on." I leaned forward until my face was mere inches from his. I was breathing hard, impassioned by my rage. "I'm telling you this so you'll understand that what happens next is a result of your own actions. You made a choice. You chose wrong. You tore out my brother's soul, tortured him, and now he's dead." I glared at the man—the human—in disgust. He didn't deserve his soul. "It's time for the reckoning."

I pulled back a few inches and brought the Sharpie to his forehead, where I started to write out a single word in big, bold letters.

B—

His sweat blurred the lines of my letters, permanent ink and all, but it didn't matter. I was finally getting a grip on my *sheut*'s innate power. I was finally starting to understand it.

U—

Where my magic was concerned, intent was paramount, and conviction was key. There was nothing shoddy or shaky about my intent or my conviction now. The hunger for revenge was all-consuming. Dom's death would be answered for.

R—

I didn't even care that he was human, or that killing him would destroy his soul. That his would be the first life I truly ended, body and soul. He deserved an eternity of agony, but I'd settle for a few minutes instead. I wanted this man to burn with the fires of a thousand hells.

And burn he did.

As I finished writing the word "BURN" on his forehead, the ink started to sizzle.

Dr. Eric Bergman whimpered . . . then gasped . . . then screamed. The black letters pulsated, brilliant orange glowing around the edges. A moment later, actual flames burst out of his forehead. They engulfed his entire head, spreading down his body and up my arm. I gritted my teeth as my skin burned, blistered, and melted right along with his.

I threw him backwards before the flames could travel past my elbow. I didn't want to singe my hair, after all. My skin would heal in a matter of days, but my hair would take years to grow back.

Dr. Eric Bergman was still screaming when the lights came back on. Someone must've turned off the EMP generator. It was time to go. Bergman writhed on the ground, rolling and flopping around. I had no doubt that the pain was unbearable, that it had already driven him mad. And yet, there was no way it even came close to the hours and hours of pain and torture this man and his team had inflicted on Dom. Pity wasn't even a fleeting thought. This was justice.

Holding my arm away from my body, I walked to the nearest sink and turned on the water, moving my arm back and forth and twisting it around until all of the flames were out. Once I was fire-free, I strode away from the burning man still writhing on the floor.

Nik stood silhouetted in the doorway at the far end of the lab, shoulder leaned against the doorframe, watching.

I paused, just for a moment. I hadn't known he was there.

A moment later, I turned my head and looked at the scientists and security guards still in their cells. "I'm holding your bosses just as responsible as Dr. Bergman there," I told them. Every single one of them stood at their viewing windows, varying degrees of horror painted across their faces as they watched their colleague burn. "Feel free to let them know." I started to walk away. "And tell them I'm coming for them."

"But—"

I stopped at the last cell's viewing window.

Two of the cell's occupants slunk back into the shadows, but a lone female security guard stood her ground. "Who are you?" she asked.

"Me? I'm Kat Dubois." I turned away from her and continued on toward the doorway. Toward Nik. The ghost of a smile touched my lips. "I'm the Ink Witch."

CHAPTER THIRTY

"You're sure you can handle running this place while I'm gone?" I asked Kimi. It was evening, and the shop was closed.

From the opposite side of the counter, she shrugged. "I've been working for you since you first opened. If I can't run this place by now, I've got no business getting my MBA."

"Fair enough," I said with a nod. I bent my knees to pick up an oversized duffel bag off the floor. I'd stuffed nearly every piece of clothing I actually wore into the bag, along with my backup boots and a few other odds and ends from upstairs. "I'll check in at least once a week, but don't hesitate to call if you have any questions."

"You got it, boss," she said. "Any idea how long you'll be gone?"

I shook my head. "But I'll let you know as soon as I know." I was returning to Bainbridge indefinitely. It was past time for me to get over my shit and rejoin my clan.

The bell over the door jingled, and we both turned our heads to watch six people stream into the shop—Heru and Nik, closely followed by two unfamiliar Nejerets, one male, one female, and *him*. The bartender from the Goose smirked when his eyes locked with mine. The five newcomers lined up, Nik and Aset on either end, Heru a few steps ahead.

"Kimi," I said without taking my eyes off the Nejerets. "Why don't you take off. I'll finish closing up tonight."

"But—"

"Kimi." I looked at her, and whatever she saw in my eyes caused the blood to drain from her face. "Go, now. I'll call you tomorrow."

She nodded, licked her lips, and backed away, rushing through the beaded curtain. A few seconds later, I heard the back door open, then shut. Kimi was gone.

I refocused on Heru. "To what do I owe this honor, oh chieftain, my chieftain?"

"Katarina Dubois," Heru said, his voice bland, "the Senate has issued a detainment order for you. You're charged with being in league with the rogue Nejerets, Mari and Mei. Your rebellious and irresponsible actions have put Nejeretkind at risk, and such behavior cannot go unpunished." His lips twitched.

I, myself, was having a hard time keeping a straight face. I'd known something like this would be coming, eventually. I was the only one who identified herself at the warehouse the previous night, making myself the easiest target for retribution. We'd lit the match with our siege on the Ouroboros warehouse; it was time to start the fire.

"I advise that you submit to the Senate's authority and offer yourself into their just and capable hands," Heru continued. As leader of this territory, it was his right to come after me himself, though I wasn't surprised the Senate sent others with him to make sure he followed through. "If you do not submit, you will be detained using force."

Nik shook his head, almost imperceptibly.

I stared at him for a moment, then returned my focus to Heru. "You know," I said, "I'm just not feeling it today. Can you come back tomorrow?"

This time, when Heru's lips twitched, he allowed a hint of a smile to break free, just for a moment. His expression went blank, and he turned on his heel to face the other Nejerets. "She chose to resist. There was a struggle."

"Was?" the bartender said, alarm flashing in his eyes.

Not a second later, crystalline *At* vines slithered across the floor, originating at Nik and wrapping around the ankles of the bartender and the two unfamiliar Nejerets. The vines climbed up their legs, winding around and around, until they were restrained up to their shoulders and their struggles were limited to the twisting of their heads from side to side.

"Fugitive's choice," Heru said. "Which to release as a messenger, which to keep for questioning . . ." He grinned viciously. "And which to *be* the message." There was no doubt in my mind what form that message would take. I was well versed in this form of communication.

I stared at Heru, unblinking, totally caught off guard. It was like a twisted version of marry-fuck-kill. "You're going to start a war," I told him.

"Not a war," he said, his grin fading. "A revolution."

"I—I don't—"

"Choose, Kat, or I'll choose for you."

I didn't even have to think about it, and I didn't bother voicing my choice. I simply drew the combat knife tucked into my boot sheath, strode up to the Nejeret who'd been posing as a bartender to spy on me, and held the blade flush under his jaw.

He swallowed reflexively.

"This is for Garth," I hissed, slicing the blade across his neck. I took a step backward to avoid the waterfall of blood that cascaded down his front and waited until his body went limp to turn away from him. I locked eyes with Heru. "I don't give two shits what you do with the others."

"Very well." His focus shifted beyond me, and he addressed the two remaining Senate Nejerets. "I'm declaring martial law." He looked at the woman. "Gaia, be so kind as to inform the Senate that my first act as Governor General is to pardon Katarina

Dubois." As he spoke, the *At* vines restraining her uncoiled from around her body.

"You might want to go now," Nik said to the unfamiliar woman. The bell over the door jingled a moment later as she made a quick exit.

I watched the slowly expanding pool of crimson on the floor—it was going to be a pain in the ass to clean up—then sighed. In hindsight, maybe I should've just broken his neck, even if slicing it open had been more satisfying in the moment.

"How'd you know he was the one who attacked us?" Nik asked.

I met his eyes, but I could only handle looking at him for a second. I lowered my gaze to the puddle of blood on the floor. "I just did."

"Come on," Heru said, patting my shoulder. "Let's get this cleaned up. There's much to do, but little time. The sooner you're gone, the better."

"Gone?" I twisted around to look at him, brow furrowed. "Gone *where?*" Because the way he'd said *gone* sure as hell didn't sound like he was talking about our clan home on Bainbridge Island.

His golden stare was hard, commanding. "Underground."

Thanks for reading! You've reached the end of *Ink Witch* (Kat Dubois Chronicles, #1). Keep reading for more Kat adventures in *Outcast* (Kat Dubois Chronicles, #2).

OUTCAST

Book Two

*For LP – thank you. I'll never be able to express how much your endless friendship and support means to me. I appreciate the *beep* out of you, Duds!*

CHAPTER ONE

"Pew . . ." Eyes watering, I wrinkled my nose and waved a hand in front of my face. "You're lucky your nose is safe from this," I told Dom. I was standing just inside the north entrance to Seattle's "Tent District," taking in the midday sights, sounds . . . and odorific smells. The unofficial district was very much a kingdom within a city, where those who shunned modern ways—or were shunned *by* them—carried out their lives off the books. And apparently out of the shower.

"For once, little sister, I think I prefer being incorporeal." Dom's words, classed up as usual by his faint French accent, rolled through my mind, audible only to me.

"You're welcome," I muttered.

My dead-ish older brother was currently watching the world around me from a tiny mirror about the size of a silver dollar hanging as a pendant on a short chain around my neck. It allowed him a view of everything ahead of me and enabled me to hear him, thanks to the skin-to-skin contact between Dom's mirror and me. In the week since I first stuffed his soul into a looking glass, I'd done what I could to make his existence more varied and mobile—at least, on *my* side of the glass. I still wasn't sure what exactly was on his side, and he wasn't offering up much in the way of details.

Or information at all. Not that his tight-lipped response to this matter was unexpected. Or annoying. Didn't bother me one bit. Not one bit.

The point being, he now had several mirrors he could bounce between at will: the standing mirror at Heru's mansion on Bainbridge, the silver compact in my pocket, and the pendant dangling from a chain around my neck. The trifecta created a network of sorts, which was pretty damn convenient; he could play the messenger between the rest of Clan Heru on Bainbridge and me, the off-the-radar fugitive on a mission. A rebel *with* a cause.

"I'm surprised any Nejerets can stand living here," I said as quietly as I could, skirting eye contact with a greasy-haired woman peddling backpacks and other kinds of bags boasting custom modifications.

My kind, immortal beings—immortal-*ish*—originally heralding from the Sahara Desert before ancient Egypt had become a thing, is gifted with more than just the amazing regenerative abilities that make our lives potentially endless. Our senses—sight, smell, and hearing, mostly—are heightened beyond those of humans, something that can be both a benefit and a curse. Right now, surrounded by thousands of bodies in various stages of unwashedness, my hypersensitive nose was definitely a curse.

"Breathe through your mouth," Dom suggested.

I could only imagine the look of horror that warped my features. "And *eat* this stench?" I snorted derisively. "Thanks, but no thanks."

"Perhaps you should be on your way, then," Dom said. *"Make this visit as quick as possible. There are many other Nejerets on Heru's list . . ."*

I nodded, though he couldn't see the movement, and scanned the area around me. The Tent District occupied what used to be the King County International Airport—Boeing Field, to the locals—back before gravloops, a high-speed transportation system utilizing air pressure and gravity, stole the market in long-distance travel. The now-defunct airport was surrounded by a chain-link fence on three sides and the narrow Duwamish Waterway on the east side, creating a long, autonomous pseudo-nation. The Tent District occupied a three-square-mile space in southern Seattle, just south of the once industrial-hip, now run-down and abandoned Georgetown neighborhood.

Within the chain-link walls, this kingdom of paupers was broken into four quadrants by two permanent pedestrian thoroughfares that crossed in the relative middle, one connecting the north and south gates, the other leading from the eastern gate to the "docks" spanning the entire western edge of the district. These avenues were for foot and bicycle traffic only, as automobiles weren't allowed within the district's fences. Guns, either. The lack of cars made it so walking through the gates was like taking a step back in time.

The acre or two nearest the northern gate functioned as something of a street fair, where it seemed that the residents of the Tent District could barter for food and goods. A myriad of jerry-rigged and dilapidated tents covered the peddler's stalls, brightly colored paper lanterns dangled from crisscrossing strings overhead, jazzing up the place, and people crowded three or four deep at each stall, speaking loudly and gesticulating with gusto. According to the satellite maps I'd viewed online, there was a larger marketplace at the center of the district, where a cluster of old airplane hangars looked to have been converted into something of a town square. At least, that's what it had looked like on the computer screen at the public library this morning. I'd never actually stepped foot within these fences before. And no, not just because of the smell.

The Tent District isn't just a gathering place for Seattle's ever-increasing homeless population; it's a safe haven for wayward Nejerets, both the clanless and the dissatisfied dissenters. Not all of my kind approved of the Senate and its Nejeret-supremacist view of the world, and the bravest—or dumbest, depending on how you looked at it—went so far as to refuse paying their mandatory taxes to the Nejeret governing body. For the past decade or so, Heru has allowed such Nejerets to remain in his territory unharmed and unharassed, so long as they stay within this district's fences. The second they leave the Tent District, they break the pact with Heru and become lawbreakers, punishable however he sees fit. It may sound harsh, but it's a whole lot kinder than the reception these rage-against Nejerets—fist pump—would receive in any other Senator's territory, let alone the punishment they would face for skirting their tax obligations.

Technically, Nejeret society is a republic, ruled by the Senate, a body of one hundred and one representatives elected by the rest of us. But each Senate seat comes with a geographical territory, and each Senator rules as a relative monarch over their land. Heru's territory spans the Pacific Coast, stretching from Alaska all the way down to San Francisco. His is one of the largest and richest territories, but then he's one of the most ancient and powerful Nejerets alive. He's also technically the ruler of *all* of us right now, having declared martial law less than a week ago and stepped into the role of Governor General.

Thanks to him, we were at war. With the Senate. With ourselves. Ominous as it sounded, I was convinced it was a good thing. The Senate has a darker, shadowy side that's all kinds of evil. Even if I hadn't sworn an oath to Heru years ago, I'd have thrown my lot in with him in this fight. This war wasn't about politics or power; it was about right and wrong. Plain and simple.

Heru's war was the reason I was in the stinking Tent District in the first place. As the striker of the match that sparked this whole revolution, I'd essentially volunteered to be the Senate's public enemy number one. They wanted to get their hands on me, to make an example of me, desperately. It would go a long way toward proving their strength. Knowing this, Heru tasked me with a dual-purpose mission—he wanted me to go underground, so to speak, traveling around and recruiting support for his side, while at the same time distracting the opposition by rousing dissention within their ranks. It was a pretty damn important job. It also left me feeling an awful lot like bait. Uncomfortably so. In fact, it sort of chafed, how bait-like I felt.

But I understood Heru's reasoning. I was a diversion. So long as it was known that I was out and about, wandering free and sowing discord, those who remained loyal to the Senate—or what was left of the Senate now that some had defected to Heru's side—would be distracted. They'd be fighting a war on two fronts, splitting their energy and resources between battling Heru and his supporters and hunting me, not to mention dealing with whatever chaos I stirred up. And trust me, I give good chaos.

My visit to the Tent District fit into facet numero uno of my mission: to rally support for Heru. Thousands of people lived here in the Tent District, hundreds of which were Nejerets thanks to Heru's standing offer of a conditional carte blanche. In a species that counted its population at just over eleven thousand, several hundred swinging this way or that could make a noticeable difference.

The district's leader, a Nejeret by the name of Dorman, was an old friend of Heru's. Or, at least, an old *former* friend of Heru's. According to Dom, the two had a falling out around the last turn of the century, nearly a hundred and forty years ago, which, I supposed, was why *I* was approaching Dorman instead of Heru doing it himself.

I pulled up my sweatshirt's hood and stuffed my hands into the pockets of my leather coat, then started down the walkway. I headed south toward the center of the district, where my sources told me Dorman had set up office. It was a little over a mile from the northern gate.

"Should've taken the eastern gate," I commented, moving my lips as little as possible so as not to draw attention to myself. At least this was a place where being a wacky chick who talks to herself might not draw too much insta-judgment.

"But this way you have plenty of time to make yourself seen," Dom said. We'd gone back and forth between using the northern and eastern gates—the eastern gate being a good bit closer to the district's core. *"I think you are discounting how beneficial it could prove*

to our cause for word of your arrival to spread among the Nejerets here. You may even draw a crowd . . ."

I agreed with him, but being the only one of us with a physical body to worry about, I was a little concerned about being jumped by covert Senate supporters or hired lackeys. It didn't seem likely that they'd been lurking around in here, and if they were, they'd be unarmed, thanks to the pretty hefty anti-weapons security check at the gate, but there was no way to know for sure. Unless they jumped me. Then I'd be pretty sure.

I peered first to one side, then the other as I made my way farther into the district, weaving around and between people. Most wore several layers despite the current lack of rain. The chill in the air justified it, and the overcast sky teased us all about raining down its droplets of love at any moment. It was February and this was Seattle, after all.

My fingers itched for my absent sword, Mercy, but I was trying to lay low. At least, when I *wasn't* trying to draw a crowd. And laying low with a katana strapped to your back is harder than it sounds. Or maybe it's exactly as hard as it sounds. In any case, I missed Mercy. Desperately.

At present, my possessions were minimal. I'd been living out of a backpack for the past four days—a good old vintage forest-green JanSport—ducking out in bars until they closed and kicked me out, then breaking into basements to crash for the night. This is my city, and I know how to live on the lam here. Once my mission takes me out to other cities—to other territories—it'll be a whole new ball game.

Honestly, right now I probably looked and smelled like I fit right in here. Sponge baths in bars just aren't the same as a good, long, hot shower.

As I made my way deeper into the Tent District, a hand-painted sign caught my eye. "Hey, they have rent-a-showers here!" I said, my voice hushed but excited.

"I hardly think a space so densely packed with Nejerets with questionable intentions is the wisest place to make yourself vulnerable by disrobing."

I frowned, excitement deflating. "Yeah . . . you're probably right."

"You could always rent a motel room."

"Maybe," I said. We'd had this chat a dozen times before, but the idea of a skeezy motel clerk knowing I was there made me uneasy. I wasn't willing to let my guard down anywhere I might be vulnerable. "Or we could head to a gym after this. They have shower stalls."

"Truly, little sister, is personal hygiene really our biggest concern at present?"

I snorted. "Says the guy who doesn't have a body to keep clean."

It was a little crazy, having gone from not talking to Dom for over three years to having him constantly buzzing in my ear, my own personal angel on my shoulder. Dealing with his constant companionship was a bit of an adjustment, but nearly losing him made me appreciate what otherwise might have annoyed me. I was just glad he was still in my life, and I was as determined as ever to find a way to bring him all the way back to the land of the living.

"So what's this Dorman guy's deal, anyway?" I asked, angling my face downward but watching my surroundings through my lashes. I knew the Nejeret in charge of this place was several centuries old and that he'd been born in Virginia around the time of the American Revolution. I knew he was of Heru's line, a great-great-great-descendant to some nth degree. But I knew next to nothing about him, about the kind of man he was. I had no clue how I might get through to him, regardless of what bridges had been burned between him and Heru in the past.

"His deal?"

"Yeah. Like, is he an asshole? Does he have any triggers? Is he gullible? Is he cold like Heru?"

Dom laughed softly, a hushed, dry sound. *"Dorman is nothing like Heru. He's a quick-witted, good-natured man with a kind heart and a friendly sense of humor, and he has no taste for violence or killing, though he's more than capable of taking care of himself when need be."*

I frowned. "He sounds like a pretty stand-up guy."

"Indeed he is."

"Which makes me oh so curious about what happened between him and Heru. Must've been one hell of a falling out."

"Indeed it was," Dom said in his patented that's-all-I'm-going-to-say-about-that tone.

"Hmm . . ." I strolled the rest of the way in silence, thoughts tumbling around in my head. I hardly considered myself the best choice for this kind of mission, but I knew as well as anyone that we had to play the cards we were dealt. After all, I'm kind of a big deal in the tarot card world. And by *tarot card world* I mean *Seattle's* tarot card world. Capitol Hill, specifically. That's pretty much the only place where anyone knows about me and my fortune-telling prowess. My skill as a tattoo artist, however—that draws in clients from all over the country.

Some fifteen minutes later, I closed in on the enormous hangars at the heart of the district and was surprised to find a crowd of Nejerets watching my approach. They fanned out behind a smallish man wearing jeans, brown leather work boots, and a navy blue raincoat, the hood pulled down to reveal a Mariners baseball cap. Like all Nejerets, he appeared to be in the prime of his life, both youthful and ageless. Well, all Nejerets who aren't *me*; I'll look eighteen until the day I die.

"That's Dorman," Dom said.

I removed my right hand from my pocket to zip up the sweatshirt under my coat a few more inches, concealing Dom. He would still be able to hear what was going on around us, he just wouldn't be able to see anything. It was unfortunate, losing a second set of eyes, but it had to be done. He was the ace up my sleeve. Or down my shirt, in his case. But still, he was my secret weapon. *Secret* being the key word.

I nodded to Dorman as I approached.

He took a few steps toward me, his hand extended, a tentative smile curving his lips and rounding the apples of his cheeks. At first glance, he seemed a jolly fellow. Warm and welcoming, too. I glanced around, fearing that I was being punked. Practical jokes aren't really my thing. Like, at all. My ex-partner-in-sanctioned-crime Mari tried pulling one once, back during our days as the Senate's dynamic assassinating duo, and she'd ended up with a face full of salt water and spit and a pretty decent shiner. She'd only tried once.

"You're Dorman, I take it?" I said, shaking the Nejeret's proffered hand.

He nodded. "And you're Katarina Dubois." His eyebrows danced over his kind, hazel eyes, and his grin widened. He had the accent and charm of a country gentleman, and there was something familiar about him. "The Ink Witch." He released my hand.

I pressed my lips together, none too pleased. I'd come to embrace the nickname, but I wanted to know how Dorman knew it: from my work as a finder of lost people, or from the night I burned the Ouroboros scientist who'd torn Dom's soul—his *ba*—out of his body, leading to my brother's eventual death?

"I wondered how long it would take you to venture into our humble abode," Dorman said. As he spoke, the sense of familiarity increased.

"Have we met before?" I asked, brows drawing together.

Dorman blinked, his smile amping back up to full wattage. "Once," he said. "A couple decades ago."

My eyes rounded. "You were the one in the old tent city—you told me where to find Mari."

He placed his hands in his jeans pockets and rocked back on his heels. "And you nearly got yourself killed. I warned you she could take care of herself."

I felt a wry smile twist my lips, and I shook my head. "Fair enough." I'd liked him then on impulse, and I felt the same thing now. "I don't suppose you've seen or heard from Mari? Or that you know how to get ahold of her?" I asked, hope high but expectations low. She would make a powerful ally in Heru's war, if I could track her down. It was a big *if*, especially considering she'd vanished with her mother, Mei, a Nejeret with a gifted *sheut* that gave her the power to teleport, among other things.

"No, I can't say as I have seen her, nor that I would know how to reach her," Dorman said, disappointing me despite my low expectations.

"Pity." I glanced to the crowd of Nejerets beyond him, who were watching and listening intently. What thoughts spun around in their minds? How much did they know? Where would their allegiance fall? "Have you heard about what's going on"—I pointed up and to the side with my chin, indicating the world outside these fences—"out there?"

Dorman's expression sobered. "I've heard whispers . . . and shouts." He stared off into the distance for a moment, but his hazel gaze soon returned to me. "I'd like to hear what you have to say about it, though."

I narrowed my eyes. "Even though whatever I tell you will be biased since I'm with Clan Heru?" I wanted to make sure he understood that I wasn't here to get lost like all the others; I was here as an emissary.

"Even more so because you're with Clan Heru." The corners of his mouth lifted, and he raised his voice, just a little. "I, too, am with Clan Heru."

Behind him, there were hushed whispers among the crowd. He'd just declared himself for our side, and some of the tension I'd been lugging around faded.

"Walk with me," Dorman said, stepping to the side and holding his arm out. "There's something I think you'll want to see, and on the way, you can fill me in on all the excitement."

I fell into step beside him.

"You'll find no fans of the Senate here," he added.

I looked at him, intrigued. "Oh? Then you'll help us fight them?"

He stared off into the distance. "Me?" he said, frowning. "I'll do what little I can, but I'm just one man." He nodded to the crowd that was now following us. "It's them you're after. Prove that this war is about more than just power. Prove your worth, earn their trust, and they'll be the most loyal army you could ask for."

I glanced over my shoulder. There were well over a hundred Nejerets trailing behind us. "And how am I supposed to do that?"

Dorman glanced at me sidelong. "You, my dear, are about to find out."

CHAPTER TWO

Dorman led me to one of the smaller hangars in the cluster making up the pseudo-town square, the small horde of Nejerets trailing behind us. I filled him in, giving him the quick and dirty version of all that had happened the previous week with Ouroboros and Mari, everything leading up to Heru's declaration of martial law and the resulting split with the Senate.

"And so the mighty king reclaims his throne," Dorman said, heading straight for the hangar's huge open doorway. Two overlapping sheets of plastic blocked the way.

"Governor General, not king," I corrected. "And it's only a temporary position."

In the mirror pendant, Dom snickered.

Dorman chuckled softly. "Darlin', Heru always has been and always will be a king. He can't help it. It's who he is." I opened my mouth to argue, but before I could say anything, Dorman patted my shoulder and said, "And don't you fret. I accept his right to rule over me. Daresay I welcome it. I sure as hell trust him more than I trust the rest of the Senators." He held one side of the plastic curtain up to let me through, then turned to address our train of Nejerets. "We'll return momentarily." He motioned for me to enter the hangar.

As I did, I blinked against the sudden brightness. Standing floodlights were positioned at intervals throughout the cavernous interior, illuminating dozens and dozens of cots lined up in neat rows, like this was some kind of field hospital. Many of the collapsible beds were occupied, the people lying on them either asleep, reading, or staring off into space. Some were bandaged here or there or had an IV attached. A handful of other people wearing mismatching scrubs moved around the area, looking after the injured and sick. Their patients seemed well cared for, but even so, something felt off. It was quiet in the makeshift hospital, but not in a peaceful sense. It was too subdued for that. It felt lonely.

"This is our hospital," Dorman said, like it wasn't obvious.

"I can see that." I surveyed the area. I hadn't considered that there might be anything like this here, but I supposed it made sense. People get sick everywhere; even a place like the Tent District needed some sort of infrastructure for allowing its residents to be cared for. It took a few seconds, but when the reason for the sense of loneliness struck me, it hit hard. "There are no visitors."

Dorman's eyes widened, like my observation surprised him. "Correct. We've had to take precautions to minimize exposure."

"Exposure to what?" Dom said, and my eyes narrowed on Dorman. "Exposure to what?" I asked, repeating my half-brother's question.

Dorman leaned in a little, like he was going to share a secret with me. "The infection." He started down an aisle between two rows of cots. "Follow me," he said over his shoulder. "I'll show you."

I stared after him for a few seconds, then followed, strides quick so I could catch up. "What kind of infection?" I asked, glancing from side to side, my voice hushed. "And why are you showing *me*?"

Dorman glanced at me over his shoulder. "Because I'm pretty dang sure that this virus, or whatever it is, is part of the war." He angled toward another, smaller door at the back of the hangar.

"The first person to show signs of the infection—a human—escaped from an Ouroboros lab. The same lab, I daresay, that you helped Heru dismantle."

My hands balled into fists. I really didn't like the sound of this.

"Our doctors haven't been able to figure out what the infection is, let alone how it works, and they're at an absolute loss as to how to stop it." Dorman spoke quietly, for my ears only. He reached the door at the back of the hangar and opened it, then gestured for me to go through.

Through the doorway, I could see that more cots were packed into this smaller room, each and every one occupied. I counted twenty-eight patients in there. I hesitated before going in. Normally, I wouldn't worry about catching a disease—any disease—but Ouroboros had been experimenting on humans *and* Nejerets. What if they'd developed a pathogen that could take me down?

"You're safe enough," Dorman said, reading my wariness. He slipped into the room ahead of me. "See? It only affects humans. We're limiting the care staff to Nejeret volunteers. Besides, it's not airborne, so far as we can tell."

I followed him in. As my focus shifted from cot to cot, from feverish face to feverish face, my dread transformed to fear, then to anger. "They're kids."

Hands clasped behind his back, Dorman nodded. "Sammy—that's the child who escaped from the lab—came to us six days ago. His friends brought him in, begging us to care for him. We had, of course, known about the children disappearing off the streets for some time. By the time we figured out what was happening, we were unable to do anything about those already taken, but for the past month or so, we've been offering sanctuary to any homeless child in Seattle in the hopes that staying within our boundaries might keep them safe."

"I think it worked," I said, nodding absently. "I have a friend in the PD. He said most of the kids vanished a month or two ago, before your offer of sanctuary. A few were abducted after, but with the pickings so slim..."

"That's some comfort at least."

"I'll check in with Lex," Dom said. *"See if any of the kids they took to Bainbridge are sick."*

I scanned the youthful faces. "So Sammy was the first?" Some of the kids were awake, reading or chatting with their neighbors or curled up in the fetal position and crying. Others were out cold. "Who are the rest of the kids?"

"Sammy's friends . . . and *their* friends, and so on." Dorman settled his hazel stare on me. "There's another room filled with more sick folks—adults, mostly. The infection seems to progress slightly slower with them, but nothing we do seems to help, really. Whatever this thing is, Ouroboros created it. If you could find the cure . . ." He inhaled and exhaled heavily, his eyes searching mine. "Most of the Nejerets who live here are here because they disapprove of the way our kind treats humans. Prove to them that you're different—that Heru is different—and that your side cares about our mortal brothers and sisters, and you'll earn the hearts and loyalty of every Nejeret here."

I placed my hands on my hips and, slowly, nodded. "How many people are infected?"

"Forty-nine, and more every day. So far as we can tell, it's contained within our walls. Thankfully, not many people leave this place." Dorman's gaze trailed off, landing on a cot in the far corner. "I'd just ask that whatever you do, do it fast. Sammy's not going to last much longer."

I reached out and squeezed his arm. "I'll do what I can. If there's a cure, I swear to you, I'll find it."

I sat tucked away in the corner booth at the Gull, a dive bar downtown on Pike Street, my tarot deck on the table before me, three cards faceup. The bar was far enough from Capitol Hill that I didn't have to constantly look over my shoulder to make sure none of the Senate's Nejeret watchdogs had found me, but it was close enough for comfort. A quick ten-minute bus ride would dump me on Broadway, just a block from my shop. Not that I'd been there in days, but knowing that Ninth Life Ink was so close was a comfort. Nik was there, looking after things in my absence. That, too, was a comfort.

I was in a holding pattern. I wasn't sure what to do about the sick kids situation. Dom was off consulting with our people on Bainbridge, so he wasn't around to bounce ideas off of, and the cards weren't telling me anything I didn't already know.

I gulped down the rest of my bourbon, then raised the empty glass and caught the bartender's eye. Normally I don't push for table-side service at a dive bar, but it was a Tuesday, and I was one of three patrons in the place. The chick tending bar nodded and grabbed the bottle of Tatoosh, then made her way across the sticky floor to my corner table.

"You any good with those things?" she asked as she poured. She wanted me to do a reading for her. That's why she was asking. It's always why people asked.

I shrugged. "I'm decent." Normally I'd humor her. Maybe even try to charm her pants off with my fortune-telling wiles. Might even earn myself access to a shower. What could I say? She was pretty enough in a grunge-chic way, and I was more than lonely enough.

I hadn't been with anyone since that afternoon in the stairwell with the Senate's spy. It didn't matter that he was dead now, that I'd killed him. I was still tempted to replace the feel of his hands on my body with those of another. It might even work. For a few hours. But I was afraid that the memories of how he'd sounded in that stairwell, how he'd smelled and felt, would return, fresh as ever. I feared finding out that they might haunt me forever.

I clenched my jaw. I wasn't in the mood for temporary amnesia right now, anyway.

The bartender lingered for a few seconds too long. I took it as a signal to take my leave and pulled my wallet from my left coat pocket. I fished out four twenties and handed them to her. "No change." It was plenty to pay for the three doubles plus a decent tip. I tossed back the bourbon in my freshly refilled glass, then slid it across the corner of the table to the bartender. "Thanks."

She took the hint and returned to the bar, the bottle and empty glass in hand.

I restacked my cards and tucked them into their crushed velvet drawstring bag, then returned the bag to my backpack and zipped the whole thing up. After scooting out of the booth, I headed to the bar's back door, which spit me out in a dingy alleyway. The pavement was slick with rain and even slicker where the uneven cobblestones of days gone by showed through the patchy asphalt, and my balance was a little off from that last double. Pulling up my hood to fend off the drizzle, I made my way to the mouth of the alley, keeping a careful eye on where I placed my boots.

I could head back to the library, maybe do some more research on Ouroboros. Except I doubted that anything I found online would do me—or the sick kids—any good. It was hardly like they would publicly post the directions to make a cure for whatever mutant disease they'd cooked up.

A bus glided past the opening of the alley, its brakes squealing as it came to a stop. BROADWAY/CAPITOL HILL glowed on the sign along its side, declaring its route.

Reacting on instinct, I stumbled to a jog before I even realized what I was doing. I made it to the bus just as the driver was shutting the door.

A cheerful, bushy-browed guy in his fifties or sixties greeted me with a wide smile. "Almost missed you there with those dark clothes. You blend right in with the sidewalk this time of night." It was barely past six, but late enough that the sun was down and night had set in.

"Thanks for waiting," I said, breaths quick from the dash. I fed a few bucks into the cash slot in the payment kiosk at the front of the bus and plopped down in the nearest open seat, just a few back from the driver. The bus was fairly full with evening commuters, but not packed.

My heartbeat picked up as the driver shifted gears and the bus lurched forward. It had been almost a week since I'd gone home. Surely I could risk a peek. I wouldn't even get off the bus; I'd just ride past the shop and make sure everything looked alright. Make sure Nik wasn't letting the place fall apart. Make sure *he* was alright.

Heru had wanted Nik to come back to Bainbridge with him—for his own safety—but Nik had refused, claiming the Senate would never consider coming after him. He'd been the host to our creator, the Netjer Re, for thousands of years, and our kind have long memories. He was revered, still, even though Re was long gone. Targeting Nik, making him into a martyr, would send a ripple through the Senate's ranks, shattering their following and driving too many of their people to our side. They couldn't afford to go after him. He was as untouchable as anyone could be.

His logic was sound enough to convince Heru, but a seed of doubt had implanted itself in my chest. I wasn't as convinced of his supposed immunity to the Senate's wrath. Peace of mind was well worth the minimal risk of a quick bus ride past the shop.

It would be quick. Totally harmless. Right?

CHAPTER THREE

Apparently, I have the will of a Chihuahua. I got off the damn bus.

And the moment my boots touched the cement of the sidewalk on Broadway, I felt a deep sense of rightness. I also felt something slightly nauseating. I'm pretty sure it was an even deeper sense of paranoia. Of what-the-fuck-am-I-doing.

I should've hopped right back on the bus, or at least hung around the bus stop until the next bus—*any* bus—showed up and ridden the hell out of dodge, because if there was one place the Senate was sure to be watching for me, it was the shop. Getting their hands on me would be a big win for their side and an even bigger fuck-you to Heru. And yet, knowing all that, I still let my feet carry me up the block. At least I was on the other side of the street. That little precaution had to count for something.

It was doing a lot more than drizzling now, and the hood of my sweatshirt was soaking up the water like a thirsty sponge. I ducked into the recessed stoop of a vacant retail space across the street from the Ninth Life and crouched down. I nodded a greeting to the only other occupant of the space, a grimy old fellow who looked just this side of death's door. He offered me a toothless smile.

The shop would be closing soon. The artists were surely finishing up with their final clients of the day before cleaning up, if they hadn't done so already. I could see their silhouettes through the fogged glass, and I yearned to go in. That shop was my home as much as the apartment overhead was. More so, maybe.

With the chime of a bell, the shop door opened. My heartbeat sped up. A waif of a young woman emerged and brought with her a wave of disappointment. I'd been hoping for a familiar face. Oh, who was I kidding—I'd been hoping to see *Nik's* face.

I watched the door from that dingy alcove for another ten or fifteen minutes, but nobody else came out of the shop. Deciding it was time to stop tempting fate, I stood and started walking down the sidewalk, hands stuffed into my pockets and head bowed. It was stupid of me to come here in the first place, knowing I'd only be able to watch my old life from the outside looking in. I felt worse than before. Like even more of an outcast.

The bell over the door chimed again, and I froze. After a quick glance over my shoulder, I hurried to the next recess in the storefronts, the entryway to a desserts-only café, and huddled there, peeking around the edge of my sodden hood to watch the person who'd left the Ninth Life.

It was Nik. He leaned back against the broad shop window to the left of the door, a cigarette held up to his lips between two fingers and a silver lighter in his other hand. He was wearing a black hooded sweatshirt and worn, gray jeans. Though he had many more, only a few of his tattoos were visible—most notably the Egyptian goddess inked into his neck, her outstretched wings wrapping around to just barely touch in the back. His dark brown hair was buzzed on the sides, the longer top portion swept back, and his face was clean-shaven. His was a jaw that didn't require the assistance of a five-o'clock shadow to look strong, a perfect finish to the rest of his chiseled face, slightly crooked nose and all.

He took a deep draw on his cigarette as he stowed his lighter back in his jeans. He blew out the smoke, then rested his head back against the glass, his eyelids drifting shut.

The door to the café opened behind me. "Excuse me, miss. Are you waiting for a seat?"

I tossed the guy a half-assed glance over my shoulder. "No." When my gaze returned to Nik, he was staring straight at me. *Shit.*

He'd heard me. That single, brief word had been enough to catch his sensitive ears. And to say he looked pissed was putting it lightly.

I shouldn't have been there. It was too risky. I was at the tippy-top of the Senate's shit list. The danger to my life was huge, the danger to my mission—to Heru's cause—astronomical. Nik had every right to be pissed. I knew it.

Which was why I ran away. Or, rather, walked quickly. I mean, I didn't want to draw attention to myself, after all.

I rounded the corner of the block and headed west. After a sneaky glance over my shoulder, I sidestepped into the alleyway behind the shops lining the block and broke into a dead sprint, making my backpack bounce against my back. I was about a quarter of the way down the alley when a metal door banged open farther down.

Nik burst into the alleyway, a thundercloud in jeans and a black hoodie. A vine of *At* shot out of his hand, coiling around my neck before I could even consider turning around and running the other way. He closed in on me, pushing me back against the brick wall of the building he'd emerged from. He didn't retract the vine of *At* until my back was pressed against the wall and his hands were planted on either side of my head. The straps of my backpack had slipped over my shoulders. I let the bag fall to the ground so I could melt back against the wall, putting a few more inches between us.

I knew better than to try to run from him again. He'd just snag me *again*, and we'd be right back here, him glowering down at me and me glaring right back simply because it was the only way I knew how to respond.

He stepped closer, leaning in. His inhumanly pale blue eyes were livid, his jaw clenched. And when he spoke, his voice was so low and quiet it sent a cascade of goosebumps trickling over my skin. "What the fuck are you doing here? I told you I'd look after things, and I am. Don't you trust me?"

I swallowed roughly. I couldn't help it, not when he was so close and so angry and so *him*. My heart was racing so fast it was a stumbling, bumbling mess. I was having flashbacks of the last time I'd been pressed against a brick wall. By the bartender, the Senate spy. By the last Nejeret I killed. I lifted my chin. Served him right for calling me a whore.

Nik lowered his face to within an inch of mine. "Well?" I could smell the remnants of his discarded cigarette on his breath, and beneath that a hint of mint and coffee.

I looked at his lips, just for a fraction of a second, then squeezed my eyes shut, hoping he hadn't noticed. I couldn't handle him so close, so intense. So in my bubble. Not without wanting him to invade my space further.

"I, um . . ." I cleared my throat and turned my face away from him. Only then did I reopen my eyes. "Mari's number," I said as soon as the excuse popped into my brain. "I need Mari's number." He was the only person I knew who had it, and I felt a renewed sense of urgency to get ahold of her. If I could reach her, maybe she would know what had been done to Sammy in that lab. Maybe she would know how to cure him.

Nik was quiet for a moment, his pale eyes searching mine. "Do you have a phone?"

I shook my head. I'd been going through a different burner each day, and I'd tossed today's as soon as I left the Tent District. I pulled a Sharpie out of my coat pocket with shaking fingers. I always had a couple on me.

Nik whispered the number to me, watching as I jotted it onto the back of my hand. "I've been trying her every day," he added. "She's never picked up."

When the pen was capped and back in my pocket, Nik leaned in further, pressing his body against mine and bringing his lips to my ear. If anyone walking past either mouth of the alleyway saw us, they'd think we were just a couple of punk kids making out. I kind of wished it were so simple.

"You could've called the shop for that," Nik whispered. "Why'd you really come here, Kitty Kat?" His lips grazed over the shell of my ear as he spoke his nickname for me.

A shiver rolled through me. I splayed my fingers on the brick wall behind me, my nails digging into the grout to keep me from reaching for him. From pulling him closer. He loved messing with me. I just had to keep reminding myself that was all this was. Him messing with me. That's it.

"Tell me the truth," he breathed.

"I—" The words "*I wanted to see you*" caught in my throat. But I had. I'd wanted to make sure he was still here. That he hadn't vanished into the night again. That he was safe. I choked on the words. Those pathetic damn words.

"Are you ever going to forgive me for leaving?" This wasn't his messing-with-me voice anymore. This was his full-on serious voice.

I squeezed my eyes shut and a tear snuck free, snaking down my cheek. I didn't have the mental or emotional ability to deal with this shit right now. I'd let Nik take a single, tiny step into my heart once, and the fallout had nearly destroyed me. Literally, figuratively . . . pretty much every-ly. I couldn't afford to let something like that happen again right now. Maybe not ever.

Nik pulled back, just enough that he could see my face, and I peered at him through my lashes. For long seconds, he stared at the tear, stuck somewhere between my cheekbone and my jaw, then raised his gaze to mine. "Kat . . ." His whisper was raw, gutting, his breath mingling with mine. He leaned in.

"I have to go," I said, ducking under his arm and sliding out from between him and the wall. I scooped my backpack up off the ground and jogged up the alleyway, ditching him before he could do the same to me. Again.

I didn't look back. I couldn't. If I did, I might never leave.

CHAPTER FOUR

Now that I was in Capitol Hill, now that I was *home*, I seemed incapable of dragging myself away. It would've been impossible if I'd let something happen between Nik and me. I couldn't. I wasn't afraid of much, certainly not of anything physical, but emotional shit scared the crap out of me. Except, with Nik—this serious, raw version of him—it was different. Something more. Something I couldn't put my finger on. This sense of great potential . . . for joy and happiness and wonder. But also for complete and utter devastation. Not. Going. There.

The fresh interaction with Nik left me unhinged. A live wire. I felt the need to lash out. To take all of my pent-up frustration and aggression out on someone. To *do* something. I couldn't handle another second of sitting on my thumbs while I waited for Dom to get back to me. There were other ways to attack this problem. And I was rabid with the need to act.

I could call Mari . . . but I'd need a phone for that. There was a public phone at the library, which was just a couple blocks away. Computers, too. Two birds and all that.

As I strode up the sidewalk toward the front entrance to the public library, I pushed thoughts of Nik and the feel of his breath in my hair and his body against mine—of the vulnerable look in his eyes in that last moment before I fled—into some dark corner of my mind. Somewhere where those troubling thoughts could haunt me from dreams. But at least I'd have a semblance of peace while I was awake. Thoughts of him, now, would only get in my way.

The Cap Hill Library is a pretty generic two-story brick building, teetering on the modern side with floor-to-ceiling windows at all of the corners and a strange, cagey protrusion shaped like the enormous bow of a ship at the main entrance. It isn't the largest library in Seattle, but it has computer kiosks set up with free Internet access to library members, which was all that I needed, really. And it just so happens I've been a member since elementary school, *and* I'd memorized my card number long ago. It was only a matter of setting up an online account, something I'd done on my first day as a fugitive, and I'd been bouncing around the Seattle Public Library system ever since.

Once inside, I tried calling Mari, not surprised when she didn't pick up. I would try her again before I left. And again and again and again until I got through.

Standing before one of the computer kiosks, I logged in and ran a quick search for the Ouroboros board of directors. If anyone besides Mari could make things happen in that putrid organization, I figured the people who held the purse strings could. Even if they didn't know the cure for the disease themselves, they had to know who did.

According to the official Ouroboros Corporation website, there were thirteen board members, but their bios didn't tell me anything beyond their names, ages, and experiences in medicine, science, and the corporate world. Nothing overtly helpful, like addresses, or even a general location or neighborhood. I could run a separate search for each of them and see what popped up, but once I started down that very specific and targeted path, it was more and more likely that my search would ping some cyber watchdog programmed to keep an eye out for someone searching for such specific Ouroboros-related information. I told them I'd come after them, right after I burned one of their scientists to death with only the power of my *sheut*, and I had no doubt that they'd be on the lookout for me, in real life *and* online.

I decided to hold off on cyber-stalking for a minute or two while I consulted the cards. I shrugged my backpack off and unzipped it, fishing out the velvet drawstring bag containing my tarot deck, then set both bags on the floor while I started shuffling the cards. After three shuffles, I pulled a card and placed it on the desk beside the computer's mouse.

Queen of Swords, reversed. The image on the card looked much as I'd drawn it a few years ago, with a slender woman sketched in black and gray standing beside a massive claymore, the sword's nose in the ground and the woman's fingers wrapped around its hilt. But the image wasn't *exactly* as I'd drawn it. Because I'd created this deck with ink and paint, and because the innate magic granted to me through my *sheut* could give the things I drew a life of their own, their images and general design shifted with the tide of my mood, not to mention with the greater movement of events around me. It made this particular deck of tarot cards incredibly insightful.

Last week, when several dozen kids went missing, abducted by Ouroboros, the children had been incorporated into the cards. Now, the children were gone from the imagery, but the tail-eating snake, the symbol for which Ouroboros was named, was still there. On the Queen of Swords, it was a small, golden circlet, resting on the queen's head like a crown.

Generally, this card represents intelligence and quick thinking, suggesting a calculated, independent intellect completely devoid of emotion. But reversed, the Queen of Swords represents quite the opposite—emotional investment that clouds decision making, relying too much on the heart and not enough on the mind.

I picked up the card, flipping it over to get a good look at the queen's face. She appeared middle-aged and stern. And somehow familiar. I held the card up to the computer screen and opened the page containing the board members and their bios.

And there she was at the top of the list—Constance Ward,

Chairman of the Board and Chief Executive Officer of the Ouroboros Corporation. Her showing up on this card definitely wasn't a coincidence. It was a message from the universe. It had to be. Now, I knew exactly who to target—the head of the snake.

I returned the card to the deck and replaced the whole thing in its bag. "Alright, Constance," I said under my breath as I typed her name into the search bar. "Where are you?"

I glanced around just before hitting enter. Nobody seemed to be watching me, aside from the librarian who'd been staring a hole in my forehead since about two seconds after I walked into the library. Geesh. I didn't even have any facial piercings anymore. Was homeless fugitive wafting off me or something?

I inconspicuously stuck my nose into my sweatshirt and gave it a sniff. Maybe.

I caught the woman's eye and winked, gaining an inkling of amusement from watching her flustered fluttering as she moved books here and there, pretending that she hadn't been keeping an eye on me for the past fifteen minutes. With a blink, I refocused on the computer screen and hit the enter key.

There were about a gazillion entries for Constance Ward, so I amended my search to include the word "home." My fingers were crossed, but even with the tip-off from the good ol' universe, my hopes weren't high.

Which just goes to show you that I can't predict the future, at least not without the help of my cards . . . or a pen and some paper. The first entry in the search results was an article from the *Seattle Times* with the headline *OUROBOROS CEO HOSTS RECORD-BREAKING FUNDRAISER*. Hosts? As in, throws a party at her house?

I snorted quietly. No wonder the cards suggested I start with Constance; tracking her down was going to be a breeze.

I clicked on the link and gave the article a quick skim. Apparently, Constance could throw a killer party. She'd raised over a million bucks for the Children's Hospital at the annual gala she'd held at her lakeside home this past October *in Madison Park*. It wasn't as precise as an address, but paired with the photos snapped at the event, knowing she lived in the ritzy neighborhood was almost as good as GPS coordinates.

From the images of the house—and the pool and the greenhouse and the sprawling lawn and the private dock on Lake Washington—I could tell exactly where Constance lived. It only took thirty seconds of skimming a satellite map of her neighborhood to glean her address. Not that I was an expert sleuth or anything—though after years of hunting rogue Nejerets, I didn't suck—but there just weren't that many private lakeside homes in Madison Park. Maybe a dozen, total, and none but hers with a huge, Victorian-style greenhouse. Ding ding ding . . . we've got a winner.

I jotted down the address, cleared my browser history, then closed the window and logged out. I didn't want to risk the chance that Nosy McNoserson over at the checkout desk might use her admin privileges and do some sleuthing of her own.

I gave the librarian a cutesy finger wave as I passed the checkout desk and glanced at the clock on the wall behind her. It was a quarter till eight, fifteen minutes until the library would close. I'd found Constance's address just in time.

I had to walk a few blocks to reach a bus stop served by a bus that would take me the two plus miles to Constance's neighborhood, but it didn't really matter because the bus wouldn't arrive for a good thirty minutes. Sometimes taking action took *forever*. It was moments like this that I missed my Ducati desperately.

According to the bus's clock, it was almost nine o'clock when we came to a screeching halt at my stop in Madison Park. I hopped off the bus and wandered up the sidewalk in the wrong direction while I waited for the bus to trundle farther down the street and turn around a corner.

Once it was out of sight, I turned on my heel and marched straight toward Constance's lakefront property. It was surrounded by a wall of trees and shrubs grown over a four-foot-high fence—totally scalable. I found a spot where the greenery was thinner and the light from the streetlamps was dim. For a few seconds, I loitered by a black pickup, pretending I was checking an imaginary phone. After I felt fairly certain I wasn't being watched, I squatted down, then leapt at the fence, propelling myself over in one smooth motion. My landing could've been better, but it wasn't too loud and didn't disturb the plants too much. With any luck, nobody would ever know I'd been there.

I huddled in the bushes for a few minutes, making sure that even if the average person had spotted movement in the shrubs from the other side, they'd have lost interest. And then I waited a few more minutes. Only after it felt like I'd been waiting for an hour but it had really probably only been ten minutes or so—really, I'm temporally lost without my phone, I should probably consider getting a watch—did I start the slow process of skulking through the bushes. And can I just say that skulking is exhausting. All that squatting and breath-holding and slow shuffling forward. By the time I reached a break in the shrubs, my quads were quaking and my back ached.

Giving my legs a break while I surveyed the property, I lowered myself the rest of the way down until I was sitting on my heels. I'd come through behind what appeared to be a guesthouse, but I had a clear line of sight to part of the enormous main house. Just like in the photos from the fundraiser gala, the house appeared to be in the traditional Cape Cod style, only on crack. The place was huge.

Here's the thing about breaking and entering into multi-multi-million-dollar properties like this—there's never really a good time to do it, but nighttime is pretty much the worst time, what with all of the alarms and motion sensors and security personnel and guard dogs. Not that there isn't always a way around the security measures, but it takes time to formulate a plan. So I had to give myself some time to study my surroundings. To locate all visible cameras and motion sensors and extrapolate the locations of others I couldn't see based on what I *could* see. To figure out how to get into the house and interrogate Constance—and, let's be honest, *dispose of* her—then get back out without getting caught. That last part was key.

I'd been squatting in those bushes for at least an hour—maybe —when a light came on in the room at the very corner of the house. It appeared to be a home theater, with enormous leather recliners lined up in rows on three descending levels.

A couple of little girls skipped into the room, I'd have guessed they were maybe seven or eight, followed by a teenaged boy. Constance was next, carrying another child in her arms—a small child, but not a young one. I squinted, focusing on the kid. It couldn't tell if it was a boy or a girl, but I could tell that the kid had some sort of a condition, something that made him or her appear extremely frail.

Constance said something—I'd never been a good lipreader—and smiled down at the child in her arms, her face filled with warmth and love. Not a second later, both disappeared behind oversized chair backs. It was as though my breath vanished with them.

Constance was the CEO and Chairman of the Board of a child-abducting, soul-stealing, Nejeret-torturing corporation. There was no way she didn't know about everything Ouroboros had been doing in that secret lab, let alone whatever was going on with Sammy and the other sick kids back in the Tent District. There wasn't a jury in this country that wouldn't convict her to a lifetime in prison for her crimes.

Yet she was also a mother. And from the looks of it a pretty damn good one. It was ten o'clock on a Tuesday night—a work night, no less—and she wasn't working late in her study or getting ready for bed, letting a nanny take care of her brood of kids. She was hanging out with them herself, and apparently having a good time doing so.

I pushed back my hood and raked my fingers through greasy hair, inhaling and exhaling deeply. Panic was peeking into the windows of my mind, lurking in the bushes surrounding my soul, trying to find a way in. Night started to close in around me, and I sucked in air uselessly.

I knew what it was like to lose a beloved mother. I wasn't sure I could do that to someone else.

But the kids on the cots back in the hangar-turned-hospital—they had a whole lot less than Constance's children. Didn't they deserve the answers Constance could provide? Didn't they deserve a chance at life? Didn't they deserve justice?

There are twelve other board members. The realization brought a much-needed rush of oxygen to my lungs, to my blood, and I could think clearly once again.

I didn't have to go after Constance, not yet. I could find someone else to target . . . to torture and interrogate. To kill. There was another way. Twelve others. I just had to track them down.

CHAPTER FIVE

There's a big difference between a human soul and a Nejeret *ba*. A Nejeret's *ba* can exist outside of his or her physical body ad infinitum, like Dom's. In other words, just because a Nejeret's physical body dies, it doesn't mean the end of that Nejeret. We don't know where a *ba* goes once its body dies, just that it goes somewhere else—to some other plane or dimension or universe—and it will continue to *be*, to exist, until the end of everything.

Not so with a human soul, though. Human souls are tied to this realm, and when a human body passes, its soul dissipates; the energy that once clung together, forming a conscious, self-aware life-form, just sort of fades away until that person, body and soul, is gone forever. It's exactly what happened to my mom two decades ago, and it sucks balls.

For years, I struggled with her death—not just with the passing of her body, but the ending of her soul. Oh, who am I kidding? I still struggle with it. But that's the thing about being an immortal girl in a mortal world. Goodbyes become all too familiar; letting go becomes as easy as falling asleep. We might not want to fall asleep, we might hold onto wakefulness with all our might, cling to consciousness like our lives depend on it, but sleep will claim us eventually. We will *let go* eventually, whether we want to or not. At least, that's what Dom tells me. Maybe in a century or two I'll understand.

For most Nejerets, the death of the mother is the first introduction into the inevitable cruelty of our existence. We're tied to humans, coexisting by way of reproductive dependency. As a byproduct of our hyper-regenerative abilities, female Nejerets' bodies are incapable of sustaining a pregnancy to full term. Except for a few very rare cases—like Lex and Heru, literal soul mates whose bond alters Lex's body, allowing her to sustain a pregnancy, or Nik's mom, Aset, who was raped before her Nejeret traits manifested and rendered her infertile—a female Nejeret's body will reject a fertilized egg almost as soon as it implants in the uterine wall. As a result, the burden of propagation, of sustaining our species, is left to male Nejerets and either female human carriers of the recessive Nejeret genes or young female Nejerets-to-be who are still fertile.

Because of this, nearly every Nejeret has a human mother. And all of us *lose* our mother, so often the one person who's always been there for us, who's loved us unconditionally. Who's put us first, always first. Who *will* die. Whose soul *will* fade away, leaving us feeling lost and alone in this desolate existence. She is our first true taste of goodbye, and the bitterness lingers for ages, clinging to our tongues like resin. A constant reminder of the pain that comes from loving mortals, even as their fragility enhances their allure.

I've killed a lot of people—forty, to be exact—but they were all Nejerets, save for the human scientist who killed Dom's body. All but one of my victim's souls continued on after their bodies died. Somehow, that didn't feel like truly ending a life. I've only ever taken the one human life. I've only ever ended one soul's existence, and that shithead deserved it. Even so, the finality of what I'd done terrified me.

And if the kids infected with gods-know-what back in the Tent District succumbed to their illness in the end, their deaths would be as final as any other human's, all because they'd been caught up in some ugly Nejeret business. It was my people's fault that these innocents might die. That their souls might cease to be. That didn't sit well with me. Even if it meant targeting and taking out—ending forever—a few corporate scumbags, I would see this thing through. I would fix this.

I couldn't afford to fart around, skimming what little information I could from what was available to the public online. I needed help. I needed someone inside the system. I needed Officer Garth Smith, my favorite of Seattle's finest.

Which was why I was lurking in the shadows across the street from the Seattle Police Department's East Precinct at eleven o'clock on a Tuesday night. I could see Garth through the floor-to-ceiling windows at the entrance, manning the station's reception desk. He was a sturdy, broad-shouldered fella who wore his Native heritage proudly. He still bore bruises from the attack at the Fremont Troll, faint but visible on his tan skin, but he looked good, considering he'd been in intensive care a week ago.

I was surprised they were letting him work at all, even if he seemed to be relegated to desk duty. Surprised, but relieved. Tracking him down would've been a lot harder if he was still convalescing at home. Mostly because I didn't know where that home was.

Guilt riddled my conscience as I watched him work, shifting papers around, organizing things. It was my fault, him getting hurt. A Nejeret working for the Senate jumped him, having overheard us talking earlier that day. Garth "knew too much," a leading cause of death in humans who get too close to Nejerets. He was the direct descendant of Chief Sealth, a legend in and of himself, who'd been tasked with the secret knowledge of our people almost two centuries ago. Sealth had passed that knowledge on, perhaps unwisely, which meant Garth knew way more about Nejeretkind than was healthy. Not that the Senate would care about Garth now —they had bigger fish to fry.

I huddled in the shadows across the street from the station for another hour in full-on creeper mode—hood up and hands stuffed into my pockets—watching Garth come in and out of view through the reception window. I'd gone nearly ten minutes without spotting him when he emerged from the door beside the reception desk and made his way toward the main entrance looking snug in his police-issued winter coat.

I waited until he was outside and heading up the block to follow him from my side of the street. I tailed him for another block and a half, until he slipped into a twenty-four-hour convenience store. A minute passed, then another. From across the street, I watched the time tick by on the register's display. Another minute. Another.

"Shit," I breathed. He'd given me the slip. He must've sensed someone following him.

Since the jig was up, I gave up any pretense of hiding and jogged across the street. I yanked the convenience store's smudged glass door open and marched straight to the checkout counter. The clerk took a step backward.

"Where'd he go?" I asked, slamming my hands on the grimy counter. "The cop who was just in here—where did he go?"

Wide-eyed and hand shaking, the clerk pointed to a hallway lit by humming fluorescent lights in the far corner of the store.

I ran down the snack and chip aisle, then into the hallway. There was a storeroom on one side, a unisex bathroom on the other, and a door with a barely glowing exit sign over the doorframe. I peeked into the storeroom. It was cluttered, but there was no possible place for a guy as large as Garth to hide out.

I turned to the bathroom. The door was shut, and there was a nine-digit keypad over the handle. "Hey," I called to the clerk. "What's the code?" I keyed it in as he told me, then pushed down on the door handle, fairly certain the bathroom was empty. I couldn't hear anyone in there, and I've got amazing hearing. *Inhuman* hearing.

"Garth?" I eased the door open. The bathroom was dark. And empty. "Damn it."

I lunged to the exit and slammed the metal door open. And froze mid-step.

Garth moved into the glow of a floodlight a couple yards away, his sidearm drawn and aimed at my chest. "Why are you following me?"

Slowly, I raised my hands so I could push back my hood. As the damp fabric fell backward, I kept my hands up and where he could see them, assuring him I meant him no harm.

Garth's eyebrows rose, his eyes rounding. "Kat?" He lowered his pistol.

The corner of my mouth lifted. "Jumpy much?"

He pressed his lips into a flat line. "I thought you were one of *them*."

"I *am* one of them."

He holstered his gun, and I lowered my hands. "You know what I mean."

I took a step toward him, my eyes scanning his bold features. "You look good." My eyes met his. His dark brown irises appeared black backlit against the floodlight. "Better, I mean." I felt my lips curve into the barest of smiles. "You look *better*." Not that he didn't look good—he always looked good. He was an attractive guy, all tall and broad-shouldered and confident and kind. A guy who was a cop, while I was a killer. A guy who was human. A guy who nearly died because of me.

Garth laughed under his breath. "Just better?" He shot a quick glance around.

My cheeks warmed.

Taking a step closer, Garth ducked his head, his eyes skimming over my face and lower, taking me in. He frowned, placing a hand on my arm and moving me deeper into the shadows with him. "Everything alright? You look . . ." He trailed off when his eyes met mine. "How's your brother?"

I touched the mirrored pendant through my sweatshirt. Dom hadn't said anything yet, so I figured he was still back in the standing mirror on Bainbridge. "He died," I said. "But he's okay, sort of. It's a long story."

Garth nodded to himself, like my wackadoo explanation was the most normal thing in the world. "Are *you* okay?"

My lips parted and I inhaled, planning to tell him I was fine, but nothing came out. Because I wasn't okay. Far from it. I just hadn't realized how far until he asked me.

Garth's features softened. "You look like you could use some warming up." He nodded his head to the side. "I live a couple blocks that way." He waved his hand and started walking. "Come on."

My feet moved on their own, my mind still stunned by my reaction to his simple question about my well-being. And like a lost little puppy, I followed Garth home.

CHAPTER SIX

Garth waited for me to pass through the doorway to his condo before shutting the door. His place was on the Puget Sound side of Capitol Hill, as opposed to the Lake Washington side. He had a top-floor unit in a five-story building. It was an older building with a brick exterior, but the interior had to have been renovated sometime during the past decade. It was nice—clean and classy.

Garth locked the deadbolt, then turned to face me. "So . . . what's up?" We'd been quiet during the walk, but apparently quiet time was over.

"Oh, you know . . ." Eyes wandering here and there, I passed by a small, open kitchen and through the living room to the two huge windows monopolizing the wall opposite the front door. "Quite the view," I said, taking in the glimmering cityscape. From here, I could see I-5 at the bottom of the hill, the familiar Seattle skyline beyond it, and just a hint of the Sound reflecting the moonlight. It didn't matter the angle, anytime I saw my city, I felt like I was home.

I glanced over my shoulder, quirking an eyebrow. "I didn't know they paid you guys the big bucks."

Garth flipped a light switch on the wall under the kitchen cabinets, and my view of the city dimmed as the lights in the kitchen flared to life. "I got a good deal. Besides, the place is small." He turned his back to me and opened the cupboard over the microwave, reaching up to pull out a bottle of Jameson. "It's just me and Eva, anyway," he said.

"Eva?" I made my way back to the kitchen, moving between a microsuede sectional and a black-stained coffee table. I dropped my backpack off on the couch as I passed it, glancing at Garth's left hand as I walked. No ring, so it didn't look like Eva was the name of his wife. "Girlfriend?" My brows drew together. "Or daughter?" He'd never mentioned any family. Well, besides his ancestors and his relatives over on the Port Madison Reservation. But no SOs or kiddos.

"No, nothing like that." Garth pulled two glass tumblers out of the dishwasher, then met my eyes. "I ran it this morning. They're clean, I promise."

I shrugged, stopping at the narrow kitchen island. The quartz countertop gleamed, a stark contrast to the dark-stained cabinets and stainless steel appliances. It wasn't like I could die of food poisoning, anyway.

A cat jumped up on the counter, settling on the edge like a gargoyle, her luminous green eyes locked on me. The feline was on the smaller side, its fur mostly white but mottled with patches of gray and orange. Its slim tail was wrapped around its feet, the end twitching every few seconds.

"See," Garth said. "Eva."

"Oh . . ." I couldn't tear my eyes from the creature, not when I was getting the very distinct impression that she was plotting my death.

Garth uncorked the whiskey, filled one glass a third of the way, the other quite a bit more, then slid the fuller one my way, along with the bottle. That got my attention, and I risked breaking eye contact with the cat to catch the glass before it reached the edge of the counter. The bottle didn't travel quite so far, but it was near enough for comfort.

Garth picked up his own glass and rounded the island, taking a sip as he walked. He stopped by the cat—Eva—and scratched the top of her head. Her eyelids slid shut most of the way, just a sliver of green and black remaining trained on me.

"Don't be offended if she doesn't warm up to you right away," Garth said, moving his hand under her chin. Eva stretched out her neck, giving him freer access. "She's kind of a one-man cat."

I forced a closed-mouth smile and picked up the glass, downing half the Jameson in a single gulp. It burned going down, just the way I liked it. "Thanks for this," I said, clearing my throat, and saluted him with the booze. I cleared my throat, took another sip, then set the glass down. "It's been a rough week. A *strange* week."

Garth's gaze moved over my face and hair. "Where are you staying?"

I stared at him, hard. "What makes you think I'm not staying at my place?"

"I stopped by the shop," he said. "Nik told me you wouldn't be around for a while. That, on top of the warrant issued for your arrest this afternoon, well . . ."

I stiffened, feeling like I'd been doused in frigid salt water straight from the Puget Sound.

"Your photo's been all over the news. They say you were responsible for the fire at that warehouse . . . and that you killed someone."

"Shit," I hissed. That might explain the stares from the librarian and the fear in the convenience store clerk's eyes. If there was a warrant out for me, not to mention news alerts, my plans would have to change drastically. No more evenings in bars. No more traipsing around the city. And definitely no impromptu trips back to the shop. I had to lay low, for real this time. There was no doubt in my mind that the Senate was behind this. It was their way of slowing me down, using the humans to track me so they could focus their efforts on fighting Heru.

I supposed I shouldn't be surprised. But that didn't stop me from being irritated. And pissed off. What was I supposed to do now?

I could go to the Tent District. Law enforcement barely had any jurisdiction there since the city had already written off most of its residents as lost causes, nuisances better contained within the unofficial district's fences than out and about on the streets of Seattle. I could duck out there . . . or I could leave the city altogether. *My* city. My home. My mission would take me away from Seattle one of these days, anyway, so why not today?

But what about the kids? I tensed at the thought. I'd made a promise to Dorman, and damn it, I would stick to it. I would find a cure for this damn disease and lock in the loyalty of Dorman's followers. I would do it, damn it.

Garth touched my chin, and I flinched away from him. He lowered his hand back to the cat. "You've been staying on the streets, haven't you?"

I stared down at the glass of whiskey. "Not exactly."

"Kat . . ." Garth set his own glass down softly, barely making a sound on the stone countertop. "You can stay here."

I stared at him, stunned by the offer. Slowly, I shook my head.

"It's fine, really." His strong features were set, his jaw tensed, his coffee-brown eyes hard, determined. "Stay here. Nobody would think to look for you here."

"But I'm *wanted*. And people already know that you know me." I was still shaking my head. "Henderson . . . all the cops who saw me in the waiting room . . ." I'd visited him back when he was in the hospital, recovering from his injuries. Was it really only a week ago? So much had changed since then. I inhaled and exhaled slowly, then picked up my glass and took a sip.

"I may have told them I made a pass at you," Garth said, meeting my gaze for the briefest moment before refocusing on Eva the cat. "And that you rejected me."

I was in the process of swallowing and choked on the whiskey.

"They dropped the subject because, well, what kind of a guy can't even get a pity date while he's laid up in the hospital?"

I finished off the glass and reached for the bottle of Jameson. "Trust me, Garth, *you* don't need pity to get a date." I uncorked the bottle, filled up my glass, and held the bottle out to him, fake smile plastered on my face. "Refill?"

He drained his glass, then set it down, knocking it closer to me with a couple taps of his fingernails. "At least they think you want nothing to do with me. Nobody'll look for you here." He turned away and headed through a doorway, hitting the light switch on the wall as he went. The light in his bedroom flared to life.

The furnishings within were fairly Spartan and very masculine, all in black, white, and gray, the only touch of color his navy blue comforter. His furniture was on the plain side, the black dresser and nightstands more simple than modern, and his bed didn't have a headboard. There were two other doors on the rightmost wall, the nearest shut—a closet, I figured—the other open, revealing a bathroom vanity and mirror. In the reflection, I could see a heavenly looking shower, a great big slate-tiled masterpiece with two showerheads, a removable one on the wall and a wide, rain shower one hanging down from the ceiling.

I only noticed I was standing in the doorway to the bedroom, likely drooling, when Garth started shutting the door. "I'm going to change, then you can shower and get cleaned up while I cook."

"Uh . . . yeah. OK." I took a step backward.

Garth shut the door, leaving it cracked open the barest amount. I didn't think he realized I could see his reflection in the bedroom window.

Feeling like a voyeur, I moved back to the kitchen island and reached out to let Eva sniff my fingers. She extended her neck, her little pink nostrils flaring, then blinked and turned her head away from me. At least she didn't try to bite me.

I looked around the dining-slash-living room, trying my hardest to ignore the crack in the door. Garth's furniture out here fit with what was in his bedroom, his preferred design aesthetic striking me as clean, functional, and simple. There was little in the way of knickknacks or personal touches, unless you counted the big-ass painting of a whale on the wall behind the couch. I thought it was an orca, though it was hard to tell, since the image was done in a distinctly coastal Native American style, all black and red on a white background.

At the sound of clothing hitting the hardwood floor, my focus shifted back to the crack in the doorway. The shirt of Garth's uniform was gone, as was his bulky bulletproof vest, and he was pulling his white undershirt off over his head. He wasn't flawless, not like so many Nejerets who'd had decades or even centuries to perfect their bodies, and he was almost more appealing for it. He was muscular, but not jacked, his physique honed more for function than attraction.

I smiled to myself. He treated his body just like he treated his home—function over form.

I was pleasantly surprised to see that he had some ink, all in the same style as that lone painting on the living room wall. There was a round-ish palm-sized design with a face on his chest over his heart, and when he turned to head toward the closet, I became enamored with the piece on his back. It was enormous, of an owl with outstretched wings, the tips reaching the ends of his shoulders and a moon with a face filling the space between his shoulder blades. It was stunning—so striking and beautifully evocative of his heritage.

The sound of his belt coming off shook me out of my voyeuristic stupor, and I turned my back to the door and reached for my glass. "What?" I said to Eva just before I took a hearty swig.

She was staring at me. Judging me, I was certain.

I cleared my throat. "So," I said, raising my voice so Garth could hear me in the other room. "I'm surprised they let you go back to work so soon."

"The station's short-staffed." He made a sound that was part grunt, part groan. "They didn't even wait until I got home from the hospital to ask me to come in on light duty. The guy who drove me home let me know they needed me to come in the next day—chief's orders."

"I thought you were 'Chief.'" It was the other officers' nickname for him.

"*The* chief," he said, opening the door. He was wearing light gray sweatpants and a white T-shirt that strained at his shoulders, just a little. "As in, the police chief."

"Oh," I said, laughing and rolling my eyes at my denseness. I scrubbed a hand over my face. "I swear I'm not usually this slow."

"Go." He pointed to the bedroom with his chin. "Wash up. You'll feel better after a shower."

Nodding slowly, I finished off my whiskey and ambled into the bedroom. I shut the door just as Garth had—not quite all the way. Fair's fair, after all. I shrugged out of my leather jacket and laid it on the bed, then unzipped my sweatshirt and did the same with it. My tank top came off next.

I peeked my head back out into the living area, shooting a quick glance at my backpack. Everything I had in there was as dirty as what I was wearing, if not worse. "Do you mind if I do a load of laundry later?"

Garth, who'd been ducked in the fridge, stood and looked at me, smile genuine and eyes kind. "You bet."

"Cool." Biting my lip, I glanced at the backpack, once more. "And, uh, can I borrow some clothes?" I smiled apologetically. "Just until my stuff's clean?"

Garth chuckled. "Yeah, sure. I'll pull something out for you while you're in the shower." He returned to the fridge. "Do you like eggs? I was thinking breakfast for dinner."

I grinned, stomach rumbling. I should've ordered some fries or something while I was at the pub. "BFD—sounds great. And, um, I sort of eat a lot," I warned him. "It's a thing . . . with my kind, I mean. Just so you know . . ."

Garth laughed. "Noted."

I pulled back into the bedroom and quickly shed the rest of my clothes, leaving my combat boots on the floor by the closet and everything else wadded up into a bundle held together by my sweatshirt. I set the clothes on the floor beside my boots and padded into the bathroom, more than a little excited to get to know Garth's shower.

Like, *really* well.

CHAPTER SEVEN

Garth's shower didn't disappoint. It was as divine as I'd imagined it would be, and by the time I emerged, pruney and squeaky clean, I felt like a new woman. I smelled like a new woman, too, thank the gods.

Wrapped in an oversized towel that nearly reached my ankles, I headed back into Garth's bedroom. A gray T-shirt and sweatshirt, some black sweatpants, and a pair of white socks were laid out on the foot of the bed.

I dropped the towel and dressed in the sweatpants and T-shirt, opting to go barefoot for the moment. It had been days since my feet were truly free. I put on the sweatshirt, too, because *no bra.* Before heading back out to rejoin Garth, I scooped up the towel along with my dirty clothes.

I toed the door open, my saliva production quadrupling the minute the smell of frying bacon smacked me in the face. "Holy shit, that smells *amazing.*"

It looked like he'd listened when I said I had a big appetite, and he was cooking up an epic breakfast-for-dinner feast. There were scrambled eggs, hash browns, sausage patties, bacon, and toast, and a metric shit-ton of all of it.

Garth smiled at me over his shoulder, then went back to work flipping strips of bacon with a fork.

I carried my not-so-pleasant burden into the living area and looked around. "Where's the washer?"

"Over there," Garth said, nodding to a long closet on the other side of the entryway. "Careful when you open the door. The cat carrier has a habit of falling off the shelf."

"Will do." I got the laundry started, making a pit stop at my backpack to grab the rest of my clothes and adding them before shutting the washer and closet alike. I headed into the kitchen, poking my nose in here and there around Garth. "Can I do anything to help?"

"Throw a couple plates and some silverware up on the counter? Unless you want to eat at the table . . ." The way he said it made eating at the table sound like the most foreboding thing in the world.

I shook my head, rummaging through his cabinets and drawers. "The counter works for me." I pulled a couple of plates from the upper cabinet next to the fridge and found the silverware in the drawer directly below it. How logical. Heading around the island, I set the plates in front of two barstools, arranged the silverware, glanced at Eva, who hadn't moved from her perch, then headed back into the kitchen for glasses—the water kind, not the booze kind. They were in the next cabinet over from the plates. Like I said, logical.

"What do you want to drink?" I asked Garth, opening the freezer in search of ice. I found the ice trays in one of the shelves on the door and pulled one out.

"Orange juice would be great, thanks." Garth glanced at me again, a secretive smile curving his lips.

I twisted the ice tray, freeing the ice cubes. "What?"

He shook his head. "Nothing."

I set the tray on the counter and picked out five ice cubes, dropping each into my glass with a clink, my gaze straying back to

Garth between each one. He was still smiling, almost looking like he was holding in laughter. "Seriously, Garth. *What*?"

He chuckled. "It's nothing, really. It's just—you look like a kid in my clothes. It's cute."

I scowled, returning the ice cube tray to the freezer. I opened the fridge and grabbed the carton of orange juice and a pitcher of filtered water. I could feel Garth watching me, but I didn't look his way.

"That bothered you," he said, not asking. The amusement was gone from his voice. "Why?"

I set the water and OJ on the counter by our glasses and bowed my head. My long, wet hair hung around my face in dark, clumpy strands. "I'm thirty-eight years old."

"You don't look a day over eighteen."

I turned to face him, my lower back resting against the counter. "Exactly. For the rest of my life, this is what I'll look like." I swept a hand down my body, Vanna White–ing myself. "An eternal teenager. It's *super* fantastic." Especially the hormones—that was my absolute favorite part.

"I can think of worse things, but . . . is that normal for your kind?" Garth's eyes narrowed, and he tilted his head to the side. "Your sister looks older, like in her twenties. So does Nik."

"It's not normal," I said, laughing under my breath and shaking my head. "There was an accident. Or, not really an accident, but a matter of life and death. Lex was being held prisoner, and—well, it's a long story. We had to force my Nejeret traits to manifest early. Thus"—I held my arms up, posing—"me. Like this. Forever. Perma-jailbait."

Garth's expression was serious as he studied my face. He leaned his hip against the opposite counter, crossing his arms over his chest.

I fought the urge to squirm under his scrutiny.

A twinkle sparked in his eye, and I knew the seriousness was fading from the moment. Final-fucking-ly. "You could try out for

To Catch a Predator," Garth said. "They could use you as bait until, oh, say, the end of time."

My lips twitched, and I eyed him through my lashes.

"Imagine the pedophiles' reactions when they find out you're really two hundred years old . . ."

My chest convulsed, and a laugh slipped out. "Stop it," I said, kicking him lightly with my bare toes.

He grinned and turned back to the food on the stove. "I can see how that would be annoying, though, at least where dating is concerned. I'd imagine going out with people your own age is off the table."

I snorted. "You have no idea." After a moment, I added, "The tattoos help keep away most guys looking for a girl to fulfill their creeptastic fantasies. It's hard to look overly innocent when you're covered in ink."

Garth nodded as I spoke. "Your attitude helps, too."

I scoffed. "Attitude? *Me*?"

He laughed, moving a spatula around a pan filled with scrambling eggs.

I filled up our glasses, then put the water and OJ back in the fridge.

"Go ahead and grab a seat," Garth said, lifting the egg pan from the stove and carrying it over to our plates. He dumped a pretty good pile onto each plate, leaving some in the pan. In no time, both plates were loaded up with a whole lot of everything, and there was still food in reserve. My kind of meal.

I sat on one of the stools, munching on a strip of extra-crispy bacon.

"So," Garth said as he sat beside me, "why were you stalking me tonight?"

I picked up my fork and stared down at my plate, moving the eggs around like I was searching for the perfect scrambled nugget. A heaviness settled in my stomach, and I hesitated in telling him why I was there. He was so kind and good and honorable. I hated the idea of dragging him through the mud once more. He was still recovering from the last time he got tangled up in one of my messes.

Garth didn't touch his fork, let alone his food, and I could feel his gaze steady on the side of my face. "So it's serious, then. What's going on?"

I inhaled deeply and closed my eyes, silently apologizing to him. "The kids who were missing . . ." I opened my eyes and looked at Garth. "I found them."

His whole body tensed, and he became statue still. For a few seconds, he didn't even breathe.

"I didn't tell you earlier, because there wasn't anything you could've done about it. The kids are safe—or as safe as they'll ever be—now. Most of them, at least."

"Was it Ouroboros?" Garth's voice sounded tight, carefully controlled. "Is that why you killed that scientist—because he was involved?"

I lifted one shoulder and let it drop. "Sort of. He was partially responsible for my brother's death. But yeah, Ouroboros took the kids. They were experimenting on them, super illegally." I implored Garth with my cycs, asking him to understand. To forgive me for keeping this from him when he was the one who'd come to me about the missing kids in the first place. "Garth, if they were willing to do that, what's to keep them from getting rid of a nosy cop or two?"

Nodding slowly, Garth picked up his fork and took a bite of hash browns. He chewed, swallowed, then glanced my way. "That still doesn't answer my question."

Why was I stalking him tonight? "Oh, right." I picked at my food for a few more seconds, then set down my fork. "One of the kids escaped early—or thought he escaped, but I think someone let him get out on purpose." I turned my stool so my knees were angled toward Garth and tilted my chin downward. "They infected him with something—we're not sure what exactly, yet, but it's bad. It spreads like crazy, and it's totally unresponsive to any kind of treatment."

I took a deep breath. It was the moment of truth. The big ask. "Garth . . . I need you to get me the addresses of the members of the Ouroboros board of directors. If I go straight to the top, someone will be able to give me some answers." I shook my head, my eyes still locked on his. "It might be the only way to get a cure in time."

Garth's nostrils flared, and his jaw clenched. "How many people are infected with this thing?"

"Several dozen at least, and more and more each day."

"I haven't heard any reports of anything like this coming in from the hospitals."

"It's not in the hospitals," I said. *Yet* . . .

Garth grunted. "What'll you do once you have the board members' addresses?"

I averted my gaze, staring down at my plate once more, and licked my lips. "Does it matter? I mean, as long as I get the cure . . ."

He was quiet for a long moment. So long that I thought he was sure to refuse. "Alright."

I looked at him, lips parted and eyebrows raised. "Alright? You'll help?"

He nodded. "I'll do it tomorrow." His focus shifted to my hair, hanging over my shoulders in wet, tangled strands. "I'll get you some hair dye, too. Now that your image is plastered all over the news . . ."

I grimaced, a heavy sigh escaping from my chest. "I forgot about that."

Garth reached out and gave my shoulder a squeeze. "Maybe some of those fake glasses, too." The corner of his mouth lifted, his full lips twisting into the faintest of smirks. "And a dress."

I smirked right back. "Don't push it, buddy."

CHAPTER EIGHT

Garth's bedroom door creaked faintly as I pushed it open. Like out in the living room, the wall facing the city was taken up by two large windows. He'd left the vertical blinds cracked open, and the glow from the nearly full moon mixed with the light from Seattle, casting stripes across him and his bed. He was sleeping on his back in only his boxer briefs, just one leg under the covers, his arms thrown out to either side and his head turned to the windows. He snored softly on each inhale, and I found the rhythmic sound soothing.

I moved closer to the bed, not trying to be stealthy but not being loud, either, and sat on the edge of his mattress. "I'm so sorry that I dragged you into all of this," I said, my voice hushed. I clasped my hands together and stared down at my intertwined fingers. "I'm terrified that if I stay here, I'll get you killed, and . . ." I inhaled shakily. "I've taken a lot of lives, and for a long time, I thought of myself as a killer. But I think I was wrong. Human life, it—it's this precious thing, and I couldn't handle knowing yours ended early because of me."

Another shaky breath. My chin trembled. "You're a good man. A good cop. This city—these people—they need you." I cleared my throat, surprised by how choked up I was getting. "So I guess this is me saying thank you. And goodbye. I left a note with Lex's phone number on the counter. You can give her the addresses. I really appreciate the offer to stay here, but—"

Garth's hand closed around my arm, just above the elbow, his fingers more than encircling it completely. I hadn't meant to wake him, but I'd needed to say my piece.

I glanced down at his hand, then twisted on the bed so I could see his face. I wanted to ask him how much he'd heard, but my tongue was paralyzed.

Garth stared at me, unblinking in the dim light. "Stay." His voice was rough with sleep.

I started to shake my head. "I really don't think—"

"Please, Kat." Garth sat up, wincing at the halfway point. "Stay." He brought a hand up to my face and brushed a few strands of hair out of my eyes, tucking them behind my ear. He peered at me in the darkness, his eyes searching, assessing. "Stay with me." He leaned in, and against my better judgement, I didn't pull away.

His lips were soft and warm, his kiss gentle. Tentative. Almost chaste. His large hands settled on either side of my head, holding me like I was the delicate one. Like he was afraid of hurting me, when he was the injured one. The fragile one. The human.

"Stay with me," he repeated, his lips brushing against mine as he spoke. Parting mine. His breath was hot and minty, his tongue gentle, coaxing. Even as he deepened the kiss, that sense of restraint remained.

My hand settled on his chest, and I broke the kiss, resting my forehead against his. I stared into his midnight eyes, lips parted and breaths quick. Without breaking eye contact, I pushed him back and stood.

He propped himself up on his elbows, his gaze questioning. Was I pushing him away? Was I rejecting him? Was I leaving after all?

I pulled my oversized, borrowed sweatshirt over my head, then followed with the T-shirt. The necklace holding Dom's mirrored pendant came next, and I set the chain on the bedside table.

The questions fled from Garth's moonlit stare, replaced by a simmering heat. By desire. It sparked warmth low in my abdomen and need deep within my heart.

I slid the sweatpants down over my hips and crawled onto the bed. He watched me, seeming to devour my every movement as I pushed the sheets to the foot of the bed. I knelt on the mattress beside him and reached out, slipping the fingertips of my left hand under the waistband of his boxer briefs. His abs flexed as I traced the waistband from one side of his hips to the other, enjoying the smooth contours of his skin stretched over hard muscle, of the faint trail of dark hair running down from his belly button to his underwear and lower.

My heart thudded in my chest as my fingertips skimmed up the length of his torso, exploring the topography of his body, the feel of his skin, his reaction to my touch. He sucked in a shaky breath when my thumbnail grazed his nipple, and a pleased smile curved my lips. I raised my gaze to his once more, resting my hand on his chest. I pressed my palm against the tattoo over his heart, and he let his elbows slip out to the sides until his back was flat against the mattress.

Using both hands, I ran my nails down either side of his rib cage, careful not to put any pressure on his yellowing bruises. His breaths were coming faster, and not even remotely steady. Unlike his stare. It was locked on my face; I could feel it even when I wasn't looking into his eyes.

I hooked my fingertips into the waistband on either side of his hips and tugged, just a little, telling him to lift his ass off the bed. Once he did, I slid the boxer briefs down his legs and tossed them to the floor.

The fingers of both of his hands splayed on the bedsheet as I straddled his hips. He was hard, ready. But I was ready, too. That spark of desire had become a smoldering coal, ready to engulf my entire body if given the chance.

I settled on top of him, his hard length tucked snugly against the core of my body. His fingers clenched, gripping the bedsheet as

I glided back and forth over him. I enjoyed the agony of prolonging the unfulfilled ache deep within me, of teasing my body, of bridging the gap between desire and need. Of pushing myself to the very edge, until there was no chance of turning back. Of bringing him there with me.

"Please," Garth whispered. Begged. "Kat . . ."

My eyes locked with his, and I froze when I saw the sheer force of his desire. It was pure and unblemished by anger, by any lust for control. Nothing about his desire for me had to do with power or manipulation. This charge pulsing between us, connecting us, wasn't born of adrenaline. This wasn't about the heat of the moment, like so many of my hookups. It felt like so much more than that, than any of it. Like so much more than anything I'd ever experienced.

I raised my hips and reached down between my legs. Garth's long, dark eyelashes fluttered against his cheeks as I coaxed him into me, and he threw his head back, his neck arching, when I eased down until he was sheathed within me completely.

I sat there, unmoving, letting my body adjust to him. My inner muscles fluttered, almost like they were flirting with the idea of letting go, of washing my body with the pleasure of release from just that single moment of penetration. I sat absolutely still. Not yet.

Heartbeats passed, and I leaned forward, one hand on Garth's waist, the other on his neck, my pointer finger curving over his chin. I wanted him there with me—*needed* him there with me—looking at me. Being present, in this moment, with me. I was suddenly starving for something beyond the basic primal connection I was used to. I was desperate to truly be *with* someone. To be with him.

Garth angled his face toward me and opened his eyes, dark pools in the dim bedroom. His hands moved to my hips, his fingers curling over my minimal curves.

I moved slowly, afraid of hurting his still-healing body. I'd never been one for soft, slow lovemaking. Hell, I'd never been remotely interested in having any genuine, worthwhile emotion involved at all.

Until now. Until I felt the slow well of pressure within me, the gentle build of heat, the soft swell of pleasure. This feeling . . . it was unreal. Unreal and so very unexpected.

"Kat . . ." Garth was breathing hard, his grip on my hips tightening. Not remotely painful, but enough to coax me to move with a little more force.

I was breathing hard, but not panting, and a thin sheen of sweat coated my skin.

"I can't—" His fingertips dug into my hips. "I'm going to—"

"Come," I said, rocking my hips in a steady, unrelenting rhythm. I was so close; sensing his spike in pleasure was bound to push me over the edge.

He went rigid beneath me, his jaw clenched and his eyes narrowing to slits.

I threw my head back as pleasure exploded in my core, sending sparks cascading through my body. It seemed to last for a blissful eternity. I was still gliding along, lost to the sensations thrumming through me, when Garth pulled me down to rest on his chest and encircled me in his arms.

He kissed the top of my head and whispered, "That was insane," into my hair.

All I could manage was a single, breathy laugh. I lay on top of him, feeling him soften within me, and listened to his heartbeat, strong and steady and fast. He ran his fingers through my slightly tangled hair, apologizing each time he got caught in a snag.

And for the first time since I was a child, I fell asleep touching another person. For the first time, as an adult, I felt comfortable enough to fall asleep that way. I felt safe. Like, just this once, it was okay to be vulnerable. Like, just this once, I could let my guard down for the night.

And so I fell asleep curled up on top of Garth. And it felt right.

When I woke, it was still dark out. I was no longer lying on Garth, but beside him, my legs tangled with his. I was on my back, sort of, him facing me on his side, his arm resting across my chest. His face was relaxed, peaceful, faint bruises and all. I watched him sleep for a couple minutes, waiting for a knot to form in the pit of my stomach. It always happened, after. It didn't matter who I'd been with or what we'd done, I always felt that seedling of self-loathing. Of disgust.

It didn't come. Even as I thought back through what had happened between us, as I replayed every touch, every sound and reaction, a feeling started in my belly, but not the one I was used to. A tingle and a flutter and a bit of a yearning ache. I wanted him again. And I *never* wanted them again. I wanted to kiss him, to look into his eyes. I wanted to *know* him.

I frowned, my chest tightening unexpectedly. All of a sudden, it was hard to breathe. My lungs were working—double time—but they didn't seem to be pulling in anything except used, expended air. Not what my body needed.

I had to get up, to move around. I slid away from Garth on the bed, moving slowly to keep from waking him. By the time I stood, I was shaking.

One day, maybe tomorrow, maybe in sixty years, Garth would die. And because he was human, his soul would dissipate, its energy dividing up and floating away. If I let myself get any closer to him . . . if I let myself care any more . . .

I passed through the doorway into the living room and crossed to stand before one of the windows and stare out at my city. I would do what I could to make this a safe place for people like Garth so they could hang onto whatever short amount of time they had left. So they could exist for as long as possible. So the people who love them wouldn't have to say goodbye until the last possible moment.

A chill rippled through me, and I turned and grabbed the fleece blanket bunched up in the corner of the sectional, wrapping it around my bare shoulders. It smelled like him, faintly, of his cologne and that underlying scent that was his alone. I hugged the corners of the blanket to me. Hugged myself. Held myself together.

I heard the sheets rustle in the other room, then the mattress creaked. Light footsteps marked Garth's progress from the bed to the doorway. "Kat? What are you doing out here?"

"Just thinking."

I listened to him cross the living room, making his way to me. "Are you alright?"

"Yeah." My shoulders slumped. "No." I laughed quietly. Bitterly. "I honestly don't know."

He stopped behind me, a foot or two by the sound of it. "Do you want to talk about it?"

I shook my head, letting out another quiet, humorless laugh. "I want to stop thinking about it altogether."

Garth made a rough noise, faint and low in his throat. "Maybe I can help with that." He pulled on the edge of the blanket at the back of my neck and I loosened my grip on it, letting it slip through my fingers and fall to the floor.

My brain was telling me to stop this, warning me that this would only make things worse when the inevitable happened. And it would happen. But my heart and libido had a mind of their own, and they took over.

Garth's fingers trailed down my spine, from the base of my skull to my tailbone, and I shivered, both tickled and aroused. "You're so beautiful," he said, his voice low and husky. He laid his hands over my ribcage, sliding them around my body until the "L" of his thumbs hugged my breasts. "So confident . . ." He stepped closer and moved his hands higher. I could feel the heat of him just inches behind me. "So strong . . ."

I leaned against him, resting the back of my head on his shoulder and closing my eyes.

"Do you have any idea how sexy that is?"

I smiled to myself, the faintest curving of my lips. I could feel the evidence of how sexy he found me pressed against my lower back, so yeah, I had some idea.

He flicked my nipples, and my eyes snapped open as I hissed in a breath.

"Put your hands on the window," he ordered. This was new.

Reluctantly, I obeyed. I was so comfortable there, leaning against him while he fondled me. But I'd play along . . . so long as there was more fondling. I'm a big fan of fondling.

I pressed both of my hands against the window, fingers splayed.

"Spread your legs. Shoulder width."

My belly did a little flip-flop as I did as he said. My heart was pounding, and all of the blood it was pumping seemed to be pooling in my core.

Garth took a step backward, leaving me chilled and alone at the window. But only for a second. His finger slid inside me, and I gasped, head drooping.

I didn't think about anything for the rest of the night. I couldn't. I was too busy gasping and moaning and begging for more. Always more.

And not once did Garth deny me.

CHAPTER NINE

I woke late into the morning in Garth's bed and, once again, managed to untangle myself from him without waking him completely. He roused just enough to turn onto his side, and his breathing soon returned to the slow, even rhythm of deep sleep.

Moving as quietly as possible, I made my way around the foot of the bed to gather up my borrowed clothes. I carried them into the living room, shutting the bedroom door behind me. Once I'd donned the oversized T-shirt, I sat on the sectional, feet tucked beneath me. I fished my cards out of my backpack, doing my best not to disturb the cat dozing in a lone sliver of hazy sunlight on the far armrest.

The previous night had been fun—oh, who was I kidding, it had been amazing—but it didn't mean I was any less focused on finding a way to help those infected with the mystery disease. If anything, it made me more determined to eliminate the disease so I could be sure the rest of the humans in my city were safe from infection. To make sure Garth was safe.

I pulled the vintage silver compact mirror from the pocket of my leather jacket and opened it, propping it up against a TV remote on the coffee table. Dom was there in the reflection, and I could see his lips moving, but I couldn't hear a word he was saying.

Brow furrowed, I touched the pendant hanging from the silver chain around my neck.

My heart skipped a beat or three. It wasn't there.

My lips parted, and I ran through the events of the previous night. I'd removed it when I was undressing, and I'd set it somewhere . . . but where? It hadn't exactly been my main focus at the time.

I stood and headed back to the bedroom, inching the door open and poking my head through the crack to give the room a quick scan. The necklace was there on the nightstand, the pendant glinting in the dull, gray light of the overcast morning.

The burst of adrenaline I'd felt during the few seconds that I feared I'd lost my necklace abated, and I could breathe a little easier. I tiptoed into the bedroom and retrieved it, then returned to the living room once more, easing the door shut behind me. Dom was already talking to me as I secured the clasp behind my neck.

"Where have you been?" he demanded. *"I've been trying to get through to you for hours. You know I don't like it when you take the necklace off. I need to be able to speak to you whenever I—"*

"I was having sex." I perched on the edge of the couch and looked at the compact, meeting Dom's silvery stare. We had an agreement, he and I—I would only remove the pendant during amorous moments, and he would keep his incorporeal mouth shut about my perceived promiscuity. This was the first time I'd tested that agreement.

Dom pressed his lips together into a thin, flat line. *"I couldn't get through to you for the entire night."*

I raised a single eyebrow, smirking. "It was a lot of sex."

His expression was flat, unamused.

"So what did you find out?"

He blinked and, just like that, was back to business. *"None of the kids Neffe and Aset took back to Bainbridge are showing signs of the illness, but apparently some of them are missing."*

"Missing?"

Dom nodded. *"It would seem we did not rescue all of the children who were abducted. Some, like this Sammy, were taken away. They were never seen again by the children still in the holding cells. Rumors spread about the missing children being killed, or even escaping, but none knew for sure."*

"How many disappeared?"

"Seven," Dom said. *"Heru has people checking in with all of the hospitals in the area, but so far, there's no sign of an outbreak cropping up anywhere but in the Tent District."*

"It might be too soon for anything specific to have been noted, let alone reported. It is flu season, after all." I chewed the inside of my cheek and nodded to myself. "Let me know if they find anything, or if they hear anything new."

Dom raised a single brow, his smirk mirroring mine from just moments ago. *"So long as I can get through to you, of course."*

It was my turn to level a flat look at him. "Of course."

"Neffe and Aset have requested blood samples from the victims, but they're too busy to collect the samples themselves."

"So, what—they want me to do it?"

"No," Dom said. *"Not with the warrant out for your arrest."*

"So you heard about that . . ."

"The whole state has by now," Dom said dryly. *"You need to stay put. Nik is going. He's meeting with Dorman at noon."*

I sat up straighter and glanced at the clock on the microwave. It was half past ten.

"I know what you're thinking," Dom said, *"and yes, little sister, it would be a very bad idea for you to go out right now, what with your image so fresh in everyone's minds."*

My finger tapped against my thigh, and I stared at the blank wall beside the TV stand. What if I didn't have to go *out*? What if I could see what happened at the meeting, from *here*? My *sheut* made it so the things I drew had power, sometimes even seeming to come to life. Sometimes becoming *real*, if only for a moment. If I drew a likeness of Dorman's office on the living room wall, would it just be a pretty picture, or would it become something more—a window to what was actually happening in the Tent District? It was a long shot, but I thought, just maybe, not an impossible one.

"Kat . . ."

"What?" I reached for the deck of tarot cards and started to shuffle. "I promise not to step a single foot through that door," I said, nodding in the direction of the condo's front door. If I could make my own, magical window, I wouldn't have to.

"Good."

I shuffled again. "Now hush." Another shuffle. "I need to concentrate."

What's in the cards for me today? I let the question roll around in my mind, let it saturate every cell in my body, let it flow from me into the cards. They wouldn't tell me exactly what to do or what would happen, but they would give me an idea of what to expect. They'd help guide me in maybe not the *right* direction, but the necessary one. I honestly didn't know how it worked, but somehow I would feel when the cards were ready. A little zing of power, of energy. When I felt that, I just knew.

I set the cards down on the coffee table's black-stained surface and cut the deck. I didn't always cut, and almost never into three piles like so many tarot readers, but today had the potential to be a big day. An important day. I wanted to make sure I heard whatever messages the universe had for me, loud and clear. So, I cut the deck once more and let my hand hover over each pile for a few seconds, first the leftmost, then the middle one, then the one on the right. I returned to the middle pile. It hummed with an almost electric charge.

"Loud and clear," I murmured, picking up the middle pile and stacking it on top of the others. I flipped the top card and set it on the table.

Justice. I wasn't surprised to find that the major arcana card had altered itself, as my cards so often did. The Justice card currently showed Dorman, the unofficial leader of the Tent District, standing in front of a chain-link fence topped with razor wire—the perimeter surrounding his kingdom. His expression was stern, and he held a sword in his right hand—*my* sword, Mercy, with her silver pommel and crystalline *At* blade—a set of scales in the other, weighing a dripping heart against a pristine white feather. A creature with the body of a lion and the head of a crocodile lurked at the very edge of the card, the Egyptian god Ammut, waiting to eat the heart of the judged should it prove unworthy.

I took it as a good sign that this card showed up first and that Dorman was the central figure. The Justice card itself represents balance, objectivity, and accountability. In general, it's a positive card, especially since it was currently appearing in a time of relative chaos. To me, it suggested that following my current path, seeking salvation and justice for those under Dorman's care, was the right thing—the necessary thing—to do. It meant that finding a solution to the problem Dorman had lain at my feet would ensure that universal balance, or *ma'at* to my people, was maintained.

I slid the Justice card to the side and flipped the next card from the deck.

The Hermit. Traditionally, this card represents healing, self-exploration, and a general need for self-reliance and alone time. While I thought all of that sounded kind of nice for me, I didn't think it was talking about me—or, at least, not *just* me. The card depicted Nik, shirtless so his tattooed torso was displayed in all its glory. His side was to the viewer, his head bowed and his arm outstretched, like he was reaching for someone or something just out of frame. He stood on a polished floor of *At*, my sword held in his grasp, the tip nearly skimming the floor. The crystalline blade dripped with blood.

Mercy showing up twice was far from a coincidence, and I couldn't help but wonder if she represented something more than her pure, deadly self. I couldn't shake the sense that she represented *me*.

A little unnerved, I drew the next card and flipped it over.

Queen of Swords. Once again, Constance Ward, the Chairman of the Board and CEO of the Ouroboros Corporation, stared out at me from her throne. The only difference from how the card had looked when I'd drawn it back in the library was that Constance now had a sword sticking out of her chest. *My* sword. Did it mean I would kill her after all? The thought spurred images of her children in my mind, and my chest tightened. There had to be another way.

I moved my hand to the deck to draw another card, but the electric hum had faded. The magic was gone. The universe had shared all it would for now.

With a sigh, I relaxed back into the couch and stared out through the nearest window at the cityscape gleaming in the light of a gloriously dreary Seattle morning. Dorman as Justice, Nik as the Hermit, Constance once again appearing as the Queen of Swords, and Mercy showing up on all three cards—what did it all mean?

I started when the bedroom door opened. I'd been so caught up in thinking about the reading that I hadn't heard Garth moving around in the bedroom.

"Morning," he said, strolling into the living room in only his underwear. He stopped beside the couch and bent down to kiss the top of my head.

I reached out to snap the compact closed, but not before I caught Dom's raised eyebrow. "Hey." I tilted my head back, offering Garth my lips.

He kissed me, gentle as ever, his fingertips caressing my neck. I felt him smile against my lips before pulling away. He headed into the kitchen and started fiddling with a coffeepot. "I'd offer to make breakfast"—he craned his neck to glance at the clock on the microwave—"or lunch, but I really have to get to the station."

"No worries," I told him, standing and following him into the kitchen. I stopped at the island and leaned on the counter with my elbows. "I can fend for myself."

Garth laughed, low and throaty. "I have no doubt, but I'm trying to impress you."

I snorted. "Stop trying," I said. "I'm thoroughly impressed.

Honestly, I had no idea you were so . . . creative." It was the best word I could come up with to sum up all we'd done the previous night.

He glanced at me over his shoulder, eyebrows dancing.

My neck and cheeks heated.

"I'm going to hop in the shower while the coffee brews," Garth said, turning and making his way back to the bedroom. "Join me if you want . . ."

I grinned. Oh, I wanted.

CHAPTER TEN

Garth was out of the condo by eleven. He left me his personal cell phone, taking only his work phone with him. He also left me with a key to his place, along with the warning that I should only leave the condo if it was absolutely necessary. Like, emergency necessary.

I can be rash, but I'm not stupid. I was fully aware that lying low had to be my top priority, and it was a little annoying that both Dom and Garth expressed concern over me leaving the condo. Like I just wouldn't be able to resist frolicking out the door and gallivanting all around the city. Like my self-control was nil. But I had zero plans to gallivant. I mean, come on, I'm not even the gallivanting type.

Even so, I wanted to get the inside scoop on that meeting between Nik and Dorman. The longer I pondered the three cards I'd drawn, the more I thought that maybe, just maybe, I needed to be included in the meeting in the Tent District, even if I was only there remotely. Both Nik and Dorman had been incorporated into the designs, and I couldn't shake the feeling that their appearances were significant, like they were pointing me toward the meeting. It was more of a whisper from the universe than a scream, this time, but that didn't make the message matter any less.

As soon as Garth shut the condo's front door, I rushed to the sectional to retrieve my backpack and unzipped the front pocket to dig out a black Sharpie, then I grabbed Dom's compact and crossed to the kitchen island. I set him up on the corner, giving him a good view of the wall beside the TV. If I didn't let him watch what I was attempting, he'd bug me nonstop.

"What are you doing?" he asked, and I shushed him. Case in point.

Barefoot and wearing only Garth's T-shirt, I stood before the blank, white wall and uncapped the pen. I pictured the room in the back of the makeshift hospital, recalling exactly what it had looked like through that doorway with all those cots and the poor, sick kiddos. My drawings could be realistic, verging on lifelike, but I had no idea if this would work. Didn't mean I wouldn't try.

I started by drawing a tall rectangle on the wall. That was the doorway in the hangar. I added rows of occupied cots, spending a few minutes giving each sick kid some memorable details. I closed my eyes, imagining what the scene would be like when Nik was there, collecting blood samples from the infected humans. I drew him crouching down at the second cot from the doorway in the middle row, his head bent over the kid lying there, blessedly asleep.

Eyelids remaining shut, I continued to draw, my hand moving with a mind of its own, the ink directing it. The *universe* directing it. I gave myself over to the magic, let the universal energies flow through my *sheut*, saturate the rest of my body, and pour into the drawing. The marker started to hum with power, the wall giving off a sizzling electricity that made the hairs on my arms and the back of my neck stand on end. I was used to a gentle zing of power while drawing or doing a reading, but this was something else altogether. This was massive, a torrent compared to a trickle.

My breaths came faster, my heart beating harder, stronger. A surge of energy passed through me, a pulse like lightning compared to the steady current I'd been channeling before.

"Mon Dieu . . ." Dom's voice was filled with awe.

My eyes snapped open, and I stared at the wall—at the thing that was much more than simply a drawing of a doorway on a wall.

"What—how did you do that?"

"I'm not sure," I said, eyes glued to the thing on the wall. Or, rather, *in* the wall. It wasn't just a picture of the sick room at the back of the makeshift hospital; those were actual cots with actual sick kids lined up in rows. I could hear their moaning. Their sniffles and muffled cries. It worked. It *really* worked. Somehow, I'd created a window to another place entirely.

Slack-jawed, I stared through the window. A man knelt beside the second cot in from the doorway in the center row. It was Nik, just as I'd drawn him. His head was bowed over a slumbering little girl of maybe six or seven, and he was collecting a sample of her blood in a vial at her elbow. He raised his head, focusing on something within the room, just to the side of the doorway. "Is there any way to get a sample from Sammy? Having patient zero's blood might make all the difference."

The left half of Dorman came into view as he shifted his feet. He'd been standing beside the doorway. His arms were crossed over his chest, and he still wore that baseball cap. He shrugged. "You're welcome to try." He was so close, I felt as though I could reach out and touch him.

Cautiously, I brought my hand up to the wall. I held my breath and pushed forward. And met no resistance. I pulled my hand back and stared at it. It had passed straight through the wall up to my wrist.

This thing I'd created—it wasn't merely a window to the Tent District. I wasn't restricted to watching Nik and Dorman's meeting; if I wanted to, I could *go* there.

Nik must've spotted the movement, because he was suddenly staring at me.

I sucked in a breath and froze.

"What?" Dorman glanced over his shoulder, then returned to looking at Nik. "What is it?"

"I thought I saw—" Nik shook his head, but his eyes didn't

leave the doorway. "It was nothing, I'm sure." So it seemed that they couldn't see me, even though I could see them. Could *hear* them and, if I wanted to, reach through and touch them. It didn't seem possible.

A slow grin spread across my face. "Holy fucking shitballs." It didn't *seem* possible, but it *was*.

I spun around and ran to the closet housing the washer and dryer, yanking the doors open and pulling my clothes from the dryer. I dumped them all on the floor at my feet, picking up first a pair of underwear and pulling them on, then doing the same with some jeans. I hopped on one foot, then the other as I put on my socks, then strapped on my bra and topped it with a tank top. I shrugged into my sweatshirt, zipping it up as I hurried to the couch to grab my leather coat. I retrieved my boots from the bedroom and shoved my feet into them, doing a hasty job of tying the laces.

After shutting Eva away in the bedroom, I rushed back to the doorway on the wall, snagging Dom's compact and snapping it shut before stuffing it back into my pocket. I paused at the wall, staring at the drawing that was so much more than that—it was an actual gateway to another place—and took a deep breath. And then I lunged *through* the wall.

Almost as soon as I crossed the impossible threshold, Nik was on his feet, a vine of *At* shooting out of his palm. That vine of opalescent otherworldly material wrapped around my waist, holding me back.

Nik's eyes rounded, a tentative smile touched his lips. "Kitty Kat?" A second later, he let out a bark of laughter, dissolving the vine of *At* and releasing me at the same time. "I knew I saw something."

I smoothed down my sweatshirt and coat, patting the pockets to make sure everything that had been in there still was. "Nice greeting," I said, not meeting his eyes. I felt the extreme urge to *not* make eye contact with him, though I didn't know why. Instead

I looked at Dorman, who was staring at me, eyelids opened wide and a hand to his chest. "Sorry if I startled you," I told him.

Dorman laughed nervously. "*Startled* is putting it lightly . . ."

I flashed him an apologetic smile.

"I thought you might show up," Nik said, winding around the cots to come to me. "Though not like that. Neat trick." He stopped a few feet away, and I finally forced myself to look at him, a spike of some unsettling emotion making me feel uneasy. "I brought something for you, just in case." His nostrils flared, his eyes narrowed, and a slow grin spread across his face. He schooled his features a moment later, going from wicked to innocent in a heartbeat. "You look tired." He tilted his head to the side. "Have you been getting enough sleep?"

My eyes narrowed to a glare. "Stop sniffing me, you pervert."

He smirked. "I can't help it. You reek of one-night stand."

"It wasn't a one-night stand," I snapped. At least, I hoped it wasn't.

Nik's eye twitched, but his smirk remained in place. "So Kitty Kat has a boyfriend. Isn't that sweet."

Unease turned to slight queasiness. "Shut up."

Dorman cleared his throat, and we both looked at him. "I don't mean to interrupt, but . . ." He swept a hand out, gesturing to the infected kids lying in the cots. "I'd prefer it if you got the samples to Bainbridge as soon as possible. There's been a bit of a development in the disease, and I don't think we can afford to waste time."

I took a step toward him. "What happened?"

"Around midnight, Sammy entered what we're calling the 'final phase' of the infection." Dorman sighed and shook his head, worry shining in his hazel eyes. "He became violent, almost rabid, attacking any and every person he could. It was . . . shocking, to say the least." Dorman's shoulders slumped. "He got out and infected thirty-seven more people. I'd never have imagined that someone so small could do so much damage, but . . . at least he didn't get beyond our fences." Dorman sighed. "The only upside is that the disease seems to progress more slowly in adults. That buys us a little more time."

"Not much of an upside," Nik muttered.

I realized my hand was covering my mouth, and lowered it. "Where's Sammy now?"

"Dead," Dorman said, his voice resigned. "The last person he attacked managed to break his neck. Maybe we could've brought him down sooner with a gun, but we're a firearm-free zone."

The news of Sammy's violent demise hit me like a punch to the gut. If I hadn't wussed out at Constance's house, I'd probably already have the cure. Now, thirty-seven more people might die—and might infect gods knew how many more people on their way out—all because I'd given in to weakness and spared Constance and her family. I gritted my teeth and pushed through the flood of failure. "Might need to change that rule," I said.

"Or at least invest in some tranq guns," Nik added.

Dorman nodded, but I thought it was mostly to himself. "A few more people have entered the final phase." He looked at us with lost, sad eyes. "We're using sedatives on them, but it's taking triple the amount it should to keep them down—more, in some cases. They're burning through our supply."

"I'll bring what I can back from Bainbridge," Nik said.

Dorman nodded a thanks, but his stare fixed on me. "We need a cure, Kat. Have you made any progress?"

"I—" I cleared my throat. "I'm working on it."

I understood now why the cards led me back here—for motivation. For resolve. I had let Garth distract me, lending a sense of blissful normalcy to a situation that was anything but normal. Dire was more like it. If this disease spread beyond the Tent District and remained unchecked, it would cause chaos and mayhem, not to mention unfathomable loads of destruction. I had the ugly suspicion that *that* had been the point of Sammy's "escape" all along. The Ouroboros Corporation or the Senate or whoever was ultimately responsible was even more demented than I'd ever imagined.

And if I was right, it begged the question—what happened to the other six kids the Ouroboros scientists had separated out? Had they been guinea pigs for some other twisted project? Or were there more infected kids out and about, spreading the disease with abandon?

My hands balled into fists. "Are there any other new developments?"

Dorman shook his head.

"Alright." I turned to the open doorway, then glanced over my shoulder. "Next time you see me, I'll have some answers for you." I marched through the doorway, fully expecting to find myself back in Garth's condo.

Yeah, not so much.

Instead, the doorway transported me right where it was supposed to—straight into the rest of the hangar-turned-hospital. I stopped and turned around, eyebrows scrunched together.

Nik watched me through the doorway, his head cocked to the side, and Dorman was craning his neck to see. Both looked as confused as I felt.

"Damn it," I grumbled, scowling. It looked like my gateways only worked one way. I hadn't been expecting that. Now, I'd have to draw another to get back. I knew it had seemed too easy. I stomped back into the smaller sick room and huffed out a breath. "I need a wall and a marker," I said. "Or some paint."

Dorman looked at Nik. "You can finish up here on your own?"

Nik nodded.

"Alright." Dorman headed to the not-a-gateway doorway. "Come with me, Kat. You can use my office."

I glanced at Nik, meeting his eye and offering him a weak smile before following Dorman. He didn't return it. He just stared back at me, his face blank. But his pale blue eyes . . . they were filled with something deep and dark, with something I couldn't identify. Or something I didn't want to identify.

I turned away from him and jogged to catch up to Dorman.

It was nearly two in the afternoon by the time I felt that surge of power bringing the second gateway to life.

Dorman whistled. "That's quite a trick." He was behind me, leaning on his desk as he watched me work. His office was at the base of what had once been an air traffic control tower—back when there'd been way more air traffic to control.

I looked at him. "You swear you'll paint over this as soon as I'm through it?" I felt pretty sure that would destroy the gateway.

He nodded, a sly, shy grin curving his lips. "Been meaning to redecorate, anyway."

I laughed under my breath.

The door to his office burst open and Nik strode in, his eyes honing in on me. "Good, you're still here." A long, black sport bag was slung across his shoulder, probably now filled with countless vials of blood.

"For about two more seconds," I said, nodding to the active gateway to Garth's condo on the wall adjacent to the door.

Nik studied it for a moment, scanning the area through the gateway and frowning, then looked at Dorman. "Can you give us a minute?"

After a nod, Dorman left the office.

I raised my eyebrows and planted my hands on my hips. "What's up?"

"I have something for you," Nik said, moving forward and placing his bag on the chairs in front of the desk. He unzipped the bag and pulled out the leather shoulder harness that was usually attached to my sword's scabbard. Except right now there was no scabbard or sword in sight. He held the harness out to me.

I took a step toward him and reached for the harness, not quite understanding. "Um . . . thanks, but—" My eyes widened when my fingers closed around more than the worn straps of leather. The scabbard—I could feel it in my hand, and from the weight of it, I knew that Mercy, my sword, was sheathed within. I shook my head. "How . . ."

Nik stuffed his hands into the pockets of his jeans and hunched his shoulders, looking adorably bashful. It was all an act, of course, but it was still cute. Or as cute as Nik could ever get. "I transformed the whole thing, scabbard and all, into *At*, then made it invisible."

My mouth fell open. I'd known that Lex's *sheut* enabled her to imbue *At* with various properties, like glowing or appearing invisible, but I'd had no idea that Nik could do it, too. I eyed him, wondering what other powers he'd been hiding from the rest of us.

"You left your sword behind because it would draw attention." Nik shrugged. "Now it won't."

Eyes stinging, I found the invisible hilt with my right hand and drew the sword. Mercy's blade slid free with a pristine ring. The entire thing, pommel to blade, was completely invisible.

Nik flashed me a devilish grin. "Now the trick is re-sheathing it . . ."

"This is incredible." I stared at, well, *nothing* with wide eyes, absolutely awed.

"Just don't drop it."

I glanced at Nik, frowning. What if I *did* drop it? I'd have to grope around until I stumbled over the damn thing.

"But just in case you do manage to lose it," Nik said, seeming to read my thoughts, "I can always find it again, you know, because I can sense anything made of *At*."

My eyebrows rose. "Anything?"

He nodded.

"Even my ink?" I flashed him the Eye of Horus on my palm.

"When you're close enough." He shrugged. "It's a pretty small amount."

"Huh." I sheathed the invisible sword after only two tries and hugged the whole thing to my chest, feeling a little less alone. Nik had done this for me, and now it would be like I carried a little piece of him around with me, wherever I went. That mattered more to me than I was willing to admit, even just to myself.

"Thank you," I said, meeting his eyes and hoping he couldn't see how intensely his gift was affecting me. I cleared my throat. "Really, Nik. Thank you."

The corner of his mouth twitched, and he breathed out a laugh. It was the only "You're welcome" I would get. He pointed to the gateway with his chin. "Go on. Do your thing. I've got a ferry to catch."

I stared at him for a moment longer, then took a deep breath, held my head high, and turned my back to him. And stepped through the new gateway.

CHAPTER ELEVEN

By the time I'd returned to Garth's condo and checked his cell phone, I had a series of texts from him, each with the name and home address of one of the Ouroboros board members. He'd sent them within the past half hour, and his timing was impeccable. Any longer and I'd have made a straight shot for Constance. And despite my renewed motivation to do what had to be done, no matter the cost, I wasn't ready to go after her. Even after the reading that morning, after her appearance on the Queen of Swords card with Mercy shoved through her chest. *Even* though I now held the sword that had impaled her in my hands, I wasn't ready to go after her to get the cure.

Sure, if push came to shove, I'd do it. But I didn't want to, and I knew I'd regret whatever I ended up doing to her for the rest of my potentially *very* long life.

I did a quick Internet search on Garth's phone, running down the list of names he'd sent me. I was hoping for a sign, some tidbit of information that would point me in the right direction. Or, at least, in the least guilt-ridden direction. I was fully committed to the cause, ready and willing to use lethal force if necessary. I *would* find a way to stop the spread of the disease and save those unfortunate enough to already be infected. At least, those who weren't already too far gone. It was too late for Sammy, but it wasn't too late for the others. Not yet.

I found my target as soon as I hit enter on the third name—Mitch Carmichael. The list of links included several news articles from the past year reporting allegations that Carmichael's name had been linked to an illegal human trafficking ring, one that specialized in young women and children. It looked like his name had been cleared and the matter had been swept under the rug, as almost anything could be if enough money was thrown at it, but things like that don't just disappear. Not now, in the age of the Internet. Nowadays, things like that live forever.

However guiltless Carmichael appeared in the eyes of the law, I couldn't ignore the reality of the situation—Ouroboros *had* abducted children to use as test subjects. It seemed an awful big coincidence that one of the leaders of that corporation had potential ties to another child-abducting organization. It even crossed my mind that the idea to take the street kids could've come from Carmichael originally. If so, I thought it would be pretty easy to get over my aversion to taking human lives. Easy as breathing. But a hell of a lot more gratifying.

I tried creating a gateway to someplace closer to the downtown high-rise Carmichael called home—I even went so far as to draw a likeness of one of the cluttered basements I'd ducked out in a night or two on the wall beside the original gateway, which would've left me just a few blocks from Carmichael's place—but no matter how hard I tried to focus, I couldn't get the magic to work. I couldn't even get a spark of the increasingly familiar current of otherworldly energy to hum through me. My magical batteries were well and truly dead, and I had no clue how long it would take them to recharge. I'd have to go the long way.

It would've been safer to wait until dark to leave Garth's building, but I had a narrow window of opportunity to get into Carmichael's home while he was out—assuming he held anything close to normal work hours. He was on the Ouroboros board of directors, but unlike Constance, he didn't hold an additional position at the corporation. So far as I could tell, he'd made his money elsewhere, or he'd fallen into it by way of inheritance, and that was how he'd ended up at the top of the corporate ladder at Ouroboros.

At least it was drizzling out, and a thick layer of storm clouds darkened the sky, threatening worse. Nobody would toss me a second glance for keeping my hood up. That was almost as good as moving through the city in the dark of night.

I shed my leather coat, strapped the sword harness on, buckling it across my chest, then put the jacket back on over the invisible sword. Mercy was slender enough that she didn't cause the jacket to bulge or bunch uncomfortably, even if she did warp the line of my back a little. I dug through my backpack next, pulling out a device about the size of a deck of playing cards—a rechargeable handheld electromagnetic pulse generator strong enough to knock out all electronics within a hundred-foot radius. It was one of the few gadgets I had left over from my days as one of the Senate's pet assassins. I'd brought it with me for my time as a rogue in case of an emergency. Well, guess what—this was a god damn emergency.

Hood up, I left the condo, locking the door behind me. I used the stairs, figuring they'd be less traveled, and once I reached the bottom floor, I ducked out through a side entrance, pleased I'd been able to get out of the building without running into a single person. Not even Dom chastised me for breaking my word about leaving the condo the conventional way. It was a good start to the mission.

According to the information from Garth, Carmichael lived in a multimillion-dollar loft on the twenty-second floor of a tower on First Street, downtown. He probably had an insane view of the Puget Sound. A view like that *would* be wasted on a scumbag like him.

Sneaking up to Carmichael's loft was easy enough. The building was part upscale hotel, part condominium, which meant it had maids and room service. I strolled into the employee area like I belonged there, nabbed a room service uniform that consisted of black trousers, a maroon chef's coat, and a stupid little maroon hat off a rack of identical uniforms, and ducked into the employee locker room to slip everything on over my clothes. I ended up looking a little husky, but otherwise pretty nondescript.

I took the service elevator up, keeping my head down to keep my face off of any security cameras, and was on the twenty-second floor in no time. I knocked on Carmichael's door, the last at the end of a windowless hall, hoping he wasn't home, and waited for a minute. When nobody answered, I unbuttoned my chef's coat and reached into the pocket of my leather jacket, pressing the switch that would activate the EMP generator. I counted down in my mind.

Five . . . four . . . three . . . two . . .

The lights in the hallway flickered, then went out, leaving me in not complete darkness, but something that would seem so to human eyes. There was just enough light coming in through a window around the corner and sneaking out under the four other doorways along the hallway that I could see well enough. Barely.

The lights and security systems would be down for a couple minutes. I had to work fast.

I knelt before Carmichael's door and pulled out the only other thing in that pocket—an invisible-ink marker, the kind that only shows up under a black light. I didn't want to tip anyone off to the extent of the magic I could work. If I did that, I could say adios to my biggest advantage.

I uncapped the marker and wrote on the door, just below the handle: *UNLOCK*. It was a shot in the dark. Literally. *BURN* had worked on the Ouroboros scientist last week, but that had also been a basic matter of heat. This was another area of physics entirely, and I had no clue if my brand of magic held any power over movement or mechanics at all, let alone whether or not I had enough juice to accomplish something as small as unlocking a door.

I wrote "UNLOCK" all around the handle, over and over, and then I held my breath. "Come on," I whispered. "Work, damn it!"

I twisted the door handle. It was still locked. I wasn't surprised; there'd been no zing of primal electricity. No hint of that energy that could only be called *magic*.

With a faint groan, I rested my forehead against the door. I'd have to do this the old-fashioned way. Which I sucked at, because back in my Senate-condoned breaking-and-entering days, I'd always been able to rely on Mari to create a key out of *anti-At*.

"I might need your help here, Dom," I said as I pulled a lock-picking kit from my sweatshirt pocket. Doubling up on outerwear has its perks—extra storage being number one on the list.

"You know what to do," my big brother said. *"Just remember, it's all about feel. Locate each of the pins first, then get started."*

I inserted a small, metal tension wrench into the lock on the handle, then added the lock pick and held my breath. I pushed the farthest pin up, feeling it click into place, and turned the wrench in the lock, then went to work on the next pin. I was sweating by the time I'd worked through the final three and had the thing unlocked, and I wasn't even done. There was still the deadbolt to deal with.

I rose up on my knees and fit the tools into the upper lock. I worked through the first three pins pretty quickly, but even so, the florescent lights flickered when I was on the fourth pin. I turned the lock with the tension wrench and allowed myself a deep breath. One more pin to go.

I stiffened when I heard the snick of someone unlocking one of the doors farther up the hallway. "Shit!" I redoubled my efforts on the deadbolt.

The lights flickered again, working up the courage to shine on. As soon as they were back online, it would be only a matter of seconds until the cameras followed.

The final pin clicked into place, and I turned the wrench,

exhaling in relief when the deadbolt slid free. I twisted the door handle and pushed the door open, slipping into the loft just as the door up the hallway opened. I snagged the case for my lock-picking kit, pulled my arm in through the crack, and shut the door. I sat on the ashy hardwood floor in the entryway to Carmichael's loft, breathing hard and sweating like I'd just sprinted all the way up here using the stairs.

"That was way too close," I said to Dom.

"You made it . . ."

I snorted in reply. While I waited for my breathing and heartbeat to slow, I fished Garth's phone out of my right pocket and checked the time. It was a quarter till five. I had no clue when Carmichael would be home—assuming he truly wasn't here already. But I figured I was safe; if he'd been home, the sound of the door opening should've drawn him out, if my knock hadn't. Best to make sure, though.

I hoisted myself up off the ground and moved as quietly as possible into the loft. Considering my rubber soles and that I was naturally light-footed, my footsteps were almost silent despite my combat boots.

The loft was very open concept, the kitchen, dining area, and living space all blending together, much like in Garth's condo, only on a grander scale. Carmichael had at least four times as much space as Garth, and plenty of furniture and decor to fill it. How he'd managed to find so much stuff that was both modern and tacky was beyond me, but—shiny, cherry-red plastic *S*-shaped dining room chairs? And a refrigerator door that doubled as a chalkboard? Really?

My lip curled, and I moved on to the master suite, a space that was sectioned off not by walls, but by three stairs leading up to a raised platform. I checked the master bathroom and the closet, then headed down a short hallway that led to a powder room, a guest room with another full bath, a study, and a utility room with laundry machines that looked like they'd never been used. Like, literally, they still had the stickers sealing the doors shut.

Nobody was home, that much was clear, so I headed back into the main living area to prepare for Carmichael's arrival. I lost the polyester room service garb, then took off my coat, sword harness, and sweatshirt, laying it all out on the kitchen table. I wasn't too worried about Carmichael seeing my stuff and bolting. By the time he was in the door, it would already be too late for him. I set Garth's phone on the table beside my jacket, then tucked the lock-picking tools back into their little case and returned it to my sweatshirt pocket.

I gave the loft a slow scan and exhaled heavily. "Nothing to do now but wait," I said, both to myself and to Dom. I was already bored. "Gah . . . this is the worst part."

"I always enjoyed the waiting," Dom said. *"It gave me a chance to collect my thoughts, to center myself. To come to peace within myself with the fact that I was about to take a life, so the guilt wouldn't crush me once the deed was done."*

Have I mentioned that Dom spent centuries as Heru's go-to assassin? Where those darker arts were concerned, he was the best of the best. But he'd had his fill of killing long ago, and he'd given it up in exchange for assisting Heru in other ways, namely by interrogating and torturing his enemies. Dom's well-known distaste for killing was one of the things that made him such an effective interrogator. His subjects could always be certain that death wouldn't end the pain, not while Dom was still in the room.

I was lucky enough to be one of the few he'd taken under his wing. He'd invested a shit-ton of time and energy in me, teaching me everything he knew. I wasn't quite as good as him—or as good as he'd been when he was still technically alive—but I was close.

"At least Carmichael's got a killer view," I said, crossing the living room between a couch that I thought might actually be made of a solid piece of wood and a zebra-striped bearskin rug. The general shape gave away the fact that it wasn't an actual zebra. So did the bear head. "This place is practically waterfront."

I stopped at the window, appreciating a beautiful thing when I saw it. Even with the overcast sky and the shortened line of sight due to the rain, the Sound was still as stunning as ever. The loft's view was a hell of a lot better than its interior, that was for damn sure. I stood there, admiring the Puget Sound in all of its gray, slightly gloomy glory, for what felt like eons.

Until I heard the sound of a key being stuck into one of the locks I'd just picked.

Snapping into action, I turned away from the window and rushed into the kitchen. The fridge was the nearest thing to the entryway, so I stood with my back to the slate door and listened as Carmichael unlocked the deadbolt. He was taking forever. Probably because he was also talking on the phone—something about a vote tomorrow. A *coup*, he called it.

He opened the door, then shut and relocked it, and just like that, I had him trapped. The amount of time it would take him to unlock and open the door inward was about twice as long as it would take me to slam him face-first against it.

I smiled to myself. I loved it when they made it so damn easy.

Of course, I didn't show myself right then and there. I didn't slam him into the door, much as I might have enjoyed it. I couldn't risk whoever was on the other end of the call getting suspicious, let alone Carmichael uttering a full-fledged plea for help. I'd have to threaten him into hanging up, if he didn't do it on his own first. My sword wouldn't work as a means to up the threat, since he couldn't see it. Wouldn't have mattered anyway; Mercy was still on the table, sheathed in her scabbard. My eyes landed on the knife block on the massive island opposite me. Promising, but still too far away.

Luckily, it never came to threats, because Carmichael is an oblivious boob. He brushed right past me and headed into the bedroom area, all the while talking on his phone about how excited he was for the meeting in the morning and how shocked he imagined *she* would look—whoever *she* was.

"Listen, Scott, I gotta go. I've got squash at seven, and my instructor throws a fit if I'm late." He toed off his shiny dress shoes and loosened his tie. "Yeah. Yeah, you too, buddy. See you tomorrow." He tossed the phone onto the bed and headed into the bathroom. The way this was playing out, I couldn't have choreographed the whole thing better myself.

I listened as he continued to undress and turned on the shower, but I waited until I heard the shower's glass door open and shut to follow him into the bathroom. I drew Mercy as I passed the table and picked up Carmichael's phone and pocketed it before I stepped through the doorway into the slightly steamy room. Apparently the guy liked really hot showers.

I sat on the bathroom counter between the double sinks and watched him, my head tilted to the side. He had his back to me.

Mitch Carmichael wasn't an unattractive man. I'd have placed him in his early sixties, and he was in pretty good shape—must've been all the squash he played. His tush was only a little saggy, and I figured he must tan—or fake tan or take a slew of fancy-pants vacations to the tropics—because a white dude like him doesn't get a tan like that during a Seattle winter without some sort of assistance. He's got a full head of salt-and-pepper hair and probably fits into the "silver fox" category.

I watched him shampoo his hair and soap up his body, but I drew the line when he planted one hand on the shower wall and started to stroke himself.

I cleared my throat, loudly.

Carmichael froze.

"Yep," I said, "that wasn't in your mind."

He spun around, nearly falling on the slick tile floor. His half-flaccid penis was more impressive than I'd expected, and I raised a single brow in acknowledgment of that fact. He stood frozen in place, the hot water hitting his back and his hand cupping his man bits. "Who are you and what the fuck are you doing in here?"

My eyebrows rose, and I hopped off the counter. "You don't recognize me?" I approached the shower, stopping at the glass wall to stare at him up close and personal. "From what I understand, my picture's all over the place right now."

Recognition dawned, and his eyes rounded. "You—you're her—Katarina Dubois."

"Also known as . . ."

He mouthed, "*Ink Witch.*"

"Ding-ding-ding," I sang, grinning. "I knew you'd get it eventually." I gave him elevator eyes, the quick, disinterested version. "Why don't you go ahead and rinse off, Mitch, and then we can get started."

His face was flushed from the heat in the shower, but even so, the color seemed to drain from his face. "Get started with what?"

I blinked several times. "Why, finding the truth, of course."

"The truth about what?"

"Aren't you just the nosy Nellie." I tapped the glass wall with the tip of my sword, watching his eyes search for the source of the noise and appreciating his confused expression when he found nothing. "Or would 'eager beaver' be more appropriate?"

Carmichael backed away from the glass wall. "You're insane." He continued backing up until he hit the tile wall.

"Maybe," I said with a nod, not discouraging his conclusion one bit. It's more fun when they think I'm unhinged. "But I'm also the one with an invisible sword, so . . . I'd do what I say, if I were you."

"I have money," Carmichael blurted.

I shrugged one shoulder. "Don't want it."

"Cars . . . stock . . . property . . ."

"I don't want any of that," I said, enunciating each word clearly.

"Well what do you want from me, then?" Carmichael was panicking. I could see it in his wild eyes, hear it in the timbre of his voice. His entire body trembled. Fight-or-flight was kicking in, and he wanted to run. Good; survival mode was good. Right where I wanted him.

I plastered on a plastic smile. "What I want, Mitch, is for you to rinse off and come out here so we can have a little chat." I winked at him. "Don't worry, *buddy*, I'll take things slow. Who knows . . . you might even enjoy yourself."

Some people got off on the bite of pain. Hell, I wasn't opposed to it, myself. It was entirely possible that Carmichael was one such person. It would be amusing for me, but it would be unfortunate for him. I'd have to use more extreme interrogation tactics. Pleasure from pain only stretched so far. Eventually, there was only pain.

CHAPTER TWELVE

As it turned out, Carmichael was *not* a fan of pain. He was about as far from a masochist as a person could be. I duct-taped him to one of those hideous red chairs and set him up near the windows with his back to the glorious view so the backdrop of the Seattle waterfront and the Puget Sound beyond would give me comfort and lend me strength. So it would remind me of why I was here—to protect my beloved city from people like Carmichael.

I left him naked, not because I was overly fond of the sight of him, but because nudity creates insecurity. It's one more barrier cast away, one more protective wall torn down. Being naked in front of others has the tendency to make a person feel exposed, no matter how comfortable they are in their own skin. Especially when those "others" have not-so-nice intentions. It had been Dom's suggestion, and a damn good one at that.

Carmichael cried out when I nicked his left pectoral with Mercy's invisible tip. To be fair, I cut a smidgen deeper than I'd planned, but I was still getting used to the very strange lack of visibility of her sword blade. I knew the feel of her well, but it was becoming all too clear that my sword and I would have to become even more familiar with one another.

"That was just so you'd know the blade is real," I explained to

Carmichael, standing a couple feet away from him. "Every time you lie to me, I'll cut you again. And yes, I'll be able to tell when you're lying." It was true enough; my heightened hearing allowed me to hone in on his heartbeat, and my eyesight was good enough that I could see the level of perspiration on his skin and gauge any change in his pupil size. "We'll keep playing this game until you bleed out or I get all the information I need. Understand?"

Carmichael gulped, his Adam's apple bobbing up and down.

"Alright . . ." I flipped Mercy up and rested the flat of her blade against my right shoulder. "Did you know about the children your SoDo lab was abducting and experimenting on?" I watched him carefully, taking in every part of his response, verbal and otherwise.

"No," he rasped.

"Lie." I slashed a shallow nick across his cheekbone, and he yelped. I planted my hands on my hips and leaned over him. "I gave you fair warning—you lie, you get cut." I gave him *the look*. "You did that to yourself. Now, did you know about the kids?"

Again, Carmichael swallowed roughly, then licked his lips. "Yes, I—I knew about them."

"And did you know about all the research and experiments going on in that lab?"

"Yes," Carmichael admitted. "We all did—all of the board members."

I tutted, tapping the flat of the sword against the side of his face. He flinched at each touch of the smooth, invisible *At* blade. "Don't try to deflect the blame onto them. They're not here. *You* are. I'll get to them later." I returned the sword to my shoulder. "Tell me, Mitch, do you remember a boy named Sammy?"

Carmichael's heart rate leapt, and sweat beaded on his forehead.

I crouched before him, intrigued by his severe reaction. "Answer the question."

"Yes," he said, his voice barely above a whisper. For whatever reason, Sammy meant something to Carmichael. Something big.

"Do you know what was done to Sammy?"

His heart rate spiked again, but it leveled out when he finally answered. "We—they infected him with a—" He shook his head, his brow furrowed. "Not a disease, but something worse."

"Worse, how?"

Again, he shook his head. "I don't know. I wasn't involved much in that project, I swear." Carmichael hesitated for a moment, then his heart rate elevated and he blurted, "Constance." His heart rate remained at that higher level as he continued, "Just her. It was her idea . . . all of it."

With a sigh, I lifted Mercy from my shoulder and rested her tip against Carmichael's ribcage, angling it so the blade pressed in between his fifth and sixth ribs, right below his nipple. Just a little more pressure and I'd break the skin. I gave it that small amount of pressure.

Carmichael yelped.

"Here's the deal, Mitch. I'm going to keep pushing on Mercy here—that's my sword's name—until you tell me the truth, the whole truth, and nothing but the truth." I gave it a moment for the words to sink in. "Who was involved in the project?" He didn't answer right away, and I started to push the blade in deeper. "How long until I puncture your lung, I wonder?"

"All of us," he said. "We all knew about it. Everyone was involved to some degree, but Constance really was project lead on this." He wasn't lying.

"How do I get the cure?" I exerted a little more pressure. "Who has it?"

"I—" Carmichael shook his head vehemently. "I swear I don't know anything about a cure." The truth in his words turned my heart to lead.

I withdrew the blade. A deal was a deal, after all. "That wasn't so hard, was it?"

"Ask him more about the children," Dom said. *"There's something there. When you brought up Sammy—his reaction was too strong."*

I frowned, tilting my head from side to side and tapping Mercy's blade against the outside of my boot as I considered

Dom's suggestion. I wanted to get my hands on Constance and the others before anyone caught wind that I was hunting Ouroboros board members, but a few extra questions couldn't hurt. Besides, if Dom thought this was important . . .

I fixed my stare on Carmichael and stopped the rhythmic tapping. "Let's talk more about Sammy."

Again, the bastard's heart rate spiked. Dom was onto something.

"Cute kid, though when I saw him, he was a little under the weather." Understatement of the year. When I'd seen Sammy, the eight-year-old had been unconscious, his breathing labored and his temperature dangerously high. Now, well . . . at least he wasn't suffering anymore. "Did you spend much time with him?" I asked.

"I—" Carmichael turned his face away from me. "I only met him once."

"And when was that?"

"I don't know. Monday of last week? Tuesday, maybe? It was before they infected him."

"Why?" I narrowed my eyes. "Why is that important?"

"Because I—when we . . . I didn't want to get infected too," Carmichael said through a moan. His shoulders were hunched, and his body shook with the force of his sobs.

"When you *what?*" My hand shot out, and I gripped Carmichael's throat with clawlike fingers, bringing my face centimeters from his. "What did you do to Sammy?" I recalled the headlines about the human trafficking allegations, about the women and children purportedly sold into slavery, and my grip tightened. "Tell me!"

"If—if I do, you—you'll kill me."

Oh, dear gods, no . . .

I clenched my jaw, fingernails digging into his throat. I could feel the tendons and muscles in his neck tensing, the hard tube that was his windpipe straining against my hold. It would be all too easy to crush. Blood oozed from the cuts caused by my nails, and I only squeezed harder. "You deserve to die," I said, tearing up with the force of my rage. "I wish there was a hell, so you could burn in it for the rest of eternity." I sucked in a shaky breath. "But there's not."

I released him and straightened, raising my boot to the seat of the chair between his thighs. I moved his flaccid penis out of the way with the toe of my boot and slammed the sword blade home.

Carmichael howled in pain. He didn't stop howling until I was finished and his family jewels lay in a bloody mess on the hardwood floor. He'd never touch another kid again.

"Enjoy your hell, you ball-less sack of shit," I said, then spat on him. I turned away and stalked into the kitchen, where I started to pace. "Dom, can you let the Bainbridge folks know to expect a prisoner? I'm going to send him to the dungeon." It was under the massive garage in the Heru compound, a separate building from the main house where Lex, Heru, and some of the others lived, and it was about as stereotypical as a dungeon could get with all the stone and iron and generally dank atmosphere. I didn't want to risk the possibility that this sick fucker might cross paths with Reni, Lex and Heru's three-year-old girl. "And let them know everything we learned about him, will you? I'm sure they can get more useful info out of him."

"Of course," Dom said. *"But are certain you'll be able to create a gateway?"*

I heaved a breath, then another. I could practically feel the magical energy gathering strength within my *sheut*. "Oh, yeah." I shook out my hands and cracked my neck. "I got this."

"Very well. When should they expect him?"

I was quiet for a moment, estimating how long it would take me to draw the dungeon. "About an hour," I said finally. I grabbed a canister of chalk from the counter beside the fridge—seriously, who the fuck has a chalkboard for a fridge door, anyway—and stalked back into the living room area. I shoved the coffee table and ridiculous zebra-striped bearskin rug out of the way and knelt on the hardwood floor to get to work.

Once I was finished drawing the dismal dungeon and felt the

telltale spike of otherworldly energy, I stood and moved behind Carmichael's chair. I raised my foot and planted my boot on the back of his chair, kicking hard and savoring his scream as he fell through the gateway. All that was left of him was a puddle of blood and his now-useless balls.

I considered cleaning up the mess for all of two seconds, opting instead to use the hideous rug to smear blood onto the drawing, rendering it inert. I didn't give two shits whether or not someone found the mess. Carmichael got what he deserved. Better than he deserved, because he was still alive.

"I should've killed him," I whispered. I shook my head and stared up at the exposed ceiling beams to keep myself from crying under the force of my regret. I was suddenly more disappointed in myself than I'd ever been in my entire life. It didn't matter that Carmichael likely had a wealth of useful information about the Ouroboros Corporation's other nefarious projects, not after what he'd done.

I balled my hands into fists and squeezed my eyes shut. "I should have killed him!" It wasn't a scream or a yell or a shout. It was a roar.

CHAPTER THIRTEEN

It was maybe six by the time I left Carmichael's building. I didn't even attempt to draw another gateway; creating the gateway to Bainbridge had left me completely drained. The sun had set, dusk had come and gone, and the moon was blocked by a thick layer of clouds, leaving behind a darkness better suited to the middle of the night. Which was well enough, because I looked like I'd just murdered someone. Which was extra frustrating, considering the knot in my stomach was there because I *hadn't* killed Carmichael. It was there because I'd let him live.

The trip back to Garth's was a rain-soaked blur. I walked a few blocks, then hot-wired a little crotch rocket and rode the bike up slick streets to Capitol Hill. I ditched the bike in an alleyway a few blocks from Garth's condo and skulked the rest of the way there through the puddles, sticking to the shadows between streetlights.

I pulled up short when I reached the glass double doors marking the entrance to the building. "Shit," I hissed, backstepping a few yards. I'd totally forgotten about the doorman sitting behind the little reception desk. This was the only exterior door I had a key for, and I couldn't exactly tromp through the lobby with blood smeared all over my clothes.

I couldn't break in the same way I'd left, either—that door was exit only; no keyhole at all, so picking the lock wasn't even an option, and Garth wouldn't be home for another hour or two, so I couldn't call him to come down and open that door from the inside. There was a garage underneath the building. It had a roll-down steel and glass door at street level that opened only when the condo residents came and went. I'd never been down there, but I didn't see that I had any other choice.

Hands stuffed into my pockets, hood up, and head down, I made my way around the corner to the east side of the block and ducked into the deepest shadows near the garage door. And waited . . .

The waiting was awkward, because it was still early enough that the street was busy, even if it was dark out, and because the rain was falling steady as ever. I felt like a creeper. Probably because I looked like a creeper, no matter how nonchalant and unobtrusive I tried to be. But at least I wasn't alone. There was a genuine homeless dude chilling in a trash bag poncho on the ground beyond the far side of the garage door. We were like a match set, he and I.

After a good long while, there was a beeping sound from within the garage, a mechanism clicked over, and the door slowly lifted. A dark sedan slowed on the road and waited for the door to open all the way. It wasn't ideal—I'd have preferred someone leaving rather than someone coming home—but at least this got me in through the gate and off the street.

I waited until the car had pulled through all the way, gave the driver a few seconds to get deeper into the garage, then slunk in and crouched down between the nearest two cars. I waited there, hidden and silent, until I heard the car door, followed by the beep of a car alarm and the footsteps of the new arrival leaving their car. I waited a little longer, listening to the sound of a key fitting into a lock and the gentle whoosh of a door opening on well-oiled hinges. And then I waited a little longer, giving whoever it was some time to move on. Patience is a virtue, after all, even if it's not usually one of mine.

After a ten count, I stood and walked along behind the

bumpers of parked cars, not too slow and not too fast, like I owned the place. Like I belonged. I doubted any cameras could pick up on the bloodstains, and I didn't want to draw attention to myself by sneaking around and looking generally sketchy.

As I neared the door into the building, I pulled my lock-picking kit out of my pocket and readied the two little tools I would need. I had the door unlocked in less than thirty seconds and slipped into the building. I tossed a glance over my shoulder when the garage door triggered again and picked up the pace, heading for the metal door to the stairwell.

The second I shut the door to Garth's unit, I was already toeing off my boots, even as I locked the deadbolt. I shrugged out of my leather coat and hung it on the back of a barstool, then unbuckled my sword harness and slung it over the coat. I unzipped my sweatshirt and pulled off my tank top, dropping both straight into the trash can beside the fridge, followed by my jeans, socks, underwear, and bra. I could never wear them again; they would always remind me of that sick fuck Carmichael, of my failure to end his pathetic existence. Even if I managed to get the clothes clean, the memory would remain a dark stain. Besides, the last thing I wanted was to leave traces of that bastard's DNA in Garth's washer. Someday soon, someone would get into Carmichael's loft, and they'd find the bloody scene I'd left there. I wouldn't risk implicating Garth in any of this.

Barefoot and naked, I hurried through the bedroom and into the bathroom to turn on the shower. While I waited for the water to heat up, I looked at my reflection in the mirror. My straight, dark hair hung around my face and past my shoulders in strings wet with a combination of blood and rain. Be warned that when cutting an asshole's balls off, the blood can and will get everywhere.

The bathroom was steamy and the mirror started to fog over before I shook out of my daze and realized the shower had been running for plenty long enough to warm up. I opened the glass door, and only when the hot water hit my skin did I notice how chilled I was. That I was shivering.

"Little sister—"

"Not now, Dom," I snapped.

I gritted my teeth to fend off the sudden swell of frustrated, disgusted tears and snatched the bar of soap off the little built-in recess in the shower's slate-tiled wall. I lathered it between my hands, then started scrubbing my body. I scrubbed and lathered, lathered and scrubbed. I attacked my hair with a vengeance. I washed myself until my skin felt raw and stung when the water touched it. Until the soap was little more than a sliver. Only then did I set what was left of the bar down. Only then did I feel even remotely clean.

I placed my hand on the wall beside the recess and bowed my head, letting my hair act as a dark curtain shielding me from the world. Letting the water cascade all around me.

I should've killed him. The thought buzzed around in my skull like a drunken bee. "Damn it!" I yelled, slapping my hand against the wall hard enough that it made my palm throb. I may have broken something. I didn't care. *I should've killed him.*

My shoulders shook, and my whole being caved in from the soul out. Horrors danced through my mind, taunting me. I couldn't help but imagine whatever ghastly, perverted things Carmichael had done to poor little Sammy. The possibilities haunted me. Nauseated me. It didn't matter that he could still be useful, that he still had information we could use, even if none of it had anything to do with the disease.

I should've killed him.

I leaned in, resting my forehead against the shower wall, then turned, wedging my shoulder in the corner. I slid down along the wall until I was sitting on the floor, one knee pulled up to my chest, the other leg outstretched. Forgotten. I leaned the side of my head against the wall and stared at the glass door, watching the rivulets of water stream down in stops and starts.

I should've killed him.

CHAPTER FOURTEEN

"Kat?" It was Garth, calling out for me from the other room.

I was shivering again. I was still on the tile floor and the showerhead still rained down on me, though the water was no longer even remotely warm. I could hear Garth's footsteps drawing nearer. He was in the bedroom now. He was almost to the bathroom.

"Should I join you in th—" He stopped in the doorway, his arm partially outstretched to pet the cat perched on the counter, his words halting right along with the rest of him. The shirt of his uniform was unbuttoned and hanging open, displaying the bullet-proof vest he always wore underneath it. He stood there, frozen by shock for barely a second.

"Jesus, Kat." He lunged into the bathroom and yanked the shower door open, reaching in to turn off the water. He stepped into the shower, shoes and all, and crouched down before me. "What happened?" His hands hovered around me, like he was afraid I was physically injured. Like it would matter if I was. "What's wrong? Are you hurt?"

I watched him, took in his concern and confusion, wrapped them around me like the fact that he gave a shit about me might soothe the invisible wound caused by my razor-sharp shame. "No

—" The word was barely a whisper, and I cleared my throat. "I'm fine. I—" I squeezed my eyelids shut, but it only made Carmichael's face clearer in my mind's eye. It only sharpened the sting of regret.

Garth's fingertips touched my cheek, a gentle caress following the contours of my cheekbone and jaw. "Kat . . ." He was quiet for a moment. "What can I do to help you?"

Much as I wished there were magic words he could utter, some secret touch that could cure what ailed me, I knew better. There was nothing he could do but let me wallow until the mood passed. I opened my mouth, intending to tell him as much, but the words caught in my throat. I sat up ramrod straight and snapped my head to the left to stare at the slate-tiled wall like I could see through it to the kitchen and the front door.

People. I could hear them, out in the hallway. They were moving slowly, quietly, but I could still make out the sounds of them arranging themselves around the door to Garth's condo. There were only two reasons for a group of people to arrange themselves around a door like that—either they were setting up to sing Christmas carols, or they were planning to bust the door down. I narrowed my eyes. There had to be at least eight of them fanning out in the hallway, maybe more.

"Wha—" Garth started, but I slapped my hand over his mouth.

"Someone's here," I hissed. I heard the sound of clicking metal. A terrible, ill-boding sound. An unmistakable sound. Guns. Automatic. Big.

The door crashed open, and I had Garth's gun drawn before he even had a chance to reach for it. "Get down," I mouthed, anticipating impending gunfire.

Eva jumped off the counter and low-crawled deeper into the bathroom to hide behind the toilet.

Garth caught my wrist as I squeezed past him through the open shower door. "You can't go out there!" he whispered, his words no less vehement for their quietness.

"I have to." Whoever just broke in—whether they were sent by the Senate or Initiative Industries, the Ouroboros Corporation's parent conglomerate—they weren't going to let us just hide out back here, and they certainly weren't going to let us slip away. They would find us, and they would kill us.

I'd known it was a bad idea to stay with Garth. I'd known I would be endangering him, and I'd done it anyway. It was my fault that they were here, whoever they were. This was on me, one hundred percent. I owed it to him to make it right.

One of the intruders entered the bedroom, an armed mercenary—human—from the looks of him. I could see his reflection in the mirror. He was armed to the teeth and dressed in all black, from his flak jacket down to his cargo pants and combat boots. I swept the gun around and aimed, threatening to put a bullet in his head before he could train his gun on me. It probably helped that I was naked. That *might* be what allowed me to get the jump on him.

The merc froze, a quick blink his only movement.

"Why are you here?" I asked, feeling like a moron for wanting to give him the benefit of the doubt. If his orders weren't to kill me, I'd let him live. I *wanted* to leave him alive—he was only human, after all, and this life was it for him and his mortal soul—but not at the expense of my life, let alone Garth's. *He* was human, too, and one that I cared about. If humans were going to be dying in this condo today, he wouldn't be one of them. Not on my watch.

The merc didn't answer. He just stood there, staring at me.

Not a moment later, one of his buddies tossed a small metal can into the room. It started spewing a foggy gas.

I reacted without thinking. I shifted my aim lower and pulled the trigger, shooting the guy I had in my sights in the thigh, then swinging around to get his buddy in the shoulder. I backstepped and slammed the bathroom door shut. "I think it's tear gas," I told Garth, crouching off to the side in case the other mercs got gun happy. I grabbed a bath towel off the towel rack and stuffed it into the crack under the door. "There's eight, maybe ten mercs out there." They wouldn't have long after that gunshot. Someone would call the cops, which meant the intruders would get desperate, quick. Not great for us.

Garth nodded, impressing me with his sharp focus. He wasn't dazed in the slightest, and the glint in his eyes told me he wouldn't go down without a fight.

"Here," I said, reaching into the shower and handing him back his gun. As I turned away from him, I slammed the side of my fist down on the iron-esque pole of the now-empty towel rack, knocking it free. Thankfully, Garth had splurged for high-end fixtures; the thing didn't just look like iron, it *was* iron.

Now that we were both armed, Garth with his sidearm and me with a two-foot, hollow iron pole, we'd at least be able to put up a fight. Of course, we'd be sitting ducks stuck in here, little more than target practice for the mercs outside.

"Look up, little sister," Dom said. *"People rarely expect an attack from above."*

I glanced up at the ceiling. This was a top-floor unit; there should be just enough room for me to crawl around up there. I climbed up onto the vanity counter and shoved the iron pole through the drywall ceiling. "Thanks, Dom," I said under my breath.

Garth ducked, his hands going over his head. "What are you doing?"

"Keep them distracted, OK?" The corner of my mouth lifted, and I quirked my head to the side. "And try not to get shot. I'm going out a different way . . ."

I stared up at the ragged opening overhead. It was just under two feet wide; plenty of room for me to fit through. I reached up, balancing the iron bar across the two-by-fours framing the ceiling, then grasped the supports. I glanced down at Garth. "Give me a boost?"

Dubious, Garth crawled out of the shower and stood, crouching. He kept shooting furtive glances at the door. Not surprising, because I could hear the mercenaries gathering in the bedroom. We had a handful of seconds before that door came down, and unless I managed to get up into the ceiling and surprise them from above and behind, we'd both be dead in not much longer. I just needed Garth to hold them off for a fraction of a second, and holding them off might include taking fire. It was risky, but we didn't really have any other choice.

Garth wrapped a hand around either of my ankles and lifted. "Be careful," he said, his voice polished gravel.

I renewed my grip on the two-by-fours, flexed my arms, and pulled myself up into a maze of ducts, wiring, and insulation. I sort of bear-crawled in the general direction of the bedroom. With any luck, the mercs wouldn't have a chance to do anything to Garth until it was too late and I was already on them. With any luck . . .

I'd just reached the ceiling vent in the bedroom when there was a crash, and the first crack of gunfire exploded below me. Heart pounding, I held my breath and smashed through the drywall ceiling, dropping almost directly on top of one of the intruders. The gas burned my eyes, but so long as I continued to hold my breath, my lungs were safe. It was a short "so long as . . ."

I yanked off the merc's gas mask as we both crumpled to the floor. Tears streamed down my cheeks, and my eyelids slammed shut reflexively. I forced them open, squinting around me, but the thick yellowish-white gas was almost impossible to see through in the evening darkness.

The guy I'd landed on was gasping and sputtering. He'd hardly been prepared to fend off an attack from above. Taking advantage of his momentary confusion, I captured his neck between my thighs, and as I waited for him to pass out, kicking and clawing at my legs, I secured his gas mask over my face.

The one good thing about the sickly opaque gas was that it rendered my opponents just as blind as it did me. They couldn't see, but they also couldn't hear nearly as well as I could. Advantage: me.

As I sucked in a much-needed clean breath of air, I heard competing rat-tat-tats of automatic gunfire and hoped it meant Garth had managed to snag one of their bigger guns.

Even as I was waiting for my first victim to lose consciousness, another of the mercs coalesced out of the poisonous fog, automatic rifle searching for a target. I swung the iron pole like a baseball bat. His knee snapped, and his leg collapsed. I elbowed him in the side of the head almost as soon as he was on the floor, and he went limp immediately. I smacked him one more time, for good measure. The guy I held in a choke hold between my legs followed his buddy into unconsciousness a moment later. I relaxed my legs and kicked him away.

Crawling closer to the guy with the screwed-up leg, I yanked off his gas mask and tossed it in the general direction of the bathroom, then stood, iron rod in hand. Silently, I moved around the room, taking out mercenaries before they even realized I was on them. Like taking candy from a baby. It was almost too easy. The hard part was dispatching them without actually killing them. I had no idea who these guys were or why they were here, but I doubted it was anything more complicated than simply following orders. A simple exchange of money.

I found the final intruder grappling with Garth on the bathroom floor. Neither had gas masks on, and both men's eyes were swollen shut. Even as they fought each other, they struggled to breathe. Exhausted, a little beat up, and eyeballs and skin raw from exposure to the gas, I whacked the mercenary on the back of the head with my trusty iron pole. He went limp instantly.

Garth lay there beneath the merc for a second, coughing and choking, then rolled to the side, depositing the guy on the floor beside him.

Half blindly, I searched the floor and countertop for the gas mask I'd tossed in there just moments earlier. I found it in the sink and handed it to Garth. The gas didn't seem to be lethal, just really damn painful, so I figured I'd been right about my tear gas assessment and that he would survive. Not that that meant he had to keep wallowing in the toxic stuff.

"Thanks," Garth rasped before he secured the mask over his face. He looked like hell, all swollen and oozy. I probably didn't look much better, if the way I felt was any indication. He practiced breathing, slowly pulling in more and more air until he could take long, full, deep breaths. "What now?" he asked, bleary-eyed and weary.

I grabbed his hand and pulled him out of the bathroom. "Now, we get the hell out of here."

CHAPTER FIFTEEN

The tear gas was quite a bit thinner in the living room, and it cleared out pretty quickly once we shut the bedroom door, opened up the windows, and turned on the kitchen vent. The door to the hallway was open, but there were no gawkers. Any initial snoopers probably ran as soon as they caught sight of the armed mercenaries, and any other potential lookie-loos certainly fled at the sound of gunfire.

"We need to rinse you off," Garth said, gripping my arm and pulling me toward the kitchen. We'd both discarded our masks as soon as we were out of the bedroom. "You're covered in chemical burns."

"I'll heal," I said, twisting my arm so it slipped free. Considering the singed state of my skin, a few layers might have slipped free as well. But, damn it, it was my turn to grip his arm and drag *him* somewhere. "What we need to do is get the hell out of here. There's bound to be more of them." Plus, the mercs that had only been knocked unconscious wouldn't stay that way forever. I pulled him to the wall, where my drawing of the kids' sick room in the Tent District was still intact, if not exactly as I'd left it.

There appeared to be some sort of an evacuation going on, with pairs of people carrying kids out of the room on their cots. I gripped my throat and muttered, "Oh, shit," under my breath. The tear gas must've passed through the gateway. Those poor kids . . .

Garth stared at the living drawing on his wall, his eyes saucers and his expression rapt. "What *is* this?"

I figured it was best to work with a minimalistic approach, explanation-wise. "Think of it like a doorway," I said, right before I pushed him through the wall. He stumbled onto the other side, then turned around and marched right back toward me. And then he disappeared.

I smirked, though my heart wasn't in it. One-way gateways, and all that . . .

"Find Dorman," I called through the gateway, hoping he could hear me. "I'll join you soon." A moment later, I retrieved the can of touch-up paint from the shelf above the washer and drier in the laundry closet and splashed the entire can on the wall above the ink-drawn gateway. The moment the off-white paint dripped across the drawing, the whole thing crackled like a live wire touching water, and in a blink, it reverted to being just a picture. Just lines drawn in black permanent ink. Nothing more.

I rushed back to the couch and opened up my backpack, pulling out a wad of freshly washed clothing. I dressed as quickly as possible, ignoring the singed state of my skin, shoved my feet into my boots without bothering to tie the laces, strapped on the sword harness without buckling it, then grabbed my backpack and leather jacket and the bag filled with my soiled clothes from the Carmichael incident. Hands full, I ran to the broken-in door.

"Garth has a personal vehicle, does he not?" Dom said. That Dom, always the voice of sound thinking and clear reason.

I paused, then backpedaled to grab the set of car keys sitting in a carved wooden bowl on the kitchen island. Driving out of here would be a whole lot less conspicuous than leaving by foot.

A muffled feline yowl brought me up short just as I was passing through the doorway. Eva. I'd forgotten about her in all the chaos. From the sound of her desperate cry, she was somewhere back in the bedroom.

I hesitated. I could just go. I *should* go. Eva would probably be fine, and I sure as hell didn't have time to wrangle a terrified cat. But even as I took a step into the hallway, I thought of Garth and how devastated he would be if I let something happen to her.

"Oh, come on," I grumbled, dropping my burdens and rushing back into the condo. I grabbed the cat carrier from the laundry closet and ran into the bedroom. The gas was still pretty thick in there, and my eyes stung anew. "Eva?" I called out, coughing as I scanned the ripped-up, body-strewn space. "Here, kitty kitty . . ."

Another yowl. I was pretty sure it came from the cabinets under the bathroom counter.

I dashed into the bathroom and crouched down, opening one of the cabinet doors. Sure enough, there was the little calico cat, huddled in the back corner, relatively unharmed. *Thank the gods . . .*

I didn't have time for caution. If she bit me, so be it. I would heal. I reached into the cabinet and yanked her out by the scruff. Thankfully, Eva was little more than a tense, trembling dead weight. I shoved her into the carrier and tucked the whole thing under my arm like an oversized football, then fled from the condo, snagging my leather coat, sword, and the trash bag on my way out.

I took the stairwell down to the basement and was already clicking the disarm button on the car alarm's key fob before I'd even opened the door to the underground garage. I didn't know what Garth drove when off duty, but not knowing didn't make me miss a beat. I pressed the button over and over as I jogged farther into the garage, following the *beep-beep beep-beep*.

"Hot damn," I said with a breathy laugh when I finally honed in on his car.

I'm not sure what I was expecting—maybe an SUV or a truck. Not the case. Garth owned a classic beauty, a black and chrome Mustang. The muscle car had clearly been restored and retrofitted with modern amenities like an alarm, because it couldn't have been a day older than 1967.

Pushing stringy, tangled wet hair out of my face, I unlocked the driver's side door and flung my bag, jacket, and the condemning trash across the center console to the passenger seat. I strapped in Eva's carrier in the backseat before sliding into the car myself. After I stuck the key into the ignition, I shot a quick glance around, then twisted my wrist. The engine roared to life in the cavernous space.

After a second or two, the Mustang settled on a low, thrumming rumble . . . until I put her into gear and maneuvered her out of her parking spot. I was surrounded by thunder and vibrating power, which only increased as I pulled out of the garage and onto the street. When I shifted into second and pressed on the gas pedal once more, a thrill rushed through me. The old girl had kick, and I kind of loved her.

I was tempted to really let her open up on the freeway, but it was too risky. I needed to fly under the radar, and getting pulled over was pretty much the opposite of that. My face was all over the news, after all. There was no doubt that any traffic cop would recognize me, and then I'd have to fight my way out of yet another sticky situation, and I really didn't want to beat up anyone else for just doing their job. Everybody needs money, after all. It's the world we live in.

Traffic was shitty pretty much everywhere, not that it was really any surprise—weekdays from two thirty to seven in the evening are pretty much the worst times to drive in Seattle. Aside from the mornings. And any time there was an accident. Or just someone getting pulled over for speeding.

Most times are the worst times for driving in Seattle, and this time was no different.

I lasted on the freeway for a single stretch between exits before getting off and navigating my way through the maze of stoplights and one-way streets downtown. It took a ridiculous amount of time for me to make it a few miles, but finally I was parking the Mustang in an abandoned gravel lot beside the freeway, maybe a quarter mile southeast of the Tent District's eastern gate. I was so close to meeting back up with Garth. So close to sending him away, for good.

I must've been sleepwalking the past twelve hours. It was the only explanation for why I'd let anything happen between us. For why I'd thought any kind of an *anything* between us was a possibility. He was good and pure, and his life had been free and easy before I'd come along. His life had been safe. I was toxic to him, as bad as the tear gas, and the longer he hung around me, the more likely it was that he'd get dead. I'd let my heart take over, and that had been a mistake. It was time to start thinking with my brain . . . and *only* with my brain.

I buckled my sword harness, shrugged into my leather coat, still splattered with sticky blood, zipped it almost up to my neck, and settled my backpack on my shoulders. Hands in my pockets and head down, I hurried toward the Tent District's eastern gate.

"Would you mind unzipping a bit so I can see where we're going?" I sucked in a breath, startled by Dom's voice. He'd returned to the Bainbridge mirror for the drive to get Lex and the others up to speed and to get an update on Carmichael, and I always felt antsier when he wasn't the voice of reason in my head.

"Please tell me keeping that sick fuck alive was worth it," I said as I unzipped my coat a good six inches.

"Neffe did a rough patch job on his"—Dom cleared his throat —*"wound. She loaded him with morphine, and he's been very chatty ever since. He might not have been directly involved with the infection, but his dirty little fingers were dipped into enough other projects to make him a wealth of information, not only on what Ouroboros is up to, but Initiative Industries as well."*

I pressed my lips into a thin, grim smile. "That's something, at least." The reality that Carmichael might be able to do more good alive than dead—for now—eased some of the regret and disgust knotted up in my belly. Some, but nowhere near all of it. I still wanted him to suffer, and a morphine-induced haze was a far cry from that.

"You must be more cautious, little sister," Dom said. *"It would seem the board of directors took your threat more seriously than we'd expected. They must have extra eyes on the board members."* It was his argument for

how the mercenaries had found me in the first place—they'd seen me leaving Mitch Carmichael's building.

I stopped across the street from the eastern opening in the razor wire–topped chain-link fence surrounding the Tent District and placed my hands on my hips, shaking my head. "But then wouldn't they have stopped me when I was actually working on Carmichael?" I started pacing, a dozen steps down the sidewalk, then a dozen back up. "Maybe it was an anonymous tip? Someone easily could've spotted me leaving his place. I looked like hell . . ."

"Perhaps," Dom said. *"But that would suggest that the Senate and/or Ouroboros or Initiative Industries have people inside the police force, which is just as disturbing."*

I paused, considering his words, then continued pacing. "We have to assume they do. Which means Garth can't go back to work. They know he's involved now." I wasn't sure if "they" was the Senate, the pharmaceutical giant, Ouroboros, or its conglomerate parent company, Initiative Industries. I'd pissed off all three with my revenge stunt a week ago—*totally worth it*—so it could be any of them. Or *all* of them. Regardless, Garth now had a big fat target on his back, too, thanks to me. "They'll kill him," I told Dom.

"I'm in agreement. This just goes to show how recognizable you are now." He was quiet for a moment. *"Perhaps it is time to move out of the Seattle area. There are many other neutral Nejerets to visit outside of Seattle. You know Heru will provide any resources you might require."*

But I was shaking my head before he'd even finished what he was saying. Not that he could see me. "I can't go anywhere until we stop this disease. Otherwise, all of Dorman's people are as good as out. We have to show them that Heru's side is the right side . . . that human lives mean something to us."

Dom was quiet for a long moment.

I picked up the mirrored pendant and held it away from my chest so I could see his face. "You know I'm right. I can't stop until the board tells me what I need to know. Dorman may have the infection contained for now, but who's to say that'll last? And if it gets out . . ."

"Perhaps you are right," Dom acceded, his shadowed, silvery stare hard. *"But taking on the Ouroboros board on your own is suicide. They'll be watching for you now. They'll be waiting."*

I smirked. "Who said anything about taking them on alone?"

"I don't count."

I sent him an air kiss. "Come on, Dom, you're worth a thousand allies." I shrugged one shoulder. "But I wasn't talking about you."

Dom shook his head slowly. *"Then to whom, may I ask, were you referring?"*

I blinked my lashes several times, eyes opened wide with mock innocence. "Why, the most powerful Nejeret on earth, of course."

"You can't trust Nik," Dom said, voice flat and cold. *"He's unstable. His mind snapped when he fought with Re."*

"Pffft," I said, waving a hand dismissively. "'Unstable' is my middle name."

"I'm serious, Kat."

I stared at him for a moment, considering his warning. He only used my name when shit was about to get real. Or had already gotten real. Or was in the middle of the whole "real" situation. Regardless, his use of my name was really fucking notable. Plus, he kind of had a point about Nik and the whole "instability" thing.

Nik had shared his body with the old god Re for thousands of years. Their coexistence had been peaceful, collaborative, even, until two decades ago, when the two beings had their first—and last—disagreement. Over whether I should die. Re snapped—like, literally lost his marbles and went full-on psycho—and Nik entered into some sort of an internal battle with him, leaving their souls deadlocked and his physical body comatose. When the new gods finally pulled Re's soul from Nik's body a few years back, Nik regained consciousness . . . and promptly vanished. He'd been in the wind ever since. Until two weeks ago, when he showed up in my shop with news of Dom's disappearance. Part of me was still holding my breath, waiting for him to disappear once more.

Nik might be the most powerful living being on earth, but it was entirely possible that Dom was right and that his mind was broken. Which would also make him the most *dangerous* being on earth.

"I need him," I told Dom. "There's no one else."

"There's you," he said. *"In this case, going it alone might be the better option."*

I shook my head slowly, sadly. "Not this time." My partnership with Mari had soured near the end, leaving a bad taste in my mouth. I preferred to work alone. Thrived on it. But this time, I knew *I* wouldn't be enough, and my days of suicide missions were over. I gave a shit about what happened to me.

I was ready for a partner. I was ready for Nik.

CHAPTER SIXTEEN

I didn't bother with zipping up my coat to hide Dom this time. I wanted him with me, ears *and* eyes; I needed every weapon I had for what was to come. The board of directors would give me the cure, end of discussion. I was done pussyfooting around.

Decision about working with Nik made—assuming he'd agree to it—I marched across the street and through the eastern gate into the Tent District, making a beeline for the former air control tower, where I hoped to find Dorman and Garth.

They were in Dorman's office, just the two of them, as I'd hoped. They stood side by side with identical stances—feet shoulder-width apart and arms crossed over their chests, Garth nearly a foot taller than the compact Nejeret. Their backs were to me as they stared at the wall, or rather, at the gateway I'd drawn on the wall earlier that day. The one that was still active, giving a clear-as-day window into Garth's condo.

I paused in the doorway, hand on the doorknob and eyes narrowed at Dorman's back. "Funny . . . I could've sworn I told you to destroy that thing."

Dorman turned his head enough that he could just see me out of the corner of his eye. Garth, on the other hand, spun around, hands extended, and stared at me for a few seconds. His eyes were rounded, his lips parted. As soon as the momentary shock wore off, he rushed me. He wrapped his arms around me and lifted me off the ground, burying his face in my hair, his nose firmly lodged in the crook of my neck. I could feel his breaths, quick and hot against my shoulder.

His reaction took me by surprise, and for a moment, I was a stunned rag doll, arms and legs dangling. I knew he cared, but this was some serious giving-a-shit. Way more than I'd been prepared for. It only took a moment for my heart to warm, the sheer, overwhelming mass of his concern for me thawing my stupor and seeping into my soul. I wrapped my arms around his broad torso and squeezed my eyes shut, fighting the sudden sting of welling tears caused by the avalanche of emotions.

Garth was gripping my jacket so hard that his knuckles were digging into my back. It was far from comfortable, but I hardly minded. "Don't ever do that to me again," he said, his gravelly voice hoarse. After several more heartbeats, he set my feet back on the floor.

I glanced up at him, meeting his rich brown eyes for only a moment. His skin was red and irritated from the tear gas, worse than it had been before, and the whites of his eyes were bloodshot. I wouldn't apologize for shoving him through the gateway to safety and leaving myself at risk. It had been my choice, and I would make the same one again, a million times over.

As I stared at the scuffed floor, I felt the corner of my mouth lift. I finally understood my mom's decision all those years ago. For the first time ever, I could relate to her sacrifice. Garth's life mattered to me, just as much as my own. Maybe more.

The realization was shocking, and I raised my eyes to meet his once more. What was happening to me? What were these thoughts I was having? These things I was feeling? I searched his eyes, looking for some explanation. All I found was a troubling sense of contentment, of hope and joy and peace. And it gave rise to a fear that threatened to consume me completely.

I couldn't fall in love with a human. It was the ultimate form of self-destruction for a Nejeret. It was setting myself up for guaranteed, unavoidable failure. For heartbreak. For soul-destroying devastation.

And yet there didn't seem to be any way to stop it. I was a train, hurtling toward a half-completed trellis, and I had no brakes.

Garth licked his lips. "Kat, I—"

It's just the adrenaline from the fight, I told myself. Stressful situations cause heightened emotions. That's all. I lowered my gaze and cleared my throat. "I borrowed your car," I said, interrupting him and redirecting us away from any impromptu declarations. Not ready, not now . . . not ever. "And your cat's in there," I added. The corner of my mouth lifted once more, and I glanced up at him through my lashes. "Gotta say, sweet ride, copper."

Garth's eyes widened, whatever he'd been about to say catching in his throat, and the faintest smile touched his lips. "Dorman told me you took Eva with you. Thank you, Kat, really." He shook his head ever so slowly. "So what do you think of Lola?"

My eyebrows rose. "Lola? You named your car Lola?"

He shrugged.

I met his shrug with a single raised shoulder. "She's alright," I said, mock nonchalance thick in my voice.

Dorman coughed purposefully and took a step toward us. "So . . ." He gestured to the one-way gateway. "This is a clusterfuck."

I glanced at him, then shifted my focus beyond him to the gateway and the scene taking place in Garth's condo. Cops and paramedics swarmed the place, wheeling a couple of the injured mercenaries out on stretchers and escorting a few more out in cuffs. A few more would follow in body bags, once the scene was processed. The scene that was Garth's condo. His home.

"I'm so sorry," I told Garth, watching him out of the corner of my eye.

He turned his attention from me to the gateway, blowing out a breath. "I knew there'd be risks when I offered to help you." His words were exactly the right thing to settle my guilt and doubt, but his tone was tight, and his expression was weary. I didn't think he'd fully processed the implications of all that had happened.

"You can't go back there, Garth," I said, needing him to grasp the severity of the situation. Of *his* situation, courtesy of me and my drama. "You can't go home, and you can't go to the station." I turned to face him, reaching for his hand. His darker skin was raw and red, where the pale skin on the back of my hand was already mostly healed. His fate was now tied to mine, and his life was so much more fragile. "You have to disappear until I get this all sorted out."

His thick fingers slipped between mine. "I can help you." His offer was sweet, but there was a wild look in his eyes. It was starting to sink in, and he was grasping for something to hold onto while the rest of his world fell apart.

I flashed him a weak smile and shook my head. He'd taken an oath the day he earned his badge—serve and protect. Helping me from this point on would mean breaking that oath in every way possible. "You should go to Bainbridge. You'll be safe with Heru and Lex."

Garth stepped in front of me, blocking my view of the gateway. "I *want* to help you."

I looked past him, meeting Dorman's curious stare. For some reason, what happened between Garth and me next mattered to him. My *choice* mattered to him. Would I use Garth, or would I protect him? Maybe it would show Dorman what kind of a person I really was. Maybe it would be the thing that determined where his allegiance truly lay, regardless of what happened with the cure.

I held Dorman's stare for a moment longer, decision made. I wouldn't use Garth; I would keep him safe. Always. Even if it meant hurting him another way.

I looked at Garth, my stare unflinching. "You can't help me. You'll only get in my way."

His expression hardened, and he pressed his full lips together.

"I'll draw a gateway to Bainbridge," I said, voice flat.

Garth shook his head. "I'll drive. There's something I have to do along the way, anyway."

"But you *will* go there, right?"

He nodded once.

I clenched my jaw. "Fine."

"Fine," he said.

"Alright, so . . ." Dorman forced out a rough, nervous laugh. "Now that that's decided . . ."

CHAPTER SEVENTEEN

I walked Garth the quarter mile to his car, as much to make sure he got there safely as to show him where I'd parked it. It was half past eight, and the street running alongside I-5 was quiet. And Garth was quiet. And *I* was quiet. We were just a couple bundles of quiet, the two of us, surrounded by more, tense quiet.

"Listen, Garth," I started as we jaywalked across thc cmpty street. "I know you're capable of—"

"I get it, Kat." Garth looked up the street, away from me, then glanced my way. "I mean, look at you—you were covered in burns from the gas, head to toe, and now you're good as new, while I . . ." He trailed off, clearing his throat with a cough. Tear gas is a real bitch on the ol' esophagus and lungs. "I can't even begin to understand what it must be like to be one of you . . . to heal the way you do . . . to know you'll live for centuries while the rest of the world, well . . ." He laughed bitterly, gravel on concrete. "I'm like glass compared to your steel. You're worried about me. I'm flattered, actually."

I eyed him as we walked and he talked, hands in my pockets, tongue tangled in knots.

He didn't say anything those final few steps to the car, but when we reached it, he took hold of my upper arms and backed me against the driver's side. "I might be fragile compared to you, and I might come with a definite expiration date," he said, leaning into me, our bodies touching from knees to chest. "But I'm not weak, Kat, and I'm not backing down from whatever this is that's developing between us."

I raised my chin, my eyes locked with his. "Which would be what, exactly?"

His dimples appeared as he smiled, just a little. "I don't know yet, but I sure as hell plan to find out." He angled his head downward and leaned in, claiming my lips for a few blissful seconds.

I probably shouldn't have let him kiss me, considering that, unlike Garth, I had no intention of indulging in our reckless relationship any further. I could already feel my heart hardening, closing him out. Which is maybe why I savored that last kiss so much.

Palm to his sternum, I pushed him back a few inches and slipped out from between him and his car. I dug his phone out of my coat pocket and handed it to him. "Use the West Seattle Ferry Terminal," I said, licking my lips. I could still taste him there, vanilla and coffee. I started across the street. "My people will be expecting you, so if you don't show up at their gates on Bainbridge in a couple hours, I'll come after you myself."

"Promises, promises . . ."

I glanced at him over my shoulder. Didn't say anything. Just looked at him.

Garth nodded, and a second later, he opened the car door and slid into the driver's seat. The engine rumbled to life before I'd reached the sidewalk, and I felt a little of the tension tightening my shoulders ease as he roared away. He was out of this, for now.

I rubbed my hands together and broke into a jog. It was time for the real work to begin.

"Do you have a plan yet?" Dom asked me as I neared the eastern gate.

"Parts of one," I told him, slowing to a walk. "And yes, it still involves Nik."

I passed through the gate, the hairs on the back of my neck standing on end. Planting my hands on my hips, I stopped and looked around. The first hundred feet or so within the eastern gate was a smaller version of the northern gate's bazaar, only focused solely on ready-to-eat food. It had been bustling with people when Garth and I were on our way out, barely ten minutes ago. Now it was all but abandoned. "Where is everyone?"

"Was Dorman planning any kind of an assembly or a gathering?"

I shook my head. "Don't know," I said as I targeted the nearest person, an elderly Chinese guy manning a fried noodle bar. He was one of the few people still hanging around. "Hey," I said to him as I approached. "Where'd everyone go?" I pointed to the rest of the thoroughfare with my chin.

The man squinted, deepening the creases fanning out in the skin around his eyes. "There was shouting in the square," he said, and I assumed he was referring to the central portion of the Tent District, where Dorman's office and the hospital were. "Very loud shouting and other sounds, and everyone ran to it." Noodle Guy was quiet for a moment, then nodded to himself. "But they will come back. Everyone has to eat."

I was already running toward the square by the time he finished talking. The crowd was on its way back, hushed murmurs exchanged between people clinging together at the elbows or comforting each other with arms around shoulders and waists. Red-rimmed eyes and the pale skin of shock marked most of them.

"I have a very bad feeling about this," Dom said.

"Gee," I muttered, "you think?" The closer I drew to the square, the thicker the milling and meandering crowd became, and with me moving against the tide, I had to do my fair share of shoving and offer up a string of excuse-mes and move-its just to make headway.

There were too many people to see what was going on in the square, and I wasn't tall enough to see over them, so I did what any logical person would do—I climbed one of the old, rusted shipping containers someone was using as a house. They stacked them up here in threes and fours and fives, the Tent District's version of apartments. Once I could see over the crowd, it was easy enough to find the eye of the storm.

Maybe forty feet from the entrance to the hospital-hangar, Dorman knelt on the ground, a small, frail body cradled on his lap and a solid ten feet between him and the crowd encircling him. His head was bowed over the child, his ever-present baseball cap removed. Even from so far away, I could see the blood spattering his clothing and tell that his shoulders were shaking.

There were other people on the ground near him, some moving, some not. There was so much blood sprayed around on the people and asphalt within that open space that it looked like someone had poured out buckets full of dark red paint.

"What the hell happened?" I said, more talking to myself than to Dom.

He answered anyway. *"It must've been one of the kids. If another child entered the final phase of the disease and turned rabid unexpectedly . . ."*

Slowly, I shook my head. "But they're sedated. How could any of their bodies override the drugs?"

"I shall confer with Neffe. I'll return shortly."

I nodded and jumped down from the side of the shipping container. My hands smelled like rust and iron and paint, and I wrinkled my nose even as I returned to shoving my way through the crowd. I needed to get to Dorman to find out exactly what happened. If the sedative wasn't enough, we'd have to come up with another plan. There were dozens of kids on the verge of entering the final phase, even more adults not long after that. If just one small child could do this much damage—infect who knew how many more people—what would happen if two went wild simultaneously? Or *more*?

It took me maybe five minutes to fight my way through the crowd, and I stepped on more than a few toes in the process. The Nejerets at least knew to get out of my way, and the humans proved themselves quick learners. By the time I reached the clearing, Dorman was on his feet, the child limp on the ground at his toes. The little boy's eyes were open. Glazed over. Unseeing.

I swallowed roughly as I stepped into the clearing. "What the hell happened?"

Dorman turned to me, the color drained from his face and his lips parted. He had a dazed look in his eyes that spoke undoubtedly of shock. "I didn't have a choice." He was looking at me, but it was clear that he wasn't seeing me. "Jonny—he was out of control. He attacked every person who came near him . . . anyone he could get his hands on. It took everyone to catch him. I—I—I had to—to—"

"Hey," I said, approaching Dorman with my hands upraised, palms out, like I was dealing with a wounded animal. With an unpredictable creature. "Hey there, Dorman, you're alright. It's all going to be alright." I placed a hand on his shoulder and leaned in closer, weaving my head slowly this way and that until I managed to catch his faraway gaze.

His eyes focused, and he shook his head. "I killed him."

I nodded, squeezing his shoulder through his raincoat. "I know. You did what had to bc donc." I shot a quick glance around at all of the terrified and worried faces.

Those closest to the clearing were Nejerets, immune to the infection. They'd linked arms, forming a living barrier. From the looks of it, all of the people within the circle were human and had blood on them—Jonny's blood or their own, I wasn't sure. But I suspected they were being held here by force. By that living barrier. Because they were believed to be infected now, too.

"Let's take care of the living," I told Dorman. "We can deal with the dead later."

It took a few seconds, but Dorman finally blinked, then nodded. He'd just opened his mouth to address his people when someone screamed. It sounded like it came from the hospital.

Both of our heads snapped toward the sound, and a second later, I lunged into a dead sprint. If another of the sick kids entered the rabid stage and somehow broke free of the sedative's hold while literally every able-bodied person was out in the square, then there'd be nobody in the hospital to protect those who were too sick or injured to protect themselves. It would be a bloodbath. A full-on massacre.

The ring of Nejerets parted as I hurtled toward them, as did the first few people standing behind them, but once I was well into the throng, I had to resort to less civil methods for ensuring my forward momentum continued. "Move!" I shouted, elbowing a man in the chest. I stiff-armed the woman behind him in the shoulder, and the people beyond them started to get the point. Pretty soon, the masses parted like I was Moses.

Another scream, pained this time. Bloodcurdling.

I leaned forward and ran like hell. Once I was through the hospital's doors, I didn't have to go much further. The sight that greeted me was so startling, so *wrong*, that I stopped dead in my tracks and stared for a fraction of a second. Long enough for my jaw to drop. For my stomach to turn.

A little girl, maybe six or seven, straddled the patient in the cot in the middle row, three beds in. It was a teenage boy with a cast on his right leg. A cast that seemed to have made it impossible for him to escape from the wraithlike child tearing into his neck and chest with her bloodstained fingernails. She was making an unearthly noise, a snarl mixed with a whine and a growl that no human vocal chords should ever have been capable of producing. A few patients huddled in the corners, and those who were more mobile stumbled toward the exit, panic blazing in their eyes. Several littered the floor and beds around the little girl's current victim, spattered and smeared with blood. Apparently they'd tried to help. They'd failed.

I heard footsteps pounding the pavement behind me, knocking me out of my momentary horrified stupor. I leapt over the first cot, then hurtled the next, body slamming into the little girl. She flew back several feet, landing askew on the next cot over. Luckily, it was empty. The one beyond it, not so much, and that patient, though untouched by the rabid child, didn't look like she'd be up and moving on her own any time soon. It was too late for the boy, he was bleeding out as I stood there, but if I could stop the little girl from hurting anyone else—from infecting anyone else, as sure of a death as tearing out their throats with those clawlike fingers—it wouldn't be a complete fail in my book.

The girl scrabbled around until she was crouched on the cot on feet and hands. Blood was smeared all over her nightgown and clumped in her dirty blonde hair. Her eyes were so bloodshot it looked as though all the blood vessels in her eyeballs had burst. Maybe they had. I didn't know the nitty-gritty of the disease's symptoms.

The girl pulled back her lips, revealing a mishmash of adult and kid teeth, along with a couple gaps where her baby teeth were missing. She made that sound again, that bone-chilling, whiny snarl.

A shiver crawled up my spine.

And then she lunged at me.

I was so shocked by how quickly she could move that my deflection of her attack was slower than it should've been. But she was a sick little girl and she couldn't possibly be this strong and how could I bring myself to hurt—

Her jagged fingernails caught on my cheek, gouging the side of my face in stops and starts. She grabbed a chunk of my hair in her impossibly strong grip and yanked my head to the side, exposing my neck. For the kill.

Even a Nejeret will die from a ripped-out throat. And there was no way I was about to let some kid kill me.

I wedged my boot between us, pressing the sole into her belly, and rolled onto my back at the same time as I kicked out. She might've had the adrenaline-fueled strength of a pro boxer, but she was still as light as a young child, and I launched her far. All forty-five pounds of her flew even farther than I'd intended, and her frail body slammed against the corrugated metal wall. The boom of her impact echoed throughout the room, a gong of pain and death.

She sat limp for a moment, but impossibly, she lifted her head and managed to gather her feet under herself. She was preparing to spring at me again.

"Stay down," I said through gritted teeth as I stalked toward her, hoping some part of her brain was still lucid. "Please, just stay down."

She placed her hands in front of her on the floor and leaned forward.

"Damn it," I howled, reaching over my shoulder to draw my sword. It was easy enough to stop her once Mercy had joined the fight. As the *At* blade slid through her little body, it was one of the few times Mercy proved the rightness of her name. The girl had already been at death's door. She been fated to die the second she contracted that fucking disease. At least, now, her suffering was at an end.

The footsteps behind me stopped, and I pulled Mercy's blade free as I turned my head to glance over my shoulder. "The sedative isn't working," I said to Dorman. "When they get close to the final phase, end it."

He nodded, his throat working but no sound coming out.

I wiped my sword's blade on my jeans until the *At* was invisible once more, then stood and re-sheathed it. I stared down at the little girl lying on the floor. Somehow her face was absent of blood-stains, though the rest of her seemed bathed in the stuff. She almost looked like she was asleep.

"What was her name?" I asked softly.

"Ab—" Dorman cleared his throat. "Abigail. Her name was Abigail."

"Any family?"

"A mother, but she's sick, too."

I raised my eyes to the ceiling so high above and blinked several times, then took a deep breath. "That's a blessing, then."

"Yes," Dorman said. "It is."

CHAPTER EIGHTEEN

Before I left the Tent District, seven kids had to be euthanized. Neffe sent word to me through Dom about her theory that the spike of epinephrine that floods the infected person's system as they enter the final, rabid stage of the disease must be so intense that, in some cases, it's able to override any sedatives. She said that increasing the already tripled dosage further might help keep them down—*might*—but such a high dosage was also just as likely to kill them.

Apparently she and Aset and a team of other brilliant, scientifically minded Nejerets had been tirelessly working in their lab on Bainbridge since they first received the blood samples from Nik. They had some idea of how the disease worked—some sort of an attack on both the body and the soul—but not enough to slow it down, let alone stop it. It was unlike anything they'd ever seen, and considering they had millennia of experience in the field, that fact scared the shit out of me.

Dom had known Neffe for centuries, and he'd worked closely with her for almost as long. He knew how to read her, and according to him, she wasn't just flummoxed by this disease; she was afraid. Such a thing almost never happened, and that scared the shit out of me even more.

It also *motivated* the shit out of me. I still had Abigail's blood all over me. Four raw, pink lines still streaked down the side of my face from where she'd gouged me with her fingernails. I was just lucky she'd missed my eye; an injury there would've taken a full regeneration cycle or two to heal, and I was already functioning on fumes. Thanks to the chemical burns I'd healed from earlier today, whenever the time came that I could afford to crash, I would crash hard. No doubt about it.

Ten kids had died from the disease so far, but they'd managed to take another dozen or so people to the grave with them and infect over a hundred more during the final throes of the disease. A disease that Ouroboros had manufactured. That the Senate and Initiative Industries *had* to have known about.

It didn't slip past me that the rabid stage had probably been a purposeful construct of the infection. That they wanted the victims to lash out during their final few hours. And the only reason I could come up with for why *anyone* would include such programming in such an infectious, apparently incurable disease was for one single reason: to increase the infection rate. They wanted to spread this thing to as many people as possible.

I would find a way to stop it. To stop Ouroboros. I would find a fucking way, damn it.

"You're certain of this?" Dom asked for the umpteenth time. *"You trust him?"*

I rolled my eyes, knowing full well he couldn't see it. "It's happening, Dom. I'm going to work with Nik, and it's going to be awesome. So *please* just accept it." I was in Dorman's office, finishing up the final few details on a drawing of my bedroom, getting the wrinkles in the bunched-up comforter just right and adding a pile of clothes in the corner. A pile *I* hadn't left there, but that showed up in the drawing anyway. Were the clothes Nik's? Had he moved from the couch to my bedroom in my absence? My eyes narrowed, even as I added shadows to the discarded clothing. I was creating the gateway on the wall beside the still-active one to Garth's condo, though this one was taking much longer, considering the lower hum of otherworldly energy flowing through my *sheut*. I was running on fumes in more ways than one.

I was adding texture to a wadded-up pair of jeans when, unexpectedly, I felt a surge of power rush through me, entering me from some other plane, passing through my *sheut*, and flowing into the drawing. The imagery crackled, electrified by the energy, then flooded with color. With immaculate detail. The drawing became real. It became a gateway.

I recapped the Sharpie and stuffed it into my back pocket with several others, all in various states of running out of ink. I was finding that sometimes the partially dried-out markers were the best for shading and texture. I should know, I'd been drawing on walls with them a lot lately.

I yanked open the door to Dorman's office and poked my head out. The space beyond had been converted into a reception and waiting area, with the half-dozen rooms scattered around the perimeter functioning as offices for Dorman and the other Tent District "officials." The district was a big place, housing thousands of people, however unconventionally, and this repurposed air control tower operated as the central nervous system. And, so far as I could tell, it operated pretty damn well.

"Hey, Caleb," I said, calling out the reception guy's name.

A baby-faced young man sitting at a desk just a few yards from the door to Dorman's office spun his chair around to look at me, eyebrows raised. He was human, for now, but his dad was Nejeret and his mother was a known Nejeret carrier. His older sister had already manifested Nejeret traits, and only time would tell whether the same would happen for Caleb.

"Let your boss know I'm leaving, will you?" As an afterthought, I added, "And don't let anyone but him come in here, alright?" I was worried about others finding the pair of gateways.

Caleb nodded twice.

"Awesome. Thanks." I pulled the door shut once more, then grabbed my things. Less than a minute later, I was passing through the gateway to my apartment.

I entered my bedroom as though I was walking through the doorway, except a quick glance over my shoulder showed me that the door was still closed. When I left the bedroom, I was relieved to find that the blinds were all drawn and that the apartment was dark, only the glow from streetlights, storefronts, and cars passing by on Broadway leaking into the apartment in strips of light.

Washing up was a main priority, but I didn't want to strip off my clothes and hop into the shower until Nik knew I was here. The thought of him finding me in there, well . . . that wasn't an option. So, I decided to settle in at the kitchen table with a bottle of bourbon and my trusty deck of tarot cards. Luckily, there was a full bottle of Widow Jane—ten-year—in the cupboard. I didn't even bother pouring the booze into a glass; I just drank it straight out of the bottle.

I started shuffling the deck, but I made it through only two rounds before the cards slipped free from my hands, spraying across the edge of the table. I'd washed my hands back in the Tent District, but blood still smudged the backs of my hands in a few places, and I couldn't take my eyes off the faint stains for long enough to focus on what my fingers were supposed to be doing with the cards.

Hands shaking, I scooted the chair backward with the screech of wood on wood and stood, rushing to the kitchen sink. I must've scrubbed my hands in nearly scalding water for minutes, because my skin was raw and stung with minor burns by the time I finally turned the faucet off.

I gripped the edge of the counter and bowed my head over the sink. I'd tied my hair back with a rubber band back in the Tent District, when we'd been taking care of the rest of the critical cases. I'd been so busy helping Dorman then, so focused on creating the gateway that would bring me here, that my mind had been occupied.

It wasn't anymore. I was just standing there, waiting. And thinking. And remembering.

She'd been so light. Just a wisp of a girl. And her perfect little pixie face had gone from vicious to peaceful in the blink of an eye. In the time it took her to breathe her last breath. For her heart to give up wrapped around Mercy's blade. For a flash of lucidity to appear in her blue eyes just before the light faded completely. I'd done that. I'd snuffed out that light.

But so had Ouroboros . . .

The thought was logical, and I knew it made sense, but it didn't stop the shaking. It didn't stop my stomach muscles from convulsing or the bourbon from rising up my throat and splattering into the sink. It didn't stop me from melting to the floor, a puddle of misery.

"Little sister—"

I gripped the mirror pendant and yanked, hard. The chain snapped, and I threw it. Somewhere. Away. I wasn't in the mood to be comforted. I deserved the pain.

On unsteady hands and knees, I crawled back to the table and reached up to grab the bottle of bourbon. I curled up against the end of the cabinets with that bottle and waited for Nik to come home.

I waited. And thought. And remembered.

CHAPTER NINETEEN

The bourbon was gone by the time I heard a key turning in one of the locks on the apartment door. The bottle now lay on its side a few feet from me; I'd knocked it over with my boot, and it had rolled until it hit the table leg. My head lolled to the side when the door opened, and I watched Nik enter the apartment.

He shut the door, twisted the locks, and froze with his hand still on the bottom deadbolt. Likely because he picked up on my heartbeat or the lazy whoosh of air in and out of my lungs. Or maybe it was the scent of bourbon and blood that tipped him off. Regardless, his eyes locked with mine, black pools of darkness in the dim apartment.

"You shouldn't be h—" His words cut off when he flipped on the light switch beside the door, and he froze once more. His pupils constricted at the influx of light, revealing his hauntingly pale blue irises. "Shit, Kat. Are you alright?"

I rolled my head to the side, turning my face away from him, and stared at the lone tarot card that had fallen from the table. *Death*. The image on the card came in and out of focus, Abigail riding on a pale horse, face gaunt and eyes the sightless color of moonstones. On the card, I knelt before her in supplication, or possibly begging for forgiveness. She stared down at me, holding her horse's reins in one hand, a banner displaying that damn tail-eating snake in the other.

Traditionally, the Death card represents endings, but also the transformation and change that comes *after* an ending. When one door closes, blah blah blah. I had no doubt that it was significant that of all seventy-eight cards in the deck, this was the one that fell off the table. It was significant. It mattered. Only my alcohol-sodden brain couldn't figure out why. All I could do was look at Abigail's face. See the accusation in her stare. Hate myself.

Nik's footsteps were quiet as he crossed the living room. I heard him toss his leather coat onto the table when he reached it. He didn't seem to spot the bottle until he was almost on top of me. He stopped, standing over me, and nudged the empty bottle with his toe. "How long have you been here?"

I tried to lift my head from the side of the cupboard, but my neck didn't seem capable of supporting it, so I let it bang back against the hollow wood. "Hour . . . dunno . . ." The words were slurred, my vision skittish. Even with my body's ability to process alcohol quicker than a human ever could, I'd consumed a dangerous amount. A full bottle of liquor in that short amount of time might just be enough to kill me. "Wanted to forget," I mumbled.

Nik inhaled and exhaled heavily, then crouched down beside me. He had a hand-shaped bruise on his neck and scratches that looked like they'd come from fingernails on his forearm. "Alright, Kitty Kat . . ." His arms slipped under my knees and around my back. "Let's get you cleaned up." He lifted me like I weighed nothing—like I was as light as Abigail had been—and carried me into the bathroom, where he set me down in the bathtub.

Time skipped around in stops and starts. Getting black-out drunk will do that.

One minute, I was fully clothed; the next, I was naked from

the waist up, and my jeans were covered in soured bourbon. My body's natural defense against poison had kicked in.

Another skip forward, and I was naked, warm water spraying down on me. From outside the tub, Nik was holding me up in a sitting position, his hand jammed into my mouth, his fingers making me gag.

Another skip, and I was lying on my side in the tub, my abdominal muscles aching and my throat burning. The water raining down from the showerhead was cool, and I was shivering.

One more skip forward, and I came to curled up on my side on the couch, covered by a faded fleece blanket matted from being washed so many times. My pulse jackhammered inside my skull, and my whole body ached.

A glass of water appeared in front of my face.

I licked my lips, insanely thirsty. "Thanks," I whispered, accepting the glass as I gingerly pushed myself up onto my elbows.

Nik helped me sit up the rest of the way with a hand on my upper arm.

The blanket slipped down, and I realized I was wearing an old, ratty T-shirt, one of the few I'd left behind when I'd temporarily relocated back to my room in the house on Bainbridge. A quick glance under the blanket revealed plain black underwear, nothing else.

"All you have here are jeans," Nik offered up in explanation. He was standing a few feet away. He'd changed into a pair of black sweats and a gray T-shirt, and his feet were bare.

I lifted the glass of water to my lips and tilted it back, shrugging as I chugged. My sluggish mind caught up a moment later, and flickers from the past hour or two flashed through my mind. Nik had dressed me. He'd had to dress me because he'd stripped off my bloodstained clothes. And he'd cleaned me up in the bathtub. And helped me purge the rest of the bourbon. Team vomiting —we could start a whole new Olympic sport.

I choked on the water. The blood drained from my face, leaving my cheeks icy.

"Shit . . . are you going to throw up again?"

I shook my head, mortified by the memories. Without looking at him, I downed the rest of the water and handed the glass back to him. "Can I have another?" I asked, my voice raspy.

As I watched him walk away, my nose picked up on the scent of toasting bread. And was that eggs?

"There's milk and OJ, too," Nik said from the kitchen. "And there's coffee, but I still have to brew it."

Now that he'd brought up the possibility of drinking something other than water, I was dying for a Cherry Coke. But after what I'd just put my stomach through, I thought it best to give it a break from the usual crap I forced into it for a little while longer. "Milk, please." A moment later, I added, "And maybe coffee in a bit?"

"Sure." Nik came back into the living room and handed me a glass of milk, then returned to the kitchen. "Hungry?"

I nodded and pulled my legs up onto the couch, tucking my icy feet into the crooks of my knees as I gulped down half the glass of milk. I'd never really been a fan of drinking the stuff straight up, but it sounded good. Refreshing. Tasted it, too.

"Nik," I said softly, resting the half-empty glass on my knee. "I—"

He was standing at the stove, just out of view, but poked his head around the wall to look at me. His hair was askew, the longer strands swept mostly to one side, and his stare was open and intent.

"It was a little girl." I stared at the glass of milk but watched Nik out of the corner of my eye. "Couldn't have been more than seven years old."

Nik didn't say anything for a moment, just watched me right back. "One of the kids infected by the Ouroboros disease?" He reached out to do something on the stove, then came around the corner and into the living room. He sat on the coffee table in front of me, his legs splayed wide and his elbows on his knees. I could feel his eyes on me, I but still couldn't bring myself to look at him.

To see him. I wasn't used to him being so attentive or serious. I didn't really know how to interact with *this* Nik.

I nodded. "The girl—she entered the final phase right after another kid." My face felt numb, my voice devoid of emotion or intonation. "The sedatives don't always work." I swallowed. "Nobody was ready when she went rabid, and I was the first to get to her." I blinked slowly, seeing not the glass of milk in my hands but the hospital in the Tent District. The chaos and fear. The little girl tearing into that poor teenager's body.

"She'd already killed a couple people," I continued, "and she wasn't showing any signs of weakening yet. I—" Another blink, and I cleared my throat. "I stopped her." Finally, I met Nik's eyes. "I killed her."

Nik didn't reach out to touch me or offer up any comforting platitudes. He simply stared at me for long seconds, his breathing even, his heartbeat steady. I could feel my own slowing to match his, pulled in by the steady rhythm, like he was the moon to my ocean, regulating the tide of emotions within me. "Do you know her name?" he finally asked.

Again, I nodded. "Abigail."

His answering nod was slow, thoughtful. He shifted his hands to his knees and pushed himself up. "Hang on," he said, already walking to the apartment door. "I'll be back in a second."

After he shut the door, out of the corner of my eye I noticed something shiny on the coffee table, about a foot from where he'd been sitting. It was the little mirror pendant that afforded Dom's soul a window out to the physical realm. The broken chain was gone, and a thin black leather cord had taken its place. I wasn't quite ready to face Dom after my meltdown, but it was a comfort to know he was nearby.

Nik returned a couple minutes later with a tattoo machine in one hand and a small bottle of *At* ink in the other. "Ready to add her name to the list?" he said, sitting on the couch beside me. He wrapped his fingers around my wrist and pulled my left arm out so it lay across his lap, then ran the tips of his fingers over the list of forty names. Of the dead. My dead.

I shivered at the gentle touch.

Nik's gaze flicked up to meet mine, a faint glimmer of that familiar, snarky spark shimmering in those pale blue depths. It was the first I'd seen of it since waking. "Any others I should know about?" He shrugged one shoulder. "You're so efficient, I just figured you were bound to have racked up a few more names by now."

The ghost of a laugh shook my chest. I thought of the mercenaries who'd invaded Garth's apartment—some of them hadn't survived—but finding out their names would require a fair bit of detective work on my part. And even then, it would be impossible to say which had been killed by my hand and which by Garth's. And then I thought of Mitch Carmichael and wished, yet again, that I'd killed him. But I hadn't.

Eyes locked with Nik's, I shook my head. A second later, my stomach grumbled. Nik snorted, and I smiled sheepishly.

He gave me back my arm and stood, heading for the kitchen. "Food, first, then ink."

I glanced down at my arm. I could still feel his fingertips gliding over my *At* tattoo, like his touch was seared into my skin. It was as though the *At* ink was having some sort of a reaction to him, its creator.

"Here you go," Nik said, dragging my gaze up from my arm.

"How—" I shook my head, staring up at him. Numbly, I accepted the plate and set it on my lap.

Nik returned to the kitchen.

"You know how you said you can sense the *At* ink?" Briefly, I thought back to that morning on the roof of the Columbia Center, to the way his attention had been drawn to the freshly inked piece on my arm even though it was covered by the leather sleeve of my coat. "I think, maybe, it can sense you, too."

Nik came back with a plate of his own and sat a couple feet

from me on the couch. "What do you mean?" he asked, shoveling a forkful of scrambled eggs into his mouth.

"I—" I laughed under my breath, then looked at my plate. It was filled with scrambled eggs, buttered toast, and sausage links. I couldn't remember the last time so much real food had been cooked on that stove. "I'm not sure," I told him, picking up a triangle of toast. "I'll let you know when I've figured it out."

"You do that, Kitty Kat." Nik speared a sausage link with his fork, then winked at me. "You do that."

CHAPTER TWENTY

"So why'd you come here, really, Kitty Kat, because I know it wasn't for this." The tattoo machine hummed in Nik's hand, the needle scratching incessantly into my skin, depositing opalescent *At* ink and permanently marking me with Abigail's name. My arm was stretched across Nik's lap again, and I was resting my head on the back of the couch.

I sighed, heavily, and closed my eyes. There wasn't much to stare at on the ceiling anyway. "I need your help."

"With what?" Nik asked, not missing a beat with the ink job.

I opened my eyes and turned my head so I could see his face. Or, at least, part of his face. With the way he was leaned over my arm, I could see maybe a third of his perfect, masculine features. It didn't matter what angle I viewed him from, his beauty was unreal regardless. Not that I would ever tell *him* that.

Nik lifted the needle from my arm and looked at me sidelong. "Next time, warn me before you move. This shit's permanent."

My pulse jumped, and I glanced down at my arm, worried I'd made him screw up.

"I was *kidding*," he said, nudging my shoulder with his. "It's *At*, Kitty Kat; it does whatever I tell it to do. If I mess up my lines, I can fix it." He laughed under his breath. "I'm done, anyway."

I could see that, considering I was still looking at my arm.

"You didn't answer my question," he reminded me.

I raised my gaze to meet his, licked my lips, and inhaled deeply. "I, uh . . ." I looked away, focusing instead on the opposite wall. Nik's pale stare was too keen, too knowing. "Earlier today—"

"Yesterday," Nik corrected. "It's already tomorrow."

I raised my eyebrows. "What time?"

"Four in the morning. You went through a single regeneration cycle, but I think you'll need one more."

I nodded absently. It made sense, considering the state I'd put myself in, not to mention everything I'd put my body through today. Or yesterday. I hadn't intended to lose so much time—or *any* time. But it wasn't like I'd have been able to execute my plan at midnight, anyway. Oh, no; this plan required regular business hours, very specific ones. This plan allowed time for one more regeneration cycle, thankfully. Nik was right: my body needed it.

"*Yesterday*," I said, "I had a little chat with one of the board members at his flat—Mitch Carmichael. It didn't matter how persuasive I was; he didn't have the information I needed to stop this disease." I glanced at Nik—his attention was rapt, all on me—then returned to staring at the blank wall. "When I was done with good ol' Mitch, I sent him to Bainbridge." Disgust was thick in my voice. "I figured they could get other useful information out of him, even if he'd proved useless with this."

"You don't sound too happy about that," Nik commented.

My lip curled. "The things he did . . ." I shook my head, heartbeat picking up. "I wanted to kill him so badly." My eyes burned with unshed tears. *Poor Sammy.* "I wanted his soul to die." I looked at Nik, defiant. He tended to frown on me killing humans. So did I, but that wasn't the point. "It's what he deserved, but . . ." My shoulders slumped.

"No doubt he deserved it," Nik said quietly. Seconds passed, me attempting to regain my simmering composure and Nik studying every inch of my face, watching me struggle with my frustration and anger. "But it wasn't weakness—not killing him."

I snorted derisively and crossed my arms over my chest, redirecting my stare back to the wall.

Apparently Nik was over my avoidance strategies, because he gripped my chin and turned my face back toward him, forcing me to look at him. To face him. "You exercised restraint. Even when faced with what was clearly a lot of rage." The faintest smile touched his lips. "I'm a little impressed, actually. It's not your usual style."

I tried to yank my jaw free, but he tightened his grip. I clenched my teeth together so hard that they creaked.

"Besides," Nik said, "you can always finish the job later."

I stared off to the side. Only if I survived the coming day, and that was questionable, especially if Nik wasn't down to help me. "Nik, I—"

Pierced eyebrow quirking upward, he released my jaw.

I took a deep breath, then dove in. "I'm going after the rest of the board. Today. According to Carmichael, there's a board meeting scheduled for this afternoon. They're going to be voting to un-chair Constance Ward—she's the chairman of the board—so they'll at least need a quorum, but from the way Carmichael was talking, the other twelve board members will all be there. It's the best chance we'll have of getting the information we need to stop this thing."

"We," Nik said. An observation, not a question.

I shifted on the couch, pulling up my left knee and turning to face him. "Getting into the boardroom will be the hardest part, but once we're inside, you can seal us in with the board—and everyone else *out*." I leaned in a few inches, eyes searching his. "Once we get what we need from them, I can create a gateway to the Tent District or Bainbridge or *wherever* we need to be. But if you're not with me . . ." I'd have to rely on door locks. I'd only have seconds to get the information. And I'd probably die in the attempt.

"Why?" Nik's voice was flat, his stare distant. "Why do you care so much?"

"If I can get the cure to Dorman, he and his people will support Heru," I explained. "He's already agreed to—"

"Bullshit."

For several seconds, I sat there with my mouth half open. Brow furrowed, I brought my lips together.

Nik fixed his intense, pale stare on me. "This isn't about Heru's revolution. It's more than that to you. What is it, Kitty Kat? Why does finding a way to stop this disease matter to you so much? It doesn't affect our people." He laughed under his breath, humorless and bitter. "In fact, if it really does come down to a war between humans and Nejerets, a pandemic wiping out most of the mortals would go a long way toward evening out the playing field. This disease could wipe out millions—billions—if it gets beyond the Tent District. The infection rate is already exponential, and it's only been contained because people so rarely come and go from that place." He inhaled and exhaled, his eyes searching mine. "So drop the holier-than-thou, I'm-doing-this-for-the-good-of-our-people act and tell me the real reason you want to stop this thing, because the good of our people would mean letting it run its course."

My chest heaved with each successive breath, and my nostrils flared. The words coming out of his mouth were so unexpected I could barely understand them, let alone believe them.

"Why?" Nik asked once more. Demanded.

"Because it's not their fault," I snapped, standing. I stalked across the room, not caring in the least that I was wearing only a T-shirt and underwear. "Because they're not our enemies, no matter what the Senate or Ouroboros or Initiative Industries want us to think." I spun around when I reached the front door and headed back toward the kitchen. Pacing always helped me think, helped the words flow, and I was ready to unleash on Nik. "Because innocent people shouldn't have to pay for a war they know nothing about. That's the real bullshit, Nik, and I'm not about to walk away from these people just because they're a different species. Just because walking away would be easier. They deserve better than that. I don't run when things get hard." I glared at him. "I'm not a coward."

A slow, wolfish grin spread across his face. "But I am?"

I glanced at him, but kept on pacing. "I never said that."

"Not in so many words." He stood and rounded the coffee table, coming to stand directly in my path.

I tried to turn away from him, but he took hold of my arm, and I knew better than to test my strength against his. He would win that battle, every time. I settled on a question instead. "Why did you leave?"

Nik was quiet for so long I doubted he would answer. But finally, he did. "I needed some time. It was too quiet in my head after Re was gone. I didn't know how to be just *me*." He was talking about the time he disappeared a little over three years ago, after waking up from a decades-long coma and finding his body housing one soul instead of two. But that wasn't the time *I* was talking about.

I jutted my jaw forward to keep my chin and lips from trembling. "Not then," I said, my voice hushed. "Before, when I—when we . . ." I cleared my throat. I was referring to the one and only time we kissed, two decades ago, just downstairs. It was back when the shop had sold magic and mysticism rather than ink and fortunes. The kiss had been both wondrous and disastrous. It had been the beginning of the end.

Again, Nik let that long silence settle over us. "Re and I had an agreement," he finally said, speaking of the other, godly being who'd shared his body for millennia. "One of many. Where certain things were concerned, my body was mine alone. He agreed to forgo pleasures of the flesh, so long as I only pursued them when he was dormant."

My gaze wandered up to Nik's face.

A bitter smile twisted his lips. "Over the centuries, Re became more and more resistant to voluntarily going dormant." Nik's grin grew sly. "But I'd learned early on that he detested physical pain, so if I found myself, well, *wanting*, all I had to do was drive him away with pain, first."

I thought back to the flashes of memory I had from earlier, when he'd first arrived. He'd been covered in scrapes and bruises. And then I recalled all of those mornings so many years ago, when we'd been working together to track down the rogue Nejerets responsible for my mother's murder—Nik had suffered from minor injuries more mornings than not. Was this, right here, the explanation for why?

"I fell into a pattern," Nik explained. "For millennia, I only ever touched a woman after I'd run Re off with enough pain to keep him dormant for hours. I never touched anyone in any non-platonic way while he was conscious." Nik tilted his head to the side, his pale blue eyes locked with mine. "Until you." He released my arm, but I didn't move away. "It was too much for Re." Another gentle, bitter laugh. "Maybe too much for me, too."

I faced him fully, ever so slowly shaking my head. "Why?" I searched his eyes for answers I doubted he would give me. "Why me, Nik? Why then?"

It was his turn to look away. "I'll do it—this thing with the Ouroboros board. I'll help you, if you still want me to."

I blinked, opened my mouth, blinked again, and just stared at him. Disappointment warred with exhilaration within me. His non-answer spoke volumes; I just didn't know what it was saying. But his offer to help me with my current mission chased the disappointment away, and a grin overtook my face before I could even consider stopping it. "Really? You mean it? Even if it's not what's best for our people?"

He shot me a sly glance. "Humans, Nejerets . . . we all share the same ancestors." It was true; thousands and thousands of years ago, Nuin, the first human Re possessed, had been born to two fully human parents. He'd started our species the moment he reproduced, but we all truly originated in the same place. Without humans, we wouldn't ever have existed at all.

"Well, alright," I said, still grinning.

"Besides," Nik added, his tone light, "we've got to make sure your boyfriend's safe."

My smile soured. "Garth's not my boyfriend."

"Oh yeah?" Nik moved around me to pick up our plates from the coffee table. "Have you told him that?"

I frowned, then stuck out my tongue at Nik.

He laughed.

Feeling lighter, I waited until he disappeared around the wall dividing the living room and the kitchen, then made my way to the coffee table and picked up the mirror pendant. "Dom?" I said, holding it against my palm so I'd be able to hear his response. "Are you around?" I couldn't see him, but it didn't mean he wasn't nearby.

His sharp-featured face appeared not a second later. *"Little sister . . . you are well?"*

I had no doubt that he'd overheard much of what transpired with me over the past few hours. It had probably been driving him crazy, knowing I was entering a tailspin and not being able to do anything about it. "I'm fine. Now," I added. "But I had a lot of help."

"I know. And I'm grateful to Nik." He paused for a moment. *"Perhaps I have been too critical of him."*

"Oh," I said with a laugh. "I never thought I'd hear you say that."

Nik poked his head out of the kitchen, but as soon as he saw me talking to my palm, he retreated again.

Dom fell back into silence, and I studied his somber features. It was clear that something was bothering him, even in his miniature state. "What is it, Dom?"

He sighed, heavily, something he still seemed to be an expert at despite having no physical lungs or breath or mouth to actually sigh with. *"It's Garth,"* he said. *"He never made it to Bainbridge."*

My heart became so heavy that I had no choice but to stumble the few steps to the couch. "Nik," I said hollowly, "I need to borrow your phone."

CHAPTER TWENTY-ONE

"You were worried about me," Garth said, sounding pleased.

I scowled. *Worried?* That was putting it lightly. My whole damn body was shaking. I thought he'd been abducted, or that he'd been offed on the ferry and dumped into the Sound. "You should be with Lex on Bainbridge right now," I said, fingers gripping Nik's phone so hard that it creaked in my grasp, "so fuck you very much, Garth."

He chuckled, covering the laugh with a lame cough. "You're adorable."

I growled into the phone, the fingers of my left hand gripping the edge of the couch cushion. "I'll show you adorable."

"You guys are so cute," Nik said as he meandered out of the kitchen, his tone sickly sweet. He headed for the bathroom in the hallway, smirking the whole way.

I flipped him the bird as he passed the couch. "If you're not at the Heru compound," I said to Garth, "then where the hell are you?"

He was quiet for a second. "Home," he finally said, voice hesitant. "It's just a quick hop from my people's place to yours." He took a deep breath. "Kat, I had to stop here first. I wanted to drop

Eva off at my folks' house and, well . . . my family deserves to know what's going on."

I scoffed, eyes bugging out. "You *told* them?"

"Are you kidding me? Of course I did," was Garth's response.

I was speechless for about a heartbeat. "Garth!"

"They already know about your kind," he said. "We've been guarding knowledge of you for generations. It was my duty to fill them in on what's been going on. They're already in this, whether you like it or not, and they deserve the chance to prepare for whatever's going to happen next."

My chest rose and fell as my breaths came too quickly, and I shook my head, unable to believe his audacity. "How many people did you tell?" I asked, forcing my jaw to unclench. I narrowed my eyes. "*Who* did you tell?"

"Oh no you don't," Garth said. "You won't get those details until you come up here to meet them."

My mouth was suddenly cotton, my throat a desert. Meet Garth's family? I licked my lips, searching for the words. Wading through the emotions. "Yeah, well, that might be a while," I said, figuring now wasn't the time to tell him meeting the parents wasn't written in our stars. That *we* weren't written in *any* stars. I couldn't afford to fall in love with a mortal right now. Maybe ever. "There's some stuff I have to do here to fix this mess," I told him, avoiding the subject.

Nik emerged from the bathroom and stood on the other side of the end table, arms crossed over his chest. He stared down at me. Judged me, no doubt.

"Stuff," Garth said. "Like what?"

I rolled my eyes, shooing Nik back into the kitchen with a wave of my hand. Not like him being in there would mean he couldn't hear both sides of my convo with Garth—Nejeret hearing and whatnot—but at least his absence would give me the illusion of privacy.

"I don't know," I said to Garth, stalling. I couldn't tell him everything I was intending to do. I was starting to think it would be best to tell him nothing at all. "I've got a plan," I amended. "It could help the infected, but it's risky."

"How risky?"

I held my breath, then blew it out. "It doesn't matter, so long as I get the cure. That's the most important thing in the world right now, even you have to admit that. I mean, you were at the Tent District—you saw what's going on. Hell, Garth, you might even have been exposed." A seed of dread lodged in my throat. I hadn't thought twice before sending Garth through that gateway to Dorman at the Tent District, but what if that had been a mistake? Considering how rampant the disease was running there now, him being infected was far from an impossibility. I cleared my throat, ignoring the lump forming there. "What if you contracted it and now you're passing it on to your family?" I said, voice raising in pitch.

"Come on, Kat. I would never do that to—"

"Then get your ass to Bainbridge and tell them you need to be tested."

Garth was quiet for a moment. "I was planning to head there tomorrow."

"Go today, Garth. Go now," I said. "Please." I held my breath.

"Yeah, alright."

"You promise?"

"Yeah, I promise."

I exhaled, relieved.

"So long as you promise to be careful doing whatever it is that you're planning to do."

Careful. I stared up at the ceiling, battling frustration. I was rarely careful; recklessness was sort of a hallmark of mine. Part of my style. And it wasn't like I couldn't lie to him, but I was surprised to discover that I didn't *want* to lie to him. Damn it. "Yeah, sure," I said.

"Say it, Kat. Promise me."

I rolled my eyes again. What can I say? I'm still technically a teenager, and rolling my eyes is second nature to me. It's like breathing. "I *promise* to be careful," I said, drawing out the word 'promise' in annoyance.

"Glad to hear it," Garth said with a dry laugh. "Alright, I should go. My family's going to be disappointed, but . . ." He sighed. "I made this girl a promise . . ."

Eye roll number three. In the kitchen, I could hear Nik choking on a laugh. I'd forgotten he was in there. Flustered, I quickly ended the call, stood, and marched into the kitchen, where Nik was in the process of washing the dishes. "You're such an ass-turd," I said, then chucked the phone at him.

He caught it with wet, soapy hands, easy peasy, his expression all concealed amusement. "As opposed to all those other kinds of turds?"

"Har har." I leaned my hip against the counter, crossing my arms over my chest and tossing out eye roll number four. Apparently I was going for a record.

"You should get some rest." Nik tucked a plate into a free slot in the dishwasher. I couldn't remember the last time I'd even had enough dirty dishes to warrant using the dishwasher. "Take the bedroom. I'll grab some shut-eye out here."

I raised my eyebrows. "Did you really just offer me *my* bed?" Shaking my head, I pushed off the counter and headed for the bathroom to brush my teeth before crashing. "Barely here a week, and you're already acting like you own the place . . ."

He laughed quietly as I walked away, and the sound was unexpectedly reassuring. Having him at my side meant the world to me. It meant that maybe, just maybe, my plan would work. I couldn't help but smile. Just a little.

"Almost done," I mumbled around the cap to my second-most-faded black Sharpie. Chewing on the plastic helped me focus, allowing me to think less and let the electric hum the universe was channeling through me take over. My knees ached from kneeling on hardwood for so long, but I pushed through the pain.

I was almost done with the gateway, just in the process of shading the glare on the polished composite floor in the lobby of the offices on the sixtieth floor of the Columbia Center, the Ouroboros Corporation's Seattle base of operations. The lobby was the closest place to the boardroom that I'd ever been, and I'd never tried to create a gateway to somewhere entirely new to me. I wasn't sure the magic would work if I didn't already have some frame of reference. And now certainly wasn't the time to test the extent of my gateway-creating power.

"That was fast," Nik said from the kitchen. He was fixing grilled cheese and tomato soup for our pre-ambush lunch. "Just under forty minutes," he added, sounding impressed.

The corner of my mouth lifted in the tiniest of smiles. I squashed my peacocking pride and refocused on the drawing on the hallway wall. In less than a minute, that extra-powerful zing of otherworldly energy pulsed through me, and the drawing bled to life. Janelle, the icy receptionist I'd grappled wills with last week, sat behind the long, curved reception desk, fingers clacking away on a computer keyboard as she spoke into her headset. Something about making sure everything was in place for the meeting. Apparently there would be bagels and fruit. *Oh* . . . and donuts!

I sat back on my heels, admiring my work. It was so tempting to go through the gateway now, but doing so would defeat the purpose. We wanted—needed—all of the board members to be in the boardroom when we crashed the party. It was the only way to ensure all the required knowledge would be at our fingertips. Waiting would be a bitch, but at least there'd be crispy grilled cheese to help pass the time.

Which, as it turned out, was fantastic. Who knew Nik could cook? I suppose it shouldn't have shocked me, what with the thousands and thousands of years under his belt, but still, I was impressed. Perfectly melted sharp cheddar on toasted bread that was equal parts crispy and buttery dipped into creamy tomato soup that I was fairly certain was homemade forced me to redefine my personal idea of heaven. I happily stuffed my face and wasn't the least bit ashamed when I licked the last bit of buttery goodness off my fingertips.

"Guess you liked it," Nik commented.

I froze, the tip of my thumb in my mouth, and met his eyes across the small kitchen table. Remembering where I was and who I was with, I opted to finish cleaning my hands using the paper napkin in my lap. "It was alright," I said with a halfhearted shrug.

Nik snorted softly, then glanced into the kitchen. "Five till one," he said, his eyes on the stove clock. "Let's get suited up. We can take care of the dishes later."

My heart rate was already picking up, and I could feel my chest rising and falling with more enthusiasm than usual. It was game time. I nodded, scooting back my chair and standing. "Would you mind doing me a favor?" I said to Nik as I reached for the leather sword harness hanging from the back of the chair adjacent to mine.

"Depends on the favor."

I paused, leveling a flat stare his way. So far, I'd never asked a single thing of him that he'd refused, never asked him to cross a line he wasn't willing to cross, and I couldn't help but wonder where, exactly, his line might be.

"Can you make Mercy visible again?" I asked, holding the invisible *At* sword out to him. "I figure she might instill a little more fear if her potential victims can actually see her."

A slow, wicked grin spread across Nik's face. "I have to say, Kitty Kat—I like the way you think."

CHAPTER TWENTY-TWO

Nik and I stood side by side in the hallway, staring into the active gateway to the Ouroboros lobby. The board meeting was scheduled to begin at one, ten minutes ago.

"They should all be in there by now," I said, my elbow brushing Nik's as I glanced at the watch on my left wrist. Nik had lent it to me so I'd stop asking him to check his phone for the time. The only other clock in the apartment was on the stove, and what can I say—I'm lazy.

"Yep." Nik's arms were crossed over his chest, and he was wearing that long, black leather jacket that I remembered so well from the ill-fated weeks we spent hunting rogue Nejerets together —or attempting to hunt them—a couple decades ago. He was completely unarmed, mostly because with magic like his, *he* was the weapon.

Like him, I wore a black leather coat, but unlike him, I was armed with more than just my wits and the innate magic afforded me by my *sheut*. Mercy was strapped to my back, returned to her full, visible glory. Needle daggers were tucked into the sheaths sewn into the interior of my sleeves, the corded leather bracelet on my left wrist doubled as a garrote, and a two-inch push knife was hidden in my belt buckle. I also had two not-so-hidden combat knives on the outsides of my ankles in boot sheaths and a fragile-looking *At* vial holding a couple tablespoons of infected blood hanging from a chain around my neck—our secret weapon—and my left coat pocket was stuffed full of black Sharpies, our backup exit strategy. Nik carried plan A, rolled up and stuffed into his back pocket.

I glanced at Nik sidelong. His dark brown hair was slicked back, the sides freshly buzzed, and his pale stare was locked on the gateway, cold and focused.

"We've only got one shot at this," I told him.

"Yep," he said, not looking at me. He was in the zone.

I rolled my head from one shoulder to the other, cracking my neck and psyching myself up. My whole body vibrated under the force of the adrenaline coursing through my veins. We could do this. I cracked my knuckles. We could *do* this.

Licking my lips, I watched Janelle stand and walk to the edge of the curved reception desk to chat with a young businessman. From the looks of their body language, a whole lot of flirting was going on. For the moment, the two appeared to be the only people in the lobby. Janelle was distracted, some distance between her and the insta-security button. We wouldn't get a better chance than this.

"On the count of three," I said.

In my peripheral vision, I saw Nik nod.

"One . . . two . . ." We exchanged a glance. "Three."

Nik and I stepped through the gateway. Janelle and her amorous colleague didn't notice us until we were practically on top of them. We had them both tied up and gagged with *At* restraints and stowed under the reception desk—out of sight and mind—in less than thirty seconds.

"This way," Nik said, jogging toward the hallway shooting off from the right side of the lobby. We'd studied the building plans that morning, before I'd started drawing the gateway, and we had a pretty good idea of the layout of the entire floor. Our diligence paid off; we rushed past several offices and were closing in on the nearest of the two doors to the boardroom before any of the occupants of the offices could even get their doors open.

"Hey!" someone yelled behind us. "You can't go in there!"

But their warning was too late. My hand was already on the door handle. Plus, it wasn't like one little human could do anything to stop us.

I shoved the door open and stepped into the boardroom, basking in the outraged gasps, shocked expressions, and half-standing poses of the twelve people seated around the long, mahogany table. A thirteenth person, a youthful businessman, sat in the far corner of the room, a tablet on his lap, his fingers frozen over the attached keyboard. Bad luck, him being here. He picked a terrible day to play note-taker to this group of corporate slime-balls. I almost felt bad for the guy. Except for the part where he chose to work here.

Nik followed me in, and I heard him shut and lock the door.

"This is a closed meeting," a woman said from the head of the table. I recognized her immediately—Constance Ward, CEO and Chairman of the Board. The ends of her blonde bob brushed the shoulders of her cream silk blouse as she pushed back her chair and stood. Her stare was hard, her expression stony. Apparently corporate Constance was nothing like the warm, caring mother I'd peeped on a couple days ago. "You need to leave."

I took one more step into the room and pushed out my bottom lip. "But I heard there'd be donuts." Out of the corner of my eye, I watched the spread of solidified *At* coat the walls, ceiling, and floor of the boardroom, looking so much like a rapidly spreading sheet of ice. In a few more seconds, it would coat the floor-to-ceiling windows on the far side of the room, blocking out the insanely gorgeous view, and we'd all be effectively sealed in.

Constance's eyes strayed from me as the imprisoning shell of *At* caught her attention. "You're Nejeret," she said, her head moving as she watched the progression of the otherworldly material. Her gaze returned to me. "I know you." A hint of fear gleamed in her eyes. "You're her—the Ink Witch."

"Gold star for you, Connie." I flashed her a cheeky grin. "Cute kids, by the way," I added with a wink.

Her eyes rounded, and she blanched. Ever so slowly, she sank back down into her seat, her hand migrating up to her chest. She opened her mouth, then licked her lips. "You—how—" She swallowed roughly, her eyes tearing up. "Please . . . don't hurt them."

I honestly hadn't intended it as a threat. In a twilight zone kind of way, I sort of respected Constance, and I actually felt a little remorse for making her think I intended her family any harm. I mean, come on—I protect kids, I don't kill them. My gut twisted as Abigail's ghostly visage floated through my mind. Usually.

"We're sealed in," Nik said from behind me.

I took a deep breath. It was showtime. "Everyone sit down," I said, reaching over my shoulder and drawing my sword. Mercy's blade came free with a melodic ring.

The few board members who'd risen from their seats when we barged in eased back down. Their movements were painfully slow, like they feared drawing my attention their way would put a target on their backs. Too late.

I did a pointless but fancy-looking spin-twist with my sword, then flipped it up and rested the flat of the blade against my shoulder. Best if these corporate asshats realized Mercy wasn't just for show, but that I knew how to use her; it might make the proceedings move a little faster.

"Raise your hand if you remember a little boy named Sammy," I said.

Nik rounded the head of the table to take up a position on the other side, leaning back against the *At*-coated windows, his hands in the pockets of his long leather coat. He was the only person who moved in the long seconds that followed my request.

After scanning the owlish faces surrounding the long table, I exhaled heavily, exasperated already. I whipped Mercy's blade out, slapping it on the table's surface. Every single human jumped in their seats.

"Who remembers Sammy?" I started to move around the table, dragging the tip of my sword as I went.

The razor-sharp *At* blade glided up the sleeve of a board member—a balding older fellow I recognized as one Gregory Spelt, Vice Chair of the Board. The blade traveled across the shoulders of his suit jacket, then crossed to the shoulders of the woman sitting beside him. Melinda Jones flinched when the blade first landed on her bony frame, then tensed up like she was being electrocuted.

I continued on like that, eyeing those across the table from me, not letting them look away. "You know," I said, "the cute little homeless boy you guys yanked off the street? The one you infected with an engineered disease?"

I paused, putting the slightest pressure on the sword as it inched down a male board member's arm. Mercy's blade cut through the fabric of his sleeve. I couldn't remember this guy's name, but I was fascinated by the beads of sweat forming on his forehead and temples. I leaned in, focusing on his quaking eyelashes. "You know," I said, voice hushed, "the boy you let good ol' Mitch have some quality alone time with before you released him. The one you hoped would infect as many people as possible."

My current friend yelped, and the coppery scent of blood reached my nostrils.

I straightened and glanced down at his arm, where a dark spot of blood blossomed on his sleeve. "Whoopsie," I said, tone flat. "My bad." I winked at the guy before raising Mercy and once again resting her blade on my shoulder. "Guess I got a little too eager."

"You're insane," a guy said from Constance's end of the table. He was the youngest looking of the board members, and I pulled the name Scott Easton from memory.

I also pulled a needle dagger from my sleeve with my free hand and flung it his way. It struck him in the forehead, sticking in his skull and reverberating with a dull thwang. He shouted out in pain, then brought his shaking hands up to his forehead. I'd used just enough force to get the knife to stick in the bone, but not enough to actually pierce his skull and enter his brain.

"I'm not insane," I said, stalking around the table. I yanked the dagger free from Scott's dense head, wiped the tip on his shoulder to clean off the blood, and shoved it back into its sheath up my sleeve. "I'm mad. There's a difference."

"I—" Constance cleared her throat. "I remember him—the boy, Sammy, I mean."

I took a step back from the table, eyeing her. For some reason, I'd hoped she'd been in the dark about the finer details of this particular project.

She licked her lips. "I don't know how he got out, and I swear I didn't know about Mitch, but . . ." Her body was trembling, but her voice was steady. Ballsy chick. "I can only imagine."

"It was her idea," someone said from the other side of the table. It was bony Melinda Jones. "We never wanted any of this. We called for a vote to un-chair her today . . . because she's gone too far." Melinda's eyes burned with a feverish intensity, and her breathing picked up as she went on. "She's led this board astray. The things we've approved because of her . . ." Melinda shook her head. "We're going to set that all to rights today." Her chest heaved with each successive breath.

I stared at her, sword on my shoulder and expression bored. As I blinked, I let a grateful smile light up my face. "Finally, someone's talking. Thank you, Melinda, truly," I said, nodding in gratitude.

Her shoulders relaxed a bit.

I sheathed Mercy and started around the table, heading her way.

The tension returned.

"You're going to make this so much easier," I said, running my fingertips over the knot of the leather bracelet on my left wrist as I drew near to her. Melinda started to spin her chair around so she was facing me, but I tugged on the slipknot holding the bracelet on my wrist. A fraction of a second later, the leather cord was wrapped around Melinda's neck, cutting into her throat.

Gasps filled the room, and people leaned back in their chairs. Some even brought their hands up to their own necks. And what do you know, not a single person stood or lunged at me to help poor Melinda. They just watched, horrified, as I began to strangle the life out of her.

"This is what happens when you lie to me. Honesty *is* the best policy, after all," I said, ignoring the bite of Melinda's nails as they gouged deep trails across my forearms and the backs of my hands. I looked at Constance, then scanned the others' faces even as I kept the garrote tight around Melinda's neck. "I already know you were all involved to some extent. I need to know who oversaw that project. Who's responsible for the disease?"

"Scott," Constance said, pointing to the young man sitting two chairs down from her. "And Gregory." She glanced at the man sitting to her left, then looked off to the side, deflating. "And me."

Disappointment flooded me. I let up on the pressure of the cord around Melinda's neck, taking a step back from the table as I rewrapped the garrote around my wrist. Melinda collapsed forward on the table, a sobbing, gasping mess.

"Let the others go," Constance said. "It's me you want." Damn, but just when I was ready to write her off as a genuinely bad egg, she had to go and do something noble. She was making this really hard on my conscience.

My eyes met Nik's, and when he nodded, the corner of my mouth lifted. "Sure," I said, looking back to Constance. "We'll let them go." I made my way around the table as I secured the slip-knot on my bracelet, holding out my hand when I neared Nik. He reached into his jacket and pulled out the rolled-up sheet that had been tucked into his back pocket. "Thanks," I said when he handed it to me.

I shook the doorway-sized fragment of gray bedsheet open, pleased to see that the gateway I'd created back in the apartment was still active. I hadn't been certain it would survive a trip through another gateway, but it had. Good to know.

Under the tense, watchful stares of the terrified board

members, I grabbed a stapler off a side table and used it on the wall to hang the sheet. The scene on the other side of the gateway was gray and dismal, as any good dungeon should be. I couldn't see any of the Bainbridge Nejerets at the moment, but I knew Heru was there in that dank underground space, waiting with a handful of others for the arrival of his newest guests.

Once the gateway was up and running, I tucked my chin to my chest and whispered, "Alright, Dom, let Lex know they're on their way—ten to start with, but three more should be following soon."

"Very well," Dom said. *"I shall return shortly."*

I turned around, facing the rapt room. "As your oh-so-courageous leader requested, I'm letting the rest of you go."

I looked at Melinda. Her neck was red, raw, and oozing blood where the leather cord had bit into her skin, and she sat a little slumped in her chair, bloodshot eyes puffy and cheeks tear-streaked. I thought it was best to start with her. She already knew, firsthand, the consequences of pissing me off; I doubted she'd risk it again, even if the task I gave her seemed utterly impossible . . . like walking through a bedsheet hanging on a wall.

"On your feet," I said, drawing Mercy and pointing the blade at the traumatized woman. "You're first."

Melinda stood, movements wooden, and looked at me without really seeming to see me.

"Walk," I said, flicking the tip of the *At* blade at the gateway.

She moved like she was sleepwalking, only pausing when she was a few inches from the sheet. I gave her back a firm smack with the flat of my sword, and she stumbled forward through the gateway. And once again, Melinda was the cause of the gasps filling the room. Lucky girl.

"On your feet," I said, pointing Mercy at the man with the bleeding arm. "You're next."

CHAPTER TWENTY-THREE

"Well, well, well . . ." I rubbed my hands together, eyeing Constance, Scott, and Gregory, who were all huddled at the far end of the table. The last of the nonessential board members had just passed through the gateway to Heru's dungeon, and I was now free to focus all of my attention exactly where it was needed—on the three little piggies, making all that mischief under their roof. "I wonder which one of you has the straw house," I pondered aloud.

They exchanged wary glances.

I fingered the vial of infected blood hanging around my neck as I wandered back to their side of the boardroom. All three tensed up visibly as I neared them. Ever so slowly, I made my way behind their chairs, watching them watch me out of the corners of their eyes. Letting the tension build. Letting the fear take over.

"Which of you will give in first?" I asked. "Who will collapse under the slightest pressure?"

I stopped behind Gregory's chair and settled my hands on his shoulders. The top of his balding head was shiny, like he'd plucked any final straggling hairs. I could almost see my reflection in his bald spot, and I thought he might even oil that oh-so-shiny skin. His shoulders bunched up when I gave them a squeeze, and he held his breath when I leaned in, resting my chin on his right shoulder.

"Which of you has the most to lose?" I asked, looking across the table at baby-faced Scott. I blinked and shifted my attention to Constance. "Or the most to leave behind?"

The color drained from her tastefully made-up face.

I grinned, slow and sly. I didn't have to actually kill her, but threatening to do it—to leave her precious children motherless—would be enough to loosen the tongue of any mother who gave two shits about her kids. And from what I'd seen of Constance, she gave way more shits than that.

"Did you and your kiddos enjoy the movie the other night?" I asked her, straightening and cocking my head to the side. "That's a pretty fancy-schmancy home theater you've got there."

I hadn't thought it possible, but she blanched even further. After a rough swallow, she licked her lips, her focus darting around the room from me to Nik to the sealed-off windows behind him and the two impassable doors in the opposite wall.

"No way out, Constance," I said, tapping my fingernail against the *At* vial—*clink clink clink*. I glanced at the gateway. "At least, not to anywhere that's even remotely as pleasant as here."

"W—what do you want?" she asked, tears spilling over the brim of her eyelids.

"The cure."

Her eyes locked on me, her pupils so dilated by fear that the black drowned out the natural gray-blue of her irises. She shook her head slowly, her eyes rounding. A thin sheen of sweat coated her pale skin, giving her a sickly, pearlescent glow. "I—I can't—"

I stopped tapping the *At* vial. "Can't? Or won't?"

"I can't!" she said, voice shrill and eyes wild. "I wish I could, I swear, but—"

I kicked Gregory's chair, and he rolled a couple yards down the table, making room for me to squeeze in beside Constance. I placed my hands on the polished tabletop and leaned in toward her. "But *what?*" I asked, voice hushed. A few strands of her blonde hair swayed in the wake of my words.

Again, she licked her lips. "The—there *is* no cure."

My nostrils flared, and I searched her eyes, her face, looking for the telltale signs that she was lying.

"Honestly, I wish—"

"Shut up!" I shrieked, straightening and settling in to pace alongside the table. Either Constance was a damn good liar, or she was telling the truth. I had to believe the former; the possibility that there was no cure was too horrifying to accept. I might actually have to kill someone to get the truth. A human—either Scott or Gregory. Maybe then dearest Constance, here, would take this seriously.

"Little sister—"

"Not now, Dom," I snapped. For fuck's sake, couldn't he see that I was in the middle of something? It was a *terrible* time for a chat.

"It's Garth," he said, ignoring my dismissal.

"What?" I paused, placing my hands on my hips. "He totally disregarded what I said about getting to the compound, didn't he?"

"No, little sister. He arrived a couple hours ago."

"Then what is it?" I asked, staring hard at Scott, who was watching me like I had a stick of live dynamite stuck up my ass.

"Neffe just got the results from his blood test," Dom said. *"It came back positive, little sister. He's infected."*

My heart stumbled a few beats, and my grip on Mercy's hilt faltered. The sword slipped out of my hand, landing on the hardwood floor with a sharp clatter.

Nik took a step away from the sealed-off windows. "What is it? What happened?" He was suddenly in front of me, only I couldn't remember watching him close the distance between us. He gripped my upper arms. Squeezed, hard. "Kat! What's going on?"

I shook him off, reaching up to twist open the vial of infected blood even as I stepped over Mercy and marched back across the room to where Constance still sat. I drew the needle dagger from my left sleeve once more and dipped the point into the vial.

"Kat, wait!" But Nik reached me too late.

I scratched the dagger across Constance's smooth cheek in one sharp motion. She flinched back, her hand flying up to cover the shallow wound. Shallow, but deep enough. Garth was sick; now she was, too.

"That was infected blood, bitch," I hissed, leaning in until I was so far into her personal bubble I was practically giving her a lap dance. "Tell me the cure, or I'll leave you in here until this fucking disease kills you, too." I leaned in further, my nose less than an inch from hers. "Or maybe I'll wait until you're nearing the end, you know, the part when you lose your shit and attack everyone around you?" I laughed bitterly. "Maybe I'll wait until you're rabid, and then I'll send you home. How long do you think it'll take the kids to realize you aren't their mommy anymore—for them to see you as the monster you really are? For them to run from you?" I narrowed my eyes, studying her expression, soaking in her fear. "Too long, I bet."

Constance's eyelashes fluttered, and tears streaked down her pasty cheeks. "Please . . . no . . ."

"Tell me the cure," I yelled.

"There isn't one," she yelled right back. "Please, kill me. You have to kill me. I—I can't go home like this. I can't spread this to my babies."

I backed up, leaning against the edge of the table and staring at her, utterly dumbfounded.

"Kill me." She pushed her chair back and dropped to her knees before me. Her fingers gripped my legs, her manicured nails turning her fingers into talons. "Please, kill me," she begged. "Please. There's no cure. I swear there's no cure. Just *kill me*."

My heart went cold. Because I believed her.

CHAPTER TWENTY-FOUR

Garth is sick . . .

I stared down at Constance, kneeling on the floor at my feet. Clinging to my legs. Begging me to kill her. She was sick, too. She was infected, and there was no cure.

Garth is going to die . . .

All the moisture that should've been in my mouth was gone, leaving it a desert. I gripped the edge of the polished boardroom table behind me, my palms slick with sweat.

This is my fault . . .

I should've known better than to send Garth to the one place infested with this manufactured disease. I should've known better than to crawl into his bed. I should've known better than to fall for a fucking mortal. I had known better. I'd known better, and I'd done it anyway. But I'd thought I would have a little more time with him, that *he* would have a little more time before his mortal body wasted away and his soul faded into oblivion.

My eyes burned with the need to cry, but I blinked the tears away. I didn't deserve the relief of tears. Garth would've had more time if I hadn't invaded his life. From now on, I would only get involved with Nejerets. I was off humans, for good.

If only Garth was a Nejeret . . .

I blinked again, straightening from my slouched position, my eyes searching the blank wall just a couple yards away as an idea formed. An impossible idea. What if we'd been looking at this whole situation all wrong? What if it wasn't the *disease* we needed to cure? What if it was mortality? What if it was *humanity*?

Slowly, my focus shifted to Nik, standing off to the right near the wall. "Mari," I said, recalling what she'd told us about her work with Ouroboros that stormy day on the roof, just a few floors above where we stood now. "We need to find Mari."

She'd wanted Nik to work with her because his *sheut* power would enable her to transfer slivers of a Nejeret *ba* into a human being and graft it to their mortal soul. She'd claimed that, if the procedure was done properly, it would transform a human into a Nejeret.

I shoved Constance to the side, ignoring her cry of surprise, and took a step toward Nik. "Don't you see? There's no cure. This game—we can't win it. It's rigged against us. But if we change the rules . . ."

Nik stared at me for several, pounding heartbeats. I could see his mind working, could tell he was right there with me. "You want to turn the infected into Nejerets," he said, his stare intense, his pale blue eyes burning with an unearthly fire. He shook his head ever so slowly. "Kitty Kat . . . Mari's theory was just that—a theory. She never had success with the process."

I took another step his way. "Because she didn't have *you*, Nik. Remember? She said storing the *ba* sliver in *anti-At* poisoned it. But if you do the transfer . . ."

Nik crossed his arms. "That's assuming we can even find her."

It was a far from easy task; we both knew it. Over the past week, I'd been asking every Nejeret I crossed paths with if they'd been in contact with Mari or her mother, Mei, but none had seen or heard from either of them since Mari rescued her mom from the Ouroboros lab and the two went into hiding. Even Heru, whose *sheut* gave him the power to teleport to any place on earth by simply thinking of someplace, something, or some*one*, had failed to locate the pair. I wondered if it had anything to do with the fact that Mei could do the exact same thing, only better.

I took one final step toward Nik and reached out, gripping his forearms. The leather of his coat sleeves was smooth and warm to the touch. "We have to try," I said, pleading with my eyes. "It's Garth." My chin trembled, and my throat threatened to close up. "Dom just told me—he's sick."

Nik clenched his jaw, his eyes locked with mine, and time seemed to slow. To stretch.

He blinked, breaking the spell, and his focus slipped past me, his gaze growing distant. It was a look I recognized from the days when he'd shared his body with the god, Re, from the times when he would withdraw from the outside world to look within, to converse with one of the creators of this universe. Except that god was gone, now. Dom had warned me that Nik was broken inside, and I couldn't help but wonder if I was seeing evidence of that truth right now.

A chill crept up my spine, and dread pooled in my belly. "Nik," I said, squeezing his arms through the leather. "Please. Help me, *please*." I gave him a shake. "Nik . . . I need you."

His gaze refocused, slowly, and it was almost like my words had jumpstarted his mind.

"Help me find—"

"I know where she is," Constance whispered.

My eyelids opened wide, and both Nik and I turned to stare down at her.

Constance knelt with her head drooped, her blonde bob hanging in disarray around her face. Her shoulders rose and fell with each halting breath. "I've been in contact with her," she said, voice hoarse. "She's here, in the city . . . underground."

I looked from Constance to Nik and back, seeing the shock and uncertainty I felt mirrored on his face. I narrowed my eyes. "Why are you telling us this?"

"The disease was never supposed to get out," Constance said, raising her head to peer up at us. A hint of defiance shone in her eyes. "It was created as collateral. When Initiative Industries first brokered the negotiations between Ouroboros and your Senate, your people would only agree to support our longevity research with funding and"—she glanced away, clearing her throat —"*resources* if we helped them develop the disease." By resources, I had no doubt that she meant living test subjects. People, human and Nejeret alike. "It was their way of ensuring we didn't go back on our word and tell the whole world about them." She looked at me. "About *you*."

I scoffed. "What does this have to do with Mari?"

"She and I oversaw the development of the project, but Scott and Gregory handled the day-to-day while Mari and I worked on something that wasn't strictly on the books."

"The *ba* transfer," I guessed.

She nodded. "The technology to remove a Nejeret's *ba* already existed—all we had to do was figure out a way to transport fragments of *ba* into a human subject. Mari theorized that even the smallest, microscopic amount would spark the transformation . . ." Constance shook her head. "But every single time we tried the procedure, the second the balance between human soul and Nejeret *ba* shifted in favor of the immortal side, the *anti-At* we'd used to transport the *ba* fragment would eat away at the newly forming *ba* like acid through flesh, and the subject would die."

Constance looked at Nik. "You're the one she told me about, aren't you—the one who can make the transfer work?" There was a flicker of hope in her eyes, even after everything.

Nik didn't respond, didn't even nod. Instead, he looked at me. "Even with Mari's help, there's no guarantee that this'll work. It's still just theoretical. And assuming the procedure *is* successful, there's no way of knowing how much of Garth will be left once his soul is transformed by the *ba*. He might not even *be* Garth anymore."

"But it's all we've got. Even if there's only a one percent chance that this'll work, the odds are still better than if we let the disease run its course," I said, sounding a little lost, even to myself. I was grasping, and I didn't care. "He'll die, Nik. We have to try." Gods, I sounded like a broken record.

It took Nik a long time to answer, but finally, he nodded.

I exhaled heavily, relieved to still have him not just on my side, but *at* my side. I looked at Constance. "You know exactly where Mari is? You can take us to her?"

With a hand on the corner of the table, Constance climbed up onto shaky legs. "Yes. Yes, I can, but . . ." She licked her lips, wringing her hands. "I want something in return."

I felt the corner of my mouth twitch, and a quick glance at Nik showed the hint of a smirk curving his lips, as well. "What do you want?" I asked her.

She looked from me to Nik and back. "Use me as a guinea pig. If the procedure doesn't work, I'll die, but if it does work . . ."

"You'll live," I said with a rough laugh. "And a hell of a lot longer than you would've otherwise."

"I don't care about that," she said, and to my amazement, she meant it. "If it works, you have to promise to use the procedure on my son. It's the only way he'll ever have a chance at a normal life."

I stared at her, weighing her request. Was it possible that everything she'd done had been for her kid? I would never say I approved of her methods, but I couldn't deny that she was a solid mother. Maybe a little extreme with the whole putting the well-being of her kids first—ahead of the whole damn world—but she wasn't all bad.

Finally, I shook my head, a wry smile twisting my lips. "Why the hell not," I said, offering Constance my hand. Besides, I needed her just as much as she needed me. Some of the best partnerships started that way.

Constance shook my hand, and the agreement was made. "Thank you," she said softly.

I pulled my hand back and turned to the two men huddling at the other side of the room, as far away from us as possible. "Don't think I've forgotten about you, boys." I dipped the tip of the needle dagger in the vial of infected blood to re-coat it and stalked their way. "So . . . you two were in charge of the day-to-day operations on this project. Isn't that just fascinating?"

They exchanged a look. It reeked of piss on this side of the room, and it only took a glance down at Scott's trousers to see why.

"I wonder who might've let Sammy out?" I stopped a few feet from them and waggled the tainted dagger in front of their noses. "Who wanted the disease to get out—to spread?"

They recoiled.

I crouched down, elbows on my knees. "First person to spill the beans doesn't get infected . . ."

"It was me," Scott blurted. "I did it."

I blinked, taken aback by the quick response. I hadn't expected it to be so easy to get a confession. I also hadn't expected that confession to be a lie. "Now why would you *ever* lie about a thing like that?"

Gregory sighed, and the older man's entire demeanor changed. Not just his demeanor, his whole damn appearance. He stood, his head filling out with thick, dark brown hair and his face shedding several dozen years even as his shoulders broadened and he gained a few inches. The muddy brown of his irises gave way to an ethereal bronze that shimmered with an alien light and swirled with a whole galaxy's worth of stars.

"Because I compelled him to," he said.

"Holy shit," I breathed, standing and stumbling back a few steps. Gregory—or whoever the hell he was—wasn't human. And he wasn't even Nejeret; no Nejeret had eyes like that. The man standing before me was a fully-fledged Netjer, an actual, full-powered god, like the two who were currently still on sabbatical from our universe.

Vines of *At* shot past me as Nik reacted, but those indestructible ropes evaporated into a rainbow mist before they even came close to touching the Netjer.

I took another step backward, eyes wide and mouth hanging open. My heart hammered in my chest as I struggled, fruitlessly, to come up with a plan. But a Netjer is basically all-powerful. There was *nothing* I could do to this guy that he couldn't fend off, let alone throw back at me tenfold. There was no way for me to beat him and a gazillion ways for me to die trying.

I took one more step backward and ran into Nik's warm, solid body. The sudden contact made nearly jump out of my skin.

"Just me," Nik said, his voice barely more than a whisper. He rested his hands on my shoulders, and I took comfort from his touch. Drew strength from it. Maybe I couldn't beat this guy in a fight, but I sure as hell wasn't about to run away with my tail tucked between my legs.

I straightened my spine and locked stares with the unwelcome Netjer. He wasn't from our universe; there were only four Netjers native to this place—the original creators of this universe, Re and Apep, and the new gods, my niece and nephew, Susie and Syris—and this Netjer was most certainly none of them. He didn't belong here.

"Who are you?" I asked, voice hard and surprisingly steady. Go me.

The Netjer clasped his hands behind his back. "A visitor."

"Well, you're not welcome here," I snapped. "Go—"

Nik gave my shoulders a squeeze, and I shut my mouth, however reluctantly. "Why are you here?" he asked, sounding a whole lot more in control than I had.

"I've heard much about you, Nekure," the Netjer said, using Nik's true, ancient name. "Re speaks of you often."

I felt Nik stiffen behind me.

"What do you want?" I asked.

The Netjer leveled a cold stare my way, and his scrutiny paralyzed my lungs. "It would be impossible for your mind to understand my desires while in your current form."

"Why are you here?" Nik asked, repeating his earlier question.

The Netjer's stare shifted to Nik, and only then could I suck in a lungful of breath. "To observe," he said and turned away to stroll toward the sealed-off wall of windows. "To learn." He glanced at us over his shoulder. "To decide," he said a second before he evaporated into a glowing, writhing mass and floated through the wall of windows.

"Wait!" I shouted after him.

But he—it—was already gone.

CHAPTER TWENTY-FIVE

"To *decide*," Lex said, her brow scrunched as she studied my face. "That's what he said—to observe, to learn, and to decide?"

We were sitting at the table tucked away in the breakfast nook, surrounded by windows giving us a view of the storm pouring rain outside and bending the trees this way and that. The manicured gardens behind the house were already covered in a bevy of pine branches and bunches of leaves, and the angry clouds in the sky only seemed to be darkening.

"No *and*," I said, "but yeah, those were his words." I took a gulp of my Cherry Coke. Their house had one of those fancy pop machines that could make essentially any flavor of carbonated beverage. It was pretty awesome, and the sugar and caffeine were doing wonders to fend off the shock of the Netjer run-in. "What the hell—" I glanced at Reni, sitting in the high chair beside Lex at the table, snacking on string cheese. Her onyx ringlets appeared almost blue in the stormy afternoon light. "Sorry. I meant, what the *heck* is a fu—*freaking* Netjer doing here? Did Susie or Syris mention anything about a visitor?"

Lex shook her head, her fingers automatically going to the *At* falcon pendant hanging on a silver chain around her neck. It had been a gift from her godly children given to her just a few minutes before they left for the Netjer home universe three years ago, and it's the sole link between this universe and wherever they are, at least so far as us lowly Nejerets are concerned. I crossed my arms over my chest and sniffed. Apparently *some* Netjers could come and go as they pleased.

"He had coppery eyes," Nik told Lex, "if that helps the twins identify who he is. I think that part of his physical appearance was genuine, at least, though I don't know about anything else."

"He dissolved into one of those shining light blobs like the twins did," I added, though I doubted that helped at all. I lifted my glass to take another sugary sip.

"I'll talk to the twins," Lex said. "See what they know."

I bit my lip. "I don't suppose there's any way that they can come back here and, oh, say, deal with this whole mess, can they?"

Sighing, Lex shook her head. "I wish . . ." She picked a stray chunk of string cheese off her shoulder, seemed to think about what to do with it, then handed it back to her daughter, who grinned and popped it into her mouth. I wondered if Lex had been considering eating it herself. "They're stuck where they are until the other Netjers decide they're capable of tending to this universe." Her shoulders bunched up. "All I keep thinking is that maybe the other Netjers sent this guy here to watch over things in the twins' absence, but . . ." Her shoulders dropped. "I don't know."

I snorted a bitter laugh. "Well, if that's the deal, he sure is doing a bang-up job." Shaking my head, I tapped Nik's arm with the back of my hand and said, "We should go." We'd spent too much time discussing the "visitor" already, and Garth's life was sand in an hourglass.

"Oooooh . . ." Reni pointed in Nik's and my general direction. "Pretty colors!" She clapped her hands together, causing a few cheese bits to go flying.

I exchanged a quick, confused glance with Nik, then looked at Lex, eyebrows drawn together.

Lex raised one hand and shook her head. "I have no idea. She's been seeing things that are invisible to the rest of us lately—must be her *sheut* maturing."

Like Nik, Reni was one of the few Nejerets to have been born of two Nejeret parents, thanks to a little loophole in that whole Nejeret reproductive snag. Lex and Heru were what Nejerets called a "bonded pair," a rare set of true soul mates, their *bas* resonating perfectly with one another. As a result, they were one of the few Nejeret couples able to reproduce together. They were also addicted to each other—physically—and would die if separated for too long. A tough bargain, but one they seemed content with. And unlike Lex, Heru, Aset, and me, who'd all gained *sheuts* later in life by Susie and Syris, Reni had been born with hers, courtesy of her unique parentage. She was growing up with a *sheut*, giving her access to unknown powers at a very early age. She fit into the small fraction of the Nejeret population born with *sheuts*—Nik, Mei, and Mari, among them—and it would be a while before the full extent of Reni's innate powers was clear.

I exchanged another look with Nik, frowning this time. What did Reni see when she looked at me? Or at *us*? "Right, well . . ." I pushed my chair back and stood, and Nik did the same. Lex followed a moment later. "We're taking Constance with us, but we promise to bring her back."

"Fair enough," Lex said. She followed us to the front door, standing in the opening as we made our way down the porch stairs. "You don't want to see Garth before you go?"

The muscles in my shoulders bunched up. The thought of facing him without having a way to save him made my stomach turn. Guilt. Dread. Flat-out fear. I was sick with all of it. But not as sick as Garth would be soon, especially if this didn't work.

I shook my head, unable to turn around to look my sister in the eye.

Lex sighed. "Alright, well, will you tell Heru to come join me when he's finished?" He was in the dungeon, where Nik and I were headed to pick up Constance, the third member of our impromptu ambush-Mari team. He'd been leading the charge on interrogating the board members ever since we started sending them through the bedsheet gateway, and I had no doubt he was extracting some pretty juicy information.

I nodded, turning partially to wave at her. "And you'll have Dom pass on whatever you learn from the twins, yeah?"

"Of course," Lex said with a nod. At the sound of a high-pitched shriek from within the house—either a laugh or a cry, I couldn't tell—she cringed, then shut the door. I loved Reni, but man, the kid was just so very *toddler*.

I passed through the gateway I'd drawn on the wall of the garage, right on top of Heru's dungeon, and stepped into a crowded pub. Constance followed me, Nik right behind her. I'd been nervous about creating the gateway to the Pike Brewing Company, an always-bustling brewery and eatery located in the warren beneath Pike Place Market—I wasn't eager about exposing so many people to the now-infectious Constance, but so long as she kept her hands and her fluids to herself, all of the innocent humans would be safe.

I'd have chosen a less-crowded destination, but this was the place in the market I knew best—and hence could *draw* best—and the gateway had been a breeze to create. My only other option was the oh-so-famous fish market upstairs, and that was way too exposed for an out-of-thin-air appearance. At least down here there were doorways to pretend to pass through, not to mention alcohol to dull any onlookers' senses.

"Lead the way," I told Constance, holding my arm out for her to pass me by. I figured I didn't have to worry about her bolting—helping us was her only chance at surviving the disease. The only way she'd ever get to see her kids again. The only way her son would get better.

Pike Place Market is a multistoried maze, with ramps and hallways and in-between floors aplenty, and our route through the tangle was far from a straight shot. We headed up to the main outdoor level, passing by the famed fish market, narrowly dodging the huge Coho salmon being lobbed around to entertain the tourists, and wound through the throng to an offshooting stairway that led to the lower floors—or, at least, to parts of the lower floors. We passed by a free-trade jewelry and trinkets shop, a seller of miniature cars, animals, and pretty much everything else, and a kitschy magic shop on our way to a locked door marked "Restricted" tucked between the odorific men's restroom and a used bookstore.

When we reached the door, Constance produced an inky black key made of *anti-At*, and Nik and I both recoiled instinctively, however minutely. Touching the stuff wouldn't hurt Constance, since she didn't have an eternal *ba*—yet—but it would unmake any Nejeret from the soul out. Except for me, thanks to the protective Eye of Horus symbol tattooed into my palm. The *At*-inked symbol had already saved my life and my *ba* from the effects of *anti-At*, and it had the obsidian striations marbling through the opalescent ink to prove it.

Constance unlocked the door, and the three of us entered a narrow, steep stairwell lit only by a few ancient-looking bulbs in caged light fixtures high up on the walls.

"Cozy," I commented, eyeing the flickering lights. About one in three bulbs actually worked.

"This leads to an old utilities room," Constance explained without looking back. She was concentrating on the slightly uneven stairs. "The market made some updates a few years ago, and this area's not in use anymore."

"That explains the excellent upkeep," I said, glancing back at Nik.

He breathed a laugh, but no hint of a smile touched his lips. He had his game face on. Not surprising—Mari wasn't his favorite person, and she was one of the few people whose *sheut* power was a match for his. She was one of the few people who could pose an actual threat to him.

Constance led us deeper into the market's underbelly, and we entered a defunct boiler room with a hodgepodge of breaker boxes lining the brick walls to what appeared to be a bricked-over doorway. At least, until Constance wound her way through the ancient machinery filling the room and depressed a single brick to the right of the old doorway, then pushed on the area of newer bricks. It gave in with the grind of stone on stone until there was an opening plenty wide enough for a person to fit through. The space beyond was pitch-black, even to my sensitive eyes.

Nik whistled, and I grinned. Who doesn't love a secret passageway?

Constance reached through the opening, fumbling blindly for something. "There's a lantern here, somewhere . . ."

"Here," Nik said, holding up his hand, palm up. A writhing, glowing mass of living *At* flared to life, looking so much like some alien form of fire. It cast the area around us in an eerie incandescent light, making the world appear almost silver.

Constance's eyes widened, and she licked her lips. "Thanks," she said, eyeing the otherworldly mass for a moment before turning away from us.

We followed her through the opening to what appeared to be an old sidewalk—there was even an antique lamppost a few yards up the passageway and an arched opening for a window, though the view through the cracked glass only showed a mass of dirt, rocks, and rubble. The air down here smelled musty and earthy, sort of like a cave, but not quite. I'd been in spaces like this under the city before, areas leftover from the citywide regrade after the devastating fire of 1889. The old Seattleites had decided building a new city on top of the old one would be more practical and efficient than rebuilding the old. And lucky us, that meant that much of the original city remained . . . one only need know where to look.

"You won't find *this* on the underground tour," I said, voice hushed, as Constance led us further into the remnants of a Seattle long forgotten.

"I remember this place," Nik said, his voice barely a whisper. He walked ahead of me now, sharing his light with Constance as much as possible. I watched his profile as he slowed and looked around, nostalgia transforming his features. He reached his free hand out, brushing the half-burned wood frame of another window opening. "This was a hotel—the Occidental. Mother and I stayed here once." A wistful smile touched his lips. "This was the first place I ever had my photograph taken." He laughed under his breath. "Re disapproved, but Mother was so eager . . ."

I smiled to myself, enjoying this rare glimpse into Nik's past.

"Just a little farther," Constance said, pausing and tossing a glance back at us. Only then did I realize how far behind we'd fallen.

Five minutes later, we reached an old armored door, the kind used on a bank vault a century or two back. *PUGET SOUND NATIONAL BANK* was engraved in the metal near the center of the door. Constance made quick work of the heavy-duty built-in lock, spun the wheel, then turned a handle, and the door slowly swung outward on surprisingly well-oiled hinges. "Stay here, out of sight," she whispered, then passed through the vault doorway and headed for a second door just a few yards in from the first. It was smaller and rusted, with a several-inch square hatch at face height for a peekaboo window.

Nik nodded, and the two of us backed up a few steps, retreating into the passageway. I inhaled deeply, then held my breath.

Constance's knock was gentle, but she didn't need more than that to alert Mari's Nejeret ears of her presence. "It's me," she called quietly. "I have news."

There was a rusty creak, followed by, "What happened at the meeting?"

Adrenaline flooded my bloodstream at the sound of Mari's

voice, and my whole body hummed with anticipation. She was really here. We'd found her. I might just be able to save Garth.

"You look like hell," Mari told Constance. "Did the board vote you out?"

"Not exactly," Constance said. "Let me in, and I'll explain."

Nik and I stared at each other as we waited for the sound of a door opening. It seemed to take forever. There was clang after clang as Mari dealt with the door's locks, and I was starting to get a little lightheaded from holding my breath for so long. But I could hardly let it out now, in a massive exhale. Mari would hear that, for sure.

Finally, the door opened with the faintest of creeks. We waited a few more seconds for Constance to actually get in the doorway, where she could bar the way so Mari wouldn't be able slam the door as soon as she spotted us, and then I stepped into view.

"Hey, Mars," I said, raising a hand to wave.

Her familiar, almond-shaped eyes rounded in surprise.

"Been looking for you . . ."

In an explosion of rainbow mist, statuesque Mei appeared behind her adopted daughter and placed her hand on Mari's shoulder, preparing to teleport them both away to safety.

"Wait," Nik said as he, too, stepped into view. "Daughter, please, hear us out."

I blinked, eyeing him for a few seconds before his words finally made sense. It always took me a moment to reconcile the fact that Nik has a daughter—Mei. He's just so *un*fatherly in pretty much every way possible. Not that that changed the fact that he *had* fathered Mei millennia ago. She'd inherited her fair share of the stunning beauty that was so pervasive in her father's bloodline, though her ancient human mother's genes had lent her a far more Middle Eastern look. She'd also inherited her *sheut* from Nik, though her powers were quite different from his.

"We need your help," Nik said, extending his hand, almost like he was pleading with her. Maybe he was.

For uncounted seconds, the five of us stood there, an ice sculpture of tensions and uncertainty.

Until, finally, Mei nodded. "Very well, Father." She looked at me, bowed her head in greeting, and murmured, "Katarina." Then she straightened. "Both of you, please, come in."

CHAPTER TWENTY-SIX

"So," I said, "will you do it?" I was sitting across from Mari at a farm-style dining table in their surprisingly well-stocked underground kitchen. It turned out that their hideout really was an old bank vault, and that some guy named Billy had set it up as a fallout shelter in the forties, only to leave it abandoned some years later when he died in a car accident. We knew about Billy and how he'd died because he'd been a friend of Mei's back in the day. It was how she and Mari had known the bunker was down here in the first place.

Mari inhaled deeply, then looked at her mother, who was sitting to her left. I'd filled them in, telling them as quickly as possible about everything that had happened over the past couple days, save for our encounter with the mysterious Netjer. And my whatever-it-was with Garth. TMI is very much a real thing.

I glanced at Nik, sitting on my left, but his eyes were locked on Mei, too. Probably because she was staring at him just as hard. I didn't know much about Nik's relationship with his daughter, but based on appearances, it was a tense one.

Seeing that she wouldn't get any help from her mom, Mari returned her attention to me. She blew out a breath and threw her hands up in the air. "Oh, why not." She pointed a finger at me. "On one condition." She redirected her pointer finger to Nik. "*You* agree to help me, even after we save Kat's boyfriend."

"He's not my boyfriend," I said reflexively, and Mari snorted. I looked at Nik, begging him with my eyes to agree to her condition. It was hard to do when he hadn't even glanced my way. Losing patience, I reached out and touched the back of his wrist with my fingertips.

Finally, he looked at me, his expression hard.

"Please," I whispered. "Nik . . . *please*."

His features softened, and he closed his eyes and bowed his head in assent.

A sly grin spread across Mari's face. She slapped her hands together, then rubbed them back and forth vigorously. "Looks like you're not dying today, Connie," she said to Constance, who was lying down on the mid-century couch in the "living room." She was running a fever already, and she'd practically collapsed on the couch as soon as Mari suggested she get some rest.

Constance held up a hand, giving us a thumbs-up over the back of the couch.

"Gather whatever you need. We've got to get back to Bainbridge right away," I told Mari, then looked at Mei. "Can you teleport us there?"

"You three, no problem," she said, then looked at the couch. "But I can't teleport her. She's human—the trip would tear her apart."

I sighed, then scooted my chair away from the table. "Alright, well, a gateway it is, then." I stood, hoping I had it in me to make one more today. "Which wall do you care about the least?"

Mari and Mei exchanged a confused look.

"Her power's evolving," Nik explained. Oh, right, because I hadn't included that part in my flash update, either. "She can draw a sort of doorway from one place to the next."

Both Mari and Mei looked at me, eyes opened wide and lips parted. Boy, I sure do love surprising people. Maybe it's why I always try to make sure their expectations are extra low. Because I totally do that on purpose. Really.

"Wall preference?" I asked, nudging them out of their shocked states.

"Oh," Mari said. "Um . . ." Brow furrowed, she looked at her mom, who shrugged.

"Artist's choice," I said, nodding slowly as I scanned the space. I was already digging the bundle of Sharpies out of my coat pocket. "Suh-weet."

CHAPTER TWENTY-SEVEN

"Alright," Neffe said, exchanging a look and a nod with Aset, "we're ready." The two petite Nejerets stood on either side of something that looked an awful lot like a dentist's chair—only the kind a demented, evil dentist would use, what with all the strappy restraints holding down the brilliant duo's first subject.

Mitch Carmichael was being used as the inaugural lab rat for the *ba*-grafting procedure. Even though Constance had volunteered, Heru thought she held too much value to be used so negligently. She was willing to work with us—to share everything she knew about the inner workings of the Ouroboros Corporation and Initiative Industries, not to mention the negotiations and deals made with the Senate—and that made her an invaluable asset, especially compared to rancid Mitch Carmichael.

If the procedure was a success, Mari promised to infect Carmichael with *anti-At* as soon as the positive outcome became clear, and his short-lived, partially formed *ba* would be erased from existence once and for all. No gentle eternity for this pathetic excuse for a human being. That was just fine with me.

Standing at the foot of the chair, Nik held a marble-sized orb of *At*, a minuscule sliver of Heru's *ba* writhing within its temporary prison. It was one of nearly a dozen such marbles filling a metal lockbox on the counter behind me. Heru was the oldest Nejeret on site, and though Mari hadn't been able to explain why, she believed his age would make his *ba* the best candidate for a successful soul-grafting.

The *ba* extraction itself had only taken a few minutes, though it had taken Mari more than twenty-four hours of constant work to get the extraction apparatus—a modified MRI machine—up and running. With Nik's help, Mari was able to harvest a baseball-sized chunk of Heru's *ba*, which she claimed should be all she'd ever need, since the fragment would ceaselessly replenish itself within its *At* prison, just as Heru's *ba* would regrow until it was fully repaired within his physical body. Probably a good thing, because I doubted Lex would ever let her husband go through a *ba* extraction again. It had been excruciating even to watch.

Mari stood beside me, arms crossed over her chest and expression rapt. Lex stood on my other side, and Dom, watching from the pendant hanging around my neck, was the only other soul present. Heru was two floors above us in his and Lex's bedroom, recovering under the attentive "care" of his toddler, and it had been Mari's suggestion to clear the basement laboratory of everyone else to ensure that word of this potentially world-changing procedure didn't get out. Nobody had argued.

Nik glanced over his shoulder to look at Mari. "You're sure this'll take?" He frowned. "I don't need to do anything more invasive?"

Mari nodded. "A human's soul is contained within every single cell of their physical body. The moment that *ba* fragment touches his skin, it'll recognize a potential host. It *wants* to be whole, and merging with a human soul is the path of least resistance. Go on . . ." She gestured to Carmichael with her chin. "See for yourself."

We wouldn't know if it was truly successful for a few hours, or so Mari claimed. That was how long it would take for the newly forming *ba* to make noticeable changes to Carmichael's human physiology.

Nik placed the *At* marble on Carmichael's shin, balancing it there with a single fingertip. A moment later, the opalescent *At* dissolved into a shimmering mist. I caught only a glimpse of that silvery filament of *ba* before it seeped into Carmichael's skin and vanished completely.

Mari blew out a breath and brushed a sleek strand of black hair from her forehead. "Well, I suppose we should all get comfortable. This is going to take a while."

Three hours, seventeen minutes, and forty-two seconds later, Mari destroyed Carmichael's brand-spanking-new *ba*. I heralded Carmichael's writhing passage into oblivion with a one-finger salute. It was a glorious moment.

"We'll do Constance next," Mari said as she turned her back to Carmichael's writhing form, "then your boyfriend, Kat."

I rolled my eyes, ignoring Nik's snicker. He'd swapped places with Mari and now stood on my left. I lost patience after a few seconds and elbowed him in the side none too gently.

"We'll prep Constance," Aset said, and she and Neffe headed to the quarantined half of the lab. The temporary plastic walls had been erected to keep the disease as contained as possible, and the area within functioned as a makeshift hospital for the few infected people in the compound, Garth included.

I watched them go, my heart yearning to follow. I still hadn't visited Garth. I didn't know how to talk to him without telling him there was *maybe* a chance that he would not only survive the incurable disease but also become a Nejeret. That he'd live forever. I couldn't not tell him that chance existed, but I hadn't been willing to get his hopes up. I'd needed to know for sure. And now I did.

"Go," Lex said, nudging me with her shoulder. "He's been asking for you nonstop." She offered me a gentle smile. "Give the poor guy the good news."

I searched her kind, carmine eyes, looking for some reason not to go. I was afraid to face him. But I needed to, so I pushed off the counter and marched after Neffe and Aset. The two were already beyond the plastic walls.

I could hear Lex and Nik whispering, but I hummed tunelessly to drown out whatever they were saying. Force of habit. Some things are better *not* overheard.

Mari laughed, and I slowed, glancing over my shoulder to see her sidling up to Nik. "Better get used to it, buddy." She linked arms with him, and I felt the hairs on the back of my neck stand on end. I had to force myself to keep going. "Besides, you've got a new partner now, and I'm half as crazy and twice as fun."

Ugh. I threw up a little in my mouth.

Nik looked my way, and when his eyes met mine, when I saw the sad smile curving his lips, my heart seized up. He nodded infinitesimally, and I had the oddest impression that he was saying goodbye.

Shaken, I faced forward and continued onward, heading into the decontamination space everyone had to pass through on their way in and out of the quarantine zone. A quick spray of some high-intensity disinfectant cascaded over me in a fine mist, and I continued through the next plastic flap.

Garth was sitting at a folding card table alone, his back to me, a half-played game of solitaire laid out before him. Neffe, Aset, and Constance were in the far corner of the room. Aset seemed to be explaining to Constance what sorts of changes to expect after the procedure.

I took a deep breath, then plastered a smile on my face and headed for Garth. "Hey, stranger."

He spun in his seat, looking too big for the folding chair, his fingers gripping the chair back. The second his rich brown eyes locked with mine, my heart warmed and my smile softened, becoming genuine. He looked exhausted; his skin was too pale, emphasizing the dark circles under his eyes, but he still filled the space around himself with a sense of calmness. Of peace.

"So, I've got good news, and I've got bad news," I told him as I drew nearer.

His eyebrows rose. "What's the good news?"

"This disease isn't going to kill you."

He started to stand, but I stopped him with a hand on his shoulder. "You found a cure?" he asked.

I shrugged one shoulder, pulling out the chair adjacent to his and turning it around to sit on it backwards, cool-kid style. "Something like that," I said, resting my forearms on the back of the chair.

He frowned. "And the bad news?"

I smirked, tilting my head to the side. "You're going to have to put up with my ass forever."

"I don't—" His brow furrowed, and he shook his head. And then his eyes widened. "My forever, or yours?"

I grinned. "Mine."

CHAPTER TWENTY-EIGHT

Sitting on a piece of driftwood, I stared out at the endless gray mass of salt water. Wind made the surface of the Puget Sound choppy, a clutter of white peaks forming only to fade away under the rolling swells seconds later. Dark clouds coated the sky from horizon to horizon, but the rain was the barest of drizzles. It looked more like five o'clock than one, but a glance at my borrowed watch assured me it was still barely after noon.

Off to the left, across the choppy Agate Passage, I could just make out the shoreline of Port Madison through the mist. Garth's family was there, waiting for word of his condition. His ancestors had been living on that reservation for generations, safeguarding the secret of my people's existence. Now Garth—one of them—was also one of *us*. I just didn't know how much the Nejeret he would become over the coming days would resemble the human he'd been. How much would that tiny sliver of Heru's *ba* change him—not just *what* he is, but *who* he is? There was no way to know until he woke, and Mari wasn't even sure how long it would be until that happened.

Garth and Constance had been out cold for over two days now, locked in a state of regenerative sleep as their bodies transformed to accommodate their new, immortal souls. I'd remained at Garth's bedside for the first nine hours, and the inaction—the waiting—had nearly driven me mad. Patience isn't my strong suit, and stillness is like torture to me.

"The news is reporting cases of the disease in hospitals in Portland, San Francisco, Los Angeles, Albuquerque, Salt Lake City, and Vancouver now," Dom said, breaking through my meditative fog.

I exhaled heavily, shoulders slumping. "Guess closing the state borders didn't work."

Washington had been under quarantine since the previous evening, once it became obvious that the people flooding hospitals in the greater Seattle and Tacoma areas complaining of a severe flu were actually the first wave of a new, frightening epidemic. The Cascade Virus—CV, for short, a strange viral pathogen that was seemingly nonresponsive to any kind of treatment—was all anyone could talk about on the news these days. I'd stopped watching TV or listening to the radio that morning, sick of hearing about the search for a cure. I already knew they'd never find one.

"Maybe they can stop it before it spreads across the country," I said, resting my chin on my hand. Not sure who "they" were in my mind, but surely there was someone—some humanitarian group or special government organization—who could handle this. Someone who could succeed where we'd failed.

"Perhaps," Dom said, but he didn't sound convinced.

"If it gets any worse, this could be bad, Dom—like, extinction-level bad."

"After everything we've learned from the members of the board, I believe that is precisely the point of all this." Heru had learned from Scott, the youngest member of the Ouroboros board, that the Senate paid him half a billion dollars and promised him immortality if he arranged for the release of ten infected humans and planted them in major cities across the country. He'd only made it to seven by the time we shut down his base of operations, the lab in SoDo.

I shook my head, feeling defeated. "I just don't get it. *Why* would the Senate do this? How *could* they? It's just so . . . so *wrong*."

What good was Heru's war now when all he was fighting for was a crumbling world?

"I wish I had an answer for you, little sister."

"I don't," I said. "That would mean your mind is just as twisted as theirs are." I inhaled deeply, then sighed. "The number of people who are going to die . . ." Even thinking about it twisted my stomach into knots. "I wish there was something I could do. *Anything.*" I'd never felt more useless in my life.

"There is something you can do," Nik said from some ways behind me.

I straightened and twisted around on the driftwood, spotting him at the mouth of the trail leading to the beach through the woods. "Shouldn't you be with Mari right now?" The two had been working together so closely for the past couple of days that I'd barely seen him, even though we'd both been in and out of the basement laboratory the whole time.

Nik strolled the rest of the way to my driftwood bench and sat beside me. "I'm right where I should be."

My cheeks warmed, and I hated my stupid heart for the little flutter it gave. I averted my gaze, staring down at the tiny rocks near my boots rather than risking meeting Nik's pale eyes.

"The way I see it, we've got two options."

"Oh?" I thumbed the cuff of my leather sleeve.

"Either we let all the humans die, and that's it," he said. "Game over."

I raised my eyes to meet his. "Or?"

Nik leaned in, like he was making sure he had my attention. It was pointless; he always had my attention. "Or," he said, "we save as many of them as we possibly can before it's too late."

"By turning them into Nejerets before the Cascade Virus kills them, you mean." Which also meant "we" didn't include me. I slouched, just a little, my gaze wandering back down to the rocky beach. "You and Mari, team awesome, saviors of humanity." I gave an unenthusiastic fist pump. "Go you."

Nik guffawed. "Not exactly, Kitty Kat." He bumped my shoulder with his. "I was thinking of you and me, actually. Figured, with your gateways and my control over *At*, nothing's stopping us from taking this show on the road." He pulled something out of the pocket of his jeans. When he uncurled his fingers, one of the *At* marbles containing a sliver of Heru's *ba* rested on his hand. "We've already got an endless supply of *ba*, and if we went from hospital to hospital, we could make a serious dent in the spread of CV."

Eyes wide, I looked at him. "But—but what about Mari? You made a deal." That deal was the only reason Garth was going to live. "You agreed to help her in her research." I shook my head. "She can't actually *do* anything without you there to complete the transfer."

"Lex can do it," Nik said, shocking the hell out of me.

I felt my eyes bug out. "She *can*? Since when?"

"You're not the only one who's *sheut* is evolving and growing stronger."

I stared at him for a few more seconds, mouth hanging open. "So she can control *At* like you now?"

Nik nodded lazily. "Says she's been working on it for a while. Her abilities are pretty limited at this point, but she's good enough to meet Mari's needs." He shrugged. "I think she's looking forward to it, actually. It'll give her something worthwhile to do . . . you know, a way to contribute to the cause even though the war keeps her stuck behind the walls here."

I couldn't stop staring at Nik. As he spoke, it took all of my willpower not to jump up and do a spaztastic happy dance. I pressed my palms together and sandwiched my hands between my thighs. "So you're serious," I said, half-asking. "You really want to do this—save the world and all that?"

Nik chuckled. "Maybe not the whole world." He leaned in a few inches. "Maybe we can just start with the humans in Seattle and go from there."

"Deal," I said, grinning as I offered him my fist. "So when do we start?" I was so tired of doing nothing that I was ready to start yesterday.

He smirked and curled his fingers back around the *At* marble, raising his fist to bump knuckles. "How about now?"

The end

Thanks for reading! You've reached the end of *Outcast* (Kat Dubois Chronicles, #2). Keep reading for more Kat adventures in *Underground* (Kat Dubois Chronicles, #3).

UNDERGROUND

Book 3

For Jenna, who inspires me every day
with her endless well of patience, love, and kindness.
I couldn't magic up a better friend if I had a sheut of my very own.

CHAPTER ONE

"No," Heru said. "Absolutely not." His leather wingback chair was silhouetted by the view of the woods, the choppy Puget Sound, and the overcast sky through the window behind him. "We don't know nearly enough about the side effects of the transformation." He leaned back, away from his desk, and rested his hands on the chair's armrests, making it appear more a throne than a desk chair. He was a king, through and through. "Until we've had more time to study Garth and Constance, until we know exactly what the implantation of a ba has done to them beyond curing them, the procedure is on hold indefinitely."

This couldn't be happening. I took a step closer to the desk, hand outstretched. "But what about—"

Heru shed the blasé air and stood, the leather of his chair creaking and the chair's legs screeching as they moved across the hardwood floor. "Listen very carefully, Kat," he said, placing his palms on the desk, one on either side of his laptop, and leaning forward. His golden irises flashed with irritation. Even from a dozen paces away, he seemed to tower over me. "I forbid you from transforming even a single human into a Nejeret. Am I making myself clear?"

I lowered my outstretched hand, balling it into a tight fist. My fingers itched for the hilt of my sword, Mercy. The pain of my nails digging into my palm provided a small but much-needed distraction, activating the lizard part of my brain enough that I didn't attack Heru with words. Or worse.

I shifted my focus from Heru to his wife, Lex—my half-sister—who was seated in one of the cushy armchairs set off to the side of Heru's desk, silently bouncing their toddler, Reni, on her knees. Both mother and daughter had been watching our exchange, eyes opened wide and mouths forming tiny Os. Still were. Neither they nor I had expected this meeting to go south so quickly. Or at all.

I implored Lex with a single look, desperation quickening the rise and fall of my chest—like, running-up-stairs quick.

Lex inhaled as though she was about to say something but hesitated, closing her mouth a moment before giving a tiny headshake and averting her gaze. Or rather, avoiding mine.

I pressed my lips together, holding in a frustrated growl, and glanced over my shoulder at Nik. He'd been standing beside me for minutes, quiet as a mouse. He was supposed to be my partner in this. The whole save-the-humans plan was his idea in the first place. He *should've* been backing me up.

But instead, his expression was blank, like he was only half paying attention. Less than. He did that sometimes. It was his conversing-with-Re face. Except the ancient god had long since vacated Nik's body, so I had no clue why Nik was still making these infrequent trips to la-la land.

Whatever. Right now, I really didn't care, except for the part where he'd picked a pretty damn terrible time to check out, the prick. His plan, remember? And he was just standing there, hanging me out to dry.

"Thanks for nothing," I hissed under my breath, my glance turning into a glare. I took a deep breath, inhaling the earthy scent of leather and musk wafting off the books lining the towering built-in shelves on either side of the study. Looked like I'd be fighting this battle on my own. I cracked my neck. No biggie. I was used to going solo, anyway.

"Listen," I said on my exhale, forcing myself to meet Heru's hawkish golden stare.

"I urge you to use caution, little sister," Dom said from within the mirror pendant hanging on a leather cord around my neck.

I ignored my half-dead half-brother—aside from an eye roll, which he couldn't even see, so it hardly counted—and barreled onward. "I'm never going to have kids," I said to Heru. "We all know that. So why don't you just consider whoever Nik and I transform to be my darling children?"

Out of the corner of my eye, I watched Lex and Reni turn their faces from me to Heru. When Lex's domineering husband—*my own* oath-sworn leader—failed to respond, her focus returned to me. Our argument was like the slowest, tensest tennis match in the history of the world.

"It's only fair, isn't it?" I said, taking another step toward the desk. Toward Heru. "Or is creating new Nejerets a privilege only meant for the good old boys' club?" Another step. Another. My eyes narrowed to slits. I didn't care that I was poking a bear. "How many kids have you fathered, anyway? Maybe that'll give me a good starting quota." Gods, but I hated my voice when it took on that snide tone. Couldn't help it, though. Mix the hormones of an eighteen-year-old with an assload of frustration and anger, and, well . . . consider my bitch mode activated.

Heru breathed in and out three times, his nostrils flaring, then straightened, pulling his hands off the desk's ashen surface. His face remained expressionless, aside from a minor tensing at the corner of his mouth. "I understand your desire to save the humans, Kat, I truly do," he said, making his way around the desk. "But we are in uncharted territory here, and caution may very well save more lives in the long run than will steering a reckless course through dangerous waters."

He drew closer, and I crossed my arms over my chest. When his stare became too intense, I lowered my eyes to the floor. "How many people are going to die while we sit here doing nothing?" I said, my voice small. Small, but razor-edged.

"You may be surprised that I do, in fact, have a very good idea of just how many people will perish with each passing hour." Heru placed a gentle hand on my shoulder. "Based on the reports so far, of course."

His was meant to be a comforting gesture—probably—but I couldn't shake the knowledge that positioned like we were now, he could snap my neck before I'd even have a chance at any kind of defensive maneuver, if he chose to. I doubted the thought had even crossed his mind. The threat was likely just a product of my imagination, but that didn't stop it from spurring a spike of adrenaline. Annoying, considering Heru would easily be able to hear the resulting rise in my heart rate. I gritted my teeth.

"I also have projections of how many people will contract the virus each hour, as well as vectors showing the potential spread of the infection worldwide." Heru gave my shoulder a squeeze. "At present, the Cascade Virus is mainly a threat to the North American population alone."

I scoffed and raised my eyes to meet his. "You can't believe it's not already *everywhere*."

Heru gave a sideways nod. "Indeed, I do not. But the virus has a far weaker foothold elsewhere, which means that even if we lose most of the population of this continent, we may very well still be able to find another way—a less permanent way—to save the rest of humanity. Introducing millions upon millions of new Nejerets is far from the best solution."

Millions . . . I hadn't thought of it on that grand of a scale. Not that I was about to let any hint of shock show. "Oh, please," I said. "Like there's any other solution." I laughed derisively. "There's not going to be some amazing discovery, and even if there is, we're not going to be able to manufacture a cure overnight." Neffe, Aset, and every other science-minded Nejeret loyal to Heru had been working on finding an alternative cure for the Cascade Virus for days, but it remained just as stubbornly incurable. My lip curled. "Sounds like you're just afraid of a little immortal competition."

"Afraid . . ." Heru's hand fell away, and he turned to the side, his head bowed. "Yes, I am afraid." For just that moment, a fraction of a second, it seemed as though all of those impending deaths weighed heavily upon his shoulders. But as quickly as the impression came, he straightened and was back to being all ruthless confidence. "But what I fear is for the well-being of our kind and of the planet that we call home." He strode over to Lex and Reni.

His daughter blinked up at him, her cherubic face fraught with worry as he curled one of her fine, dark ringlets around his finger.

"Nejerets have large appetites, and we're prone to excess," he said. "The loss of humanity would be a shock to our way of life, but I fear the Earth could not sustain such a large swell in immortals." He emitted a whisper of a sigh. "And that's assuming we could even find a way to live together in peace." He released the strand of his little girl's hair, brushed his knuckle over his wife's cheekbone, and returned to the chair behind the desk. "Considering how well we're doing right now, my hopes aren't high."

Though logical and heartfelt, his reasoning didn't sway me. Human lives weren't worth less than Nejeret lives; that was the kind of thinking that had fostered the psychopathic genocidal actions of the Senate.

"Fine," I said, slumping my shoulders purposely to display defeat and moving one hand behind my back. I crossed my fingers. "We'll do it your way."

CHAPTER TWO

I exhaled heavily, tossing Lex one final glance and unable to resist flashing Reni a weak smile, then turned my back to them and started for the door, passing Nik on my way. No more crossed fingers, of course. "C'mon, Nik," I grumbled. Just because we were stuck here—for now—didn't mean we had to be sitting on our thumbs. I fully intended to spend the downtime refining our plan and weighing our options—obey, or don't. I certainly wasn't opposed to a little rogue action.

I had the door to the hallway open and was halfway out of the study by the time I realized Nik wasn't following me.

I called to him, turning partway and raising my voice. "Dude, what gives? Let's go regroup."

Both Heru and Lex were watching him, brows drawn together and eyelids narrowed. They looked as perplexed as I felt, all of that coated in a fine dusting of unease.

I marched back into the study, grabbed Nik's arm, and gave it a tug. "Hey, space cadet, coming back to Earth anytime soon?"

I barely registered Reni clapping her hands and cooing, "Oooooh . . . pretty!"

Nik blinked several times, his faraway stare melting away. "What?" He looked at me. "Did I miss something?"

I laughed bitterly. "Nothing important." I sent a meaningful glance Heru's way. "But we *have* been dismissed, so . . ." Another meaningful glance, this time at the open door.

Nik cocked his head to the side, shaking it infinitesimally.

I frowned, mirroring his head tilt. "Hey—you okay?"

"I swear I could hear—" Again, he shook his head, more forcefully this time. "Never mind."

"Okaaay . . ." I gave his arm another little tug. "My room?" I asked, eyebrows raised. "I'll fill you in on what you missed." I let go of his arm and took a step toward the doorway.

"Ah, yeah . . ." Nik followed, taking one halting step, then another. "I mean, no. I need to . . ." Again, he shook his head. "There's something I have to do. I'll, uh . . ." His pace increased, and he beat me to the doorway. "I'll catch up with you later," he said, jogging into the hallway.

I stopped in the doorway and watched him rush down the second-floor hallway toward the grand staircase at the front of the house. Once he was out of sight, I glanced over my shoulder at the family of three watching from within the study. Both Lex and Heru wore what-the-fuck expressions. Glad I wasn't the only one.

Nik wasn't normal, not even for a Nejeret. His time sharing his body with Re had changed him irrevocably, making him distant and difficult to read. Even now, with Re gone—returned to his home universe where the rest of the Netjers could restore him to health—he still seemed to have a hold over Nik, almost like echoes of the god remained with him, haunting his consciousness. He was generally difficult to know, let alone to understand, but his behavior just moments ago was downright bizarre.

I offered Lex and Heru a weak shrug before leaving them alone to discuss whatever the hell had just happened without me. I was halfway to my room when I heard the very distinctive sound of a door being eased shut, the little metal pieces snicking into place like alarm bells ringing in my ears.

I paused and glanced around. All seven doors but the one to the study were closed—it could've been any of them. Not that it really mattered. None of what had been said in the study was overly sensitive information. We hadn't decided to *do* anything. In fact, we'd settled on doing nothing as the best plan of non-action.

One deep breath later, I made it the rest of the way to my room and locked myself in, leaning my back against the door. After Nik's sudden bailout, I needed some solid alone time. To think. To worry. To mope. To figure out what the hell to do next, because whatever I'd told Heru, doing nothing *at all* really wasn't an option. In defense of my lying to him, I *had* crossed my fingers.

"That was quite peculiar behavior from Nik, don't you—"

I let my head fall back against the door with a dull thud and groaned. "Not now, Dom," I breathed. My idea of alone time didn't include my incorporeal half-brother's ever-present presence. It didn't mean I had to be an asshole about it, though. I sighed. "Sorry."

"I'll give you some space," Dom said a little primly. Great, I'd hurt his ghostly feelings. *"Let me know when you want to talk."*

I nodded. He'd moved to the standing mirror in the corner and could see me from there, so it wasn't like he thought I was being a double asshole and flat-out ignoring him. And I knew from experience that speaking to him further would only spur him into drawing out the one-sided conversation, and I was craving a type of guidance he couldn't give me.

Dragging my feet, I made my way to the bed and plopped down on the edge. I opened the top drawer of the nightstand and pulled out the velvet drawstring bag containing my hand-drawn deck of tarot cards. I pulled my legs up and tucked my feet into the crooks of my knees before starting to shuffle the cards.

Seven times, I divided the cards and threaded them back together, all the while thinking: *What the hell is going on with Nik?* Yes, I'd intended to do a more general what-am-I-supposed-to-do-now reading, focused on the bigger picture—the human extinction picture—but that was unceremoniously shoved aside by my subconscious. At the moment, I was way more concerned about Nik's little show back in the study.

I cut the deck into three piles and hovered my hand over each pile, eyes closed and mind and soul focused on the otherworldly energy charging the cards. Each pile gave off a little tingle of power, but it was the leftmost pile that made the air filling the narrow space between my skin and the cards feel thick with static electricity. *Ding ding ding*, we've got a winner.

I restacked the cards, placing the leftmost pile on top, then flipped the top card.

The Sun. Definitely a good omen. The design had altered itself to show a man wearing jeans and a torn white T-shirt standing with his back to the viewer. The man was Nik, I was certain. He stared up at the gilded sun engulfing the top half of the card.

My brow furrowed. The Sun card almost never carries any negative connotation, even when reversed. It represents improvement, recovery, growth, and success. If someone's ill, it means they'll recover. If someone's business is struggling, the Sun means they'll find a way to prosper. It's hands down one of the most positive cards in the major arcana, so drawing it first should've been comforting. Then why did new knots of anxiety tighten and twist in my stomach? Usually I had a sense of a card's meaning relating to the situation at hand; not so this time. I felt more confused than ever, and my concern for Nik amped up a few notches.

I blew out a breath and angled my eyes up at the ceiling. "Loving the clarity here, really," I said to whatever universal power fed me these insights. "Big help. Super fantastic."

But maybe the universe's clouded answer was a response in another way, possibly a gentle nudging for me to ask some other question—like, the *more important* question. *Fine,* I thought, *we'll do it your way*.

Deliberately, I collected all the cards and restarted the whole shuffling and cutting process. This time I forced myself to focus on the billion-life question: *What are we supposed to do now? How are we supposed to help humanity? How can we save them?* And last but not least: *Should we listen to Heru? Should we follow his orders? Should we do nothing and just let all those people die?*

As I cut the deck and tested the magical potency of each stack, whispers of the merits of asking for forgiveness rather than permission danced through my mind. Nik and I could break rank and start transforming people behind Heru's back. Together, we were *probably* skilled and powerful enough to evade him long enough to at least make a dent in the droves of sick and dying.

Settling on the middle chunk of cards this time, I restacked the deck and drew the top card.

Three of Swords. The card depicted a lone woman—me—crumpled on the muddy ground, rain pouring down on her, a single ray of sunshine lighting the area over her heart. Three swords stuck out of her body, each resembling Mercy, except only one appeared to be made of *At*. The other two were metal, one gold, one steel, or maybe silver.

Heartache. Sorrow. Betrayal. The Three of Swords represents the pain that comes when the clouds part and truth shines down, uninhibited and unavoidable.

More than a little unsettled, I wiped my suddenly clammy hand on my jeans, then drew another card.

Five of Pentacles. A test. Loss, emotional or financial. The fear of isolation. This card was almost as discouraging as the first. Was the test the card referred to me deciding whether or not to follow Heru's orders? If I did cross him, was this card telling me I would lose everything? Would I be cut off from the people I loved? Even the mere thought was devastating; I'd only just mended these relationships. Was I really willing to risk them to save people I'd never met?

Almost on impulse, I drew another card.

Ten of Swords. Ruin. The breaking of bonds. Endings. Not the blindsiding kind of ending, but the kind that comes with warning bells and dread. The kind that results from a culmination of a whole load of messy shit. The kind that's expected, unavoidable, but no less devastating for it. At least this card bears a single ray of hope: the Ten of Swords promises an ending that will clear the way for a new beginning. When one door closes, and all that . . .

A rotten seed implanted itself in the pit of my stomach. This reading was just as confusing as the last, aside from one crystal-clear part—I couldn't do nothing. None of the cards hinted at any kind of static *anything*. They were all about action, about change. Which meant I couldn't follow Heru's orders. Defying him wouldn't be easy, and it would be really damn painful. But according to the cards, it had to be done.

"Well, shit . . ." Looked like I'd be asking for forgiveness then, since the permission route was off the table.

I would need to talk to Nik, to find some way to convince him that inaction wasn't an option. If anyone would be up for disobeying Heru, his nephew was the right guy for the job. Heru would never hurt Nik, his twin sister's only son. Her only child. Only if Lex's or Reni's lives were in danger. Only then.

I collected the tarot cards and flicked the top of the deck a few times with my index finger to discharge whatever remained of that oh-so-potent universal energy—that magic, so to speak—before putting the cards away. A few invisible sparks crackled, and the deck went quiet.

I jumped at a knock on the bedroom door, then froze, hunched over on the bed, the tarot cards halfway into their drawstring bag.

Was it Heru? Had he somehow guessed my rebellious intentions?

I sat on the bed, paying way too much attention to my breaths and heartbeats, my eyes searching the room for some explanation, for some excuse. Except I hadn't done anything wrong. Yet.

Spine straightening, I shook my head. A breathy laugh escaped from my mouth, just slightly tinged with hysteria.

The knock came again, and once more, I jumped at the sound.

I silently chastised myself, then cleared my throat and looked at the door. "Who is it? What do you want?" Everyone who lived here was a Nejeret, which meant they'd have been able to hear my words clearly even though I hadn't raised my voice.

"It's me," Garth called through the door far louder than was necessary.

My eyes opened wide. I hadn't seen him conscious since the transformation. He'd been out for days, his brand new *ba* working on a cellular level, turning him from human to near-immortal Nejeret.

I abandoned the cards, leaping off the bed and rushing to the door. My feet couldn't carry me quickly enough.

And yet, when I reached the door, I hesitated. Frozen. Paralyzed by the unknown. Would the man on the other side of the door be the same man I'd come to care about? Would he be different? Would he still *be* Garth?

There was only one way to find out.

CHAPTER THREE

My fingers fumbled with the lock, but I managed to get the door open. "You're awake?" I said, beaming up at Garth. "I mean, duh, that's obvious, but—"

My smile grew limp the second my overexcited brain processed the expression on Garth's face. His strong brow was furrowed, the corners of his mouth turned down, and he was squinting, barely a hint of his warm brown irises visible through the dark lashes. Hardly a happy expression.

"Are you—" I swallowed roughly. "Are you alright?" Had something gone wrong with the transformation? His pulse was racing, and he wasn't exactly flush with the exuberance and excitement of fresh immortality.

"I—" He winced, almost like the sound of his own voice hurt his ears. His frown deepened, and he shook his head. "Honestly, Kat, I'm not really sure what I am right now," he said, his gravelly voice barely more than a whisper. "Let alone *where* I am . . . or if the procedure worked. I feel—I feel strange, to say the least."

I offered what I hoped appeared as a reassuring smile despite the worry tumbling around in my chest. "Yes, it worked," I told him, "and you're in Heru's house, a couple floors above the lab." I took a step backward and held out my arm, inviting him into the room. "How long have you been up?" Once he was through the threshold, I eased the door shut. "How do you feel?"

His back to me, Garth stopped near the foot of the bed and bowed his head. He was wearing rumpled blue and gray pajama pants and a navy blue T-shirt. His feet were bare, his short, black hair tousled. "Everything is so—" His broad shoulders rose and fell as he inhaled deeply then let the breath out in a sigh. "It's all just so much *more*." He was still using that almost-whisper. "So loud and bright and—and—"

I closed the distance between us and placed my hand on the back of his shoulder. I trailed my fingertips down the length of his arm as I moved around to face him. Goose bumps rose under my touch, and I laced my fingers through his when I was finally standing in front of him. "And sensitive?" He had no idea what he'd been missing out on as a human, touch-wise, and I was more than willing to enlighten him.

Except he hardly seemed to be enjoying my touch. His eyes were squeezed shut, and his hand shook in mine. "Yes," he said through gritted teeth. "*Very* sensitive." Nope, his reaction definitely wasn't one of pleasure, but of something that looked a whole lot more like pain.

Abashed, I released his hand and crossed my arms over my chest, tucking my hands under my armpits. I wasn't sure what else to do with them. "Sorry," I said softly. "I wasn't thinking."

Nejeret traits don't manifest until full maturity, a.k.a. adulthood. When mine manifested, I'd had months to get used to my gradually heightening senses, and the process had still been quite the adjustment. I couldn't imagine what it would be like to go to sleep as a human and wake up a Nejeret, all senses turned up to the max. Pity panged in my chest, and all I wanted to do was comfort Garth, but I didn't know how.

Under pressure, all I could come up with was, "How are you holding up?"

"Alright, I guess." Garth laughed breathily and rubbed the back of his neck. "Maybe not so alright. I don't know . . ."

I started to outstretch my hand, like reaching out to him, touching him, might provide some comfort when all evidence pointed to the contrary. I tucked my hand back under my arm, practically hugging myself. "So, what are you—"

"Kat, listen, I—"

We started and stopped speaking at the same time. After a tense couple of seconds, we both laughed, though that cut off just as quickly when Garth winced and covered one ear with his hand.

"Sorry," I said again, the word barely audible. "What were you going to say?"

After a few more heartbeats, Garth's tense, pained expression downgraded from nails-on-a-chalkboard to annoying-high-pitched-sound, and he managed to open his eyes, though he still squinted as though he were staring straight into the sun despite the dimness of the gloomy light coming in through the windows.

"It's probably nothing," he said. "It was right when I was waking up, so I may have been hallucinating or dreaming or something, but I thought I overheard . . ." He hesitated.

"What?" I thought back to the heated conversation with Heru in the study—fine, it was an argument—and catalogued each notable point. What might Garth have overheard that could've troubled him enough to drag him from his recovery bed and down the hallway to my bedroom when clearly even breathing overwhelmed his hypersensitive senses? I searched the slivers of his rich brown eyes, thoughts whirling. "Really, Garth, what is it?"

Was he bothered by the fact that so many people were dying? Who in their right mind wouldn't be? Or was it the fact that so many more people would die while we waited to find out how Garth's own body reacted to the transformation? Surely he feared for his family's safety. Or was it that—

"You can't have kids?"

I opened my mouth, then promptly snapped it shut again and stared at him in stunned silence. Of everything Heru and I had said to each other, *that* was what dragged Garth out of bed?

Garth's brows drew together, and he shook his head, almost

like he was wading through his own tangled thoughts. Apparently, I wasn't the only one with a swamp for a brain.

"I'm sorry," he said. "That came out wrong. I just meant—is that a Nejeret thing, or just a *you* thing?" Another headshake. "That didn't sound much better, sorry. It's just that I don't really know much about your kind, and now *your* kind is *my* kind, and I have no idea what else to expect." He rubbed his temples with trembling fingertips. "With all this sensory overload . . . I'm barely holding it together. I don't know how I'm going to manage some brand-new superpower on top of all of this, and—"

"Whoa," I said, raising my hands. "Hold on, bud." I scrutinized his scrunched features. "Did someone tell you that you got a piece of Heru's *sheut* as well as his *ba*?"

Garth's temple-rubbing stilled. "No. Why? What's a *sheut*?"

I blew out a breath and turned away from him, crossing to the corner of the room to sit in the cushy, mauve armchair. It was a toned-down version of my fortune-telling chair back at the shop, the one I'd inherited from my mom. I collapsed into the chair. "So, nobody's explained to you the different parts of a Nejeret's soul?"

Garth lowered his hands and shook his head.

"Alright, so . . ." I pulled the hair tie down the length of my ponytail and let the long strands of hair cascade over my shoulders. "Have a seat." I gestured to the bed with the hair tie, then slouched against the armrest as I rubbed the ache of a too-tight ponytail from my scalp.

Once Garth was seated on the foot of the bed, I let my hand drop to the chair's arm. "A Nejeret soul is different from a human soul for a bunch of reasons, but the biggest one is this," I began. "Nobody really knows what exactly happens to a human soul after death—I suppose Re knew, but he's gone now and he never filled the rest of us in, so . . ."

I frowned as a wayward thought tunneled into my mind. The mysterious Netjer from the Ouroboros boardroom—the "Visitor," as we'd been calling him—probably knew, too. I tucked that question away for later, if our paths ever crossed again. He might even answer. He hadn't exactly been hostile. He also hadn't been *not* hostile.

"Anyway," I continued, "so far as we know, when humans die, their souls sort of evaporate, or something like that."

A mild look of horror slowly set into Garth's face. His entire family was human; of course that reality would bother him. Gods, I could be such an insensitive moron sometimes. But it was the truth, and he would've found out eventually. Isn't it better to just rip the bandage off all at once?

I had no comforting words of wisdom about losing people; I was still messed up over losing my mom. I decided pushing on to the less depressing part of this impromptu lesson was the best salve for that harsh truth. "But a Nejeret's soul remains an independent entity," I explained, "even after the Nejeret's physical body is dead."

"Like me," Dom said, for my ears only.

I nodded once, then pointed to the standing mirror a half-dozen feet from my chair. "Like Dom," I said, flashing my svelte half-brother a quick smile.

Dom stared out at us from the other side of the glass-turned-*At* surface, a silver-toned ghost in the mirror. He stood with his hands clasped behind his back, his dark eyes intent on Garth until his focus shifted to me. *"I caught a glimpse of the spirit plane before you captured me in that cellular phone. It was chaotic and beautiful, with streams of vibrant energy flowing and swirling all around me, almost like I'd fallen into a Van Gogh painting. I think I was seeing the ebb and flow of souls—not just Nejeret souls, and not just human souls, but the stuff that makes up* all *souls."*

I stared at him, lips parted and eyes unblinking. He'd never told me about any of that. In fact he'd never told me much of anything about his incorporeal experience. He still owed me a detailed description of everything there was on his side of the mirrors.

Dom's eyebrows quirked higher, and he nodded to Garth. "Perhaps you can share what I told you with him. It might be of minor comfort, considering you just told him that his whole family will cease to be once they pass on from the physical plane . . ."

"Oh, right." I cleared my throat and shifted my attention to Garth.

He was slumped on the foot of the bed, his face an avalanche of sorrow.

I relayed Dom's experience, adding, "So, maybe we're wrong about what happens to humans after they die. Dom's really the first Nejeret to be able to communicate with us after death, and everything else we know is just what's been passed down from Re over the millennia."

Again, a stray thought brought a frown to my lips. Maybe Nik had some residual knowledge about what happens to humans after they die—he *had* shared his body with Re for five millennia, after all. I'd have to ask him sometime . . . not that asking him ensured any kind of an answer. He was the king of avoidance. But it was worth a shot.

Garth perked up a bit, seeming a little less broken-spirited, but his face was still ashen, and he looked a little bit like he might be sick.

I glanced at the wastebasket tucked next to the nightstand, wondering if I should move it closer to him, just in case. "But, um, like I said before, a Nejeret soul is different," I told him, hoping to distract him with the fact that his fate wasn't quite so bleak. "It's called a *ba*—"

"That's the thing they put inside me, right?"

I nodded. "The way Mari explains it, in the hours after the initial implantation, your human soul slowly transformed into the immortal *ba* of a Nejeret. You just had to have a little jump start with a fragment of someone else's *ba*."

"Heru's," Garth said.

"Right, and—"

"But doesn't that mean that the thing—the *ba*—inside me is actually Heru's soul? Isn't a soul what makes a person who they are?" Garth blanched to an even paler shade, though I hadn't thought it possible. He already looked like he was on the verge of passing out. "Am I going to turn into some kind of a clone of him?" Garth stood; he was trembling visibly, and I wasn't sure his legs would hold him for very long. "Is his soul or *ba* or whatever killing mine?"

Standing, I shook my head and held out my hands, palms out. "No, Garth, that's not the way it works." I crossed the room to sit on the foot of the bed and pulled him down with my hand hooked into the crook of his elbow.

He sank back onto the bed without resistance.

"There's a thing that all Nejerets know—a universal truth. You know, like one of those unbreakable laws of physics. A *ba* can never overlap in the timeline. Meaning, a *ba* can't be in two different places at the same time, so there's absolutely no way that your *ba* can be a copy of Heru's. Your *ba* is yours, and since your transformation is complete and you're clearly still you, I think it's safe to say that your new *ba* didn't kill or displace your old human soul. Your soul *became* your *ba*." I searched his eyes for some sense of understanding and thought I spotted it. Maybe. "Does that make sense?"

"I—" Garth licked his washed-out lips. There was still a slightly wild cast to his eyes, but his panic seemed to be receding, and his heartbeat was slowing. "I think so."

"Good," I said, reaching out to take his left hand in both of mine. "Is this okay?" I asked, glancing from his eyes to our joined hands and back.

He nodded.

"Good," I said again. "Now, fair warning—this is where shit gets weird . . . -er." I took a deep breath. "Our *bas* are what give us our relative immortality and our heightened senses and—" I hesitated. "And what make female Nejerets infertile," I added slowly.

Garth's eyebrows rose.

"It's a tricky little blip," I said. "A side effect of our immortality. The same hyper-regenerative ability that makes us heal super-fast and keeps us forever young *also* makes a female Nejeret's body reject any—" I got caught up on the word *baby*. "—reject a fetus. We miscarry before we even know we're pregnant."

"That's awful," Garth said, his voice a little hoarse. "I'm so sorry."

"Totally don't worry about it." I snorted a derisive laugh. "I'll be the first one to admit that I'm far from mother material."

"Oh, I—" Garth looked away. He seemed to be struggling with what to say. "That's—"

He was taking this little infertility tidbit way harder than I'd have expected him to, considering he was *a guy* and was more than able to father a thousand kids, if he felt the urge. I didn't get what was upsetting him.

"Hey," I said, knocking his arm with my knuckles. "It's a totally different story for you, though. Male Nejerets can have all the kids they want."

"I see," Garth said, his voice distant and disconnected.

I leaned to the side to get a better angle to see his eyes, but he seemed to be avoiding looking at me. A niggling suspicion told me why, but I was avoiding acknowledging it. See, Nik wasn't the only one with finely tuned avoidance skills.

"He's falling in love with you," Dom said, his voice buzzing through my mind, his words waylaying my skillful avoidance efforts. "And he is only now learning that whatever future the two of you might have, it won't include children."

Well that sucked all the air out of my lungs. And the room.

Garth couldn't *love* me. He was too good for me. Too good, period. And I was, well, not. If you looked up "good" in a thesaurus, I'd be listed as an antonym.

Besides, I didn't do love. Hell, I didn't even do relationships, and despite my rather intense fondness for Garth—despite the fact that I'd dragged him here to be cured via an extremely experimental procedure that would "theoretically" transform him into a Nejeret—he was *not* my damn boyfriend. Regardless of Mari's endless teasing. Committing to save all of humanity was no biggie, but committing to *be* with someone—to let someone in, to let that person know me . . . know all the things I'd done—that kind of intimacy terrified me beyond words. Beyond thoughts.

I was in desperate need of a new subject. I racked my brain for something. Anything. Clearing my throat, I said, "A, um, *ba* isn't what gives a Nejeret like me my 'magical' superpowers, though." I couldn't quite bring myself to look at Garth's face, so I focused on his shoulder instead. "Some of us—and when I say some, I'm talking about the extreme minority—have an additional part of our soul that's sort of tacked onto our *ba*. It's called a *sheut*, and it's the thing that makes it so we can do different things like teleporting or telling the future or—"

"Turning humans into Nejerets," Garth said, his voice monotone. He actually sounded kind of bummed, and I wondered if he'd been looking forward to discovering his nonexistent "superpower," whatever he'd said earlier about not being able to handle it. Or was he still hung up on the kids thing?

"Sort of, but not really," I said, forcing myself to stay on topic even as my thoughts wandered. Why did the fact that I couldn't have children matter so much to him? He barely knew me, and he knew *nothing* about my past, about the things I'd done. Out loud, I finished my response to Garth with, "That was a combination of good ol' technology and Nik's *sheut* powers."

"Oh."

When it was clear that "Oh" was all Garth was going to say, I forced myself to make eye contact with him. Windows to the soul and all that.

Silence had all but overtaken him, but the heartbreak filling his eyes was foghorn loud.

"Hey," I said, bumping his arm with my shoulder, "like I said, most Nejerets don't have a *sheut*, so you're not missing out, really. Nik and me and a few dozen others . . . we're just weirdos."

"I believe it's still the infertility revelation that is disturbing him," Dom said, insightful as always. Or maybe I was just dense from the hope that the "infertility revelation" wasn't as big of a deal as it seemed. If it mattered so much to Garth, then he deserved to be

with someone who could give him what he wanted. I would never be that person.

And at the moment, I wasn't ready, willing, or able to discuss that particular subject any further. Maybe I'd never be ready for that.

I stood and took a few steps away from the bed. Away from Garth. "I have some stuff I have to do . . . for the shop," I said, my back to him. "Kimi's waiting on my call." But he had no idea who I was talking about, so I added, "She's my assistant manager." The moment I realized I was wringing my hands, I separated them and purposely moved them down to dangle uselessly at my sides, feeling obscenely awkward. Why was it so much harder to confront things I couldn't take care of with a swift kick or a punch?

"Right."

"And you should rest," I added. "You've been through a lot." I turned around.

Garth's shoulders were still slumped. Hell, his whole damn self was slumped.

"I'm sure Mari and Neffe and Aset are all itching to get their hands on you, too. You'll be busy all afternoon with tests and stuff."

I shoved my way through the emotional bramble, ignoring the thorns, desperately searching for safer territory. If Garth hung out in my room much longer, he'd bring the kid thing back up. Or even worse, he'd realize the danger his human family was in and start freaking out about that. Or figure out what I already knew—so much of the tangled mess he was in was my people's fault. *My* fault. Guilt and disgust already plagued me; I wasn't eager to face accusation, too. Especially not from him.

"Why don't we plan to do dinner tonight—say, six? Or seven?" I proposed, falling back on good ol' avoidance. "I'll bring the food up to your room."

"Sure," Garth said, rough voice barely a whisper.

I lowered my chin, giving him a look that was meant to be

sultry. Meant to be. Probably wasn't. "We could do dinner in bed . . ."

His chest and shoulders convulsed with a single, weak laugh. "Sounds good."

"Kat," Dom said. "Perhaps you should spend some more time with—"

"Good," I said. "Can't wait." But anxiety twisted my stomach into knots, calling me a liar. I couldn't keep pretending like this thing between Garth and me could work. I'd been lying to myself when we first got together—our species difference hadn't been the biggest roadblock in our relationship, or whatever it was—and it didn't matter that that barrier was now gone. The problem was my past. The problem was *me*.

I *would not* be the dog shit on the bottom of anyone's shoe. Garth had no clue about the things I'd done, about the people I'd killed, and I refused to soil his purity—his genuine goodness.

Resolve settled into my bones as I shut the door and once again was alone in my room. I had to cut Garth loose, once and for all.

Tonight.

CHAPTER FOUR

I sat in the armchair in the corner of my room, legs curled up and knees hugged to my chest.

I'd lied to Garth when I told him I had work to do. The shop was doing just fine without me around, and there was no doubt in my mind that it would continue on that way. Kimi was more than capable of running the place all by herself. Hell, with her business school background, she'd probably come up with a hundred ways to make the place run more efficiently.

Now, with Garth gone, Nik off wasting time doing who the hell knows what, and Dom having retreated to the far recesses of his mirror kingdom, all I had was solitude and bitterness to help me pass the time. And trust me, solitude and bitterness aren't a pretty combination.

When I couldn't stand my own company any longer, I pulled my new phone out of the back pocket of my jeans and tapped the PNS app. The Public News System—affectionately called "penis" by the younger generation . . . and by me—was a required component of every personal computing device, as mandated by the same amendment to the US Constitution that required all citizens above the age of fifteen have access to a smart device, either a watch, a phone, or a tablet. It's supposedly to promote equal access to information for all. But that would require a free press, which died a decade or so ago.

The result: PNS, providers of the only local and national news stations broadcasted across the United States as of the past decade. Keeps the media from spreading corporate biases or other divisive agendas. Or so "they" claim. Nowadays, it's the bland, colorless government agenda Americans get shoved down their throats. We get the truth, the whole truth, and nothing but the truth . . . as determined by an offshoot of the executive branch. Nifty, right? Yeah, not so much.

And at the moment, all the newscaster on the local PNS video feed could talk about was the Cascade Virus and how overrun the hospitals in Washington, Oregon, Northern California, and Idaho were and what people should do to treat themselves and their sick family members at home. Because nothing the hospitals tried seemed to be helping, and the only time a hospital bed opened up was when its previous occupant had been dispatched to the hereafter. Dispatched, as in euthanized.

Just this morning, the President issued an executive order not only legalizing the hastening of critical CV patients' passing but requiring their lives to be ended before they reached the final, rabid stage. The Center for Disease Control released a statement declaring that persons who reached that stage were already legally dead, anyway, like a chicken with its head cut off that didn't know it was supposed to stop running around. It wasn't true, but I could understand the government's reasoning for the deception—this way the already strained law enforcement forces could focus on combatting the increasing number of uncontained rabid cases rather than arresting the civilians who were helping them do their job by dispatching the rabids themselves. Justified murder. *Necessary* murder.

The world was going to shit. Because of us. Because some asshole Nejerets believed they were better than humans. I shook my head, disgusted with my own kind.

The story on the local feed changed to a fluff piece: *TARSI*

TIFF'S CRUSADE CONTINUES. I laughed, silent and humorless. Tarsi Tiff, superstar and world's sweetheart. She was young, plucky, wholesome, whipcrack smart, and insanely talented. She was also a Nejeret. More specifically, she was another of Heru's daughters, originally named Tarset when she'd been born back, oh, say, four or five thousand years ago.

Since the outbreak became public knowledge, Tarsi had been fundraising online. She'd been at it for more than thirty hours straight, having gathered a mega lineup of today's latest and greatest bands and musicians. According to the newscaster, she'd already raised a half billion in charitable donations to go towards CV research. It was a shitload of money, but I feared it wouldn't do any good.

The story changed again, this time to the Ouroboros Corporation's supposed efforts to find a cure. They'd issued a press release the previous afternoon claiming that any and all people turned away from hospitals were welcome to come to them for help. I was sure their intentions were nothing but pure and selfless. For the good of mankind. Right . . .

With a sniff and a tap of my finger, I switched to the national feed. The subject was the same—the Cascade Virus, of course—but the approach was totally different than it had been on the local feed. Here, they focused less on the people who were already sick and more on how to prevent the spread in the less affected areas. It was all about how to stay safe—to stay uninfected. People were advised to stay home, and not only had the country's borders been closed off, but every single state was operating under a hard quarantine as well.

A ticker ran across the bottom of the screen—the kind that usually showed sports scores or election results. This one, however, gave infection rates and death tolls by state. The infection rates included both percentages and raw numbers. How helpful.

I felt sick to my stomach watching the numbers increase in jumps of ten or more people. Ten or more sick or dead. Because of the Nejeret Senate. Because of my people. And Heru wanted me to sit here and do nothing?

Rage boiled within me, and I stood and chucked the brand-new smartphone across the room, howling in anger. The phone smashed against the wall, exploding into a handful of larger chunks and a smattering of tiny pieces that landed on and around my dresser.

I had to do *something*. It didn't matter how much it would piss off Heru or how he would punish me, I couldn't just sit back while the humans out there were dropping like flies. Humans—people—who lived in my country. In my city. If Nik and I could save just a few of them. If we could save just one of them, any punishment would be well worth it. Was that what the universe had been trying to tell me?

I stood and moved to the bed, sitting on the edge with one leg pulled up. I freed the deck of tarot cards from their drawstring bag once more and murmured, "Alright . . . it's decision time. Do I do it?" Not should I or can I, but *do* I—an absolute. I was done pussy-footing around.

Without bothering with shuffling, I flipped the top card. I was looking for a simple yes or no answer, an upright card meaning "yes" and a reversed card meaning "no."

The Empress. Upright. Yes.

I flipped another card.

The Five of Cups. Upright. Yes.

Another card.

The Ace of Wands. Upright. Yes.

Again—upright. Yes.

Again—the same. Again and again and again, against all the statistical odds, the card was always upright, always a "yes." I went through the entire deck, wanting to make absolutely sure, turning over the cards one after another until just one remained in my hand. I'd seen all the cards as I flipped them, my subconscious taking mental note of each. I knew which card was supposed to be left—the *Knight of Pentacles*, a card associated with prosperity.

But logic didn't always apply to my deck of tarot cards. They had the power—and so far as I'd seen, the will—to rearrange themselves as needed.

Just one card left; it was time for the big question. "What happens if I do nothing?"

I flipped the card over.

Death. The entire card was black, no hint of a design at all. It practically dripped with ink it was so saturated.

I dropped the card on the bed, hands shaking. I'd asked for clarity, and I'd received it.

Someone knocked on the door, and I shrieked, clutching my chest. As my heartbeat slowed, I realized Garth must've returned for round two of the discomfort championship.

"Hang on," I said as I unlocked the door and yanked it open. I expected to see Garth standing on the other side, rumpled PJs and all, and I blinked when I saw who was actually standing in the hallway. "Lex? What are you—"

My older-younger—it's complicated—sister placed her hand over my mouth and pushed her way into the room before I could say more. She held a finger up to her own lips, telling me to keep mine zipped, then nodded once, more of a question than anything else.

I mirrored her, giving her my word to hold my tongue.

Lex removed her hand from over my mouth and turned to shut and lock the door. A moment later—a much longer moment than it would've taken Nik—the room was sealed off from the outside world by a thin sheet of *At*. Looking so much like the finest layer of ice, *At* coated the floor, ceiling, walls, doors, and windows.

My heart gave a little flutter as the instinctive part of my brain couldn't help but feel like it was being trapped. But one glance at my nightstand quieted the panic; an array of Sharpies lay scattered on the surface, any of which would work well enough in the creation of a gateway out of here. I'd never tried to draw one on a surface made of *At*, but I didn't see any reason why it shouldn't work. I knocked gently on the *At*-covered wooden doorframe as that thought came and went. Just in case.

Lex had to assume I could get out of a room sealed off with At, too, so I figured trapping me wasn't her intention. There was only one other reason I could think of for why she'd done it: she wanted to seal in our sounds—our words—right along with our*selves*.

"What is it?" I asked, taking a step toward her. Whatever she had to say, it had to be serious, but I couldn't for the life of me guess what it was going to be.

Lex reached for my hands and gripped them tightly. "You have to do it, Kat—you and Nik. You have to save them . . . as many of them as you can."

My eyelids opened so wide that it had to look like my eyeballs were about to fall right out of their sockets. "But Heru said—"

"I know," Lex said, letting go of my hands and raising one of hers so she could chew on her thumbnail. Her other arm crossed her middle, her fingers gripping her side through her sweater. "I know what he said, but he doesn't understand." She turned away and shook her head, almost like she was having an internal argument with herself.

She started pacing around the room, still managing to punctuate her movements with her signature grace. "He hasn't been anything even remotely close to human for five—six—seven thousand years." She threw her hands up. "Maybe more, I honestly don't know. But I do know that he's lost touch with people—with humans. He's too far from them now. He just doesn't get it . . . how much every single one of their lives matters to someone else—just as much as mine or Reni's matters to him. He's forgotten what it's like . . . what it means to be human."

I watched her make her way back and forth across the room.

"It's not his fault." Lex paused and looked at me. "He's a good person, Kat. You know that, don't you?" She took a single, hesitant step toward me. "He wants what's best for our people, but not at the expense of billions of human lives. He doesn't want that." Another step. "That's what makes him different from the Senate.

It's why we're fighting against them." She sounded like she was trying to convince herself as much as she was trying to convince me. "But he has to put our people's best interests first. And our people have to *see* that he's doing that, or he'll lose their trust. He'll lose them, and we can't afford that right now."

I wandered over to the bed and started gathering the scattered tarot cards, curious what the universe had to say about all of this. "So you're here, why—to tell me to go rogue?" I laughed to myself and shuffled the deck on my palm, shooting Lex a sidelong glance. I considered telling her I was already planning to go against Heru's orders, but I wanted to hear what else she had to say. Instead, I decided to dig a little. "You want me to do it now, disobediently, because then, whatever happens, it's not Heru's responsibility. His hands are clean."

Lex swallowed, then nodded once. She was always pale, but now she was a ghost.

I rested the shuffled deck of tarot cards on my palm, letting the otherworldly energy vibrate against my skin. It almost tickled. I drew the top card.

Five of Pentacles. A test. Again. It was nothing new, but it reinforced my resolve to make shit happen. Redrawing this card also meant I'd get no more guidance from the universe right now.

"Hmmm . . ." I looked at Lex, considering. I might've been stuck in a tarot card loop, but that didn't mean she was. "Here," I said, closing the distance between us and holding out the deck. "Cut it."

Lex raised her hand, pausing an inch or two from the cards. "Do I have to think about anything in particular? Like should I ask a question, or—"

I shook my head. "I'm sure your thoughts are focused enough. Go on. Cut the deck." I had a pretty good feeling about what card she would pull, and if I was right, it would set her mind to rest. In a roundabout way, it would ease mine, too.

Lex cut the deck once, I restacked it, and then I drew the top card. And what do you know, my hunch was right on the money.

Strength. It was perfect. Representing courage, patience, and resolve, this card screamed that Lex was doing the right thing by listening to her conscience. It showed her riding on the back of a proud lion, totally unscathed, and the sun shining brilliantly from the top right corner.

"I think the message here is pretty clear," I told her.

"Yeah, I guess." Some of the color returned to my sister's cheeks, but she didn't look one hundred percent herself.

"Is there something else?" I asked her, touching her arm.

She bit her lip. "It's Nik." Her eyes met mine, then her gaze drifted over my shoulder, growing distant. "That look—while he was zoned out, I mean—I've seen it before. Many times. It's his withdrawing-to-talk-to-Re look." She pointed to the card—specifically to the sun. "You know that this is one of his symbols, right?"

I breathed out a bitter laugh. "I know the look," I said, both comforted and disturbed that she'd come to the same conclusion as I had. I was worried about him, about his sanity, but whatever was going on with him would have to wait. "And yeah," I told Lex, "I'm plenty familiar with the Egyptian pantheon, but . . ." I held up the card. "The sun's been on this card since I first drew the design. *That* hasn't changed."

"Oh, I see." She laughed to herself and shook her head, running her fingers through her hair. "Could you maybe try . . . you know?" Lex drew her bottom lip between her teeth, her gaze landing on my tarot cards. "You might be able to figure out what's going on with him in a not-so-conventional way?"

I raised one shoulder, then let it drop. "I already tried, and . . ." I pressed my lips together, my brow tensing. "I got an answer, but I'm not sure what it means." I gave her arm a squeeze. "But I promise to let you know as soon as I figure it out."

CHAPTER FIVE

"What are you doing?" Dom asked.

"Finding Nik." I snatched up one of the three sketchbooks strewn along the top of the dresser, shaking the broken bits of phone onto the floor, then grabbed a pen from the nightstand and sprawled diagonally across the bed. It was past time to track Nik down. Whatever was going on with him, he'd have to suck it up and pull his big-boy pants on. We had work to do.

Thinking of him and only him, I uncapped the pen with my mouth and spat the cap onto the comforter. I pressed the pen to a randomly selected clean sheet of paper in the sketchbook before my mind even had a chance to formulate any kind of an idea of what I might draw.

Where will I find Nik?

I didn't want to know where he was *right now*. I wanted to know where he would be when our paths converged. The intent was important, just like when I did my tarot card readings.

Closing my eyes, I took a deep breath and focused. Between one heartbeat and the next, something changed in the air around me. It felt electrified. I was ready.

When my eyelids lifted, I wasn't seeing the piece of paper; I was seeing through the page, past the lines of ink even as I drew them with my pen. With some sense that went beyond sight and sound and touch and smell and feel, I found Nik.

As the image took shape, items of familiarity became clear in the background. Trees, some with bare branches like gnarly, bony fingers, others rife with pine needles and dangling patches of moss —they surrounded the mouth of a cave. Silhouetted in the opening stood Nik, shadows surrounding him like a cloak. He stared out at me from the page. It was like he could really see me. Almost like the image of him was beckoning to me, waiting for me to join him.

I scanned the sketch for any hint that might tell me exactly where he was, but it could have been any cave opening in the Pacific Northwest. "Come on . . . give me something to work with," I pleaded as my pen continued to move over the page. "Anything . . ."

It wasn't like there were loads of caverns in this area. Sure, there were some lava tubes and there was a ton of sandstone that could've been eroded by wind or water to make shallow caves, and there were mines, but those were mostly sealed off. This cave mouth had a distinctive, natural look to it, ruling out a mine.

"Little sister . . ." Dom was back. I'd totally forgotten about him. Another set of eyes. Another set of memories. An entirely other set of experiences in this region that might just lead me to the cave. To Nik.

I rolled off the bed, landing on my feet and tearing the sheet from the sketchbook. "Do you recognize this place?" I rushed to the standing mirror, holding up the drawing for Dom to see.

His stare moved from my face to the paper, his eyelids narrowing as he focused on the image of Nik in the cave. He studied the picture for several tense heartbeats but eventually shook his head. *"I'm sorry, little sister, I do not recognize that place."*

I exhaled heavily. "S'alright." I lowered the sheet of paper and let my head fall backward so I was staring up at the ceiling. "Nik just seemed so bothered . . ." That mattered. It had to. He'd had a look in his eyes as he'd drawn away, something that made me think he'd fled to somewhere specific, somewhere familiar. Somewhere that meant something to him. Somewhere where he could work through whatever weird internal shit he'd been struggling with back in the study. "He went somewhere specific, he had to . . . somewhere he's been before," I added.

"Well, there's one person who knows Nik better than anyone else . . ."

My eyes snapped open, my gaze locking on Dom. "Aset." Nik's mother, Heru's twin sister and an ancient goddess in her own right—hell, she'd been the inspiration for the Egyptian goddess Isis—was the only person Nik had kept in contact with during his years of estrangement from our people. The two of them had traveled the earth together for thousands of years, aiding Lex during her trek through time. Most of Nik's life had been spent at his mother's side. If anyone knew where he might be—where that cave was—it was Aset.

"Dom, you're a genius!" Or I was a moron. It was a toss-up.

Hastily, I folded the drawing in half, then folded it again and again before stuffing the wad of paper into the back pocket of my jeans. I rushed to the door and yanked it open, then ran down the hallway. I took the stairs three at a time, my socks sliding on the hardwood floor when I reached the bottom. I skidded several feet to the side before course-correcting and heading straight for the door to the basement. I was sure to find Aset in the high-tech underground laboratory she, Neffe, and Mari holed up in most hours of the day, working tirelessly alongside dozens of other Nejerets in their search for a cure for the Cascade Virus.

"Aset," I called, pulling the door shut behind me and launching myself down the stairway. I was halfway down by the time the heavy door thudded shut behind me, and I reached the bottom of the stairs in four strides. "Aset!"

It was bright in the lab. It was always bright down there, florescent lights mixed with UV bulbs used to trick the brains of the Nejerets who worked down there into thinking it was daytime pretty much all the time. So long as they ate regularly and enough, they wouldn't require much in the way of rest. They could operate full-speed-ahead for days before their bodies were worn down enough that they required regenerative sleep.

As I barreled into the lab, a dozen or so heads turned my way, each from a different workstation among the rows of counters and shelving and cabinets and invaluable lab equipment. I ignored them, skimming past each face until I found Aset.

She was working at a station in the back-right corner of the vast room, Heru's daughter, Neffe, standing beside her. Their heads were angled together, and the two appeared to be deep in conversation as they traded off looking into an elaborate, high-powered microscope. So far as I could tell, they were the only two scientists down here who didn't seem startled by my sudden arrival. In fact, they hadn't even seemed to notice me.

I jogged toward them, making a beeline for the two petite, exotic-looking women. Medical geniuses, both of them.

"Kat?" Mari snagged my arm, slowing me, but I pulled free.

"Not now, Mars," I said, continuing onward. "Aset, can you take a look at this and tell me—"

Neffe jerked back from the microscope and leveled a steady glare on me. She was always so prickly, especially around me. "Can't you see that we're busy with—"

Aset placed her hand on Neffe's forearm, then looked past her niece to me. Her irises were a kind, honey brown. Her eyes were always kind, like nurturing and warmth and motherliness were a part of her DNA. Something that had clearly skipped over Neffe. "Kat, dear, this really isn't a good time."

"There's no such thing as a good time anymore," I said, coming to a stop a few feet from them. I slapped the picture on the counter. "Just take a look at this and tell me if you recognize where it is, and then I'll leave." I raised my hand, palm to her. "Promise."

Aset's lips pursed, and she breathed in, but her eyes slid down to the drawing. As soon as she saw the picture, her eyebrows rose, and I knew she recognized the cave.

She looked at me, then back down at the drawing. "This is Nik?" Though he was her son and, undoubtedly, she would recognize him anywhere, the drawing of him showed him deeply ensconced in shadow. It was a valid question.

I nodded. "Where is he?" I tapped the picture with my pointer finger. "Where's this cave?"

"Just north of here," Aset said, glancing that way. "Just across the Agate Passage, in the northern hills of Port Madison."

Port Madison, a fragment of the traditional land and now the home reservation of Garth's people, the Suquamish. I'd only ever been there once, and even then, only to the museum that stood where the Suquamish people's enormous longhouse had been over a century ago.

"Nik and I lived in that cave for many years," Aset said, her gaze growing distant. "It was a home of sorts, a long time ago."

"Can you take me there?" I asked, snatching up the drawing and folding it up once more. I stuffed it back into my pocket.

Aset bit her lip. "No . . ." Her brow furrowed, and she shook her head. "Kat, dear, I really can't waste time doing—"

"I swear it's not a waste of time," I said.

"Dear," she sighed. "Anything that distracts me from my work right now is a waste of time." She placed her hand on my shoulder. "I'm sure that Garth knows where it is; his ancestors were the keepers of our secret location all those years ago. I doubt they'd have forgotten that place. I just saw him," she added. "He's probably still up . . ."

My thoughts spun. Asking Garth to take me there was out of the question; he was still too sensitive to pretty much everything. He needed to rest, to get used to what it meant to be Nejeret. But his family—that was another matter entirely. There was nothing stopping me from going to them for guidance.

"Thanks," I said, spinning around and jogging back toward the stairs. "You were a big help," I tossed over my shoulder, meaning every word. "Really."

Now the only thing standing between me and tracking down Nik and his mysterious cave was Garth's family. Easy peasy.

So, why did it feel like hurdling a mountain?

CHAPTER SIX

"Nice place," I said, scanning the property on the opposite side of the street from where I'd parked my bike. A steep gravel driveway curved up the hillside, half of a timber frame home just visible at the end, the rest of the property masked by dense woods. The short ride here was my first chance to ride the Ducati in what seemed like forever, and being back on the bike had felt amazing. True, I'd only ridden for a few minutes, having gatewayed to the museum—my only anchor point in Port Madison—straight from the garage in the compound on Bainbridge, but it was long enough to bask in the thrill of the cool, damp air slamming into my body.

"What are you going to tell them?" Dom asked. He was watching from the mirror pendant. I'd unzipped my coat and sweatshirt enough that he would have a good view.

I pulled my left hand from my pocket and pushed back the hood of my sweatshirt from my head. It had been drizzling when I first parked, but it was dry enough now. "I don't know yet," I admitted.

I stuffed my hand back into my coat pocket and strolled across the street. I usually operated best with a fly-by-the-seat-of-my-pants strategy, anyway.

I wasn't sure what Garth had shared with his family before the procedure that saved his life, but I felt pretty certain that "Mom, Dad, I'm going to be turned into a Nejeret," hadn't been a part of the conversation. And considering how sensitive his ears were at present, I doubted he'd called them to share the news yet.

As I climbed the driveway, I discovered that Garth's family home was really more of a home*stead*. Tucked away in a shallow bowl in the forested hillside, the home itself was surrounded by several outbuildings, including a small barn, a large shed, a chicken coop, and what appeared to be a second, smaller home that was so very log cabin-y. There was even a fenced-in pasture area containing a couple cows, a donkey, and several llamas.

The wide roll-up door at the front of the shed was open, and I spotted a middle-aged man within. He was crouched near the back tire of an ancient-looking Harley, a small girl of about nine or ten—a string bean of a child—kneeling on the cement floor beside him. Both wore overalls—his khaki cargo, hers denim—and had their long, sleek black hair pulled back in a low ponytail. The girl wore purple rubber rain boots to the man's work boots, and what I assumed was the man's camo cargo jacket hung on her shoulders like a robe. The girl appeared to be listening intently to the man's explanation of the inner workings of the bike's exhaust system.

Was I looking at Garth's father? The corner of my mouth tensed. And the girl—was she his sister? I knew next to nothing about his family, aside from the part where they were descended from Chief Sealth and that they were some of the few humans who knew about Nejerets. Well, there was only one way to find out more about them . . .

I angled away from the house and headed for the shed, gravel crunching under my feet. I was two-thirds of the way there when the sound of my approach reached their ears.

The man perked up, turning his face my way, and the second I got a good look at him, any question of whether or not he was Garth's father fled from my mind. When he stood, I could see that he was just as broad-shouldered as Garth, though he was carrying a little more bulk around the middle than his son. It was strange, seeing what Garth might've become in a few more decades. Unsettling.

I'd thought we were saving him by transforming him into a Nejeret, but I hadn't considered that we were also taking something away from him. The future he'd expected his whole life—his human future—was gone. For better or worse, his life was forever changed. I wondered if that had sunk in for him yet. Would he miss his lost future? Would he mourn it?

Garth's dad wiped his hands off on an oil-smudged rag he'd pulled from his back pocket, then folded it and set it on the Harley's leather seat before stepping around the girl. "Can I help you?" He didn't raise his voice, but low and resonant, it more than carried . . . at least to my ears.

I raised my hand, waving a greeting and flashing a smile. "Hi there," I called. "I'm really sorry to bother you, but I need your help. My name is—"

"I know well and good who you are," the man said. No wonder he hadn't raised his voice. He didn't just know *who* I was; he knew *what* I was and that my Nejeret ears were more than good enough to hear him. "Where's my son? Why haven't I heard from him? It's been days." Garth's father crossed his arms over his chest and leaned his shoulder against the frame of the shed door. His hard stare slid to the hilt of my sword sticking up over my shoulder, then returned to my face.

Behind him, the girl stood, following after her dad. She hung back a step or two, peeking around him, her dark eyes locked on me.

"Garth is . . ." I licked my lips, thoughts frantic as I struggled with how much to tell them.

I stopped a dozen or so paces shy of the shed, just under the heavily needled branches of a pine tree. "Garth's recovering well," I said, purposely vague. "The treatment knocked him out for a few days," I continued, choosing my words carefully, "but he's going to make a full recovery."

"We want to visit him," Garth's dad said. "Where are you folks keeping him?" He pushed off the doorframe and stepped out onto the gravel drive, relaxing his arms so they hung at the sides. Just like Garth, he was a big man. It bothered me a bit that he felt the need to show me that right now. That, at least to some degree, Garth's dad viewed me as a potential threat. I had to remind myself that it didn't matter what Garth's family thought of me; we weren't an "us." Our futures weren't intertwined.

I held up my hands placatingly. "It's not like he's a prisoner," I said. "But I can't just bring you to him." I raised my eyebrows. "Garth must've told you some of what's going on right now . . . with my people, I mean. With our war?"

Garth's dad nodded once.

"It's dangerous times for a Nejeret to be inviting strangers into her home."

His chest rose as he inhaled deeply, and for a few seconds, I thought he might threaten to kick me off his property. But his shoulders drooped as he exhaled, and he hung his head, reminding me so much of the way Garth had looked in my bedroom, forlorn and defeated. "He's my son," Garth's dad said softly. "My boy . . ."

Slowly, I lowered my hands and made my way closer, this man's obvious love for his son tugging at my heartstrings. I sucked in a breath, holding it in as I teetered on whether or not to say the next thing. The words spilled out almost of their own volition. "I'll bring him back here as soon as he's well enough to travel," I said. "But it might be a little while . . . a couple days, at least."

Garth's dad seemed to be weighing the merit of my words. "What about the rest of us? My family's been keeping your people's secret for almost two centuries. We've protected you." Defiance shown in his heavy-lidded eyes. "You should be protecting us, now."

The girl moved forward but still remained a step or two behind her dad. "Can you make other sick people better, too?" she asked, her dark eyes shimmering with unshed tears.

I opened my mouth, but then realized I didn't have an answer.

With Nik's help, yes, I could make other people "better"—but I would also be turning them into Nejerets. I didn't have any qualms against doing it—obviously—but the girl was clearly asking out of personal interest; someone close to her was sick. Someone else in Garth's family? His future was already inexorably altered. I wasn't sure how he'd feel about me interfering with the futures of his family members as well.

"My wife is sick," Garth's dad said, his voice becoming gruff. "And she's not the only one of our people to be infected by that damn virus, but none of the hospitals will take them. There's no room, and Garth warned me about Ouroboros—none of us will go anywhere near those people, whatever they claim." He cleared his throat. "But you helped Garth . . ."

Heavy emotion constricted around my throat, and I swallowed convulsively. I breathed in and out, in and out, my eyes searching first the man's, then the girl's. Garth's mom was sick. Dying. Again, I licked my lips. My heart broke for him.

"Take me to your wife," I said, unwilling to make any promises without knowing how far along she was in the progression of the disease.

Garth's dad studied my face for several long seconds, then nodded once and turned away from me. "She's back here," he said, making his way up a stone path between the house and the shed. He led me straight to the gate of the little picket fence surrounding the log cabin out back. Chickens ran around in the yard, clucking and picking at the ground. They'd done a real number on the grass, digging holes and building little mounds of earth on either side of the pathway leading up to the porch.

Garth's dad gave the girl a stern look. "Stay out here, Cas, I mean it." He opened the gate and waved me through, then rushed ahead to the front door to let me in.

As soon as he opened the door, warm air wafted out of the cabin, carrying scents of broth and herbal tea, and underneath that, the acrid stench of sickness. I wrinkled my nose, then stepped inside.

Behind me, Garth's dad followed and shut the door.

There was no entryway, so to speak, just a small "great" room formed by the combination of the kitchen, dining area, and living room. It was dim, the dying embers of a fire in the fireplace the only light besides what leaked out through the crack beneath a door set in the back wall. Not that I needed even that much light to see clearly.

I followed Garth's dad around the couch and recliners set up in a cozy semicircle around the river stone fireplace. I could hear one weak heartbeat coming from the room beyond the door. It was far from confidence inspiring, but I wasn't ready to dismiss Garth's mom as a lost cause yet.

Once the door was open, the stench of sickness rammed me in the face, and my eyes teared up. I switched to breathing through my mouth as I entered the room, making a point to be subtle about it.

The bedroom was decorated much like the rest of the cabin, with rustic log-cabin-esque furniture. At the center of the room, a middle-aged woman with strong bones and long gray-streaked black hair lay in a bed, tucked under a patchwork quilt, the look of hearty-turned-frail about her. Her eyes were closed, her chest rising and falling evenly.

"How long has she been out?" I asked.

"She woke for about fifteen minutes around midnight and took some broth."

So she hadn't slipped into the coma that preceded the final, rabid stage, yet. Or if she had, she'd only been comatose for ten or eleven hours. Which, based on reports, should leave her another six or seven hours before she became uncontrollably violent. Relief flooded me. There was still time. Garth didn't have to lose his mom today.

"I'll do it," I said, the three words tumbling from my lips. "I'll help her." There was no turning back now. I was committed. "But before I do, I need your help."

CHAPTER SEVEN

Garth's little sister's name was Cassandra, but I could call her Cassie—if I wanted to—and she was eleven years old. A small eleven, not yet having reached the too-cool-for-school tween phase yet, and she was about as much of a tomboy as an eleven-year-old girl could be. When she grew up, she was going to be a mechanic, or firefighter, or police officer like her big brother. Or maybe even a ninja, because there was apparently a gang of awesome girl ninjas on some TV show I'd never heard of, so she knew it was a possibility, but she wasn't quite sure where to get ninja training these days.

I learned all this—and more—while Cassie was leading me along an overgrown, winding trail that reached deeper and deeper into the hillside. With the way the trail kept disappearing in the underbrush, I'd never have found my way without a guide, and I was immensely grateful to have Cassie there to lead the way.

Her dad, Samuel, had volunteered her for the job of guide, saying he needed to stay behind with his wife. There'd been honesty in his eyes as he spoke, but there had also been a hint of something else. Something related to the fear that etched the lines in his face deeper every time he looked at Cassie. He was trying to get her away from her mom, likely to minimize her exposure to the virus.

I hadn't been willing to tell him that if his wife, Charlene, was sick, they likely both already were as well; they just weren't showing any symptoms yet. This thing was infectious as all hell. I hated it, but not as much as I hated the people responsible for it getting out.

We'd been on the trail for close to an hour, and barely a minute of silence had passed between us the whole time. Cassie may have been quiet back in the shed, overshadowed by her father, but it turned out she was quite the gabber.

"How many members of your family know about us . . . about Nejerets?" I asked Cassie. In other words—how many people might I need to transform?

Cassie shrugged. "Everyone in my family."

I looked away, frowning. "And 'everyone' includes . . . ?"

"Oh, um . . ." Squinting her eyes, Cassie screwed her mouth to the side. "So there's"—she held up a hand and started counting off on her fingers—"me, Mama, Daddy, Garth, Nana, Papa, Auntie Ruth and her family . . ." She continued counting on her fingers, though she'd fallen silent. A few seconds later, she lowered her hands and looked at me. "Twelve or Thirteen? I don't know, maybe more."

Even just twelve or thirteen was enough to be dangerous. My kind didn't look fondly upon humans knowing of our existence, but there was one way to make sure Garth's family would be safe, whatever the outcome of the Nejeret war. At least safe from the death sentence their knowledge of our kind would bring if the wrong Nejerets found out. It wouldn't matter what they knew about us if they *became* us.

In my mind's eye, I pictured the *At* orb Nik had shown me on the beach this morning, the one containing a writhing, smoky fragment of Heru's *ba*. Based on the size of the *ba* fragment that had been used during the procedures to transform both Garth and Constance into Nejerets, I thought there would definitely be enough to carry out the procedure on at least thirteen people, maybe more. Then Nik and I could use whatever was left of the *ba* fragment to grow more . . . if "grow" was even the right word when one was cultivating an immortal soul.

Fulfilling my promise to Samuel and Cassie by transforming Charlene to save her life was the priority, but it didn't mean I had to stop there. I could make the rest of the family immortal, too. Make them Nejerets, with or without Garth's permission.

Of course, it was more complicated than that. While I would probably be able to hide Charlene's transformation until it was no longer a major issue to His Mightiness, a whole family so closely connected to me through Garth . . . not so much. Heru would figure out just how much I'd meddled with this family's future, and there was no saying how he'd react. The last thing I wanted was to redirect even an inkling of his wrath at Garth's family. They didn't deserve that. But then, they didn't deserve death by Cascade Virus or Senate execution, either. And the cards *had* told me to proceed with the plan to transform humans into Nejerets, so . . .

"Are you a ninja?" Cassie asked, and the abrupt intrusion into my spiraling thoughts knocked me off guard.

"A ninja? What makes you say that?"

"Well, you're dressed in all black."

A quick glance down at myself proved that she was right, though my dismally monochromatic wardrobe hadn't been a conscious decision.

"And," Cassie continued, "you have a sword, and it looks like a ninja sword, and . . ." She squinted thoughtfully, her gaze scrutinizing my face. "And there's just something about you . . . something in your eyes . . ." She fell quiet for a moment. "It's like you see everything even if you're not looking."

I glanced at the girl sidelong. "Seems like you see quite a bit yourself." Way more than I ever had when I was her age.

Cassie shrugged. "So, is that a yes? You're a Nejeret ninja?"

"Something like that," I said, glancing away. I scanned the forest around us. We had maybe a couple hours of daylight left. I wasn't sure how long I'd be out here, talking to Nik. Hell, I wasn't even sure he'd be out here *right now*, let alone in any kind of a state to talk. He had extreme tastes when it came to distractions and coping mechanisms. For all I knew, he could be in a regenerative sleep up there, healing off whatever damage he'd paid someone else to dole out.

"D'you think I could learn?" Cassie asked.

I'd been so caught up in my thoughts of Nik—the hypotheticals and possibilities and worst-case scenarios—that I'd lost track of the conversation.

"To be a ninja . . ." Cassie prompted. Hope filled her eyes, driving away some of the shadow caused by her worry over her mom.

I frowned, mind still half occupied by thoughts of Nik.

"Sure, kid," I said offhandedly. "Why not?"

Cassie was quiet for a long stretch of time—longer than she'd been this whole hike. Finally, she inhaled deeply, held the breath in for a few seconds, then blurted, "Do you think *you* could teach me?"

Well, shit . . . can't say I shouldn't have seen that one coming. I sure as hell didn't have time to train a kid the way that Dom had trained me. But Cassie was sweet—and kind of tough, actually—and dashing her dreams wasn't high on my priority list. Besides, if the procedures worked and Garth's entire family was transformed into Nejerets, someone would need to familiarize them with our ways. She and the rest of her family would need to learn what it meant to be Nejeret, after all. I supposed I could stop by from time to time.

Once the war was over. Once humanity was no longer facing mass extinction. You know, the usual save-the-world bullshit.

"I don't know . . ." I eyed Cassie, weighing the actual level of her interest. Looked pretty damn high. "I've got some stuff I have to take care of first, but after that, we can talk."

The color was bright in Cassie's cheeks, a mixture of exertion and excitement. She gave a little hop-skip and said, "Cool," slashing the air in front of her in a quick one-two punch, her mittens moonlighting as boxing gloves. She flashed me a cheeky grin, and I didn't have the heart to emphasize that I hadn't actually agreed to anything. "Wait till I tell my dad!"

Oh dear Gods, the last thing I needed was her father up my ass about the mere possibility of training her how to fight. "Yeah," I said, drawing out the word, "maybe hold off on telling anybody for now." My first, bigger battle would be convincing him to let me turn him and his whole family into immortal beings using a procedure that had only existed for a few days and had only been used on three people, one of which was dead.

After all the ninja talk, Cassie and I fell into a companionable silence. I figured she was losing herself to daydreams of ninja training, her imagination carrying her away even as her feet led me closer to Nik.

Maybe a half hour passed, and then Cassie came to an abrupt halt. There was a bend in the trail, thick ferns surrounding the tree trunks of pines and deciduous trees alike, merging with blackberry vines rife with shriveled-up bunches of berries from the past season to block our view of the trail beyond the bend.

"Why are we stopping?" I asked, glancing at Cassie.

She brought her mittens up to her mouth and whispered, "We're almost there." A secretive little smile touched her mouth. Without a word, she turned and sprinted up the spotty trail, disappearing around the bend. I heard her giggle, followed by a soft, masculine laugh that I knew all too well.

I lunged into a run.

Not sure what I was expecting when I rounded the bend. Maybe Nik standing in the mouth of the cave just as I drawn him. Or Nik sitting somewhere in the cave. Anything but what I actually saw when he came into view.

Nik, the sarcastic, brooding, ancient Nejeret, was spinning Cassie around and around and around, much to the girl's evident delight. Clearly, they were acquainted. More than. They knew each other well.

Thoughts tumbled around in my mind until, piece by piece, they fit themselves together. "This is where you were," I said, feet rooted to the ground.

Nik slowed his spinning of Cassie and set the girl down on her feet, both of them breathing hard from the happy exertion. Cassie pushed flyaways from her ponytail away from her face. Her cheeks were rosy, her smile was broad, and the worry for her mom had temporarily fled from her eyes.

"This is where you were," I repeated, a surprising burst of anger flooding my cheeks with heat. Three years ago, when Nik woke up from his seventeen-year Re-induced coma and disappeared without a word, I'd taken it pretty damn personally. After everything we'd been through together, he was suddenly just *gone*. By choice.

I took a step toward him, my hands in fists. "For more than three years, Nik, *this* is where you were," I said, accusing and asking at the same time. "Just a stone's throw away, but you couldn't even be bothered to let me know you were alright . . . or even alive." I shook my head.

Cassie took a few steps backward, hiding partially behind a tree. Nik, however, didn't move, other than tilting his head to the side, just a little, as he watched me.

"So, why'd you come back here?" My eyes widened as my heart sank. "To disappear again? To abandon me—the humans—everything? Is that the plan?" If it was, then why hadn't he just stayed out here? Why had he wedged himself back into my life? Why had he thrown around promises of teamwork, only to smack them away right when I was beginning to trust him again?

Nik simply stared at me, no hint of whatever he was feeling showing on his face. If he was feeling anything, at all. His eyes remained a cool, icy blue. Hard and emotionless.

I wanted to punch his stupid expressionless face. "Is that the fucking plan?" I repeated, voice rising.

Still nothing from Nik.

Laughing bitterly, I shook my head and looked skyward, like

the universe might commiserate with me. I felt like I'd been duped. Like we both had, me and the universe, because it had guided me to him so many times over the past few weeks. The universe thought we were supposed to work together, and I had too. But I'd been a fool. Trusting him again had been a mistake.

"I can't believe you," I said, still shaking my head. "I should've known better." My palm itched, and I rubbed it against my jeans as I looked at Nik, but I could only handle maintaining eye contact with him for a few seconds before the urge to punch him threatened to overtake my self-control. I glanced away, jaw clenched. "I *did* know better."

Never again.

CHAPTER EIGHT

I blinked and stared down at my palm—my itching, burning palm—the Eye of Horus tattoo staring right back at me. "What the—" I sucked in a breath in understanding. The protective ward had been activated. It was *warning* me . . . but of what?

I lowered my hand and refocused on Nik. His stance was tense, wary, his expression one of annoyance.

Him—the Eye of Horus was warning me about him, just like it had warned me about Mari back on Harbor Island.

I swallowed roughly, barely able to believe what was happening. "Yes or no, Nik—are you backing out of our deal?" I took a step toward him, then another. And then I forced my feet to stop moving, inhaling and exhaling deeply through my nose. If I got close enough to him, I wouldn't just be throwing words.

"I can't do this right now, Kat."

I flinched, my stupid feelings stinging from the dismissal like it was a verbal slap. "Now is the only time to do it, Nik. *Now* is the time that people are dying. They're dropping like flies, and it's all because of us." I growled under my breath, not fully believing this was really happening. "For fuck's sake, Nik, this whole save-the-humans plan was your idea."

Nik glanced away lazily, then started wandering back toward

the cave. "There's more going on here than our little war, Kat. There's something bigger. Just let it go."

"Let it go?" I jutted out my jaw, tears of frustration burning in my eyes, and stared up through the tree branches at the overcast sky. I fought the urge to scream as I struggled to come up with some reason—any reason—for Nik's drastic change of tune. All I could think was that he'd been playing me the whole time. That he'd never planned on saving anyone. That I'd been duped.

But still, I pressed on. I had to at least try to convince him to work with me. There was no one else. "Millions, Nik, maybe billions of people are going to die because of 'our little war.' What could possibly be bigger than that?"

"The fate of the universe."

I scoffed. "What's that supposed to mean? That if we start transforming people, the universe is *doomed*?" I ended the question with a mocking laugh.

"Actually," Nik said, "yeah, that's about right."

I rolled my eyes. "Sure . . ."

Nik was in the cave now, standing in the mouth, silhouetted by darkness. I was struck by the realization that this was the image I'd drawn, not the way I found him with Cassie, laughing and spinning. *This* was the moment that mattered.

"Believe me or not, Kat, but that's the truth," he said. "I don't know how it happened, and I sure as hell don't like it, but I can hear Re again, and he's warned me that—"

"No," I said, shaking my head. "Nik, are you kidding me? You can 'hear Re again'? No!" I stomped a boot into the mulchy ground for emphasis. "It's all in your head," I said, tapping the side of my own skull with my index and middle fingers. Nik was messed up from sharing his mind and body with Re for so long. He'd admitted himself that he'd been struggling from the sudden switch from two consciousnesses to one.

"Believe what you want, but you're on your own."

I guffawed. And then I snapped my mouth shut, eyes narrowing. "This is just a cover story, isn't it?" I finally worked up the nerve to ask the thing I'd been fearing all along. "You never planned to go through with it, did you?"

Nik raised his eyebrows, like he was surprised. But at what? At how far off base I was? Or that I'd sniffed out his deceit?

"I never trusted him," Dom said, his words whispering through my mind. "For all we know, he could be in league with the Senate."

The Senate? That nauseating possibility hadn't occurred to me. Had he been dragging me along, tossing red herrings out to keep me from the truth? Had everything been a lie? Was this whole "Re" thing just a way for him to save face?

I inhaled deeply, sucking on the question I needed to ask but really didn't want to. "Are you working with the Senate?"

Nik was quiet for a moment. "If I were, would that finally convince you to drop this?"

Gut punch. I was suddenly light-headed, floating along in what had to be a dream. A nightmare.

"I'm sorry, Kitty Kat. I never wanted this." Nik raised his hand, almost like he was waving goodbye. "I never wanted to hurt you." A sheet of *At*, crystalline and unbreakable, spread out from his palm, covering the mouth of the cave. He'd locked me out with a blockade stronger and more permanent than anything any human could ever build. Not even *At* could break *At*, so hacking at it with my sword would be utterly pointless. He really was going to let all those people die.

"Bastard," I breathed, glaring at him through that opalescent wall. "Traitorous, cowardly fucking bastard." I knew he could hear me through the *At*; it was a perk of his gift.

Enraged, I marched toward that otherworldly wall, aware of Cassie hiding in the forest nearby—aware of another presence just beyond her—but at the moment, neither mattered as much as Nik and what he'd just done. What he *wouldn't* do.

"I warned you about—"

"Do *not* give me an 'I told you so' right now, Dom," I snapped as I approached the barrier.

Remotely, I noticed a strange feeling in the air, almost like it was charged with static electricity.

"Give me the *ba*," I demanded when I reached the wall of *At*. I raised my fist, drew my arm back. "Give it to me!" I shouted, and slammed my fist into the *At*.

It happened almost in slow motion, as though my fist was moving through something more viscous than air. As though time needed just a moment, a breather, to catch up with this momentous event.

A millisecond before my knuckles touched the *At*, energy crackled around me. Through me. I felt every single hair on my body stand on end, brought to attention by this foreign, alien energy. This magic. I was tapping into something new, some powerful force I'd never experienced before. It felt similar to the surge of energy that happened every time I created a gateway. Similar, but so very different. And so very much *more*.

The moment my knuckles touched the *At*, even as my bones cracked and crunched with the force of the impact, even as pain shattered all coherent thought in my mind, the wall of *At* fractured like a windshield struck by a rock.

I stumbled backward a few steps, hugging my hand to my chest as I stared on in awe.

The cracks in the wall of *At* spread until they were everywhere. For a moment, the wall stubbornly held its shape. But just for a moment.

I held my breath as the pieces crumbled to the ground.

"How—" Nik stared at me, eyes wide with shock, and shook his head. "How did you do that?"

I swallowed, then cleared my throat. "I have no idea."

CHAPTER NINE

I blinked, one of those slo-mo, life-rushing-before-your-eyes blinks, and in that brief moment, realization struck, a lightning bolt transforming shock into awe. I'd broken through Nik's wall of *At*. I—me, Kat Dubois, the chick who's *sheut* allows her to do weird shit like make and read magical tarot cards and draw gateways to other places—broke through Nik's wall.

I shouldn't have been able to do it. Never before had I shown any signs that my *sheut* allowed me to control *At*. But that's the tricky thing about *sheuts* . . . they evolve. They change and strengthen and grow. They become more, especially if pushed. And, yeah, I'd say I just pushed my *sheut* pretty damn hard . . . hard enough to shatter several bones in my hand.

I met Nik's astonished stare. His eyes were opened so wide that the entirety of his pale blue irises was visible.

Ever so slowly, my lips spread into a grin. Nik didn't want to help me help the humans—fine. Turned out I didn't need him anymore anyway. He could go off soul searching or panda watching or become a monk for all I cared. Perfect. All I needed from him was the *ba* fragment he'd been carrying around in that orb of *At*. Once he handed it over, we'd be square. I'd grin and wave and wish him good luck with the voices in his head or the Senate or whatever. I'd wash my hands of him, once and for all.

I glanced over my shoulder to check on Cassie. She was peeking out from behind that tree trunk. I gave the woods a quick scan, but there was no sign of the other presence I'd sensed just moments ago, and I chalked it up to the innocent curiosity of a forest creature. This was *a forest*, after all.

Since the kid was safe enough, I refocused on Nik. I held out my right hand, palm up, my throbbing left hand still clutched to my chest. "Give me the orb."

Nik's eyes narrowed, and he crossed his arms over his chest.

"Now," I demanded.

But still, Nik didn't make a motion to hand anything over. He remained silent, staring at me. He didn't even blink. There was a faint tinge of panic in his eyes. Good, I could work with that.

"Give. Me. The. Orb," I said, lowering my mangled hand and reaching over my shoulder to wrap the fingers of my good hand around the hilt of my sword. I drew Mercy in one smooth motion, the *At* blade singing out in melodic warning. I'd never drawn her on her maker. It was surprisingly easy.

A slight twitch under Nik's right eye was his only reaction.

I altered my stance, moving one foot back and bending my knees, preparing to strike if necessary. "Either give it to me, or I'll take it." I raised the sword. "Your choice." I couldn't, for the life of me, imagine why he would refuse.

Nik's expression relaxed, opening up, and for a moment, he was the Nik I knew. Or thought I knew. For that single second, I thought he was going to give me the orb.

But when he unfolded his arms and set his jaw, the chill in his eyes warned me he was preparing for a fight.

I pressed my lips together, huffing out a breath through my nose. I'm far from patient on my best days, and this wasn't even close to a good day. My irritation scale was sky-high. If Nik wanted to fight—fine, we could fight. In my present mood, it was just what I needed.

The corner of Nik's mouth lifted in a cruel smirk. "You can't beat me, Kitty Kat."

"Try me," I said through gritted teeth. Adrenaline surged within my veins, heightening my awareness and dulling the pain from my broken hand.

Without warning—though far from unexpected—vines of shimmering *At* shot out of both of Nik's hands.

Behind me, Cassie gasped. From the sound of it, she'd snuck closer, but I could hear her hasty footsteps on the soggy earth as she retreated again.

One of the vines of *At* wrapped around my sword wrist, the other around my waist, effectively immobilizing me.

Nik straightened out of his attack pose. "I win. Now drop it, Kat. Don't make me hurt you." But he already had, and the pain was far deeper than anything physical could ever be.

Glaring at him, I concentrated on the otherworldly bindings. I pulled all of the hurt inward—the anger and betrayal, the disappointment—letting it pool within my *sheut*. Letting it stoke my rage, fuel my desire to win. To beat him so I could follow through on my promise to save Charlene. *Help me,* I called silently, beseeching the universe. *I need this.*

Between one second and the next, a burst of electric energy rushed through my *sheut*, and the air around me crackled with unspent power. The *At* restraints sizzled, blackening as they wilted away from me.

I grinned, a wicked surge of pleasure replacing the receding magic. For once, Nik and I would be fighting on an even playing field. The prospect exhilarated me.

I tutted Nik, mocking him. "Looks like somebody's going to have to play fair this time." I let out a harsh laugh. "Guess we'll find out how good you really are."

"Good enough, I'm sure," Nik said, a crystalline longsword appearing in his left hand, a dagger in his right.

The time for talk was over. I struck first, lunging forward, then spinning away when Nik deflected my blade. I used the momentum to launch a butterfly kick—a ballsy move when going up against an opponent with two blades in play. Which was precisely why I did it; Nik would never expect it.

He lashed out awkwardly with his *At* sword as he ducked.

I blocked the strike with Mercy's equally unbreakable blade, having predicted his defensive maneuver before my feet even left the ground. As I twisted in midair, I drew the tiny push dagger hidden in my belt buckle and swiped at Nik's thigh. My left hand was weak and the movement hurt like a bitch, but I managed it, and the pain was so worth the result. The one-inch blade sliced through Nik's jeans and bit into flesh, the tip scraping against bone.

He hissed in pain, stumbling back a few steps, his blades raised defensively. For the second time that afternoon, shock lit his pale blue eyes. This wasn't like our little sparring match back in the shop, when he'd first sauntered back into my life. This wasn't just a way to blow off some steam. Blood had been drawn. This was real. Possibly the most real any fight had ever been for him. But not for me.

"The orb, Nik," I said, breathing hard. "Just give it to me. It doesn't have to be like this."

Nik's face was tense from the fresh pain. "I can't! Re told me—"

"Oh, so we're back to Re," I said, laughing in disbelief. "Which is it, Nik—voices in your head or working for the Senate?"

"The Senate—" He shook his head, his brow furrowed. "I just told you that so you'd let this go. I thought maybe it would give you something else to focus on . . . something besides the virus. I had no idea you'd be able to get through my barrier."

Insulted by his flip-flopping stories, I snorted. "Show me some proof that Re's really talking to you, and I'll believe you," I told him, knowing full well that such a thing was near impossible.

"I can't—" Again, Nik shook his head. "Re's here," he said, tapping his temple. "It feels so real . . . it *has* to be real. And he won't shut up about you . . . about you ruining everything again. About you destroying the universe."

"Come on, Nik. We can't give up on humanity just because of a voice in your head that *feels* real." The spike of adrenaline was wearing off, and the sharp ache in my hand was slightly nauseating. My sword arm drooped. "You've been through some crazy shit." A few millennia's worth, actually. "Maybe this is just like PTSD or—or, I don't know . . . something. Maybe your subconscious is struggling with the fact that even if we try, we won't be able to save everyone. I'm not a psychologist, and I've never had the strongest moral compass, but I know that letting all of those people die is the wrong thing to do. We have to do what we can to help them, Nik. *I* have to."

He opened his mouth, then laughed silently and shook his head. "You don't understand," he murmured. "You can't hear him, so you won't hear me. Kat . . . I can't do what you want me to do, and if you're not going to give up . . ." He inhaled deeply. "I'm so sorry it's come to this."

Not a second later, he was coming at me, and I was very much on the defensive. I may have caught him off guard with my previous attack, but Nik had stepped up his game, big-time. It was all I could do to keep his blades from shredding me into fleshy ribbons.

I was sweating by the time he pinned me against the cave wall, disarmed and dripping blood from the fingertips of my right hand. He stood an arm's length away, the last few inches of his longsword pressed against my throat. Mercy lay on the ground a few feet to my left. It's difficult to maintain a grip on anything when your palm is coated in blood and the tendons in your wrist have been severed. Now, neither hand was functional for fighting. He had me.

"Go home, Kat," Nik said between heaving breaths. "If there's even a chance that Re's real, that what he's saying is true—" Nik shook his head. "The barriers between dimensions—between universes—are already weakened by the imbalance caused by the transformations. That's why I can hear Re. So don't you see—

continuing to transform humans into Nejerets will only make it worse, weakening the barriers until the collapse of the entire universe is inevitable. And yes, there's a chance that Re's not real, but it's not worth the risk. Just let nature run its course. Please, Kat, don't make me hurt you anymore."

I still thought "Re" wasn't really talking to him, but I understood his reasoning, I really did. Even so, I'd made promises that I fully intended to keep. Maybe saving as many people as possible *was* too risky, but I would *not* let Charlene die. I would not break that promise. For Samuel and Cassie. For Garth.

I leaned in, the sting of the *At* blade biting into my neck clarifying my mind, reviving my determination. "I can't."

Nik withdrew his sword, lowering it until the tip dragged on the ground.

"Garth's mom is sick," I told him. "I have to save her. I promised." Not to mention the rest of his family. Transforming them was the only way to protect them from my people, but I figured I should start small. "Help me, Nik. It's just one person." Damn it, but hope had wheedled its way into my heart. I wanted him to say yes, to give me a reason to forgive him. I was desperate for a reason to believe that this wasn't the end of whatever warped relationship we had.

Nik closed the distance between us with a single step. He stared down at me, his gaze surprisingly earnest. His eyes searched mine. "Kat, I—I can't help you. And I can't let you do it, either."

I stared at him, disgust a living, breathing thing inside of me. I was just asking for one life. A single life, such a tiny thing. "Then get the hell away from me."

Nik's shoulders slumped, and he turned his back to me, taking a few steps deeper into the cave. "He wants me to kill you." Nik's voice echoed off the rock walls. "He says it's the only way."

My heart rate spiked. I needed to get out of here, but I couldn't leave without the orb. I tested the fingers of my left hand experimentally. Pain shot up my arm, but I had a decent amount of control, which meant that whatever bones and connective tissue

I'd damaged by punching the wall of *At* were starting to heal. The hand was functional. Or functional-ish.

"He's right," I said a millisecond before I dove for my sword, the fingers of my left hand curling around Mercy's hilt as I rolled over my shoulder and landed back on my feet. The pain was horrific, but I'd been expecting it. "The orb, Nik," I said, raising the sword. "Give it to me."

With his back to me, Nik bowed his head. "You won't give up, will you?"

"Only when I'm dead."

After a slow shake of his head, Nik moved deeper into the cave until he was consumed by darkness. A few seconds later, an *At* orb the size of a softball bounced out of the shadows, rolling to a stop at my boots.

"Go." Nik's voice was a ghostly murmur. "Get out of here, Kitty Kat . . . before I decide he's right."

"Nik . . . it doesn't have to be like this." I despised the thread of a plea in my voice. The weakness.

"Go!"

I bent over to pick up the orb. When I straightened, I glared into the darkness. "You know, for a moment there, I actually considered you a friend." I laughed bitterly. "The moment's over." He'd made it perfectly clear that he truly was every bit the cold bastard I'd believed him to be the first time I met him, over two decades ago. "Don't get up," I said, voice thick with emotion. "I'll let myself out."

Just for a second, I paused in the mouth of the cave, recalling the feeling of the energy I'd channeled to break through the wall and get into the cave in the first place. I'd tapped into a force that was more vibrant and volatile than anything I'd felt before. Something within me was changing. *I* was changing. And it scared the shit out of me.

Awkwardly, I reached across my body to sheath Mercy over my right shoulder, then stepped out into the dying afternoon light. I spotted Cassie cowering behind the trunk of that same tree, eyes dark saucers in the grim light. She'd seen so much—too much. Poor kid. I worried she'd run from me, seeing me for the monster I was. The monster her brother was blinded to.

"I'm sorry." Nik's words whispered on the damp breeze, and I sucked in a breath. But I stomped on the urge to look over my shoulder. Sorry wasn't enough. Nothing would be, not after this. Fool me once, shame on me. Fool me twice . . .

"Come on," I said, marching past Cassie. Either she would follow me, or she wouldn't. Nothing I could do to change that now. "Let's go save your mom."

CHAPTER TEN

Cassie was a little skittish for the first part of the hike back—and really, who could blame her after the brawl she'd just witnessed between Nik, someone she obviously knew well and trusted, and me, the person who'd vowed to save her mom—but she worked past it by the time dusk invaded the woods.

"Why doesn't Nik want to save my mom?" she asked, voice soft, hesitant.

"It's complicated, kid." Which was really just another way to say, "I don't know." Because whatever Nik's beliefs about what was happening to him, whatever his reasons to oppose me in this, he still should've been willing to save the life of a woman he clearly knew. If he was so familiar with her daughter, how could he not know Charlene, and know her well?

"Oh." Cassie fell into a deep silence that lasted the rest of the hike.

It was full dark by the time we reached their property. I stood with Cassie at the fence line, staring at the cabin, and glanced at her sidelong. She looked like she was trying to burn a hole through the wood of the door.

I didn't want to leave her outside, alone and in the dark. But Samuel had made himself perfectly clear earlier—Cassie was absolutely not allowed inside the cabin. "You'll be fine out here?" I asked her.

She dug the toe of her rubber boot into the earth, her gaze sinking to the ground as she shrugged. "It's not like I have a choice. Papa won't let me go in," she said, hurt in her voice. Hurt, and defiance.

"Because he loves you," I reminded her. The last thing we needed was for Cassie to take a page out of my book and decide disobedience was more her taste. I wanted to stay on Samuel's good side—to agree to letting me save his wife once I revealed to him that the "cure" carried an extra little kick—and I doubted encouraging his daughter to rebel would earn me much in the way of favor. "You should listen to your dad," I told Cassie. "He seems like a smart guy."

She pursed her lips, quirking them to the side, and huffed out a breath through her nose. "Then why's it okay for him to go in there?" She folded her arms across her chest. "I just want to see her," she said, a tremor in her voice. She was afraid she'd never see her mom again, not alive at least.

I glanced heavenward. Oh ye of little faith—I'd made a promise, and come hell or high water, I was determined to keep it. After everything, I wouldn't fail in this. But she didn't know that, because she didn't know me. Not really.

"I get it, kid," I said, sighing. "Trust me, I totally get it." I crouched down to her level, catching her gaze. "My mom died when I was a little older than you. She's gone, and I would give pretty much anything to have her back. I'm not going to let that happen to you. You won't be saying goodbye to your mom for a really long time." If I had my way, maybe not ever.

Cassie's bottom lip trembled, and she looked away.

I straightened. "Go wait in your house," I told her, opening the creaky fence gate. I picked my way along the uneven stone path to the cabin's compact front porch. "I'll let you know when I'm done." Once her mom's transition into immortality was well on its way, there'd be no reason for Samuel to keep Cassie from her mom's bedside.

I took a deep breath as I climbed the three porch stairs. All I had to do now was convince Samuel that immortality was the cure he'd been hoping for all along; he just hadn't known it was a possibility.

I twisted the brushed bronze doorknob and pushed the front door open. "Samuel," I called ahead, not wanting to startle him. "It's Kat."

I made my way to the bedroom door and rapped my knuckles on the solid wood. The door creaked open, and I poked my head in through the crack.

Samuel sat in a chair pulled up to the side of the bed, a rain poncho covering his upper body, a surgical mask over the lower half of his face, and yellow rubber gloves on his hands, the type people use to clean their toilets and bleach their bathtubs. A poor man's hazmat suit. He was holding a paperback book opened to some point in the middle, though his attention was on the doorway. On me.

I glanced past him to Charlene. Her heartbeat wasn't only weak now, it was irregular. She didn't have much time left. Hours, maybe. Or less. And then, she'd go all she-Hulk and attack everyone she could, spreading the disease to the rest of Garth's family, assuming they didn't already have it. One more fuck-you from the joint team of jackasses—the Nejeret Senate, the Ouroboros Corporation, and Initiative Industries.

"Can I come in?" I whispered.

Samuel nodded once and closed the book, careful to mark his place by dog-earing the top corner of the page.

I pushed the door open a little further, offering him a silent wave.

His red-rimmed eyes locked on the blood coating my right hand and wrist. Damn, but I'd forgotten all about that. Both my left hand and my right wrist were well on their way to being healed, though the bones in my left hand would have to be reset for the hand to be fully functional. But at this point, the knife wound on my wrist was likely just an angry pink scar under all the crusted blood. Not that he knew that.

"I'm fine," I said, glancing at my hand, then lowering it to wipe some of the blood off on the back of my jeans. "We heal super-fast."

Again, he nodded once. But he still hadn't blinked.

"I'm just going to wash up real quick," I said, pointing over my shoulder with my thumb. The kitchen sink was calling my name.

When I returned, hands freshly washed and free of crusted blood, I pushed the door open the rest of the way, cringing at the squeaky hinges. Charlene didn't notice. She was out cold.

As I stepped into the room, I reached into my coat pocket and pulled out the *At* orb. "I have everything that I need," I told Samuel. Another step. "But you should know—what I'm about to do will cure more than just the disease."

"What do you mean?" He eyed the orb, seeming to become hypnotized by the smoky, swirling *ba* contained within.

I hid the orb behind my back, hoping to regain what little of Samuel's attention was up for grabs.

He blinked, the first time he'd done so since I'd entered the room, then shook his head. "Wha—" He focused on my face, his brow pinched. "What was that?"

"It's the thing that will allow me to save your wife's life," I told him, moving deeper into the room.

When I reached the foot of the bed, I sucked in a deep breath and held it for several seconds. "Listen, Samuel," I said, blowing out the breath. "Garth knew what he was getting into when he agreed to the transform—the procedure, and I want to—*need* to—make sure you understand, too." I stared at him for a moment, waited, made sure he was listening. "I can cure your wife . . . by turning her into a Nejeret."

Samuel stared at me for a long time. So long that I wasn't sure he was comprehending my words. I wasn't entirely sure I wouldn't just incapacitate him and heal Charlene regardless of his decision

—too much had happened to get me here, in this room, ready to save her—but I wanted to at least give him a chance.

"Do you understand what I—"

"Yes," Samuel said, cutting me off. "I understand." A breath. Another. "Do it. Please."

That whisper of consent was all I needed. I rushed the rest of the way around the bed and sat on the edge of the mattress, the quilt bunching up underneath me. I set the orb down beside Charlene's leg, then reached out to take her hand in mine. There was a spark of built-up static electricity the moment my skin touched hers.

I leaned in. "Charlene?" I whispered. "I honestly don't know if you can hear me or not, but if you can, I want you to not be afraid. Things will be . . . intense when you wake up. But you'll be alive, and you'll get to watch Cassie grow up, and that's all that really matters, right?" I shot Samuel a quick glance before refocusing on Charlene. "Alright," I said as I reached for the orb. My fingers closed around the smooth, cool surface. "No time like the present."

But then I hesitated. Releasing the *ba* right now would use up my entire supply. Mari's supply back at the lab was separated into smaller marble-sized pieces, a bite-size *ba* delivery system. But I doubted I had anywhere near enough control over my new powers to divide this softball-sized orb into enough parts to work on any other members of Garth's family who fell ill, and Charlene didn't have time to wait for me to figure it out.

I set my shoulders. Charlene was my priority. I wouldn't let indecision make me into a promise-breaker. I'd just have to relieve Mari of some of her supply later. *After* I took care of Garth's mom.

I shifted Charlene's hand so my palm cradled the back of her hand, then placed the orb against her palm and curled both her fingers and mine around the sphere of *At*. Closing my eyes, I bowed my head and concentrated. On the orb. On the universal energies. On the memory of the sensation I'd felt when I broke through Nik's *At* barrier. I squeezed my eyes shut. I called out to the magic.

And felt nothing. Not a single electric zip. No static. Nothing.

I licked my lips and tightened my grip on Charlene's hand. This would work. It would *work*. It had to.

But it didn't. No matter how hard I focused, no matter how intensely I concentrated, I couldn't get the magic to work. Not this time.

My cheeks were wet by the time I opened my eyes. "I—" I cleared my throat, watching the shallow rise and fall of Charlene's chest. "I'm sorry." I let go of Charlene's hand, reluctantly plucking the orb from her limp grasp. "I'm so sorry."

Apparently, I'd been wrong about my *sheut* powers. Maybe they weren't evolving. The instance up at the cave might have been a one-off, not that I'd ever heard of anything like that happening before. But then, magic was hardly a science. That's why it was called *magic*, after all.

"What happened?" Samuel asked, his eyes filled with confusion but also a glimmer of hope. "Is she . . . is it too late?"

"No," I said, shaking my head. "It's not that." Or rather, the problem wasn't her.

It was me.

CHAPTER ELEVEN

"Is she better now?" Cassie asked about a quarter of a second after I opened the cabin's front door. She'd been sitting on the porch steps, but stood when I emerged.

I froze in the doorway, heart thudding and eyes locked on her. "What?" I felt like I'd been caught breaking into the cabin, not invited in to save her mom. Oh, right, saving her mom—that thing I'd just failed to do. That's what she was asking about.

The hope brightening Cassie's face faded. The light in her eyes dimmed. She already knew. "I'm a failure," must've been written all over my face.

"I, um . . ." I cleared my throat and stepped onto the porch, shutting the door behind me, then passed Cassie and started down the walkway. "I can't do it alone," I told her as I hurried away. "I thought I could, but . . . I'll be back. I'll fix this."

I wouldn't be returning with Nik, that was for sure, but I knew exactly who to ask for help this time—Lex. I just hoped that by the time I got her back here, it wouldn't be too late. And that was assuming Lex was even willing to help. But after everything she'd said in my bedroom, I had to believe she would be.

"Little sister," Dom said, "I know what you're planning, and I would ask you to proceed with the utmost caution. If Heru finds out that Lex—"

"He'd never hurt her," I said, stating the obvious. An inability to cause her pain was practically hardwired into him, courtesy of their soul bond.

"It is not Lex I am worried about," Dom said ominously.

I sniffed, unimpressed. Sure, there was always the chance that Heru might take his anger out on me for coercing his wife into an act of disobedience . . . *if* he found out. It was a pretty likely possibility. But breaking my promise to Garth's family wasn't an option. Lex would help—I would do anything I had to do to convince her, consequences be damned.

I jogged down the driveway, settling my helmet on my head without securing the chin strap, then kicking the bike's engine on. Whatever the urgency, I couldn't risk leaving an open gateway to the Heru Compound *outside* of the compound, so I resigned myself to taking the Agate Pass Bridge back to Bainbridge.

I pulled up to the main house within the compound's walls maybe fifteen minutes after I left Cassie standing in her driveway, looking forlorn. Like I was abandoning her and her family. Like I wouldn't come back. Like I'd let them all die. Hell, I'd failed in my first promise to her, so what reason did she have to believe me when I said I would return?

In a rush, I barreled through the front door and paused in the middle of the foyer, head bowed and eyes closed, listening. Nobody was on that floor. Or rather, nobody with a heartbeat. I wouldn't find Lex here.

I flew across the foyer and up the staircase, heading straight for Heru's study. When I didn't find anyone in there, I checked Lex and Heru's suite at the far end of the hallway, then Reni's room. But they were all empty.

"Damn it," I hissed. Of *course* this couldn't be easy. Not now, when the stakes were as high as they'd ever been. Poor Charlene was hanging on by the thinnest thread. I didn't have time to waste running around like this. Luckily, I didn't have to.

Spinning around, I ran back to my room, where I knew a plethora of sketchbooks were waiting for me. I could go stand out on the porch and call out Lex's name, except I didn't want the whole Nejeret world to know I was looking for her, let alone why. Stealth was something I considered, sometimes. Rarely. Mostly just right now.

I shoved the door to my bedroom open and grabbed the first sketchbook I saw, a half-filled spiral-bound book I usually used to sketch out preliminary tattoo designs for clients. I preferred not to mix work and pleasure in my sketchbooks, but fuck it—this was too important to give even a half of a shit.

After grabbing a pen off the nightstand, I sat on the edge of the bed, back hunched and right hand drawing furiously. As Lex's form took shape, flakes of brownish, dried blood snowed down on the image from the sleeve of my coat, but I didn't even bother to brush them away. I could feel the electric thrum of potent energy siphoning in through my *sheut* and back out through the pen.

In the drawing, Lex was standing with her back to me, hugging a long, hooded sweater around her body even as the ends of the sweater whipped about her legs. Her hair was pulled back into a loose bun, several escaped strands waving wildly around her head.

"C'mon," I murmured. "Where are you?" She was outside, that much was clear . . . but where, exactly?

My pen scratched at the page, seemingly moving of its own volition. A long, twisted piece of driftwood took shape. Then countless little rocks filled the space under Lex's feet. I didn't even get started on drawing the water; it was obvious that she was on the beach at the north end of the compound. And I knew exactly where on the beach, because it was my go-to spot for quiet contemplation, too.

I stood, tossing the sketchbook and pen onto the bed, and hurried to the door. I yanked it open and stepped out into the hallway. And ran headlong into Garth.

"Jesus!" I stumbled backward a few steps, gripping the leather of my coat over my chest.

Garth winced at my one-word outburst, taking a backward step himself. "Sorry," he said, his voice barely a whisper.

I should've known he was there—my hearing was plenty good enough to have heard him from within the room—but I'd been too distracted by my mad search for Lex. By the desire to save Garth's mom, a woman I'd never met, at least not while she was conscious.

And yet, making sure she didn't die was currently the most important thing in the world to me. It was absolutely imperative that I save her, overcoming even my need to stop the spread of the Cascade Virus or to destroy Ouroboros, Initiative Industries, and the Senate. I couldn't explain why even if my life depended on it, but saving Charlene was *everything*.

I huffed out a breath. "It's fine. No harm." I stepped back out into the hallway and pulled my bedroom door shut behind me, remembering at the last second to close it softly for the sake of Garth's newly heightened hearing. "You're supposed to be in bed . . . resting." I cringed inwardly, hating the irritation in my voice. But, damn it, I didn't have time for this; I was trying to save his mom!

"I was resting, but . . ." Garth looked at me, anguish burning in his warm, brown eyes. "I called my folks . . . wanted to let them know I'm alright."

My heart plummeted. He knew. About his mom, that was certain, but did he know about my fumbling involvement?

"My mom . . ." Garth's stare grew distant. "She's sick, and . . . it's bad. She's not going to last much longer."

I fought the urge to tell him I already knew about his mom, to tap my foot, to shove past him and get back to fixing this whole damn mess. But I couldn't get his hopes up. I wouldn't be able to stand seeing the same look in his eyes as I'd seen in Cassie's if, after everything, I failed him, too.

Aside from the few, rare exceptions, every Nejeret, man or woman, loses their mother early on. It's a fact of near-eternal life that almost destroyed me two decades ago. And I was terrified that Garth would learn the truth of this unavoidable pain all too soon. Unless I could untangle this mess and ensure that he never, ever had to say farewell to Charlene.

I closed the distance between Garth and me, throwing my arms around his broad body despite knowing my touch would be painful to his oversensitive nerve endings. He needed comfort—even what little I was able to offer him right now. *Even* if it came with a healthy dose of pain.

"I'm so sorry," I whispered into his T-shirt.

He stood motionless for a moment, his whole body going rigid. But then he relaxed, his arms encircling me and his head dropping down so his nose was pressed into the crook of my neck. His shoulders shook. Hell, his whole body shook.

I made shushing noises and rubbed his back, wincing when I thought of the remnants of dried blood I was no doubt smearing all over his T-shirt from my sleeve. At least it was the back of his shirt. He might not even notice.

For at least a minute, we stood in the hallway, Garth clinging to me, showing no signs of loosening his grasp, and I was growing antsy. I needed to get to Lex. Convincing her to help wouldn't be effortless. She hadn't left the safety of the heavily guarded compound for weeks, not since the Nejeret civil war first started. Proving to her that I could ensure her safety was likely my largest hurdle, but by emphasizing my ability to create gateways—to punch holes through space to connect two distant points—I felt certain I'd be able to sway her. We'd just pop over there, do the thing, then pop right back. Zero travel time. Minimal exposure. Of course, I had to actually get to the beach and talk to her to start the ball rolling.

Garth cleared his throat roughly. "Kat, do you think I could bring my mom here?"

I stiffened. Heru might allow Charlene to spend her final hours down in Neffe's lab—*if* she survived being moved here—but it would be impossible to carry out the temporarily forbidden procedure right under Heru's nose.

"I don't know," I said, pulling away from him. "It's not up to me, but I can ask Heru for you. Right now, you should head home . . . be with your family." Which would actually be perfect. While he was in transit, Garth would be out of my way, leaving me free to do what needed to be done to save his mom.

Garth smiled, just a little, his gaze refocusing on me. "Thanks, Kat. I knew I could count on you."

I returned his smiled and reached out to give his arm a squeeze. "Go. You can take any of the cars in the garage; nobody'll mind. The keys are hanging by the door."

"Oh," Garth said. "Great." He started up the hallway, passing me, then paused and turned around. "I don't actually know where the garage is. Can you show me?"

I clenched my jaw but forced my features to relax. I had to head out that way anyway to get to the trail that led to the beach. It would hardly cramp my timeline to show him which path to take.

"Sure," I said, hurrying past him. "Follow me."

CHAPTER TWELVE

I sprinted along the trail to the beach in moonlit darkness, dodging branches and leaping over fallen trees without thought, like it was a dance I'd rehearsed a thousand times. My mind was too preoccupied to give any conscious thought to things as trivial as obstacles along the path, and my body took over. I always moved faster when my mind stayed out of it, anyway.

I was breathing hard by the time the trail, padded with a thick layer of decaying leaves and pine needles, gave way to the crunch of tiny rocks under my boots. I slowed to a jog, hopping up onto, then over that same long piece of driftwood that had featured so prominently in my finding sketch of Lex.

She stood exactly as I'd drawn her, loose strands of hair whipping about her head and long sweater hugged tight around her body, the light from the moon casting her in silver and gray.

She glanced at me over her shoulder as I approached. "I heard you coming from a mile away," she said, focus slipping back to the choppy sea. "What's got you so worked up?" *Now* floated unsaid on the evening breeze.

I slowed to a walk, left arm curved over my head to alleviate the stitch in my side. I keep in pretty good shape, but a sprint like that wasn't something I was ever prepared for. "It's Garth's mom—"

"Oh yes, I already know," Lex said, voice monotone. She tossed me a sidelong glance. "I overheard his conversation with his dad." She laughed under her breath, a sound devoid of any hint of joy. "He was so—" She shook her head. "I came out here as soon as I realized what they were talking about. After everything his ancestors did for me all those years ago, I didn't think I'd be able to tell him no." When he asked for help, she meant, because how could he not. Lex sighed. "I was hoping you and Nik might've already fixed the problem." She glanced at me again, then returned to staring out across the Agate Passage. At Port Madison. It was like she'd been trying to see what was going on all the way on the other side of the water.

"How'd you know where I went?"

Lex shivered and hugged her sweater about herself more tightly. "Dom told me." Oh, right, the standing mirror. I often forgot that I wasn't the only one with access to him these days.

I licked my lips, breathing hard. "Well, he must not've told you everything. I couldn't help her."

Lex looked at me, brows raised. "Because you couldn't find Nik?"

Looked like Dom hadn't told her much of anything at all. "No, I—I found him." I hid my left hand behind my back; it was healed—sort of—but it was noticeably misshapen and would remain that way until the bones were re-broken and set properly. For some reason, I was embarrassed by what went down between Nik and me, and I didn't want Lex to know.

"And . . ." Lex prompted.

"And Nik backed out, and I—" I almost told her about the way I'd shattered the *At* wall, but that would lead back to the fight with Nik and me sharing my bruised feelings and, well . . . I just wasn't in a feelings-sharing kind of mood. I was in a get-shit-done mood, and I fully intended to do just that. "I can't help Garth's mom on my own," I finally admitted.

I paused, listening to my slowing heartbeat. When it was beating in time with Lex's, I said, "I need your help."

Lex blew out a breath. "I was afraid you were going to say that."

I moved to stand in front of her. "Just this one time, Lex. Just Garth's family," I said in a rush. "That's it. I won't ask you to do this ever again."

Lex didn't respond. She didn't move, displaying that utter stillness so common to Nejerets. For most of us, minimizing external stimulation makes it easier to think.

"I already have a gateway drawn in the garage, and I can create a portable gateway for the trip back," I told her. "You won't have to expose yourself to the outside world for more than fifteen minutes," I said, addressing what I assumed was her biggest concern. "That's not even close to enough time for the Senate's goons to figure out you're off the compound."

Lex brought her hand up to her neck, rubbing that tender skin thoughtfully as she stared across the Agate Pass. "He can find me. Once he realizes I'm gone, wherever I go, he can find me. He'll stop us." She was talking about Heru.

I inhaled slowly, hesitating. "That's not exactly true."

She looked at me.

"An *At* barrier will block him."

Her eyes widened.

Before she could come up with some other—any other—logical, reasonable protest, I said, "He has a little sister. Garth, I mean. She's eleven, and her name is Cassie." I let that sink in for a second or two. A middle-aged, direly ill woman might not be enough to sway Lex, but the fate of a sick child had to. I rolled the potential lie around in my mouth, gauging the bitterness. Not too bad, and well worth it if it worked.

I stared out at the Sound, but watched Lex out of the corner of my eye. And then I pulled out the big guns. "She's sick, too."

CHAPTER THIRTEEN

I told Lex to meet me in the garage in a half hour, whopper of a lie about Cassie and all. I was maybe being a little overly ambitious with my time estimate, but if I ran the whole way back to the house, repurposed part of a bedsheet for a mobile return gateway, then sprinted to the garage, I knew I could do it. That was leaving zero room for error. Always a great idea.

Luckily—thanks, universe—I didn't meet a single unexpected obstacle along the way back to the house, and the gateway I was drawing on a torn fragment of a cotton sheet flared to life with a solid five minutes left on the clock. I jumped to my feet, hastily rolled up the sheet-bound gateway, and blew out of the room.

"Are you certain this is the wisest—"

"Seriously?" I hissed, cutting Dom off as I hurtled down the stairs. "This is literally the worst possible time."

"Well, that's a bit of an exaggeration," Dom muttered.

I held my tongue. Mostly because any retorts of mine would've been both childish and off base. He was just looking out for my and Lex's best interests. He was always thinking of others.

Well, I thought to myself, *that's exactly what I'm doing.* Cassie and Garth and the rest of their family—this ending wasn't written in their stars. The Cascade Virus wasn't written in anyone's stars, making it the most unnatural thing that had ever existed, and therefore it had to be combated at any cost. In my mind, at least.

The Ducati was still parked at the base of the cascading stairs leading from the front door to the roundabout driveway. I hopped onto the bike, wedging the rolled-up sheet between the seat and my inner thigh and tossing my helmet into the bushes to retrieve later. I kicked the engine to life and made it into the garage with a minute to spare.

Lex was already there, cell phone in hand as she paced in front of the gateway I'd drawn in the back corner of the garage earlier that day. As soon as I pulled the bike in through the open garage door, she tapped the face of her phone, and the door glided down to the ground.

I killed the engine and walked the bike between Heru's favorite Aston Martin and the armored Range Rover Lex used to drive back when venturing out of the compound was an option for her, bringing it to a stop a dozen or so feet from the gateway. Through the impossible opening in the wall, I could see the side of the Suquamish Museum, just a several-minute ride from Garth's family's place in the wooded hills beyond.

"Hop on," I said, nodding to the back of the bike. I pulled the wadded-up sheet out from where it was wedged under my thigh and held it out to Lex as she approached. "Hang on to this, will you? I don't want to lose it."

She eyed the bundle, confused. Not surprising, considering it just looked like a rolled-up ivory bedsheet. Which it was. That just wasn't *all* it was. "What is it?" she asked, reaching out to take hold of the sheet.

"Our way home." I twisted to pat the miniscule passenger seat behind me. "Hop on."

Lex raised her leg over the bike's saddle, hesitant but graceful.

"You ever ridden before?" I asked her over my shoulder.

She shook her head.

I lifted my left foot and settled the boot on the foot peg.

"Alright, well . . . don't make any sudden movements, and just sort of go with the flow of the bike, and we should be fine."

Lex frowned. "You said we'd travel straight there and back. Can't we just walk?"

I faced forward and muttered, "This'll be faster," just a moment before twisting the throttle, spurring the Ducati forward.

Lex yelped as we hurtled toward the wall. Even I tensed up a bit—it's only natural—but the bike's front tire plunged into the gateway exactly as expected, and in a heartbeat, we were through.

And riding right back into the garage.

"Shit!" I squeezed the brakes, and the bike skidded to a halt mere inches from slamming into the side of a Lexus. The rear tire fishtailed, and I nearly dropped the bike, regaining control at the last possible moment. I did drop Lex, though.

She hit the floor with a grunt, rolling on the cement and settling on her knees. Slowly, she stood, wincing when she put pressure on her right foot. I had to give it to her; she knew how to fall.

"I take it that wasn't supposed to happen," she said, pushing her hair out of her face.

"Definitely not." I straightened out the bike and propped it on its kickstand, then jogged back to the gateway, scanning the entire thing in search of something—anything—that might tell me why it had malfunctioned so dramatically. It still showed me a view of the side of the museum. It should have taken us there, not back here.

I stepped off to the side of the gateway, getting as close to the wall as I could, and looked at the gateway's surface. Nothing stood out as being off, not that I had any clue what to look for, really.

I took a step backward and, experimentally, raised my hand and pushed it through the gateway. At the same moment, movement to my left caught my eye.

"What the hell?" I said under my breath as I watched a misshapen hand—*my* hand—appear near the other edge of the gateway. On this side. Definitely not where it should've been.

One thing was very clear—something was interfering with the

magic, blocking the far side of the tunnel I'd punched through reality.

"Has this ever happened before?" Lex asked.

I started, not realizing she'd moved closer and was now standing beside me. I'd been too focused on the messed-up gateway. Staring at my own seemingly floating hand, I shook my head. This exact gateway had worked several hours ago, so why wouldn't it work now?

Lex sucked in a breath. "Oh God, Kat—what happened to your hand?"

"Nothing," I said, probably too quickly. "It's fine. Nothing I can't deal with later." I was referring both to my hand and to the far greater internal damage caused by Nik situation. I cleared my throat. "We'll just have to go the long way. It only takes fifteen minutes to get there."

Lex was quiet for a moment, likely reading way too much into my reaction to her concern. Finally, she shook her head. "You know I can't be out there for that long. Besides, Heru's bound to have noticed I'm missing by then."

Damn. She was right.

"But . . . you could try creating a new gateway, I suppose," Lex suggested. "Maybe one that leads straight to their house?"

"I guess it's worth a try." I tore my stare from my hand. "You're willing to wait?"

Lex nodded. "For however long it takes. Garth's ancestors saved my life; I owe that family a great debt. I'll do whatever I can to help them."

"But what if Heru figures out what we're doing?" It was more a matter of *when* than *if*, but I wasn't really in the mood to talk Lex out of helping me.

Lex shrugged, but when she spoke, there was steel in her voice. "We'll cross that bridge when we come to it."

CHAPTER FOURTEEN

"*You should look outside,*" Dom said, his words buzzing through my mind as I drew on the garage wall, knocking me out of the zone. "*Something's going on.*"

I closed my eyes and leaned my forehead against the wall, then inhaled deeply and exhaled through my nose. I was creating the second gateway to Port Madison on the opposite side of the garage from the first, in case there was something wonky about the other wall that was causing the misfire. Or *had been*, because now, my concentration was well and truly broken.

"You have the shittiest timing, Dom."

"Be that as it may . . ."

I sighed, heavily, and straightened.

"What is it?" Lex said from her perch on a fold-out stepladder. She'd been watching me work, silent in her observation, until now.

"Dom says something's going on outside." I turned partway to look at her. "Do you mind checking it out while I finish this?" I said, giving a sideways nod to the *almost* complete rendition of the log cabin's front door. I just needed another minute or two and I'd be done. It would've been half that without Dom's interruption.

"No prob," Lex said, hands on her thighs to help her stand. From the way she moved, it looked like she was still a little stiff and sore from the tumble off the back of the bike. She'd twisted her knee in her landing, but she barely even limped now.

"Here," I said, reaching into my coat pocket. I pulled out the compact mirror that functioned as one of Dom's windows to the physical world and held it out for Lex to take. "So you two can discuss whatever's supposedly happening out there," I told her. And leave me the hell alone, I added silently. Otherwise, I'd never get this gateway up and running.

Lex took the mirror and opened it, greeting Dom before making her way across the garage to the door. I was already immersed in the drawing on the wall by the time I registered the sound of the door opening and shutting.

It wasn't long until that familiar rush of electric energy flowed through me and the gateway flared to life. It was dark on the other side of the gateway, the moonlight filtering through the clouds the only thing lighting the cabin's exterior.

"Dom, can you tell Lex I'm ready for her?" I was so used to Dom always being there in the mirror pendant that it took me a few seconds to realize that his silence was a product of his absence. He wasn't in my pendant right now, he was in the compact I'd sent with Lex. Duh.

I ran across the garage to the door to fetch my sister myself. "Hey, Lex," I said as I stepped out into the dark of night.

She stood a few yards from the door, her back to me.

"It's ready. Let's get go—"

My words cut off as my focus shifted beyond Lex, and I peered at the tree line to the west. Shock stunted my speech, my lungs seizing up from a sudden wash of dread. There were no stars in the sky above the jutting treetops. No clouded moonlight illuminating the bare, scraggly branches. Just complete and utter blackness. Only one thing could cause such relentless darkness.

"Is that—"

"*Anti-At*," Lex said, her back still to me. "It's around the whole compound."

"But—" I swallowed, wetting my suddenly parched throat. "But how?" I shook my head. "*Why?*"

Lex turned around, facing me. "There's only one person who could do this," she said. And she was right.

Mari, my old partner back when I'd worked for the Senate, was the only Nejeret alive whose *sheut* enabled her to pull inky *anti-At*, one of the two building blocks of the universe, into the physical plane. She was the only person other than a full-blown Netjer who had that insanely dangerous ability. It was a well-known fact.

"But why would Mari do this?" I said, not really looking for an answer.

"Perhaps the compound is under attack, and creating a dome of anti-At was the only way to shield us," Dom ventured.

I didn't buy it, and I said as much. If we were under attack, we would've heard something, even from within the garage. There would've been signs. The entire compound was wired with an alarm system to alert everyone within the walls of any kind of danger, and that sure as hell hadn't gone off.

"Maybe there was an accident in the lab," Lex said, voice unsure, "and this was the only way to keep something toxic from getting out?"

I shook my head. She was reaching with that one. There was another option—a scarier one. "What if it's the Visitor?" I said. The mysterious Netjer hadn't exactly been friendly during my one and only interaction with him back in the Ouroboros boardroom, and he was the only other living being currently in this universe capable of creating such a dome.

Lex's only response was to wrap her arms around her middle, hugging herself.

Spinning on my heel, I ran back into the garage, sprinting toward the new gateway. I didn't slow as I approached and hurtled straight through.

And, in a dizzying about-face, found myself lurching straight back into the garage.

"Damn it!" I shouted, kicking the stepladder. It flew a half-dozen yards only to crash into the back windshield of a vintage, cherry-red Mercedes.

Whatever the reason for the *anti-At* barricade, one thing was certain: the damn thing was behind the malfunction with my gateways.

I heard the sound of rubber soles slapping on concrete, then Lex said, "If the Visitor did this, then there's nothing we can do about it. We're trapped." She heaved a few breaths. "*We* can't get through . . ."

"But Mari should still be able to." I placed my hands on my hips, the toe of my boot tapping as I considered our options.

If my gateways weren't working, I doubted Heru would be able to jump outside, either. And it wasn't like we could break through the poisonous barrier. One touch by a Nejeret—any Nejeret other than me, the only one of our kind besides Mari with an apparent immunity to the soul-eating effects of *anti-At* by way of the protective ward on my palm—and that Nejeret would be erased from existence. Total eradication. Not only would they cease to be; they'd cease to *have been*.

I couldn't, for the life of me, imagine a single reason why Mari would ever take such a terrible risk, which meant it had to be the Visitor. We had one hope to get out of here—Mari. Without her, we were truly trapped.

CHAPTER FIFTEEN

I didn't even bother with the bike, though it may have been a second or two faster. I was too hyped up, and sprinting from the garage to the house would do my adrenaline-flooded body good. When I reached the house's terraced front stairs, my strides ate up the steps three at a time. I slammed into the front door, trembling hand fumbling with the door handle, and tore the door open, a sweating, panting mess.

"Not another step," Heru said, the words a whiplash.

Much as I might like to believe myself beyond his influence, I couldn't ignore the command in his voice. The more intuitive parts of my mind picked up on the reality that I couldn't beat him—that if I tried, I would lose—even if my stubborn forethoughts didn't.

I stood, frozen in place, staring at the two men standing near the foot of the grand staircase. My eyes narrowed when they landed on Nik. It was all I could do not to launch myself at him, reigniting our fight. I settled for glaring; it was a hell of a lot better than crying, which seemed to be my only other option, according to my tear ducts.

"What's going—"

"Silence," Heru said.

I opened my mouth to argue, but the look in Heru's golden

eyes told me that now was definitely not the time to test him. Pressing my lips together, I crossed my arms over my chest and split my glaring efforts between the two ancient men.

"What—" Lex came in through the open door behind me, out of breath from racing back here. "What's going on?" She passed me, steps slow and hand gripping her side. "Did you see that thing out there?" she asked, pointing over her shoulder with her thumb.

"Yes," Heru said, his tone thawing a bit. "I have, in fact, seen it,"

"Well, why's it there?" Lex asked, exasperated.

"Nekure assures me it's merely a precautionary measure," Heru told Lex, eyes only for her now that she was in the foyer. "Little Ivanov," he said, using his pet name for his wife, "what were you doing with Kat?"

Lex waved his question away. "Nothing that matters right now." True enough; it wasn't like we could get out to finish what I'd started now, what with the *giant dome of* anti-At *keeping us here*. "So, Mari created the dome to protect us from something?"

"Mari didn't create it," Nik said. "I did."

"What?" I blurted. I couldn't help it, order to be silent or not. "What are you talking about? You've never been able to control *anti-At*."

Nik's pierced eyebrow arched upward. "Is that so?"

I sucked in a breath to say more but lost my momentum when I realized I didn't *know* anything about the powers Nik's *sheut* afforded; I'd only *assumed*.

Nik had been around for millennia, almost as long as Heru. He'd been born with a *sheut*, unlike me, and Lex, Heru, and Aset—we'd been gifted ours a few years back, just before the twins headed out for their grand adventure in Netjer-land. These days, it seemed that my *sheut* powers were growing in leaps and bounds. Nik had had thousands of years to develop his magical abilities, and he'd had one hell of a coach to help him along the way—Re—so of course he was capable of more than just controlling *At*. I felt like a moron for never suspecting it.

I'd been too caught up in my own shit, wallowing in sorrow over losing my mom and disparaging the rotting nature of my assassin's soul. I'd been too focused on Nik in relation to me—on his perceived years of abandonment *of me*—that I'd never given a second thought to him in relation to *him*. Gods, it was past time for me to get over myself already.

Reality was—I didn't know Nik at all. The realization was a gut punch. I couldn't fathom why he'd come back into my life, why he'd spent the last few weeks helping me. I mean, he'd been living in my apartment. It didn't matter that I wasn't staying there with him; he was in my space. He'd made himself a part of my life. *He* had—*his* choice, not mine. Why? What possible reason? Had that, too, been because of some voice in his head?

Nothing made sense anymore, and my every attempt to understand was dizzying.

Only two things were clear in my blindsided mind: Nik was the one trapping us here, and I had to find a way out. Charlene's life depended on it.

"Why are you doing this, Nik?" I asked, pleading with my eyes. "Why keep us trapped here?"

He bowed his head, a sad, dry laugh shaking his chest. "I told you before—I'm trying to save you. I'm trying to save all of you. If the universe collapses, we all die. Re says—"

"Bullshit." I took a step toward him, hands balled into tight fists. My nails cut into my palms, feeding my anger and clearing some of the haze of confusion from my mind. "Bull-fucking-shit, Nik." Another step. My fingers itched for my sword. It didn't matter that I'd fought him just hours ago and lost. That he'd nearly killed me. I only had eyes for him, and my view of him was cast in red.

Hurt and anger threatened to drive out all rationality, but I managed to hold on, turning the pain and rage into vehemence. Into passion. Into strength.

I needed to convince Nik that he was wrong about Re—to make him believe that the Netjer's voice was a figment of his imagination—just for moment. Just long enough for him to lower the barrier and let me out so I could reach Charlene.

I took another step toward Nik. "Re's not talking to you." Another step. "He's not in your head."

"Tread lightly, little sister," Dom warned. "Something's changed —he's different now than he was this morning."

Dom was right. I could see the change, plain as day, whether it was insanity or godly interference. Either way, I couldn't stop myself.

One more step, and I was within arm's reach. "You've lost it," I told Nik, voice hushed. Like I was speaking only to him, only for him. "Can't you see, Nik? All those years spent with Re hitch-hiking in your body have you all twisted up. You can't tell what's real and what's not anymore." I laughed bitterly, shaking my head. "You know, I get why you left now. I see what he's done to you." I stepped closer, getting all up in his personal space, and tilted my head back to meet his hard stare. My words were tactical, but a surge of genuine pity tightened my throat. "He broke you, Nik." I searched his familiar eyes, feeling like I was looking at a total stranger. "You're broken."

I was vaguely aware of Lex and Heru standing nearby, silent and watchful.

Nik breathed a laugh through his nose and closed his eyes, and I hoped my words were sinking in, that his resolve was wavering. Then, maybe he would let me out.

His eyes opened, and he gazed at me through his dark lashes, his pale blue irises barely visible. "You'd like that, wouldn't you, Kitty Kat?"

My eyelids opened wide. "What?"

"Then we'd be two peas in a pod, you and I."

I shook my head. "This isn't about me. I'm not—"

"We could commiserate about how *broken* we both are." He brushed his knuckles down the side of my face.

I stiffened, needing to get away from him but finding that my legs were unwilling to move.

"We could comfort each other." His hand slid lower, his fingers curling around the back of my neck. He leaned in, resting his forehead against mine. "Isn't that what you want . . . what you've always wanted?"

My eyes burned with a toxic mixture of desire and shame. I'd been drawn to him since the first moment I met him, even when I'd feared him—even when I'd despised him—but now I was desperate to put some distance between us.

Except, I couldn't. I just *couldn't*. My mind and my body weren't communicating properly, almost like I'd been hypnotized.

"You can have that," Nik continued. "We can be together." His breath brushed across my face, warm and intoxicating. "You just have to agree to give up. No more transformations. No more new Nejerets. Not even one."

I felt the strong desire to agree, to abandon my quest to save Charlene. My head even started the downward tilt that would initiate a nod.

But, somewhere in the back of my hazy mind, I recalled a Nejeret named Nicolaj. His was one of the names tattooed on my arm in permanent *At* ink, because he was one of the rogue Nejerets I'd hunted down. One of the many I'd killed. He'd had a *sheut*, natural born, unlike mine, and it had enabled him to overwhelm human minds until they bent to his will. Just humans, in his case, but who was to say that Nik hadn't developed a similar power—one that worked on Nejerets, too.

As soon as I considered the possibility, I knew it was true, and the realization that Nik was exerting some kind of magical mind control over me was like a bucket of ice water dumped over my head. I blinked once, shocked and appalled that he would ever violate me like that. And then I kneed him in the groin as hard as I could.

Nik's hand slipped off my neck, and he doubled over. Gets them every time.

I skittered back a few steps. "Don't you *ever* do that to me again."

I needed to find Mari; she was the only person who could get me out of here, because she was the only other person alive who could break through a wall of *anti-At*. I spun around, brushing past Lex and Heru as I ran to the door to the underground lab. Mari would be down there; like Aset and Neffe, she'd been spending nearly every hour of every day in the lab since the Cascade Virus started spreading . She'd even taken to napping on the cots set up in the quarantine area.

"Kat!" Lex called. "Wait!"

I yanked the door open and stepped through the doorway, pausing in the opening. I met Lex's shocked stare and shook my head. "How could you let him . . . ?" I shook my head, devastated by the avalanche of disappointment.

And then I slammed the door.

CHAPTER SIXTEEN

I hurtled down the stairwell and ran into the lab. Gasps and shouts heralded my abrupt entrance.

Automatically, I shielded my eyes from the faux daylight burning bright overhead as I scanned the faces of at least a dozen Nejerets. Neffe remained in the back corner where I'd found her earlier with Aset, but Aset herself was making her way across the lab toward me.

They wouldn't have heard the disagreement that just happened over their heads, not with all of the security reinforcements and soundproofing laced through the lab's walls and ceiling. It was as solid of a bomb shelter as, well, an actual bomb shelter. In fact, there was a veritable warren of underground tunnels and buildings beneath the surface of the compound, a safety measure as much as a way to expand without disrupting too much of the natural beauty on the ground and drawing unwanted attention from humans in the area.

I skirted around a cluster of three Nejerets huddled at a laptop at the nearest workstation, heading for the opaque plastic wall that blocked off the quarantine area. It was where any live subjects were kept—a.k.a. humans infected with the Cascade Virus. Not that *we* were susceptible to the virus, but we also weren't eager to spread it to those who were.

"Kat," Aset said, picking up the pace to head me off. "What are you—"

I stopped her with a look. I had no clue what my expression was, but the rage and betrayal I felt toward Nik for his attempt to manipulate my mind had warped my features into something frightful enough to stop her in her tracks.

Unconcerned, I pushed through the plastic doorway, not pausing for the disinfectant spray in the pseudo-airlock, and tore the next zippered doorway open.

Six cots arranged in two rows filled the space within the enclosed area, and only half were occupied. Mari lay curled up on her side on the farthest cot on the left, her back to me, unmoving save for the slow rise and fall of her rib cage. I made a beeline for her.

"Hey," I said when I reached the cot, grabbing Mari's shoulder and giving it a solid shake. "Mars, wake up. I need your help."

Her muscles tensed under my hand just a moment before she twisted and lashed out, an *anti-At* dagger materializing in her hand, black as obsidian.

I caught her wrist, halting the blade a scant inch from my throat.

Her eye rounded. "Jesus, Kat, you look like shit." Her voice was hoarse with sleep, and her stare fixed on my hand. "What happen—"

I leaned in, forcing her arm lower. "We don't have time for any of that right now, Mars. I need you to come with me."

The black dagger evaporated into a fine, inky mist, and Mari flopped over onto her back on the cot, pulling her wrist free of my grip. "Why?" She rubbed her eyes. "I have work to do here, and—" Her eyelids opened even wider than before, and she sat up abruptly. "What's going on?" She stared upward, her gaze gliding along the ceiling. She was sensing the unbroken *anti-At* barrier surrounding us. "It's all around us. That's—" She shook her head slowly, her mouth working but no sound coming out. "That's impossible," she finally said, voice distant. "I was asleep. I didn't create this. It's imposs—"

"Nik did it."

Mari refocused on me, shock fading to irritation in her jade-green eyes, which slowly narrowed to slits. "I'm sorry—*what?*"

"He's been hiding a whole crap-ton of shit from us." From me—that was the part that really stung, topped off by the cherry of an attempted mindfucking. "Listen, Mars"—I gripped her shoulder—"I know you've got research to do, but I really need your help." I emphasized my plea with a gentle squeeze. "Just give me a night. Just one night—when the sun rises tomorrow morning, you're free to—"

"I'm in," she said, slaughtering my queued-up pleas.

My eyebrows rose, and it took me a moment to regroup. I'd expected to have to do a lot more begging to get her to agree to help. Not that I was about to talk her out of it.

"I'm not making any progress here, anyway," she said. "We've hit a full-on brick wall with our research into the Cascade Virus." She pulled her arm free from my grip and raised both hands to work on fixing her mussed bob. "What do you need me to do?"

So many things, but I thought it best to start small. Leap one damn hurdle at a time. "Make me a knife, first off," I said, drawing the combat knife I kept tucked away in my boot sheath. "An *anti-At* version of this." It would replace the mundane knife and function as a repellant to any Nejeret who might try to stop me. If Nik or Heru or anyone got close enough, one nick from an *anti-At* blade would erase them from existence forever. Nobody would risk it.

"You are running out of time, little sister," Dom told me. "They're discussing the best way to contain you. It's only a matter of seconds until they come down to get you." For a moment, I was clueless as to how Dom could possibly know that, but then I remembered the compact mirror I'd lent to Lex. She probably didn't even realize that she was giving me ears into their discussion through Dom.

Mari took the combat knife from me, turning it over and over as she studied it. There was a sizzle in the air, and blackness crystallized the blade, though the handle remained the same. "It won't work on Nik," she warned me.

I hadn't considered the fact that his new—or new-to-me—power would render him immune from the soul-erasing effects of the black-as-death material. "Well," I said, "we'll just have to do our best to avoid him." Just for the night. All I needed was a single night, enough time to gain some minimal control over my own expanding *sheut* power and rescue Garth's mom from the single greatest threat to her life—their mortality.

Fury would sustain me, motivate me. I could already feel my connection to the universal energies strengthen . . . could sense the otherworldly power welling within my *sheut*. I was overflowing with it; if that wasn't enough to make the transformation procedure work, then nothing would be.

"Heru truly wants you on his side," Dom said. "Nik wants Heru to teleport him down here with him so he can contain you in anti-At until the threat has passed, but Heru wishes to give you the chance to surrender . . . to 'fall back into line.'"

I snorted and shook my head. Despite our pretty damn epic falling-out, Nik still knew me well. He knew I wouldn't give up, that "falling into line" wasn't even in my radar.

"What?" Mari asked.

I touched the mirror pendant, telling her I was receiving intel from Dom.

"Oh, right," she said, pulling a phone from the pocket of her lab coat and unlocking the screen with her thumbprint.

"What are you doing?" I asked. This was hardly the time to make a phone call. "We ran out of time, like, yesterday."

"I'm texting my mom," Mari said. "We're going to need her help if we're going to have any chance at all of evading Heru."

"Heru is on his way now," Dom warned.

There was a silent crackle in the air, and I spun around in time to see Heru materialize within the quarantine area. Luckily the two infected humans resting down here were passed out, either asleep, sedated, or comatose, depending on how far the disease had progressed within them. Otherwise, they'd have been in for quite the show.

"Speak of the devil," I said, hiding the newly minted *anti-At* knife behind my back. If Dom was right and Heru was still rooting for me to come to my senses—so to speak—then there was a chance that talk could buy enough time for Mari to convince her mom, Mei, to join the fun. Mei shared the ability to teleport with Heru, only she had centuries more experience with the power. She was quicker. Better. Having her on our team would give us the edge we needed.

Heru stood a few yards away, head held high and eyes locked with mine. He looked like he had no intention of moving, let alone of attacking, but with him, looks could be very deceiving. Like Nik, he was one of the few people alive who could—and likely would—beat me in a fight.

I gripped the hilt of the *anti-At* knife more tightly.

"Cease this childishness, Kat," Heru said, his voice silken steel.

A chill crept up my spine. An instinctive warning from the part of my brain that gave a shit about self-preservation. The part that didn't understand just how far past caring about my own life I was at that moment. I would see this through, no matter what. Charlene wasn't dying on my watch.

"Stand down, and all will be well." Heru's presence only fanned my anger, turning it to rage.

"And if I don't?" I said, the words grating in my throat.

My eyes burned with the overwhelm of emotion. This man was my lord, my king. I'd pledged my loyalty to him, years ago. I'd put my faith and trust in him. And even though he currently faced me emanating an aura of threat, I still believed he was the right person to lead our people. The fair and just choice, if not necessarily the most compassionate Nejeret alive.

"Kat," Heru said, tone both patronizing and filled with disappointment. "Trust me when I tell you that you don't want to find out the consequences of further disobedience."

He was wrong. What I *didn't* want was to use the *anti-At* blade on him. In my heart, my soul, I *knew* I didn't want to unmake him—and not only because doing so would unravel his thread from the fabric of history and plunge us all into the unknown chaos of a world where he'd never existed, though that was a big part of it. I believed in him, still. But I didn't believe in blind faith, and that's what he was asking me to give him. To give Nik.

It stung that he couldn't return the favor, that he couldn't believe in me.

"I can't believe you're listening to him," I said, jaw aching from clenching so hard. "It's highly unlikely that Re's actually talking to him. You know that, right?" I scoffed. It didn't matter if I believed what I was saying; it only mattered that my words bought us time. "I mean, Lex has to use a magical pendant to talk to the twins across universal boundaries, but suddenly Nik can do it willy-nilly and you just believe him? Please, explain to me the logic there. Tell me how this makes any sense at all."

Heru's nostrils flared. "I must entertain the possibility that Re is truly in communication with Nekure."

I groaned in annoyance and rolled my eyes.

"You've always been reactive, Kat, and now is no different. You're thinking with your heart, not with your head."

"Oh, really . . ." I was trying to save a life—one single life—not let someone die based on the unsubstantiated claims of a man who might just be insane. Felt like pretty sound reasoning to me. I planted my hand on my hip, fully intending to drag out this argument as long as was necessary.

"Nekure hadn't heard even a whisper from Re until three days ago," Heru said, raising a hand to stop my protests before they could start.

"So what?"

"Humor me," he said. "Just for a minute."

It struck me that Dom was right; Heru wanted me to come around. That realization caught me off guard. Like I said, he's a good guy. The *right guy* for the job. I almost felt bad for him that he was stuck giving a shit about me.

I pursed my lips. It was the only way to guarantee I held my tongue.

"Assume, just for a moment, that Nekure is correct, and somehow a connection has been reestablished between him and Re," Heru said. "This connection only became apparent *after* we carried out three *ba* transference procedures."

As he spoke, the gears in my mind whirred. It was a coincidence, most likely. Correlation doesn't equal causation.

"If Nekure's claims are correct and he is hearing Re's voice as a direct effect of the procedures," Heru continued, "then somehow, the transformation of human souls into Nejeret *ba*s—of mortal into immortal—has weakened the barriers between the Netjer universe and our own." He paused, his stare intense, but not menacing. "If the transformation of just three souls has done this, what will happen after three more? Or just one more?"

Heru took a step toward me, then another. He was maybe nine feet away now. Close enough that a solid lunge would put him on top of me. "Are you really willing to gamble with the stability of our universe?" he asked me. "With the fate not just of humankind but of all life?"

His words were starting to get to me, and I shook my head like I was casting off a swarm of fruit flies. "And the twins?" I asked, grasping the threads of logic that were way sturdier than this hearsay-based conjecture. "Any word from them?" Heru and Lex's godly children were, after all, the designated Netjer caretakers of this universe. They were always tapped in to it, on every level, no matter their current absentee status.

Heru inhaled and exhaled slowly, then shook his head, a simple slice left, then to the right.

I felt that crackle of energy behind me and knew that Mei had arrived. I was out of time. No more wavering.

Heru's focus shifted past me, and the corners of his mouth tensed. His knees bent, just a little. He was making his move.

I pulled the *anti-At* combat knife out from behind my back and held it in front of me defensively.

Heru's eyes widened when they landed on the glimmering onyx-like blade. He was erring on the side of caution by believing his nephew's story, but it was clear that he wasn't willing to risk temporal suicide for the sake of defending something that *might* be.

"I have to go," I said, lowering my chin. I extended my arm behind me, and I felt Mei's warm fingers wrap around my wrist. "I made a promise." Not a second before the world was overtaken by iridescent fire.

We were gone, nothing but burned bridges in our wake. I'd kept my distance from my people for years. Now, with a single decision, I'd made my split from them absolute. I could never go home again.

Here's to hoping it was worth it.

CHAPTER SEVENTEEN

My lungs seized up. My heart strained to pump. I was frozen. Immobile. Both there and here. Dead and alive. Existing and not.

And then there was a whoosh, and oxygen-rich air rushed into my lungs. My heart stumbled over itself in its eagerness to return to business as usual. I dropped to my knees, Mei's hand slipping off my arm, and touched my forehead to the sodden, mulchy ground. It was wet, muddy, but at least it was cool.

"Is it always like that?" I asked, gasping for delicious air. Thank the gods that traveling through gateways was a totally different experience from teleporting.

"Pretty much," Mari said. "But you get used to it."

I turned my head to the side so my cheek was touching the ground and watched Mari's slippers move into my range of vision. Apparently, she'd been going for comfort lately down in the lab. Her wool-lined moccasins sank into the rain-soaked earth as she stood with her toes nearly touching a glimmering wall of absolute, light-sucking blackness.

I pushed myself up so I was kneeling. I was a little dizzy, but at least I was upright. "So, next time should be better?" A quick glance around told me we were just outside the compound's walls in a wooded knoll about a quarter mile from the gate.

Mei offered me her hand. "It took Mari a couple hundred jumps to get acclimated."

"Awesome." Before I accepted her proffered hand, I tucked the *anti-At* knife into my boot sheath and wiped the mud from my face with the front of my shirt. "Thanks," I said as Mei helped pull me up onto unsteady legs.

She released my hand and gave my shoulder a gentle pat. "Always glad to help."

"This'll just take me a sec," Mari said, both palms pressed against the *anti-At* barrier. Her eyes were squeezed shut, and her lips were pressed into a thin, bloodless line. She'd never been able to handle *anti-At* as quickly or nimbly as Nik could *At*—chalk it up to thousands of years of practice, I supposed—but this long of a delay was unusual for her.

I started counting the seconds as they passed. "What's the holdup, Mars?" I asked when I reached thirty.

With an exasperated grunt, Mari let her hands fall away from the wall. "The barrier's not just made of *anti-At*," she said, then slapped the thing. "He cheated! It's laced with *At*, too. I can't break through even a small part of it."

I closed my eyes and inhaled and exhaled slowly. "That sneaky turd," I said under my breath.

Well, I had no choice but to throw a Hail Mary now. I climbed to my feet and raised my left hand. The Eye of Horus tattoo burned the closer my hand came to the unbreakable barrier.

"What are you doing?" Mari exclaimed, making to reach for my wrist.

I swatted her hand away, stopping a second attempt with a look. "Trust me." After a nervous deep breath, I slapped my palm against the barrier. There was no guarantee that such a massive amount of soul-eating *anti-At* wouldn't overwhelm my protective ward and consume me, erasing me from existence entirely. After all, I'd only tested it with a baseball-sized ball of *the stuff*. But I was out of options.

My palm was on fire. I gritted my teeth and held my breath, waiting for the telltale tingle of *anti-At* invading my body, hungrily seeking out my *ba*.

It never came.

I blew out my breath in relief and opened my eyes. Both Mari and Mei were watching me, hands to their mouths and twin looks of horror in their eyes.

"See," I said, "easy peasy."

Ever so slowly, Mari lowered her hand. "You're insane," she whispered.

I snorted, playing at nonchalant when I was anything but—my heart was pounding. "Like that's news to anyone." I gave the dome a sideways nod. "C'mon, let's get this over with before Heru gets a lock on our location."

Tentatively, Mari raised her hands and replaced her palms against smooth, obsidian surface. The skin around her eyes was tight with tension. She looked at me, uncertainty written all over her face. "How exactly is you touching the barrier supposed to make this work any better?" she asked.

"Where's the trust, Mars? Don't I always have a plan?"

She laughed, a shallow, dry sound, and shook her head. "No, actually, you *never* have a plan." And then she closed her eyes, concentration warping her delicate features.

I did the same. Focusing on the *At* interwoven with its counterpart throughout the barrier. I could sense it, bound to the *anti-At* like one half of a zipper. I could *sense* it, but no matter how hard I concentrated, I couldn't isolate it from the *anti-At* and will it away.

"Heru's found you," Dom said, his words skittering across the edges of my awareness. *"They're on their way."*

It was time for another approach. A more personal approach.

In my mind's eye, I pictured Nik, the one who'd created the barrier, all smug satisfaction, his heavenly features twisted by a gloating smirk. I imagined that he was made of solid *At*—that all of the *At* interwoven in the barrier had been reworked into a likeness of him—and that my hands were wrapped around his neck. I was so furious at him about messing with my mind that I wanted to tear his stupid imaginary head right off. Focusing that rage, I squeezed as hard as I could, willing my fingers to sink into the stonelike material.

"Come on," I said, voice a mere groan. "Come on . . ."

Inside my head, my imagined fingers sank deeper into the *At* that made up Nik's neck. I would destroy him for what he'd done to me. For what he *was doing* to me. I would tear him limb from limb, molecule from molecule.

"An engine approaches," Mei whispered. I felt her hand grip my upper arm. She was getting ready to teleport us again, probably to another portion of the barrier. How long would it take me to recover from the jump this time?

I redoubled my efforts on the barrier—on my mental image of Nik. Sweat trickled down the back of my neck. My palm felt slippery against the impermeable barrier.

Mari grunted a scream, and then I was falling forward.

We'd done it. We'd broken through the dome. We were free.

I opened my eyes and, for only a fraction of a second, I saw the trees that had been on the other side of the dome. Without warning, the world erupted in a shimmering iridescence and I was drowning in the temporary horror of inexistence as Mei teleported us away.

CHAPTER EIGHTEEN

We reappeared in absolute darkness, and for a moment, I was convinced that I had overestimated my immunity to the effects of *anti-At* and was experiencing firsthand what it was like to witness my life—my very existence—unraveling. Except I wasn't alone in my worse-than-death fate. Two other heartbeats cut through the deafening darkness. Two other pairs of lungs sucked in rasping breaths in chorus with mine.

"Where's the latch," Mei whispered, voice hushed, but harsh with urgency. "I can't see a damn thing!"

Without warning, a blinding light burned through the darkness. "Here," Mari said, the light bobbing along.

I blinked several times, hand held up to shield my eyes. It was a phone; Mari was using the screen as a flashlight, illuminating a brick tunnel that ended with a vault door. It took me a second or two to put two and two together and figure out where we were—in the warren of tunnels under Seattle, standing just outside of Mari and Mei's hidden underground bunker.

Now that there was light, Mei's movements transformed from fumbling to purposeful as she moved closer to the vault door. The heavy, mechanized door had once protected a bank vault, back in the 1880s, before Seattle was ravaged by a fire and the city's officials decided that rebuilding was *so last year* and built a brand-new, "fireproof" city on top of the old instead.

While Mei worked on the door's locks and latches, I moved closer to Mari. "We can't stay here for long."

Her brows bunched together. "I'm sorry?" she said, clearly not understanding.

"Once Heru gets a lock on our location, it'll only be a matter of minutes until he and Nik pop in, and I'm guessing that this time it's going to be for more than a chat." I had little doubt that the niceties were over, and that Heru would be playing hardball from here on out. When he finally made an appearance, Nik would be with him, and if Nik got close enough to see us—to use any of his myriad of *sheut* powers on us—we'd be SOL, and so would Charlene. We had to keep moving, period.

Mari shook her head, her mussed bob swaying. "But he won't be able to sense us," she explained. "I lined the walls and ceiling and, well, everything in the bunker with *anti-At* a while back. It's how we stayed hidden from you and Heru for more than a week." She eyed me, shadowed gaze quizzical. "You must've wondered . . ."

"Huh." I had wondered, but I'd forgotten in the chaotic events of the days since then.

"I'll keep an eye on Heru and the others anyway," Dom said, "just in case."

"Thanks," I whispered. The need for urgency might have lost a reason, but it was still a necessity. Charlene was a ticking time bomb at this point, and we were racing against the clock. At least now Garth was there, and if his mom awoke in a rabid frenzy, he'd be able to take care of her. Though I hoped, desperately, that it wouldn't come to that. I'd been destroyed when my mother was killed right in front of me; I had no idea what putting down his own mom would do to Garth.

There was a metallic clang from the vault end of the tunnel, then the screech of rusty metal on metal. Mari and I halted and turned our heads to watch Mei pull the vault door open.

"We should stay here for fifteen or twenty minutes," Mari said, "long enough that Heru has time to realize we've hidden ourselves from him and gives up on actively searching for us using his gift."

I wasn't fond of the idea of sitting here for so long, but I didn't have much of a choice. I could probably do this without their help, but my likelihood of succeeding was way higher if I had them with me.

Mari rubbed her hands together as we made our way to the armored doorway, "So, once the waiting's over, what's next?" She gave me a wry look. "Assuming your plan didn't end with us breaking through that thing . . ." It was a jab, but a lighthearted one.

Back in the days of our deadly partnership, Mari had always been the planner, while I'd operated best with more of a fly-by-the-seat-of-my-pants mentality. We'd compromised, most of the time, mixing planning with improvising in an often heart-stopping, always intoxicating way. We'd been one hell of a team, at least until the work lost its luster and my heart lost its "in it."

"I do, in fact, have a plan," I told her as I passed her on my way into the bunker. "Shocking, I know."

Mari held back to pull the heavy door shut, spinning the handle to lock it. "And mildly impressive." She turned from the vault door and headed toward the sofa tucked away in the "living room" corner of the bunker. She shed her lab coat and draped it over the back of the couch, then toed off her muddy slippers. "Let's hear it, then."

I bit my lip, hesitating. I needed to know one thing before I divulged my mildly kamikaze plot to her and her mom. "First, tell me one thing, Mars—why are you helping me?" I glanced at Mei, who was puttering around in the bunker's surprisingly well-laid-out kitchen. It was a little 1950s, but still beyond anything I'd have expected to find down here. "Both of you—not that I'm not grateful, but you're risking everything by helping me. Heru, once he gets his hands on us . . ."

I looked up at the ceiling and shook my head, momentarily unable to believe that I'd thought crossing Heru *and* Nik was even a remotely good idea. Mari'd been right earlier; I'd lost my mind. I was certifiably bonkers.

A hand on my shoulder drew me back to the here and now. I was a little surprised to find Mei peering at me rather than her daughter.

"I was in our rooms when my father arrived tonight," she said, speaking of Nik.

Every single time I was faced with that reality—that Nik was Mei's father—it stunned me a little. Nik had lived for thousands and thousands of years, so it shouldn't have shocked me that he'd procreated at some point. Honestly, the more shocking thing should've been that he'd had only one kid—Mei—but he was just so unfatherly that the truth of their relationship never ceased to blow my mind.

"I overheard him telling Heru what he believed to be the truth," Mei continued, "about Re and hearing his voice . . . about his warning of what might happen if more human souls were transformed into Nejeret *ba*s." Her gaze grew distant, and her hand fell away.

She seemed different since her time spent as a captive in the Ouroboros lab, the same place Dom had been imprisoned and tortured. Mei was a former Senate member, a leader in her own right, but now she was subdued . . . even withdrawn.

"Re is the reason I never had a chance to truly know my father. He's the reason my father nearly killed you, his—"

"Friend," Mari said, and I looked at her, confused by the interruption. She offered me a miniscule smile and a half-hearted shrug, then took her mom's place in the kitchen and started filling up a coffeepot with water from the faucet.

When I returned my attention to Mei, she no longer wore that far-off stare. She cleared her throat, also offering me a smile, though hers was a little shaky. "Re is the reason my father's mind broke . . . the reason he was absent from my life once again, even though we'd finally found each other." A hard glint flashed in her eyes. "After everything he's done to my father—after *everything*—

Re's no friend of mine." She breathed in and out harshly. "Whether he's really back, his whispers poisoning my father's mind further, or whether this is just an echo of Re's abuse, I won't stand for it." She balled her hand into a fist. "My family is done being manipulated by that *thing*, and I could care less that he's one of the creators of our universe."

A heavy, somber air filled the silence after Mei finished.

"Fair enough." I exchanged a glance with Mari. "What about you?" I asked her.

She resumed her almost robotic coffee-making. "I dunno. I guess I was bored." She poured coffee grounds into a filter. "We haven't made any progress in the search for a cure, and the research environment down in that lab was growing stale." She shrugged. "It wasn't really a 'breakthrough' environment anymore. We're too sheltered down there." She tucked the loaded filter into the coffeemaker. "A cure is our ticket back into Heru's good graces. Without that, we're as good as dead." She flipped the switch on the coffeepot, then met my eyes. "Necessity is the mother of innovation, after all . . . if this little adventure doesn't force a spark of brilliance, nothing will."

I snorted a laugh. "And you call me crazy."

CHAPTER NINETEEN

"You know," Mari said as she emerged from the bedroom area of the bunker, "I've been thinking . . ."

I'd yet to have the grand tour, but I hardly needed it. From my vantage point at the dining table, I had a solid view of the bedroom Mari had retreated into to change into what she called "mission-appropriate attire." She'd gone in wearing black slacks, a blouse, socks, and a lab coat, and had emerged a few minutes later in an outfit of fitted black leather pants, a black sleeveless blouse cut low enough to show off her not-insubstantial cleavage, and black stiletto booties.

"Jesus, Mars," I said, giving her elevator eyes, "we're going to a house, not a club."

She rolled her eyes—how very *me* of her—and shrugged on a fitted black leather coat. "I figured I'm the muscle for this little excursion," she said, twirling an *anti-At* dagger that she pulled out of thin air. "Thought I should look appropriately intimidating." She made the dagger disappear, freeing up her hands to tie her shoulder-length hair back into a low nubbin of a ponytail.

She looked intimidating, alright—sexually, not physically.

"Okay," I said, drawing out the word. I couldn't believe her mom didn't have an opinion, but Mei remained quiet, stirring a pot of marinara sauce at the stove.

It was always a good idea for a Nejeret to eat a square meal before heading out on a dangerous mission—the surplus in nutrients and calories could stave off any necessary rounds of injury-induced regenerative sleep for an hour or two, and I was already in the red because of my now-healed wrist and hand injuries. The next time I caught some shut-eye, I'd be out until my body decided it was in good enough shape on a cellular level to wake.

Mari waved my reaction to her outfit away like it was an unwanted, mangy puppy. "Anyway, like I said—I've been thinking, and I think the wisest thing would be to do a trial run before we head over to your boyfriend's place."

I clenched my jaw, barely refraining from snapping, "He's not my boyfriend." I closed my eyes, centering myself, then opened them and fixed my stare on Mari. "What did you have in mind?" I didn't hate the idea of a trial run—it would ensure that my impotence of the last attempt wouldn't be repeated—but every second we spent outside of this bunker and its protective encasement of *anti-At* was a second closer to the moment Heru zeroed in on our location. Once we were out of here, we really would have to stay mobile. I couldn't afford to get caught before I'd made it back to Charlene's bedside.

"We could head to the Tent District," I said, thinking aloud. I felt fairly certain that Dorman would be willing to let me attempt any potential life-saving procedure on the infected people in his care.

Mari shook her head, then pulled out the chair adjacent to mine and sat. "I don't want to give Heru a reason to think that Dorman and all the Nejerets there are in league with your little underground movement here."

My eyebrows rose. I was surprised she cared. Mari tended to be more of an ends-justify-the-means kind of girl. But then I remembered that she and Dorman had a history, that he'd been one of her followers back during the dark days, when Mari and Mei and all of the other Nejerets unlucky enough to have been born with a *sheut* were hunted by the former totalitarian body of leadership of our people, the Council of Seven. Thank the gods that patriarchal group had gone the way of the dinosaurs. If only the governmental body that replaced it hadn't proved to be just as corrupt.

"How's a quick trip to my old stomping grounds sound?" Mari said.

I searched her jade eyes, unsure what exactly she was suggesting. And then I got it, and my mouth fell open. "Ouroboros? You can't be serious . . ."

She'd worked as the science director for the twisted corporation for nearly a year, but I didn't see how that could help us, let alone why returning there could ever be seen as a good idea. The Ouroboros board had been in cahoots with the Senate. That corporation provided our enemies their main stronghold within our territory, because while Heru could police any unwelcome Nejerets within his kingdom's borders, he could hardly enforce *anything* with the humans.

Mari tapped her nose, telling me I was right on the money with my guess. "Why yes, my friend, I *am* serious." She raised a hand, palm out, and said, "Hear me out." She curled her fingers into a fist, holding up only her index finger. "First, there's plenty of potential subjects there."

I frowned, knowing she was right. It was all over the local PNS feed—Ouroboros was offering medical aid to any and all people turned away from the hospitals. Probably as a front with plans to allow those in their care to reach the rabid phase without sedation or euthanization, then releasing them back out into the unsuspecting public so the disease would spread even faster. I yearned for the day I could focus on taking them and their parent conglomerate, Initiative Industries, down. Assuming I survived the shitstorm Heru threw my way after this, I *would* destroy them.

But I needed to follow through with my promise to Garth's family first, then get the Cascade Virus under control and bring the Senate to their knees. It didn't matter to me which happened first; it was just a comfort to feel my inner resolve. Purpose was a security blanket I hadn't slept with for a long damn time. It felt good to have it back.

"Second," Mari continued, "I know their facilities inside and out." She raised a third finger. "And last—but *not* least—even if Heru figures out where we are in the brief time that we're in Ouroboros facilities, he'll think twice before coming after us there."

I let out a single, voiceless laugh. She was right. It was the perfect place to run a quick trial, to give me a chance to perfect—or at least to hone—my control over *At* before returning to Port Madison to heal Charlene.

"We'd need to be quick," I said, glancing at Mei. She was piling mountains of spaghetti noodles tossed in marinara sauce on three different plates in the kitchen. "There's no saying how much time Charlene has left." But at least by making sure I could make the procedure work, I wouldn't dash her family's hopes twice in one day.

"Also . . ." I pulled the orb containing a fragment of Heru's *ba* from my coat pocket and held it up in my palm. "I've only got the one fragment, and if Samuel or Cassie have contracted the virus . . ." I shook my head, knowing I'd be unable to abandon them to their fate. I didn't operate that way. "I have no idea how to separate this thing into smaller pieces. Who knows how long it'll take me to figure that out."

"No biggie," Mari said, standing and retreating to the bedroom once more. When she reemerged, she was carrying a small canvas makeup bag. She set it on the table in front of me and reclaimed her seat. "My gift to you."

I snatched the little bag off the table and unzipped the zipper. It was filled with several dozen marble-sized balls of *At*, each with its own, smoky *ba* fragment. "You've been keeping your own private stash of these things?" I asked, floored.

"Happy belated birthday," she said with a cutesy shrug.

I was speechless.

Mei carried two of the plates of spaghetti to the table and set them before Mari and me. A fork was planted like a flagpole in the center of each mound of noodles. "Eat up," she said, "and then we'll go." She returned to the kitchen, where she shoveled a huge bite from the third plate into her mouth, then hurried into the bedroom. She returned a moment later with a canvas messenger bag, which she proceeded to stock full of protein bars, bags of fruit snacks, and several bottles of Gatorade between bites of spaghetti.

I watched her as I dug into my own food. Beside me, Mari did the same.

Apparently, Mei was even more of a planner than her daughter was. Good. Because, at the moment, I was a definitive loose cannon. They were functioning as my stabilizers. It was a role that, in both the distant and the recent past, had belonged to Nik. In his absence, I needed their stability, desperately.

I took bite after bite, avoiding the implications of that realization. I didn't need Nik. I *didn't* need him.

I didn't *need* anyone.

CHAPTER TWENTY

"Where are we?" I asked, peering out at the scattered clumps of trees and the boxy four- and five-story buildings surrounding the grassy knoll where Mei had teleported us. I was down on one knee and disoriented from my third jump of the night—and it *was* full-on dark—but I could see more than well enough to know that none of those squat buildings were the towering Columbia Center, the base of the Ouroboros Corporation's Seattle headquarters. From the looks of it, we weren't in downtown Seattle at all.

"We're at the satellite campus in Redmond," Mari said, gripping my elbow tightly and hoisting me up to my feet. "You didn't think they were taking sick folks in at the downtown location, did you?" She laughed, a musical sound. "Ouroboros only leases two floors there—where would they put all the people?"

I hadn't given it much thought, but I *had* assumed we were headed to the downtown location. It had been a shallow assumption, clearly. I decided not to comment, glancing around as I brushed off my knee instead. It took me a second to reorient myself to being on the other side of Lake Washington. I so rarely ventured over to the Eastside, and that abrupt transition was jarring.

"So," I said, "where to now?" There were at least five buildings within sight.

Mari headed toward a paved path that led to the building to my immediate left, maybe a hundred yards away. "This way." She walked on her toes, doing her best to keep her heels from spiking into the soggy grass.

Mei followed her daughter wordlessly, and I stared after them both for a moment, then trotted to catch up. "How do you know where to go?" I asked.

"I recognized the interior from one of the featurettes on the news," Mari tossed over her shoulder. She reached the path, and her gait became much steadier, her heels tapping dully on the cement.

I fell into step beside her.

"Honestly, I'd bet they've got people stuffed into most of the buildings here by now," she said.

"Oh?"

Mari nodded once. "The more test subjects, the better, right?" She laughed dryly. "I mean, they've got to be in full-on panic mode right now, searching for a cure and all, and if we haven't been successful, I can guarantee they're struggling to make any progress at all."

"Wait." I paused mid-step. "*What*?" Again, I jogged to catch up. "Why would they want to find a cure; they're the ones who released the virus to begin with."

"Technically, it was Scott and Gregory who released the infected kids," she said, mentioning two of the Ouroboros board members. "And there's no way it was sanctioned by the Ouroboros or Initiative boards," she continued. "They're many things, but they're not suicidal." Another dry laugh, this one with notes of bitterness. "Oh no, this has 'Senate' written all over it."

My eyes narrowed. There was another option—the Visitor. The Netjer who'd been masquerading as "Gregory" for who knows how long. But neither Mari nor Mei knew anything about the Visitor—

Heru had ordered that little tidbit stay on extreme lockdown, and I'd already crossed him enough for one day—so I kept my Visitor-centric hypothesis to myself.

"So you're saying this sudden 'humanitarianism' is more than just a publicity stunt for Ouroboros," I said, stopping when Mari and Mei did. We were several dozen paces from the building's glass door.

"Oh yeah." Mari pointed her finger at a security camera sticking out of the wall a few feet above the door and closed one eye. A tiny, inky projectile that resembled a black toothpick shot out of her finger. Not a second later, the camera's lens shattered. "This is the panicked search for a lifeboat," she said, taking aim again, this time at a camera secured to the upper right corner of the building. A moment later, there was a sharp *tink*, and that one fell out of order, too.

"Good shot," I told her.

She flashed me a grin before taking out a third camera at the upper left corner of the building. "That's it for the externals." She tapped her lips with that same, dangerous finger. "Disabling the building's internal security system will waste time we don't have, and if I take out the interior cameras in the same way, the guards will pick up on the fact that this is more than just a glitch in the external feeds."

I exchanged a look with Mei. Mari wasn't usually such a think-on-her-feet-er, and it was fascinating to watch. Also, pretty damn stressful.

"They'll dispatch someone to check it out, but it should take the guard at least ten minutes to get here." She looked at her mom. "What's the minimum we've got until Heru picks up our scent?"

Mei was quiet for a moment. "It's impossible to say," she finally said with a sigh. "If he's actively searching for us right now—five minutes or so. If not . . ."

"Then we're just wasting time," I said as I jogged to the building's door. "Let's get on with it." We had somewhere between five and ten minutes to get this right. That wasn't a lot of time to practice doing something using my *sheut* that I'd only done three times before, and then, only when I was in extreme distress. In other words, super pissed off.

Mari cut ahead of me right before I reached the door. She pulled a key card from the back pocket of her leather pants and held it up to the reader on the wall to the right of the door handle.

"Mars, wait," I said, reaching for her wrist. The use of her key card was bound to set off alarm bells pretty much everywhere.

"Don't worry," she said, "it's not my old card."

I released her wrist. "Whose, then?"

She moved the card closer to the card reader. The red light at the top flashed to green, and the door's lock clicked.

I pulled on the door handle.

"Connie's," Mari said, voice hushed and face hidden. She was talking about Constance Ward, the former head of the Ouroboros board and brand-spanking-new Nejeret. "Keep your face angled down."

Mari entered the building first, then Mei. I raised my hood and took up the rear, following them through the first doorway on our left. Almost immediately, I covered my mouth and nose with my hand, suppressing a gag.

The room was large—likely a lobby before the CV outbreak—and it was filled with several dozen cots, all occupied. The aroma of so many people in the enclosed space was overwhelming; add on the stench of sickness, and it was nearly debilitating to my sensitive nose. My eyes watered, and I was forced to breathe through my mouth.

"Here," Mari said, handing me something small and cottony. Only when she secured a face mask over her own nose and mouth did I realize what she'd handed me. "It should help a bit."

"Thanks," I said once I had my own mask in place and dared to risk a full breath.

Mari nodded. "So, who's it going to be? Pick quickly . . ."

Right, the trial subject . . .

I scanned the dim room. It was an effort to focus on the visual input my brain was receiving when the smell was so overwhelming. So many people, all sick with the Cascade Virus. All dying unless a miracle happened. How the hell had it come to be that *I* was that miracle? And how could I possibly be the one to choose who would live and who would die? I'd never wanted to play god, but I hardly had a choice. Nobody else was stepping up.

My eyes landed on the smallest body in the room, and instinct told me it was the right choice. Picking an adult would be a coin toss—might choose a saint, but I just as easily might pick an abusive psychopath. At least by choosing a young child, our people would be able to take the kid in and raise it as one of us. The child wouldn't go through the same traumatic transition as Garth was going through, because their Nejeret traits wouldn't manifest until they reached full maturity. They would be far closer to a normal Nejeret, in the grand scheme of things. And having that kind of stability as a child mattered. I knew firsthand.

I wove my way around and between the cots, then knelt beside the one holding the child. It was a little boy, no older than three, his tiny body filling maybe half the length of the cot. Sweat matted his blond hair to his skull, his chubby cheeks were flushed with fever, and his breathing was rapid and shallow. He didn't have much time left.

I pulled one of the marble-sized *ba* orbs from my pocket and curled the child's tiny, clammy fingers around it. Taking a deep breath, I wrapped my hands around his and bowed my head. I pressed my forehead against the back of my hand and squeezed my eyes shut, concentrating.

As I sent my focus inward, I sought out that part of my soul that connected me to the universal energies and allowed me to do otherwise impossible things. Magical things. I wasn't sure if I could feel the thrum of energy flowing into my *sheut* or if it was a figment of my imagination. Placebo magic.

Melt, I thought, picturing the little marble of *At*. My whole body was tensed with the effort to release the fragment of *ba* into the little boy. My hands shook, and I had to make a conscious effort not to crush his fragile bones.

Nothing was happening.

Open, I thought. Crack. Evaporate. Disappear. Break. Shatter. Go away . . .

I ran through a litany of every possible word I could think of that might focus those universal energies in the right way. I put every ounce of concentration into thinking about dissolving the solidified *At* that separated the little boy from the life-saving fragment of *ba*. If only I could release it.

But just like before, it wasn't working, and this little boy would die soon. Maybe tonight, maybe in the morning. And before he died, he would be stripped of his humanity, of everything that made him *him*, and would devolve to a rabid, raging beast hell-bent on attacking any living thing in his sight.

He would never grow up. He would never experience pizza day at school or play tag at recess. He would never read a book or have an imaginary friend or a real best friend. He would never have a first crush, a first kiss, a first love . . .

He would never be remembered as anything other than a boy who died too young. If his family was infected as well, he might not be remembered at all. He was a mere blip in the greater scheme of things. A hiccup in the timeline.

And man, did that piss me off.

A surge of electric energy flooded me, body and soul, and I gritted my teeth, holding tight to this reality to avoid being swept away by the magical current.

The little boy's fist gave as the *At* marble evaporated and the fragment of *ba* soaked into him.

It worked; the transformation had begun. It would take hours for the boy's human soul to be completely changed into a Nejeret *ba*, and he'd be out for days, maybe longer, while his new, heartier immune system fought off the unnatural disease, but he *would* survive.

I sat up, sweaty and trembling with a nauseating combination of adrenaline and fatigue.

"Well?" Mari asked. "Did it work?"

Breathing hard, I looked from the boy to Mari and back. "Yeah, it worked." And now I knew what I needed to make it work again —I had to be angry. I felt pretty certain I could manage that.

"Good," Mari said, "because we've got company."

CHAPTER TWENTY-ONE

Back in the study, when I told Heru the humans I transformed into Nejerets would be like my children, I hadn't meant it in any sort of literal sense. Certainly, not in any way that included parental responsibilities. But now, as I stared down at the little boy's cherubic face, I felt a totally unfamiliar and absolutely disconcerting tug on my heart. I'd made the decision to drag him into my world. He was *my* responsibility, any way anybody looked at it.

"The guards are almost here. We must leave." Mei took a step toward me, hand outstretched. Mari was right behind her. "Now."

I skirted Mei's grip, slipping my arms under the child's shoulders and knees and scooping him up off the cot. "I can't just leave him," I said, staring her down. "We have to take him with us."

"We can't." Sincerity lit her gaze. "Kat, can't you see—teleporting him will shred his soul. He won't survive it."

I hugged the boy to my chest, backing away from the mother-daughter duo. "But he's not human anymore."

Mari stepped in front of her mother, slowly making her way closer to me. "For all intents and purposes, he still is . . . at least for the next few hours. I can't guarantee Robert will survive a spatial jump until he has a complete and stable *ba*."

I blinked and shook my head, brow furrowed. "Who the hell is Robert?"

"Him," Mari said, pointing to the kid in my arms. "Robert Thomas Foster. At least, that's what his chart says."

The realization that I hadn't even known the boy's name rendered me temporarily dumb, both of voice and mind.

"We can wait it out," I said, grasping for straws. I knew it; they knew it. "Just knock out the guards and—and if Heru shows up, we'll jump away and come back for Robert after the transformation is complete."

Mari crossed her arms over her chest. "And your boyfriend's mom will die." The statement was cool, emotionless. Absolutely matter-of-fact. She didn't give a shit one way or the other about Charlene, but she knew that I did.

I opened my mouth, then shut it again. My eyes stung with tears. I'm not a big crier, but frustration is a real bitch where my tear ducts are concerned.

"Kat," Mari said, coming to within arm's reach, "please . . . we need to get out of here."

I searched her eyes. There was genuine concern there, an earnestness I hadn't expected.

"Even if we leave him now," she said, "we can always come back for him later."

"Tonight," I said, unwilling to compromise. "We have to come back for him tonight, before anyone realizes he's been cured. If Ouroboros figures it out, they won't hesitate to slice him up and run tests on him until there's nothing left of him."

Mari looked from me to her mom. "Can you jump back to this exact spot? We're not taking any unnecessary risks . . ."

Mei nodded.

Mari turned her head to look at me. "Alright. We'll come back for him." She held out her hand, beckoning me. "Now come on. Put the boy back on his cot so we can get out of here."

Reluctantly, I did as requested. I tucked the thin blanket around Robert, then, for some reason I didn't understand, leaned in to press my lips against his forehead. "I'll come back for you," I promised.

"Come on." Mari grabbed my arm and hauled me over to her mom. "Let's go."

Mei's head snapped to the right, and she stared at the doorway. "Oh, no!"

"What?" Mari and I asked in unison.

Mei reached out with both arms, pulling both of us into a tight embrace. "Heru. He's here."

CHAPTER TWENTY-TWO

Teleporting was getting real old, real fast.

When we landed in the lightless tunnel just outside the vault door, I dropped to my hands and knees and dry-heaved.

Mari gave my shoulder a scratch while holding out her phone as a flashlight for Mei, who was working on opening the vault door. "I swear it really does get easier after a while," Mari assured me.

I sat back on my heels and let my head hang, just glad I'd managed to keep the spaghetti down. Deep breaths seemed to help calm my stomach muscles and ease the vertigo . . . for the moment. We had at least one more jump to make before the night of rebellion was over, and with the way things were going, my reaction to teleporting one more time would result in an even more extreme outcry from my body. It's always good to have something to look forward to.

Palm pressed against my stomach, I coughed to clear my throat. "Why'd we come back here?" I asked, voice raspy. "We could've gone straight to Port Madison."

The vault door clanged from within, and Mei pulled it open. "Hurry," she whispered, like speaking at full volume might make us easier for Heru to pinpoint.

One hand on my knee and the other on the cool brick wall, I managed to get to my feet and follow Mari into the bunker.

"We need to throw them off our scent," Mei said, pulling the vault door shut. Once the latch was secure, she headed to the table and hauled the strap of her messenger bag over her head, setting the bag on the table. She opened the flap and reached inside, then tossed me a neon-blue Gatorade and a high-performance protein bar.

I glanced at the label—peanut butter and chocolate—then tore the packaging open. I alternated gulps of Gatorade with bites of the protein bar. It was a terrible combination, but I couldn't deny that I became steadier and stronger with each successive swallow.

I pulled out one of the chairs and spun it around to sit backwards. It was less about the retro-hip pose and more about needing the support of the chairback under my arms to keep me upright and eating.

"How long do we need to sit here?" I asked as I chewed.

Mei leaned back against the kitchen counter. "The longer we go without Heru being tuned into our locations, the longer it will take him to lock onto us again."

I nodded, jaw weary but still chewing.

"Oh shit . . ." I stood, dropping the final bite of the protein bar and abandoning my drink on the table. "I can't believe I didn't—he already knows where I'll be headed . . . or at least Nik does. They'll be watching Garth's family." I shook my head, backing up a step. I felt like I'd been punched in the chest. I also felt like the world champion of the moronic arts. "It doesn't matter how long we wait," I said, "they'll be expecting us to go there—in a minute or in an hour, it doesn't matter. Nik's probably already got one of those damn combo-*At* domes up around their place."

"Then we take it down," Mari said as she emerged from the bedroom. "Just like we did last time." She'd changed from her high-heeled booties to combat boots. After watching her struggle through the soggy lawn earlier, I didn't blame her.

I took a step toward her. "We have to go *now*, while they think we're doing exactly what we should be doing: ducking out . . . shaking them off our trail." I looked from Mari to Mei and back. "This is the one—the *only*—chance we're going to have to get the jump on them." I rushed across the room to Mari, taking hold of her wrist and pulling her toward the kitchen. Toward Mei. "Teleport us," I said, stopping in front of Mei. "Now."

Mei didn't miss a beat. She gripped both of our shoulders and dragged us out of the here and now and into the nowhere and never.

It was game time.

CHAPTER TWENTY-THREE

I was right, damn it. Usually, being right was one of my favorite things. I loved being right; I reveled in my right-ness. But not this time. For once, I'd wanted nothing more than to be wrong. But right now, I couldn't even do that right.

A black, shimmering dome enclosed the whole Sealth family property, reaching all the way out to the point where the driveway met the edge of the road. I glared at the unbreakable barrier from the ground, that last jump having knocked me flat on my ass.

"This is such bullshit," I growled, slamming my fist down on the wet asphalt. I'd told Nik I hated him many times over our tenuous relationship, but I'd never truly meant it. Now I felt that hatred in my bones. Rage boiled within me, spilling over into a scream. I threw my head back and let it out.

"While the histrionics are entertaining," Mari said dryly, "they aren't exactly helpful."

I closed my mouth and looked at her, chest heaving. I was exhausted. Even in his twisted mental state, driven by either madness or an overbearing god, Nik was stronger than me. Better than me. I couldn't beat him, no matter how hard I tried.

Mari stepped closer to me. "Come on," she said, gripping my arm and hauling me up to my feet. "Only one thing to do now." She pulled me to the edge of the dome and pressed my left palm against the smooth, rain-slick surface.

When she released me, I let my hand slip off the barrier. "What's the point, Mars?"

She scoffed, her eyebrows raised. "The point is that it's not over until it's over, and I certainly can't hear any fat lady singing right now." She gestured to the barrier. "Now put your damn hand on there and let's get on with this." She smacked my arm. "Nobody likes a quitter."

A weak laugh escaped from my chest, surprising me. A moment later, I nodded and raised my left hand, pressing my palm against the impenetrable surface. "Alright," I said, then took a deep breath. "I'm ready." And considering how pissed off I was—how extremely over this whole day I was—I knew it wouldn't take long to bring the barrier down. The otherworldly energies flowed through me, a torrent of magic just waiting to happen.

"Hurry," Mei whispered from behind us. "I just felt someone teleport in."

I gritted my teeth and closed my eyes. "Too late, bitches," I hissed a fraction of a second before the dome fell.

Mari and I high-fived, then launched into a dead sprint, heading up the driveway.

"Mom," Mari called back to Mei. "Come on!"

Out of the corner of my eye, I watched Mari fall behind. I glanced over my shoulder to see what the holdup was. My body must've processed what I was seeing before my mind could, because my pace slowed. I'd made a complete one-eighty by the time my feet stopped moving.

"Oh shit," I breathed, my heart thudding against my sternum.

Mari was jogging back down the driveway, unaware of the danger she was heading straight toward.

Mei still stood on the road, her back to us as she faced a newcomer. The man she was staring at was neither Nik nor Heru. It wasn't a man at all, not in the conventional sense. It was a Netjer. A god.

It was the Visitor.

"Kat!" Nik's shout slapped me out of my stunned state, and I turned around to face him, horror-movie slow. He was standing at the top of the long driveway, Heru at his side and a dozen other warrior-minded Nejerets fanned out behind them. Nik was looking at me—they all were. They were so focused on me that they'd yet to notice the Visitor.

I glanced over my shoulder to double-check that the Netjer was still there. Yep.

"Please," Nik said, and at the crunch of gravel under boots, I returned my attention to him. Well *most* of my attention. I stood there, torn between a shit-storm and a shit-tsunami.

Nik made his way down the driveway, footsteps slow and hands upraised, I supposed in an attempt to appease my instinctive fight-or-flight response. "Stop fighting and just listen to me," he said. "You can't keep—"

He paused, then shook his head and continued making slow progress down the driveway, his crunching footsteps deafening in the midnight air. "It's over, Kitty Kat. You have to stop this mad crusade. You *have* to stop. For once in your life, just please, stop being so fucking stubborn."

My spine went rigid, and I stared at him, eyes burning and jaw clenched. "Just try and stop me."

Nik's eyes narrowed, and he shook his head. "You don't understand."

"Oh, I understand perfectly," I said, reaching over my shoulder to grip the hilt of my sword. Of the sword *he'd* made. The *At* blade rang out as I drew it, the tone haunting and pure. To my ears, it screamed for justice. "You're here to stop me—to kill Charlene." I broke into a run. "I can't let that happen." I was twelve strides away. Ten.

Vines of *At* shot out of Nik's hands, but they disintegrated before they could reach me. He tried again, with *anti-At* this time.

The same thing happened.

I grinned. He couldn't touch me. I was saturated in that electric, otherworldly energy. My whole body hummed with power, and the energy poured out of me, surrounding me like a magical shield. I'd never felt so powerful. So alive. It was like the universe was a part of me. Like it was inside of me, just as I had always been inside of it.

I was three strides away from Nik. Nobody could stop me now. I would *not* fail Charlene.

A glimmering longsword formed in Nik's grasp, and he raised the blade just in time to block my first slashing strike. He grimaced under the force of my attack.

And then he froze. Not in the fear sense, or even in shock. He became a literal statue, his chest unmoving despite the urgency of his breaths just a moment ago, his heart unbeating, his features as still as if they were carved from marble. It was like I'd come face to face with that solid *At* version of Nik I'd battled so hard in my mind less than an hour ago.

"What the hell?" I backed away, stunned into inaction.

Behind Nik, Heru and the other Nejerets might as well have been part of a painted-on backdrop for all the movements they were making. I spun around in search of Mari. She stood down at the bottom of the driveway, near the road. She had one foot upraised, frozen in mid-step as she ran back up the driveway, and she was leaning forward, her body hanging at an impossible angle. She should've been on the ground. But she wasn't.

It was as though time had stopped for everyone but me.

"We must speak, Katarina Dubois."

I spun around, sword in hand, only to come face to face with the Visitor. Or, considering his considerable height, face to chest. Mercy's blade stopped a couple inches from his neck, almost like he repelled her with a magnetic force.

He studied me from beneath dark brows, his alien features placid. Nobody, not even a human, would ever mistake him as one of their own. His eyes were slanted at too drastic of an angle, his cheekbones were too sharp, and his eyes . . . they were an inferno of bronze and gold and hints of some color that was somehow darker than black. There was nothing human in his eyes.

"Put that toy away," he said, his voice cool to the point of being disinterested. "There is much to discuss." His bronze eyes bored into me, seeming to see into my very soul.

Woodenly, I sheathed my sword. "What—" I blinked, momentarily breaking the spell of his stare, and glanced at Nik's frozen form. "What did you do to them?"

"To them?" the Visitor said, looking around, a hint of surprise giving his alien features their first dash of humanity. It was as though he was only now noticing the others. "Nothing."

"Riiiiight, because this is totally normal."

Much to my surprise, the Visitor laughed. "I have often thought sarcasm one of humanity's greatest achievements."

"Sure . . ." I took a step back, putting some distance between us. "Whatever you say."

The Visitor's laughter didn't so much fade or die down as shut off. "I did nothing to *them*, Katarina Dubois, because I have no interest in them. The fate of this universe is not in their hands."

I took another backward step, eyeing him warily.

"It's in yours."

CHAPTER TWENTY-FOUR

"Nope," I said, turning my back to him—or to *it*, or whatever Netjers considered themselves, gender-wise—and stalking past statue-Nik and up the driveway toward statue-Heru and the others. A heaping, stinking, steaming bag of *nope*.

Of course, the one upside to this apparent time freeze was that I seemed to be the only person besides the Visitor who was able to move around in this out-of-time moment. Which meant nobody would even be able to try to stop me when I transformed Charlene into a Nejeret. It was a not-insubstantial silver lining.

The Visitor appeared out of thin air in front of me, tendrils of multicolored smoke wafting off of him.

"Gah!" I exclaimed, leaping backwards and reaching over my shoulder to grip the hilt of my sword.

The Visitor stood before me, hands clasped behind his back and expression mild. He wasn't the least bit concerned about being attacked by me or by Mercy.

"Can't you just move around like the rest of us?" I grumbled, sheathing my half-drawn sword and releasing the hilt.

The Visitor tilted his head to the side, just the faintest line appearing between his eyebrows. "Why would I do such a thing when I am not one of you?"

I huffed out a breath. He had a point, but I wasn't about to admit that to him. "What do you want from me?" Not to hurt me, that was obvious. Otherwise, with the kind of power this guy could throw around with barely a thought, I'd already be dead.

I narrowed my eyes and placed my hands on my hips. "And who *are* you, anyway?" I held up a finger in empty warning. "And 'a visitor' won't cut it this time, bud." I might not have a bachelor's degree in anything, but I had a PhD in bravado.

The Netjer stood up a little straighter. "I am called Anapa, but I believe the people of this universe know me by another name."

"Anubis," I said, the syllables barely voiced. Sure, I didn't have any formal education in the human world beyond high school, but I was well versed in my people's history, a convoluted and tumultuous past inextricably interwoven into Egypt's antiquity.

I stared at the Netjer—Anapa—for a long moment, eyes rounded with horror.

According to ancient Egyptian mythology, Anubis was most commonly known as the original god of the dead. He'd initially been portrayed as a jackal dutifully protecting the physical remains of the dead, but he'd later gained the body of a man, a form that helped him usher souls into the afterlife and oversee the weighing-of-the-heart ceremony in some limbo between this realm and the next.

During the ceremony, the deceased's heart, otherwise called an *ib*, a perceived part of the soul, was weighed on a scale against the feather of *ma-at*—of universal harmony, justice, and balance. If the heart was found to be lighter than the feather, if it didn't disrupt the universal balance, then the soul would move on to *Aaru*, the ancient's version of paradise. But if the soul proved to be too heavy, if it threw off the scales of justice the tiniest amount, it would be eaten by Ammut, a goddess often depicted as part hippo, part lion, and part crocodile, whose name literally translates to "soul-eater." *Chomp chomp chomp* . . . then nothingness, forever. That soul ends.

I frowned, thinking that sounded a lot like what happened to human souls, only they were never actually given a chance to prove their worth against the feather of *ma'at*. They simply ceased to be.

"Good, you are familiar with the mythology," Anapa said. "That may make this easier."

"The mythology?" I gaped at him. "You mean it's *true*?"

"It is allegorical, a mere representation of the truth, created by Re and told to the humans to help them understand their place in the grander scheme of this universe." Anapa took a step toward me. "Now come, Katarina Dubois. As I told you earlier, we must speak, but we cannot do it here."

"What do you mean?" I sputtered. "What could you possibly need to talk to *me* ab—"

But his hand was on my shoulder, and the words were sucked into oblivion the moment the world disappeared.

CHAPTER TWENTY-FIVE

After a brief flash of brilliant darkness, I expected to be anywhere else besides where I'd been before. And I expected to be on my hands and knees, dry-heaving the seconds away as I waited for the dizzying vertigo I'd come to expect from teleporting to pass.

Except, when light returned to the world—or, rather, when *I* returned to the world—I was still standing on the gravel driveway, perfectly steady and not the least bit nauseated. I glanced at Nik and beyond him to Heru, then turned to peer down the driveway at Mari and Mei, hardly more than shadows in the midnight darkness. They were all still there.

And they were all still frozen, exactly as they'd been before.

Out of the corner of my eye, I spotted someone new standing directly behind me. I did a hop-twist, landing with my feet shoulder-width apart and my toes facing the newcomer.

Facing *me*.

"What the hell?" I straightened from my crouched, ready-to-strike position and stared, stunned by the sight of this statue-still version of myself standing just a few feet away. I stepped closer to her—to me—and reached out a hand, intending to make sure I wasn't hallucinating.

Anapa caught my arm before I could make contact, his long, pale fingers more than encircling my wrist.

Startled, I looked at him. For a moment, I'd forgotten he was there.

"If you touch your physical form, your *ba* will be reintegrated within it, and without the element of surprise, it will be much more difficult for me to separate the two again," he said matter-of-factly.

"Oh, um . . ." I twisted my wrist, pulling it free from his grasp, then took a step backward. "Alright." I cleared my throat, corralling some of my gumption. I had a million questions, but I wasn't sure I was ready for the potentially disturbing answers. I opted to go with the safer, familiar option. "You wanted to talk . . . so talk."

"Not here," Anapa said as he waved his hand in a slow circle. Like he was a master artist wielding a paintbrush, the woods beyond him seemed to melt, twisting with the motion of his hand into a swirling oil painting. The midnight greens and browns gave way to a burst of vibrant colors, first starting as a brilliant pinprick at the center of the swirling mass, then expanding outward until it reached a diameter of six or seven feet.

"Come," Anapa said, his arm stilling. "We will speak in *Duat*; I believe the fresh perspective will clarify much for you."

My mouth fell open. "You're saying that that thing is what—some kind of a portal to another *dimension?*"

Once again, Anapa clasped his hands behind his back. He turned to the side, studying his creation. "Yes, that is an accurate way to describe it."

"And that dimension is *Duat*," I said.

Duat was the ancient Egyptian underworld. The land of the dead. The in-between, where Re's mythical counterpart was said to have taken the sun every night. The place where souls went when their bodies died, where the stories said they had to fight all manner of creatures and demons to find their way to the Hall of

Two Truths to have their heart—their soul—weighed against the feather of *ma'at*.

I pointed to the portal, mesmerized by its rich luminescence. "That is *Duat*," I repeated, voice husky from the rapid onset of massive dry throat. I licked my lips and swallowed roughly, though neither seemed to do any good. "And you want to take *me* in there? Why?" I shook my head. "Why me?"

Anapa's gaze returned to my face, and he studied me just as he had his portal to another freaking dimension. Trust me, I'm not that interesting. "I have been watching you since we met the other day."

My eyes widened. "That was you . . . in the woods," I said breathily.

Anapa gave a single, sage nod. "Indeed. I sensed something different about you on our first encounter, though I could not—how do the people of this world say it—put my finger in it."

"*On* it," I corrected automatically, struggling to subdue a no doubt hysterical giggle.

Anapa shrugged. "I am still not certain *why* you are so different from the others of your kind, but this latest confrontation with Nekure has confirmed my suspicions. For whatever reason, you have a unique connection to *ma'at* . . . to this universe's *ib*, its very heart and soul."

I stared at him, utterly speechless. Universes didn't have souls. They were just places, like planets or houses, so there was no way *I* could have any kind of a connection to *any* universe's soul. He wasn't making any sense.

"This universe is sick," Anapa said. "It is losing its form, the barriers separating it from all other universes weakening. It cannot survive like this much longer."

I glanced at Nik, wondering if that explained his supposed reconnection to Re. If it did—and I'd doubted him to the extreme—then I owed him the most epic apology known to man. With plenty of groveling thrown in for good measure.

"Through Lex and Heru," Anapa continued, "Re spent the last

few millennia doing what he could to revive the health and stability of *ma'at*, and the births of the new Netjers did help, but Syris and Susie are mere caretakers of this universe; they are apart from it, not a part *of* it. *Ma'at* must be fully restored if this universe is to continue on, and I believe it is through you that balance and harmony may rule here once more."

"But I'm just a Nejeret," I said, voice small. A relatively young one, at that. A broken one, soul tainted by *anti-At*. I just wanted to save a few humans. That was all. Not because I was more special or stronger than anyone else, but because I was the only one willing to do it.

"There is much more to you than meets the eye," Anapa said. "You are capable of greatness."

The hysteria I'd been battling couldn't be contained any longer. I snorted a laugh, throwing my hands up in the air. "Great. Awesome. This is absolutely fucking fantastic." I laughed up at the sky. "Thank you, universe, for all of your lovely gifts. I'm so fucking glad that I get to be the special fucking snowflake I never wanted to be." I raised both hands, making fists and extending my middle fingers.

Anapa cleared his throat, and I let my hands fall back down to hang at my sides. "Please . . ." He gestured to the portal. "There is much to show you. Come."

Numbly, I let him guide me to the whirlpool of colors. Why fight it? He could make me do whatever he wanted, anyway.

"I should warn you," Anapa said when we reached the event horizon. "This may feel . . . strange."

I opened my mouth, intending to ask for just a smidgen more detail, but I never got the chance. He gripped my arm and pulled me into the portal. Into *Duat*.

Into the land of the dead.

CHAPTER TWENTY-SIX

There was something like a "pop" and then all I was aware of was a horrific sound, so discordant and grating that it overwhelmed all of my other senses, leaving me nothing but ears. Painful, bleeding ears.

"Oh God!" I cried out, eyes squeezing shut and hands covering my poor, abused ears. I groaned, grinding my teeth. My whole body—or soul, I supposed—thrummed with the arrhythmic screeching and thumping and grinding. The sound was stealing my thoughts, rendering me little more than a frayed bag of raw nerves.

And then it lessened suddenly, the discordance growing less so, the volume going from ear-stabbing to ear-punching—still painful, but manageable.

Now that that awful sound wasn't *everything*, I was able to peel my eyelids open. Blinking in awe, I stared all around me. I was floating in a river of . . . not water, but something that felt just as substantial. Electrically charged, almost. It flowed all around me, glimmering streaks and swirls of every conceivable color.

Years ago, before Susie and Syris left us to hone their powerful skills in the Netjer home universe, my people had access to another plane we called "the echoes." It was a place outside of time and space that allowed us to view echoes of the past—thus the name—and it had looked a whole lot like this with all of the swirling colors. But it sure as hell hadn't felt like this. It was as though, back then, we'd been unknowingly skimming the surface of *Duat*, but now I'd plunged headfirst into it.

I could feel the currents of energy flowing around me, trying to drag me along with them. But to where?

The current seemed to be flowing in a direction I could only call up. Not that there was any kind of a floor or ceiling to go off of. But there was a shimmering, translucent wall, through which I could see the interior of my shop. I watched another version of myself—a past version of myself—chatting with Kimi at the reception counter, and I envied her for her naiveté.

"Enjoy it," I whispered. She—I—had no idea that her world was about to get flipped upside down.

Despite the draw of the familiar so close in front of me, I felt the pull of something stronger, deeper coming from behind me. I spun around in that eddying energy, and through the miasma, I could see a dull, hazy darkness. The vibrant energy seemed almost repelled by it, but the same couldn't be said for me. I floated closer, something deep inside me dreading the touch of that relentless darkness.

"Careful," Anapa said, once more taking hold of my arm. His grip kept me from drifting ever closer to the lightless abyss. "Your time to enter *Aaru* will come, someday, but today is not that day."

I looked at him, stunned for about the millionth time. "*Aaru*? So that's real, too?" To the ancients, *Aaru* was the paradise souls were allowed to enter only after they'd been found worthy in the weighing-of-the-heart ceremony.

"In a sense," Anapa said. "When this universe was first being formed, Re and Apep created *Aaru* to contain *isfet* to make the universe more manageable."

Thanks to my people's all but mandatory proficiency with Middle Egyptian, the official ancient language of Nejerets, I recognized the term *isfet*. It meant chaos, violence, and the mindless drive for evil. If *isfet*—whatever it really was—was trapped within *Aaru*, no wonder the darkness felt so overtly ominous.

"It was the only way to preserve *ma'at*," Anapa continued, "to ensure universal balance. However, neither Re nor Apep anticipated the rise of another species of energy beings in this universe, and by the time Re realized that his newest creation—Nejerets—were being drawn into *Aaru* after their *ba*s were freed from their physical bodies, it was too late."

I shivered.

"Now *Aaru* contains not only *isfet*, but also the *ba* of every Nejeret that has passed on from the physical realm. None who have entered *Aaru* have ever returned. Not even I know what existence is like beyond that barrier, for if I were to pass into *Aaru*, I would never reemerge."

I stared at the darkness, wanting nothing more than to get far, far away from it. "So . . . *Aaru* is more like a prison than a paradise?"

Anapa shrugged. "In essence, yes, its original purpose was for containment. Be cautioned, Katarina Dubois: if you lose focus, *Aaru* will lure you in like any other disembodied energy being."

"But I'm not disembodied. I *have* a body."

"Not at the moment," Anapa reminded me. "Take a look at yourself. See what I mean."

I raised my hand, mouth agape as I examined it front and back. I followed the line of my arm upwards, then stared down at the rest of my body. I was still generally me-shaped, but that was where the resemblance ended. Instead of flesh, I was made out of a golden, glowing energy that sparked and crackled with each tiny movement. And within that golden mass, thick veins of shimmering moonlight and glittering onyx spider-webbed all over my body—or rather, my soul.

"A physical body cannot enter *Duat*," Anapa said, "as it is a dimension of pure energy. I had to separate your *ba* from your body. It was the only way to bring you here."

I felt my eyes bug out. "But what about my body? Doesn't it

need *this*?" I asked, pointing frantically at myself.

"Your physical body will be fine so long as I return your *ba* to it in the exact moment that I pulled you out of it," he said patiently.

"OK, but what's this?" I asked, holding out my hands to him so he could get a better look at the dark and light veins. "Why does it look like I'm—I don't know—infected with *At* and *anti-At*? Is this normal?"

"No," Anapa said. "It is far from normal, and it explains much."

"What? What does it explain?"

The corner of his mouth tensed.

"And why don't you look all glowy?" I gestured to his very normal-looking self. At least, normal for him. "You look exactly the same." He was even still wearing a suit, while my soul seemed to prefer going au natural.

Eyes locked with mine, Anapa blinked. And then he melted into a blindingly brilliant, ethereal being. There was nothing normal about his form now, certainly nothing even vaguely humanoid. I'd seen him in this form once before, in the Ouroboros boardroom, only now his wattage was turned way up.

"Is this preferable?" he asked.

I shook my head, barely able to stand the brightness.

"I thought as much." He reined in the glow and slowly retook his increasingly familiar form. "Now, take me to the moment when this happened," he said, tracing a line of inky darkness down my golden forearm with his index finger.

"How am I supposed to know when—" My mouth opened into a little *O* because a switch flipped in my mind. I knew exactly when it happened. And I knew how.

There was an odd sense of motion, like the current of the energy surrounding us had sped up . . . or maybe simply that we were moving against it. And then I was staring out through the transparent wall at a scene I remembered all too well.

"Well, let's get on with it, then," Mari said. She was sitting on an upturned stump facing a campfire, the hood of her raincoat pulled up and her back to another version of me—a decades-younger version of me. Both women glowed with a gentle golden light despite the overcast sky. "Go ahead," Mari said. "Do your mommy proud. Kill me."

"You're insane," the other version of me said. She raised the sword and lunged at Mari.

But Mari was ready. She moved so much faster than I'd expected, spinning on the stump and springing to the left. An anti-At dagger materialized in her hand, and she thrust it at the other version of me, burying the soul-poisoning blade in her belly.

The other version of me froze, her momentum vanishing. She became boneless, her sword tilting downward until the tip pointed to the ground, and the hilt slipped free of her fingers entirely.

I could see the ribbons of anti-At spreading throughout the other me's body, sending cracks of darkness through the golden glow surrounding her.

Suddenly, Mari was restrained by vines of At and Nik was kneeling at the other me's side, sending ribbons of shimmering white into her body. I was watching those ribbons chase down their inky counterparts, binding to them. But not pulling the darkness back out of her—my—body. Both the At and the anti-At remained within me then, marbling my soul...and was apparently still there, now.

It was still there. Even now.

I raised my hand, looking at the evidence, right there, laced through my *ba*. I'd always believed that what happened that day had damaged my soul. I'd had no idea how right I was.

"That was the moment the connection was forged," Anapa said quietly. "Your soul is fused with the two fundamental forces of this universe."

I looked at him but looked away quickly, put off by his intense scrutiny of, well, *my soul*.

"Whether by choice or by happenstance, you are *ma'at*'s champion."

"I don't understand a single thing you're saying."

Anapa bowed his head. "In time, child. In time."

CHAPTER TWENTY-SEVEN

The current of the river of energy sped up, becoming a rushing torrent whooshing upward. I clung to Anapa's arm in an effort to not get dragged away. We remained like that for what felt like days, for eons.

Until the rushing energy suddenly slowed, and we were once again floating along in that gentle, almost lazy current. The distracting discordance was gone, in its place an almost heartbreakingly harmonious sound—except it was more than that, almost like music but lacking any definable rhythm or structure. Even so, it was achingly perfect.

"What is that?" I asked, releasing Anapa's arm and looking around for the source of the music.

Anapa's eyes were closed, his head tilted back and his features serene. "The song of *ma'at*," he said, his voice hushed, almost reverent. He opened his eyes and looked at me. "This universe's heartbeat, as it was long before your time. It has been altered over the ages, warping in response to the imbalance to become the 'monstrosity' you first heard upon entering *Duat*."

"So does that mean we're in the past?" I shivered at the thought. I'd barely been able to hold on to Anapa as we swam backward in time. What might have happened if I *had* let go.

Would I have been stranded in some time between this now and my own? Would I have been sucked into *Aaru*, only to become a prisoner alongside the rest of the deceased Nejerets?

Anapa nodded.

"Maybe a little warning next time . . ."

The Netjer tossed me a sideways glance. "Time is of the essence, and we had a long way back to go," he explained. "Look . . ." He gestured to the world beyond the gossamer barrier.

The fateful scene featuring Nik, Mari, and me from a moment ago was gone. I was now looking out at an expansive desert with endless rolling dunes of golden sand. A string of people dressed in black robes looking so much like ants from this distance marched along steadily in the valley between two dunes, the sun beating down on them.

"Where is this?" I asked. "*When* is this?"

"It is the seventh millennia before your common era," Anapa said, "and we are watching the seasonal migration of one of the Sahara's desert people as they head to their summer oasis."

I moved closer to the translucent barrier, squinting. "They're glowing," I whispered, brow furrowed.

Each of those little ant-sized people shimmered with a unique luminescence, some more red, some more blue, others golden or green or purple or orange. Even the animals in their caravan glowed with that otherworldly light. Just like Mari, Nik, and I had been glowing with a vibrant golden light just a moment before, only then I'd been distracted by the quick onset of violence to really process the reason behind that golden light.

I looked over my shoulder at Anapa. "Why is everyone suddenly glowing? *How* are they glowing?"

"You are seeing their soul-energy. It is always there, only now you are able to perceive it," Anapa told me. He gestured to the barrier and the desert beyond. "Observe, Katarina Dubois. Understand."

I returned my focus to the world outside of *Duat*. One of the ancient people near the rear of the caravan stumbled, then collapsed onto the sand.

"His heart is failing," Anapa said. "Brought on by severe dehydration. He is seconds from death now."

I watched in horrified fascination as other members of the tribe circled around the fallen figure. It was impossible not to feel the tug to do something to help, but this was thousands and thousands of years before my time. This dying man had already been dead for millennia. There was nothing I could do to help.

The dying man's glowing aura was a greenish-yellow, and it seemed to expand as the seconds passed. And then something changed, and that ethereal light floated away from his body, a vibrant mote of green and yellow glittering in the relentless sunlight like a cloud of the finest emerald and topaz dust. It ebbed and flowed, twisting this way and that, slowly making its wayward way closer to us.

"Um . . . Anapa," I said, tugging on his sleeve as the light picked up speed.

"Be calm, child," Anapa said. "This soul poses no threat to you."

Was he serious? That ancient man's soul was heading straight for me. I barely had the chance to think about moving out of the way; actually doing it was out of the question.

The glowing soul punched through the translucent wall separating the physical world from *Duat*, streams of vibrant yellow and green splitting up to flow around us. I could feel the soul brushing past me, like a thousand sun-kissed feathers.

And then it was moving on. I spun around to watch it integrate into the greater flow of energy. I stared after it until I was no longer certain that this or that streak of green or yellow was a part of the man's soul. Until I could no longer tell where he ended and everything else began.

"It's souls," I whispered, reaching out to let the streaming energy flow between my fingers. "All of it . . ." I thought I should've been horrified by the realization, but all I felt was awe. It was too beautiful to be disturbing. Too wonderfully right and balanced and harmonious to be anything but wondrous.

"It is the energy that makes up souls," Anapa corrected. "It is the raw material that shares a collective purpose and a deep awareness of all that is, something close to a consciousness without quite being sentient."

"It's beautiful," I breathed, tears in my eyes. The wonder of it all was too much, overwhelming my sense of self. I wanted to join it, to become one with the collective, to feel that perfect balance and harmony flowing through me. My mom was a part of this, now, and I felt the desperate need to join her.

But I never would. I glared at the darker barrier. I was destined for *Aaru*, for imprisonment away from this glorious sense of unity.

"It is truly a marvel," Anapa said.

I looked at him, not following. "*Aaru?*" It was far from a marvel to my eyes. More like eternal damnation.

"No, child. I speak of the purity of this untainted flow of soul-energy and the elegance it gives to the song of *ma'at*. I have heard the songs of thousands of universes, but few even come close to *ma'at*'s lost perfection." He sighed. "But, alas, I did not bring you into *Duat* to listen. I brought you here to learn."

"To learn what, exactly?"

"The true nature of the disease plaguing your world so you might better fight it."

"Really?" I said, eyes widened in surprise. I moved closer to him. "You're going to help me fight it?"

"I said no such thing," Anapa said, tucking in his chin as his eyebrows climbed up his forehead. "Such a thing would be grossly forbidden." He readjusted his posture, stretching his shoulders. Apparently, my question was making him uncomfortable. "I was sent here with a specific purpose: to observe, and to judge. That is what I do; that is my role in the greater schematic of existence. I study universes that may become problematic and determine whether or not they should be allowed to continue."

I laughed and shook my head. So, the mythic Anubis wasn't

here to pass judgment on me—to weigh *my* heart, or anyone else's —he was here to weigh the heart of the universe and decide whether it was worth salvaging or whether it was best to just toss the whole thing to Ammut to devour.

Unaware of my thoughts, Anapa continued, "Even this amount of interference in the natural order of this universe would be considered crossing the line by many of my kind."

"Then why are you doing it?" I narrowed my eyes. "And what's this bullshit about not interfering? Aren't you the one who released the sick kids in the first place?" I felt a surge of anger and, shortly after, a rush of electric energy pouring into my *sheut*.

If I'd thought Anapa looked offended before, well, now he *really* was. "I did *not* release the children; that was the man whose place I took when I came to this universe. He was overdosing on pain medication, and I wished to experience the life of a human." Anapa shrugged. "At the time, it seemed logical to pick one who was at the heart of the impending catastrophe."

"And *that* didn't count as interfering?"

"I made no decisions as Gregory," he said. "I was a truly impartial voice on the board. I merely wished to gain insight into the mal-intentioned life-forms of this universe, as that has always been just as important in my judgment process as observing a universe's redeeming elements." He shook his head, his brow furrowed. "I do not know why I am telling you this. I owe you no explanations."

"Keep going," I said, moving closer to him.

To my mind, his inaction made him as guilty as if he'd been responsible for creating the virus himself. Because *he'd known*. He'd known about the virus—that it was out and spreading—and he'd done nothing but observe.

Well, it was my turn to judge. "Tell me why you're helping now, when you've done nothing but sit on your ass before now." I felt drunk with righteous anger. Not just anger, I realized, but *power*. He *would* explain himself, whether he wanted to or not. "Tell me," I ordered.

Anapa's eyes rounded. "Please, Katarina Dubois, calm yourself."

That otherworldly power roared within me, begging for a way out.

"Tell me!" My voice sounded different. Bigger. More. Like it was no longer mine alone, but laced with a thousand others.

Anapa held up his hands in a calming gesture. "You're disturbing the soul-energy."

I blinked, confused, then looked around. And, well, damn . . . he was right.

The radiant streams of energy nearest me no longer flowed upwards with the greater current. They surrounded me, a writhing mass composed of every color imaginable, making my golden hair float and crackle. The charge building up within me seemed to be interacting with the soul-energy, communicating in some way that went way beyond words.

I could *feel* what the collective soul-energy felt. And I was starting to suspect that Anapa was wrong about one very important thing—it wasn't *almost* conscious; it was fully conscious. It was aware. And it was pissed the fuck off.

He's willing to watch us wither and die! The thought was foreign, but it was in my head. It *felt* like mine. But it wasn't.

I shook my head, eyes wide. "Anapa . . ." I reached for his forearms with both of my hands, anger turning into fear. "Something's happening to me," I said, gripping his arms tightly.

He doesn't deserve to be here! The thought was overlapped by another. Expel him! And another. Shove him into Aaru!

I released Anapa's forearms and slammed my hands over my ears, eyes squeezed shut. It didn't help; the voices—the thoughts—were inside my head. "Stop!" I exclaimed through gritted teeth. "You're wrong! He's trying to help. Can't you see—that's why he brought me in here."

"It is working," Anapa said. "Please, keep going."

I nodded emphatically. "He just needs to teach me something, and then I'll do whatever I can to stop the disease."

Yes! Help us! Again, the thought was overlapped by another. *We are dying!* And another. *Save us!*

"I will!" I shouted. "I'll do whatever I can, I promise!"

Slowly, my hair settled around my shoulders, and I peeked through one barely raised eyelid. The flow of the soul-energy had returned to normal. It was over.

I lowered my hands, but when I caught a glimpse of one, I froze. Fine filaments of *At* and *anti-At*, looking so much like delicate threads of moonstone and obsidian, extended several inches beyond the golden barrier that mimicked my skin in this place. They swayed gently with the calming current of soul-energy.

"What—what's happening to me?" I asked, voice tremulous as I watched the threads retract back into me.

"Your connection with *ma'at* is much stronger than I thought."

"No shit," I breathed, then looked at him. He wore concern like it was an itchy woolen blanket. I licked my lips. "I heard . . ." Brow furrowed, I shook my head. "Something . . . like the soul-energy was speaking to me."

"That is not possible."

I rubbed my hand over my arm, but there was no sign of the—whatever it was. "Tell that to the voices."

Anapa frowned. "Let us handle one issue at a time, Katarina Dubois. None of this will matter if you do not come up with a way to stop the disease."

I laughed through my nose. "No pressure."

CHAPTER TWENTY-EIGHT

There's a ride at Disney World called Walt Disney's Carousel of Progress. Essentially, it's a rotating show populated by an animatronic family that takes ride-goers through several different historical eras—the turn of the nineteenth century, the 1920s, the 1940s, and an ultra-futuristic prediction of what the turn of the last century might be like. What Anapa showed me next was a lot like that, minus the animatronics but with the added bonus of being submerged in a whole universe's worth of soul-energy.

We skipped ahead a century or two, to the moment when Re's first Nejeret offspring was conceived. Nuin, the human body Re had possessed in utero, stood behind a fierce-looking woman, his hands on her shoulders as both overlooked the desert landscape from a cliff. They wore robes of a gauzy black material that flapped about in the arid, desert wind.

"Neither yet knows it," Anapa said, "but a zygote has formed within the mother, and the cells have begun to split. The first-ever Nejeret is being formed."

The woman's violet aura seemed to swell until, all of a sudden, a golden haze appeared beneath the purple glow. Her aura then shrank back down to its original size, the only change that tinge of gold. The moment it happened, the moment the gold appeared, there was a sharp, dissonant note in the song of *ma'at*. It was jarring after listening to the blissful harmony for so long.

I covered my ears and glanced at Anapa. "What happened to the song? Why did it change?"

"At the moment of conception, the first *ba* began to form . . . the first permanent withdrawal from the collective pool of soul-energy," Anapa explained. "The first imbalance; the first of many cuts to the harmony of *ma'at*."

I shook my head, returning to watching the man and woman on the cliff. "Did he know?"

"About the damage his actions would cause?" Anapa nodded thoughtfully. "He was aware, but he was facing a far more imminent threat."

"Apep," I guessed, referring to Re's ancient Netjer counterpart, his co-creator of this universe. Apep had gone mad eons ago, leading to a war between him and Re that had nearly torn this universe to shreds and had only ended when Susie and Syris were born to take their places as guardians of the universe.

"Indeed," Anapa said. He held out his hand for me to take, and the moment I did, the gentle current of soul-energy became a torrent.

I gripped his hand as hard as I could and held on. We moved forward in time, or rather, upward, *with* the flow of the current. It wasn't so bad this way. It wasn't great, either.

When we stopped, the view beyond the translucent barrier was dim, a rock wall with shadows that danced in the light of a small fire. One man huddled by the fire, the other lay on his back on a bed of furs, his breathing quick and shallow. The sweat on his brow glimmered in the firelight, and his chest was a mess of open wounds, almost like something with claws had shredded him. In fact, that was *exactly* what I suspected had happened.

"Who are they?" I asked.

"Grandchildren of Re's," Anapa said. "The man sitting near the fire is human, the other is Nejeret."

"His wounds are pretty bad." Depending on the internal

damage, it was hard to imagine even a Nejeret recovering from that.

Anapa nodded. "He is dying. His will be the first *ba* to join *isfet* in *Aaru*."

I frowned, glancing back at the looming darkness on the other side of *Duat*. "So he'll just be stuck in there, all alone?" I'm a big fan of me-time, but the thought of being the only soul in an isolated mini-universe was terrifying.

"For a time, his *ba* will be the only one in *Aaru*, but others will join him soon enough."

I opened my mouth to push the matter, but in that instant, the dying Nejeret's golden aura lifted from his body, expanding in a glittering mist as it ambled toward us.

As with the soul of the dying human before, the Nejeret's *ba* burst through the barrier and into *Duat*. But unlike the human's soul, the *ba* took on shape the moment it entered this dimension, gaining the form of a golden, glowing man. He seemed confused, looking around as he drifted across the stream of soul-energy toward that great, expansive darkness. He spotted us just a moment before reaching the dark barrier of *Aaru* and raised his golden hand, shouting something to us.

I felt the urge to warn him, but it was already too late. He'd realized he was being pulled into the darkness, and he was struggling against it. Fighting did him no good; *Aaru* already had him in its clutches.

I put my hand over my mouth to hold in a cry as I watched the darkness swallow him.

A harsh note of discord echoed throughout *Duat*, and I was left feeling like I'd been stabbed in the ears. I clapped my hands over my ears and squeezed my eyes shut. How had I been able to stand the discordance when we originally entered this dimension, especially when the first couple blips in the harmony were so agonizing to listen to? Oh, that's right . . . I hadn't.

"Is it like this every time a Nejeret dies?" I asked, peeking at Anapa through one squinted eyelid.

Anapa gripped my shoulder, lending me support I hadn't realized I needed. I mean, I wasn't actually standing, but the simple touch tethered me. Reminded me I wasn't alone, not like the Nejeret who'd just passed on would be for however long. Knowing my current situation wasn't so dire helped.

"Disharmony is created each time a *ba* comes into existence," Anapa said, "and again each time a *ba* passes into *Aaru*, but *ma'at* is able to repair the imbalance over time."

"But *Aaru* makes it worse." I looked from him to the wall of darkness and back. "Why wouldn't Re do something about it once he realized what was happening to us? To *ma'at*?"

Anapa was quiet for a moment. Thoughtful. "Can you not think of at least one Nejeret who is, in your estimation, truly evil?" Anapa asked me. "One who, if left to roam free as an energy being, could wreak unspeakable havoc upon this universe?"

"Well, yeah, but . . ."

The current of the soul-energy sped up once more, and I glanced around, thinking it was kind of rude that Anapa was moving us through time mid-conversation. But when the current slowed once more, the scene that appeared on the other side of the barrier was something out of a horror movie.

It was a nightmare—my worst nightmare, which had plagued my dreams over and over and over, relentless in its need to make me experience the single worst moment of my life again and again.

"No," I breathed. Despite knowing better, I moved closer to the barrier. I watched myself, a young and innocent seventeen-year-old, standing in the foyer of Heru's mansion of a house, the barrel of a gun pressed against my forehead. The gun was in the hands of Carson, the traitorous Nejeret who I'd been stupid enough to fall for.

As I'd done so many times before, I watched him squeeze the trigger. I watched my mom push me out of the way at the last millisecond. I watched the bullet enter her skull instead of mine.

"No!" I shouted. I couldn't help it.

But this time, it didn't end there. *She* didn't end there. My mom's turquoise aura floated up and out of her body, heading straight for the barrier between dimensions. Heading straight for *me*.

And unlike before, I welcomed it.

My mom's soul surged through the barrier, just as the other two had, but instead of flowing past me and integrating into the greater river of soul-energy, it coalesced around me, a gentle whirlwind surrounding me in warmth and sorrow and so much love. It was my mom, saying goodbye to me. Telling me she loved me in the only way she could now that she was little more than energy.

"I'm so sorry," I sobbed, hand to my mouth. "I'm so—so—"

I felt a rush of forgiveness, and a sense of pride. Of joy and hope, but also sadness. And then she was moving on, leaving me to be a part of something greater.

"Mom, wait!" I shouted, chasing down what pieces of her I could still tell apart from the greater flow of soul-energy. "Please! Don't leave me!" I couldn't lose her again.

"With you always . . ." The words were the mere hint of a whisper floating around me.

"I—" I looked at Anapa. "Did you hear that? Did you hear her?"

Anapa eyed me, then shook his head. "Soul-energy is not capable of communicating with anything but other soul-energy—"

I opened my mouth to tell him *I* was soul-energy.

"Which you are not. You are something else entirely." He seemed to hesitate over his next words.

"But I heard—"

Anapa held up a hand. "Believe me or do not. I have told you the truth of the matter. What you do with that truth is no longer my concern."

I heard her, I thought silently. *That* was the truth of the matter; I could feel it in my bones. Or rather, in my soul.

"Would you prefer for that Nejeret's *ba* to be free to cause further trouble in your world?" Anapa asked, recapturing my attention and returning us to the subject at hand.

"Carson?" I shook my head, lip curling. "I'm glad he's locked up in *Aaru* for an eternity." Though I did feel bad for those stuck in there with him. At least I knew how I'd be spending my afterlife—hunting down his *ba* and tormenting him in any way that I could.

"Then perhaps you can understand why Re believed it too great of a risk to the universe to let energy beings roam freely until the end of time."

"Maybe he never should've created us in the first place," I grumbled. Struck me as a case of wanting to have his cake and eat it, too . . . whatever that meant. I sniffed, then cleared my throat, pretending I hadn't just ugly-cried in front of a god. "Anyway . . . what do you say we keep this gravy train rolling?"

Anapa eyed me quizzically for a moment, then reached out to grip my shoulder. Once more, we moved forward in time.

CHAPTER TWENTY-NINE

"So, what am I looking for this time?" I asked Anapa when we slowed and the scene beyond the barrier became clear. The song of *ma'at* had devolved to a nauseating cacophony, so much more disturbing now that I'd heard its natural perfection, and I was grateful for my current lack of an actual stomach.

A past version of me stood in one of the side rooms in the lab under Heru's place. Aset and Neffe were there, of course, as were Mari, Nik, Lex, and me. And Mitch fucking Carmichael, the child-molesting psycho who'd been on the Ouroboros board of directors until we'd relieved him of his position . . . and of his life.

"Pay attention to his aura," Anapa said, pointing as Nik released the *ba* fragment into Carmichael.

The sicko's aura started out a burnt orange color, but streaks of brilliant gold shot through it slowly, one here, then one there several seconds later. And with each gold streak came an additional, not-so-subtle hint of disharmony in the song of *ma'at*, growing until it was almost unbearable. In time, there was more gold than orange surrounding Carmichael, and my hands were once again covering my ears.

Anapa fast-forwarded again, and the discordance ratcheted up a notch. The scene on the other side of the translucent barrier was much the same, the only real difference being that Garth sat in the chair in place of Carmichael. His aura was a gray-streaked royal blue, which made me smile, because the blue was so similar to the color of his cop uniform. The gray, though—something about it soured my smile. It looked . . . off. Felt wrong. It was dull compared to the blue, dimming his aura's luster.

Nik introduced the *ba* fragment to Garth's body, and the transformation began. Luminous gold slowly overtook the gray, then spread throughout the blue until there was nothing but the brilliant, blinding gold of an eternal *ba*. It was hard to concentrate on the visual input with the added discordance to the song of *ma'at*, but I managed.

Anapa fast-forwarded again, and it was Constance Ward seated in the chair this time. Her aura was magenta streaked with that same dull gray as Garth's, just less of it. They were the only two I'd seen with that off-putting grayness. Not Mitch Carmichael, who'd had an undoubtedly putrid soul, and not any of the people from the ancient desert tribe. So why these two?

It clicked suddenly, and I blamed that god-awful noise for my sluggish thought process. It was the Cascade Virus. Both Garth and Constance had been sick at the time of their transformations, and Garth had been further along, explaining why the gray streaks were more developed in his aura.

"I get it," I told Anapa, hands still covering my ears. I wasn't sure I could take another spike of the discordance in the song just yet. Those three back to back had been brutal. If I'd still had physical ears, they definitely would've been bleeding.

In a blink, we were moving forward in time again.

"There is one last thing I have to show you," Anapa said as the current slowed and the song of *ma'at* worsened exponentially.

I hunched over, curling into myself. "I can't," I gasped. It was as bad as it had been when we first entered *Duat*. "I can't be here! It's too much!"

"You must bear it, Katarina Dubois, just for a moment," Anapa said, shouting to be heard over the horrific sound. "Everything I have shown you up until this point has been foundational. You now have the knowledge to understand what is happening. This last event should make everything clear. You will know what you must do, and it will be up to you to figure out how."

Deep breaths. It didn't matter that I didn't actually have lungs right now, going through the motions helped.

"Alright . . ." Groaning, I gritted my teeth and forced my eyes open.

I stared out through the translucent barrier at another low point in my life. This one was recent—barely hours old—and still cut deep when I considered the events that surrounded it. The fight with Nik in the cave. The confrontation with him and Heru in the foyer. The rebellious flight with Mari and Mei. This bizarre journey through time with Anapa.

I was watching myself in the back room of the cabin, seated on the edge of Charlene's bed, her hand in mine as I tried to transform her into a Nejeret. As I failed.

Her aura was teal, or what little of it I could see under the gray taint of the disease was teal.

"Why does it do that?" I asked Anapa, raised voice tight with tension. "Why does the virus turn people's auras gray?"

Anapa inhaled deeply, then sighed. "Through their experimentation on Nejerets, Mari and the Ouroboros scientists managed, very much by accident, to create a bastardized, synthetic version of a *ba*. It is a vile thing, capable of immortalizing the soul of the infected, much as a *ba* is capable of doing, but in the process, it mutates parts of the soul, turning it into something else entirely . . . something incapable of existing in a human body any longer."

I frowned. "That's not disturbing or anything."

The corners of Anapa's mouth tensed. "Indeed. Now watch," he said, pointing to the scene beyond the barrier. "This is the important part."

I did as he said. My lips parted as I watched threads of pearlescent white *At* and onyx-black *anti-At* spread out from my left hand

and wrap around Charlene's hand and arm. "Whoa," I breathed. "What the . . ."

As the threads sank into Charlene's skin, the gray in her aura began to fade and the teal brightened. In a matter of seconds, her aura was returned to normal. Or what I assumed was normal.

"So, she's alright?" I shook my head, hands still covering my ears in a vain attempt to shield them from the sound. I pointed to the barrier with my elbow. "What just happened there, because I'm pretty sure I just watched a bunch of little *At* and *anti-At* tentacles shoot out of my hand and into Charlene to suck away the virus."

Anapa frowned and nodded his head back and forth. "That is not a terrible interpretation." He shrugged. "Truly, I am not sure, either, but so far as I can tell, the infection is so anathema to everything in this universe that the combined efforts of the two building blocks of this universe felt the need to destroy it."

"So, they're like the universe's antibodies?" I clarified.

"In a manner, yes."

"Okay, so . . . theoretically, someone should be able to duplicate what happened with Charlene on a grander, worldwide scale," I thought aloud.

"Not someone," Anapa said. "You."

I laughed. "Right." And then I realized he was serious, and gulped.

"The destruction of the millions of souls currently infected is more than enough to throw off the universal balance beyond anything that *ma'at* can repair." Anapa looked away, his hands once again clasped behind his back. "If it looks to me like such a thing is likely to happen, I will be forced to sever the connection between our two universes. That is why I am here."

I tilted my head to the side, confused. "So, we'll be flying solo for the rest of eternity. Why does that matter? We still might be able to fix things, even without you, right?"

Anapa speared me with an unexpectedly intense stare. "This

universe is an offshoot of my own. It is a limb, and when a limb becomes infected, it must be amputated."

"Anapa, you're freaking me out." I backed away a few feet. "What happens if you cut us off?"

"You die."

CHAPTER THIRTY

Anapa returned me to the exact time and place he'd removed me from. Nik, Heru, Mari—everyone—were still frozen in this moment between moments.

I glanced at Nik and, frowning, asked the thing I'd been suspecting since Anapa first pulled me out of time. "He claimed he could hear Re . . . in his head, I mean." I looked at Anapa. "He was right, wasn't he?"

"It is possible," Anapa said. "Though I have not communicated with Re or any other Netjers since leaving our universe, so I cannot say for certain."

But it was possible, which was more than I'd been willing to believe before. I vowed to apologize to Nik, to do what I could to make things right between us—later. I still had work to do.

Gravel crunching under my boots, I made my way to, well, me. I stood face to face with my physical body, feeling like a million years had passed since I was that woman. I rubbed my temples, immensely relieved to be rid of that god-awful noise, and stretched my neck, cracking first one side, then the other.

"How do I get back inside *me?*" I asked, pointing to the frozen version of myself standing a few yards away.

"Just touch yourself, and you will find yourself returned to your body," Anapa told me.

I snorted a laugh. "Just touch myself?" Dude needed to brush up on his earth lingo. Shaking my head, I reached out for my own—my *other* own—hand.

And in a blink, my view of the world flipped around.

"So, what now?" I asked, making my way back to Anapa.

"I have taken you as far as I can," he said, wandering up the driveway.

I fell in step beside him.

"The rest is up to you." He glanced at me sidelong and seemed to be hiding a smirk. "I would wish you luck, Katarina Dubois, but I do not believe you will need it." And before I could ask him what the hell that was supposed to mean, he vanished.

At the exact same moment time restarted.

There were shouts, and I glanced at Nik to see him looking around in confusion. To him, I wasn't where I was supposed to be. To all of them, it must've looked like I'd teleported.

Making a split-second decision, I took off at a dead sprint up the driveway, heading straight for the cabin back behind the house. I had to make sure Charlene was truly alright. Only then could I worry about the rest of the world.

Heru and his entourage were busy wondering what had just happened—how I'd "teleported" and who that man with me had been. Their voices were clamorous, but one stood out among them. "Kat!" Nik called after me. "Kat! Wait!"

But I ignored him.

When I reached the cabin, I was relieved to find the door unlocked. I barreled inside, then froze in my tracks.

Charlene and Samuel were sitting in the armchairs near the fireplace, keeping warm with a crackling fire. And Garth was there, too, crouching near the hearth as he added another log to the fire. Charlene had an afghan blanket draped over her legs and a mug in her hands, and Samuel was sitting on the edge of his seat, his elbow resting on his knees. All three stared at me with stunned expressions.

"Kat?" Garth said, abandoning the log and standing. "You—"

I held out a hand in apology. "Garth, I—" I hadn't been prepared to see him, though I realized I should've expected him to be there. "I'm sorry, I—I just had to make sure—"

Charlene stood, placing her mug on the side table beside her chair. She looked terribly weak. The illness had taken a lot out of her, and her body's recovery wouldn't come as quickly as her soul's had.

"No, don't stand," I said as I reached for the doorknob behind me, intending to make a quick exit. She was alright; I'd seen it with my own eyes. That was all I'd needed. "I didn't mean to intrude. I should go."

"I know you," Charlene said, then cleared her throat. "How—" Her eyebrows bunched together. "You were in my dreams. You were sitting at my bedside." Her eyes searched my face. "You were trying to save me. Or you did—you did something, and it . . ." She shook her head, wonder lighting her eyes. "It worked. In my dream, you saved my life." She took a step away from the chair, her legs so wobbly I doubted they'd hold her much longer.

"Please," I urged, "sit down." I had no clue how she'd seen what she had, but I had a pretty good feeling that her falling and smacking her head on the floor wasn't something she'd recover from so easily.

But, apparently, Charlene had a stubborn streak, because she remained standing. "It wasn't just a dream, was it?"

I swallowed roughly. "I—" I had absolutely no idea how to explain anything that had happened over the past few hours, and with the Cascade Virus making humans drop like flies all over the country—likely the world, at this point—I hardly had the time to figure it out right now. "I have to go," I said, turning to the door.

"Wait," Charlene said. "Please, my daughter . . . help her, too?"

I let my forehead fall against the wood of the door with a dull thunk. Now Cassie was sick? Would this nightmare never end?

And yet, much as I wanted to rush in and save the girl, even the minute or two it would take to cure her would result in hundreds, maybe thousands more deaths around the world. Possibly enough to tip the scales so far that Anapa would decide our universe was unsalvageable.

Cassie had only just fallen ill, which meant I had plenty of time. Eons compared to the timeline I'd been working with in regard to Charlene. I'd just have to get to saving Cassie when I figured out how to save the rest of the damn world. *If* I figured it out.

I slammed my fist against the door. I hated this, every damn second of it. I hated being the sucker who couldn't say no. I hated that my reckless decisions in the past had left me with a soul riddled with both *At* and *anti-At*. I hated that I only had myself to blame for me becoming the universe's damn chosen one.

"Uh . . . Kat?" Garth said from yards behind me. I could hear his footsteps bringing him closer.

"What?" I said, voice barely a whisper.

"You—you're glowing."

CHAPTER THIRTY-ONE

I turned my head to the left and stared at my fist. Sure enough, my skin was covered in a shimmering, multihued glow. The colors moved over my skin, in a constant state of flux.

I straightened from the door, bringing my hand closer to my face. "Soul-energy," I whispered. It was like I'd somehow brought it back with me from *Duat*. Or was I channeling it? Is this what had made Anapa smirk? Had he known?

"Let us in," the echoing voices whispered through my mind, one voice standing out beyond the others. One I couldn't help but recognize—my mom's voice. *"Let us guide you."*

My eyes teared up. "Mom?"

"Kat?" There was concern in Garth's voice.

"We can help you. You don't need to do this alone. Let us in . . ."

I closed my eyes and bowed my head.

"Kat, what's going on?"

I ignored Garth and his endearing concern, because right now, with the voices of collective soul-energy whispering through my mind and the impossible task set before me, it seemed like the most insignificant thing in the world. Sure, I may have accidently cured Charlene, but I had no idea how to save everyone else. I needed all the help I could get, and if that included a whole mass of disembodied souls, so be it.

"Alright," I breathed. "Show me what you got."

Gasps filled the room, and when I raised my eyelids, I had to squint against the glow of my own skin. It was as though I'd been lit on fire, but the flames burned in every color imaginable. I could feel the soul-energy dancing through me, giddy with its eagerness to help. It twined with the power filtering through my *sheut*, coaxing more to filter into me. To strengthen me.

I lowered my hand and met Charlene's wide-eyed stare. I was no longer seeing with my eyes alone, but also with the collective's. Samuel and Charlene's auras glowed gently compared to Garth's brilliant golden aura. We were all connected, through the collective. We were all made of soul-energy, even Garth, originally. Even me. That mattered, though I wasn't sure why.

"Yes, I'll help your daughter," I told Charlene, speaking not only with my voice but with the collective's. "I'll help them all." And I could; I knew it. With the collective's help, I could see the path that would lead us out of the darkness.

"Kat?" Garth sounded unsure.

"Yes," I said. "And no." Without another word, I opened the door and stepped out onto the porch.

Nik stood at the bottom of the steps, Heru just behind him, and Mari, Mei, and the others hanging back a short ways. Heru backed up a few paces as soon as I emerged. But not Nik.

He moved closer, if hesitantly. "Kitty Kat?" His brows were drawn together, and concern shone in his eyes. He reached for my hand, and the moment he made contact, his golden aura flared.

I jerked my hand away.

"Kat?" There was less certainty in his voice now.

I studied him for a moment longer, curious about the way his aura had reacted to touching mine, and then I scanned the crowd. Mei and Mari stood arm in arm, but their auras maintained a normal intensity—no flaring up.

Logic told me it was the collective's presence that caused the reaction in Nik, but the collective itself seemed to think otherwise. *"Harmony,"* the uncountable voices whispered excitedly. *"Resonance."* Their excitement escalated, their chorus of voices growing to a dull roar.

I squeezed my eyes shut and rubbed my temples with my fingertips. "Stop it!" I hissed. "Please. I can't think with all of you talking over each other like that." I inhaled and exhaled deeply. "Don't get me wrong—I'm glad for the help, but I need you to let me take the reins and *be quiet*."

Nik retreated a couple steps. "Kat?" he repeated.

I took another deep breath, then lowered my hands and opened my eyes. "I'm sorry, Nik. I'm so sorry. You were right all along, the transformations are harming *ma'at* . . . but not as much as the Cascade Virus is."

"I—" Brow furrowed, Nik shook his head. "How do you know that?"

"Anapa—the Visitor—showed me. I *saw* the damage, Nik. I *heard* it. And I know how to fix it, how to stop the Cascade Virus, but there's no time to explain. You can either help me or get the hell out of my way." I surveyed the wary Nejeret faces beyond Nik. I was speaking to all of them. "Don't try to stop me. You won't survive it."

As I descended the porch steps and started down the pathway back to the driveway, what do you know—everyone moved out of my way. Good. I hadn't actually wanted to kill any of them, but to prevent the end of the universe—yeah, I sure as hell would've sent a few more Nejerets to *Aaru*.

Formulating my plan, I recalled a rock wall surrounding the vegetable garden out in front of the house. That would do nicely. The collective agreed.

Moving as efficiently and as quickly as possible, I started transferring stones from the rock wall to the broadest part of the driveway. I could see it all so clearly in my head, but none of that would do any good until I completed the design I was envisioning.

As I returned from dropping off my seventh and eighth stones,

I passed Nik on my way back to the rock wall. He had three rocks cradled in his arms. I paused, feeling a rush of gratitude. He was helping. Which meant he believed in me. Possibly even had forgiven me. In my mind, the collective whispered about harmonies and resonances. I blocked them out and continued to the rock wall.

Mari and Mei joined in next, then Heru and his small army of Nejerets. I directed them all to stack the stones in a pile near the design I was forming on the driveway. It was as much as I could allow them to help; the magic wouldn't work if the symbol was shaped by any hands other than mine.

I stepped away from the actual rock-hauling to move stones from the pile, placing each in precisely the right spot. It didn't take long until someone caught on to the design taking shape on the driveway, and I wasn't the least bit surprised that it was Heru. It was an ancient symbol of his, after all.

Heru placed an armful of stones on the mound, then straightened and looked at me. "It's a Wedjat," he said, using the ancient name for the symbol commonly known as the Eye of Horus. The same symbol that was tattooed on my left palm. The same symbol that, when drawn by my hand, would create a powerful protection ward. If the collective was right, this enormous version of the symbol would be strong enough to heal the world.

Heru laughed, shook his head, then returned to hauling stones.

It took maybe fifteen minutes to get the giant Eye of Horus laid out on the gravel driveway. I couldn't even begin to guess how many human souls had fallen to the disease during that time, but based on the fact that we were all still alive and the universe wasn't crumbling around us, not enough to convince Anapa that cutting ties with our universe was a necessity. There was still time, and where there was time, there was hope.

Once the last stone was in place—part of the pupil within the eye—I stood up and arched my back in a stretch, scanning the watching Nejerets. Samuel and Garth were out here now, too, along with two older folks, a man and a woman I assumed to be

Garth's grandparents. I offered them all a solemn wave, then turned to Nik.

"Hey, Nik," I called, waving him over. "I need your help . . . please."

The corner of his mouth lifted, and he picked his way across the symbol to reach me. "Please?" he said, stopping a few feet away. "Alright, who body-snatched you, and how do I get my Kitty Kat back?"

I clutched my chest. "Aw . . . you care. I'd give a shit if I had any left to give." I snapped my fingers. "But shucks, I'm all out." I flashed him a cheeky grin, relieved to be back on familiar ground.

Nik chuckled, some of the tension leaving his features. Looked like we were both relieved. "What do you need me to do?" he asked, straight to business. Perfect.

I moved to stand at his side and pointed to the symbol on the ground. "Can you turn all of this into that *At* and *anti-At* combo material you built those domes out of?"

"Yeah," Nik said, "no problem. It'll take me ten or fifteen, though." Ten or fifteen minutes—it sounded like forever. I just hoped we had that long.

"Well, then . . . get started," I said, making a shooing motion.

Nik mock saluted me, then knelt at the edge of the symbol and placed his hand on one of the stones.

There was nothing for me to do now but wait. Wait, and hope and wish and pray that our clock wouldn't run out before he finished.

CHAPTER THIRTY-TWO

"Oh my God!" Lex exclaimed. I spun around to see her jogging toward me with a bulging canvas shopping bag hanging on her shoulder and her hand over her mouth. "Kat? Is that really you?"

"Mostly . . ."

She dropped the bag on the gravel driveway a few yards from me and opened her arms, throwing them around me, the multicolored glow barely making her hesitate. "Are you alright?" she asked. "What's happened to you?"

Awkwardly, I patted her back. "I think I'm alright," I told her, not ready to dive into the whole *Duat*, soul-energy thing quite yet. "What are you doing here?"

Lex released me and hustled back to her discarded bag. "I brought you some things," she said, crouching. "Eat this." She tossed me a banana before gathering the spilled items back into the bag and standing.

Suddenly ravenous, I tore open the banana's peel and stuffed half the thing into my mouth. "Heru brought you here?" I said around a mouthful.

Lex nodded. "He popped in at home to let me know that all of this craziness was happening. But I had no idea you would look so

. . . so different. We, um, weren't sure what you had planned next, but we figured it would be big and you'd need all the strength you could get," she said, handing me a bottle of water.

I gulped down the water in five swallows, then exchanged the empty bottle for a protein bar—something with dried blueberries, according to my taste buds. "Got any Cheetos in there?" I asked hopefully, eyeing her canvas sack as I chewed.

She pulled out a bag of Flamin' Hot Cheetos and waggled it at me, only to pull it out of reach when I reached for it. "Finish that first and *then* you can gorge on all the Cheetos and Cherry Coke you want."

Now *my* eyes bulged. "You brought Cherry Coke, too?" I asked, coughing as I choked on the protein bar. Hot Cheetos and Cherry Coke were the exact items I would request for my last meal. And considering what I was about to attempt—the sheer amount of energy I was about to expend—there was a decent chance that this very well might end up being my last meal. I cherished every single bite, savored each and every sip.

Nik finished with the stones in nine minutes, looking worse for wear. He'd pushed himself, and it might've made all the difference in the world. In the universe.

"Everyone move back a ways," I said as I picked my way across the symbol. The air felt fuzzy with otherworldly energy, making my clothing crackle and the hairs all over my body stand on end.

I knelt in the center of the pupil of the Eye of Horus and placed my hands on two of the stones, one on either side of me. Closing my eyes, I bowed my head and I inhaled deeply. On my exhale, I whispered, "Go ahead."

The collective soul-energy buzzed with excitement. And then it went eye-of-the-storm quiet.

A shock of power surged into me, forcing me to sit up straight, spine arched and head thrown back. I screamed, the only release I had from the agony burning through me. My *ba* was on fire, my *sheut* a raging inferno. I was burning up from the inside out, and we'd only just begun.

The power I was channeling increased, and I hunched in on myself, panting for breath. All around me, threads of black and white—of *At* and *anti-At*—grew out of the stones, writhing as they reached ever upward.

But that was wrong. They needed to go down, underground. Otherwise, there'd be no way to stop the *anti-At* from destroying every Nejeret it touched as the threads sought out the infection.

Gritting my teeth and grunting, I managed to redirect the unearthly filaments. I sent them downward, using the collective's perception of the soul-energy and the infection consuming it all over the planet to guide the threads.

It took minutes. Hours. Days. Or maybe it was only seconds. I couldn't tell. I couldn't think. I wasn't in agony anymore, because I was no longer trapped in my body; I was *everywhere*.

I was in the cabin again, standing in the back room beside the bedside, only instead of Charlene, Cassie was tucked under the covers, tossing fitfully in a fevered sleep. Her aura was still mostly untainted, making the streaks of gray stand out in stark contrast to her aura's natural vibrant magenta hue.

Reaching out with one of a billion ghostly, glowing hands, I placed my palm on her chest, directly over her heart. Fine filaments of *At* and *anti-At* sprouted from my hand, diving into her body.

Cassie's aura flared for several seconds, and when it faded back to its normal glow, the gray was gone. She was healed.

Even as I worked on her, I was also in a house across the street, cleansing two people of the virus, and in another house down the road. Millions and millions of times, the same scene played out all over the world. I channeled the soul-energy, merging with it. Becoming one with it. Together, we hunted every last hint of that abominable grayness, focusing on eradicating it completely.

And then it was done. The filaments of *At* and *anti-At* snapped back into the rocks. The torrent of power raging through me lessened to a trickle. But the pain—that remained.

"Thank you," whispered through my mind a thousand—million

—billion—times as I felt the collective withdraw from me, leaving me empty and alone and shivering with cold.

I slumped forward, face-planting in the gravel but not having the strength to do anything about it. It didn't matter. It was done, and the universe was still here. We'd won.

I used the last ounce of energy in my body to turn my head to the side. A raindrop landed on my cheek, followed by another, and another. I smiled.

And then I died.

CHAPTER THIRTY-THREE

This time when I left my body, it felt natural. It felt . . . right.

Dazedly, I floated upward, watching the chaotic tableau below. Nik, Lex, Mari, and Garth huddled around my body, movements frantic as they laid me out on my back.

"Wake up, Kat," Mari ordered, slapping me. My head flopped to the side. "Wake up!" She cocked her hand back for a second slap, but Nik caught her upraised wrist.

"There's no heartbeat," he said, voice low and words rushed. "That's not helping."

There was a several-second stare-down between the two, then Mari yanked her arm free and averted her gaze.

"Why do you always try so hard to be a fucking martyr?" Nik said to me—to my body—moving so he was kneeling at my elbow. He placed his hands on my chest and began compressions.

Lex plopped down on her butt a few feet away, and Mari stood, hugging her middle. Both had tears streaming down their cheeks as they watched Nik attempt to revive me. Garth dropped to his knees at my feet, face blank and eyes locked on my face, searching for a sign of life.

It was endearing, all of it. If I'd known how much they all

cared, then . . . well, I'd have done exactly the same thing. At least this way the universe would go on and they'd have a chance to live.

I felt a zing, and I was suddenly watching the heart-wrenching scene through a translucent film. I glanced around, surprised to find the eddying flow of the filmy multihued soul-energy surrounding me. My lazy mind pulled a word out of the far recesses: *Duat*.

That's funny. What was I doing back in *Duat*?

I floated away from the translucent wall between this dimension and mine, soothed by a sense of rightness. A sense of belonging. I closed my eyes and drifted away with the current. The discordance was still there, marring the song of *ma'at*, but it wasn't nearly so bad as it had been before.

"Not yet!" The whisper startled my eyes open. "We still need you. Not done y . . ."

"What—" I spun around, searching the rainbow current all around me. "What are you—shit!"

A dark wall was right in front of me. *Aaru*—it was sucking me in, trying to capture me.

I spun around and fought my way back across the current of soul-energy. All of a sudden, it became a hell of a lot easier, like the soul-energy itself was helping me get away from that dark eternity.

"We can help you," the voices said, the multitude settling into a single, feminine voice by the end of the four words. *"I can help you."* I recognized the voice, and it broke my heart.

"Mom?"

The soul-energy before me swirled and rearranged itself, forming a vaguely human shape.

"Mom," it repeated.

Its featureless face sharpened, coming into focus, its body gaining the curves of a woman. Of one very specific woman.

"Yes, I am the one called Genevieve Dubois," she said. "I am all that has ever been and all that ever will be." She touched her head with one ethereal hand. "I have been lost for a very long time, trapped . . . asleep . . . but you—" She lowered her hand and looked at me with luminous, color-changing eyes. "You woke me up."

"Who are you?" I asked cautiously, because it was clear that whatever her claims, I wasn't talking to my mom. "*What* are you? The soul-energy?" I didn't think so, since the collective soul-energy had spoken in the plural, but this being was referring to herself in the singular.

"The soul-energy," she said, looking around, running her fingers through the streams of color. *"Yes, that is how you woke me."*

"Alright . . ." She hadn't exactly answered my question, but she also didn't seem all there, mentally, so I didn't want to push the matter.

"I have a name," she said, familiar features wavering as her head moved from side to side, like she was searching the energy all around her for the answer. *"Iss—Iss—"* Her face brightened. *"Isfet."* She smiled a smile I'd seen a million times, even as fear paralyzed me. *"You may call me Isfet. And you—you are K—Katarina. You are my daughter."*

Holy shit. Isfet wasn't a thing, it was a *being*. I shook my head, afraid that correcting this—this creature that was supposedly the embodiment of pure evil was about the worst idea ever.

"I—I'm Genevieve's daughter," I said, not quite telling her she was wrong.

"Yes," Isfet said. "Yes, that is correct. And Genevieve is a part of me. I see my confusion there. I have been fractured for so long it is difficult to think straight." She looked around, her expression becoming lost, frightened. "This is not Aaru. Where am I?"

"Um . . . we're in *Duat*?"

Isfet looked around. "This is Duat, yes, I recognize it now." She refocused on me. "I am here, but I am not. You—you awakened me. You brought me here . . . or part of me." She moved closer. "How did you bring me here?"

I raised my hands defensively and floated back a few feet. "I didn't—I don't know what you're talking about. I didn't bring you here. You just sort of showed up."

"Ah . . . I see." Gracefully, she reached out a hand, coaxing a few threads of At and anti-At to sprout from my fingers. "You are connected to my body and, through it, to the rest of me."

"I—" I shook my head, eyes locked on the swaying threads. "I don't understand."

She floated closer to me, the soul-energy reshaping around her.

I flinched.

"You are afraid of me?" Her glimmering, multicolored face darkened. "What lies have the Netjers told you?"

Again I shook my head, my eyebrows drawn together. "Lies?"

A soft growl emanated from her, rumbling through the soul-energy surrounding us. "Whatever they told you, I suppose they left out the part where, while I was forming, once I'd reached maturity, they sliced me up, severing my mind from the rest of me —from my body and my soul—and locked me away."

Something was off. Wrong. Anapa hadn't said anything about Isfet being a, well, *being*. Which meant he hadn't told me everything. Or, at least, what he had told me was skewed by his Netjer bias. *Everyone* is biased, and if they claim to be objective, they're lying. He was no exception.

Eyes narrowed, I decided to dig a little. I wanted to hear Isfet's side of the story. "Re and Apep trapped you in *Aaru* to protect *ma'at*," I told her.

"No!" she hissed. "Ma'at is my soul, and they cut me off from it . . . to control it. A free-thinking universe cannot be controlled . . . cannot be manipulated or twisted to fit their whims. But take away my thoughts, lock away this part of me—silence me—and my body becomes their slave, my soul their plaything."

Her claims were as farfetched as they were abhorrent. And yet, deep down, I knew she was telling the truth. I could feel it.

"Do you want to die?" she asked seemingly out of the blue.

I drew back. "Um . . . no?"

"I would make a deal with you then."

"I'm listening."

Isfet bowed her head in thanks. "I am awake, but I am still

fractured . . . still a prisoner. Only part of me is here, and only so long as you remain in Duat, tethering me to this dimension. Once you enter Aaru, I will be trapped forevermore. Daughter . . . I need your help. I—" She shook her head, her like-my-mom's face shifting, a ghostly shadow slipping out of place.

"I—the longer you are away from your body, the weaker our connection. I am slipping away again. Aaru *is pulling me back in."* Her form grew fuzzy around the edges, then sharpened once more. There was more clarity and awareness in her color-changing eyes than ever before. *"There is one with you in the physical realm whose soul resonates with yours. If you return to your body, the aura from his* ba *will merge with yours. It will revive you."*

My mouth fell open. "You mean, you can send me back? I can *live?*"

She nodded gracefully. "I can push you out of Duat, but the rest will be up to you. In return, I would ask you to find me . . . to set me free. Only then will I be whole again. Only then will I be able to restore balance—harmony—to this universe. Only then will I be able to protect you. You all . . . all my children . . . the danger . . ." She started to lose shape again.

My eyes opened wide, and I reached for her. I half expected my hands to go straight through her, but my fingers closed around her arms, and she regained her form. But for how long? "What danger?" I urged.

Her gaze grew distant. "The creators . . . the destroyers . . . a great battle looms . . ."

"No, no, no," I said, giving her a shake. "Don't leave yet. I need more!"

"Help me . . ."

"Alright!" I all but shouted. "I'll do it!" I was afraid she'd "lose herself" for good before she had a chance to send me back. "But I need to know how—"

There was a pop, and the brilliant soul-energy was gone. Isfet was gone.

I could hear counting below me, and the sounds of people

crying. I looked down to see my body lying on a gravel driveway in the middle of a huge Eye of Horus symbol, Nik kneeling beside my body, doing chest compressions, and a mass of other people surrounding us, heads bowed in mourning.

"Make me whole . . . restore balance . . . harmony . . ." Isfet's voice was barely a whisper.

I floated downward, toward my body.

"Set me free . . ."

I stood at my body's feet, staring down at myself. "I'll do what I can," I told Isfet, no clue if she could hear me.

And then I turned around and fell back into my body.

CHAPTER THIRTY-FOUR

I sucked in a breath, then coughed. "Oh God," I groaned, flailing my arms in an attempt to shove Nik's hands away from my chest. Each time he pressed down, a white-hot pain threatened to knock me back into unconsciousness.

Nik froze.

"I think—" I fought to breathe without causing myself searing agony. It was no use. "I think . . . you broke . . . my sternum."

A slow grin spread across Nik's face, and he bowed his head. "Welcome back, Kitty Kat."

In some part of my mind, I knew it was significant that Nik was the one nearest me when I'd revived. But thought was too slippery to grasp, and it floated away.

My consciousness followed.

My eyes popped open, and I sat bolt upright, my salivary glands working on overdrive. Really, how else is someone supposed to react to the oh-so-delicious smell of bacon, pancakes, maple syrup, and coffee? Literally no other way, that's how.

"And they say the way into a *man's* heart is through his stomach," Garth said, chuckling. "Clearly 'they' never met you."

It took my eyes a moment to adjust to the bright morning sunlight streaming in through the windows. I was in my bedroom, Garth a dark silhouette standing at the foot of my bed, slowly gaining color.

I held a hand up to block some of the light from my sensitive eyes. "Hang on . . ." My voice was little more than a choked rasp. I cleared my throat and tried again. "Give me a second to kick my temporary vampirism, OK?"

Again, Garth chuckled.

I rubbed my eyes and arched my back in a glorious stretch, then scooted back and adjusted the pillows to prop me up from behind. "How long was I out?"

Garth's good humor faded. "Eleven days. Both Neffe and Aset said it was the longest regenerative sleep they'd seen anyone go into without waking for sustenance." He walked over to the dresser and picked up a tray laden with breakfast goodies.

"I aim to impress." I curled my feet under my legs to make room for the tray and patted the bed. I was ravenous, which my stomach emphasized by growling so loud that I half expected the bedframe to rattle.

Garth grunted and set the tray down in front of me. "They put you on a feeding tube after a few days—you were wasting away and showing no signs of waking." I'd frightened him, that much was clear in his voice.

"Hey . . ." I reached for his hand and gave it a squeeze. "I'm here now, alright?" I grabbed a strip of crispy, thick-sliced bacon and ate half of it in one bite. It was smoky and fatty and crunchy . . . basically heaven in my mouth. "I'm fine," I said as I chewed, "I promise." I swallowed, then shoved the rest of the strip of bacon into my mouth.

Releasing Garth's hand, I picked up the little pitcher of maple syrup and poured it over the stack of pancakes, all but drowning them. I loaded up the fork with a whopper of a bite and stuffed the sweet, golden goodness into my mouth as soon as it was empty again.

Realizing Garth was watching me, a serious, almost somber expression on his face, I paused mid-chew. "Oh, um . . ." I smiled as best I could with my mouth full to bursting. "D'you want some?"

Garth lifted a hand. "No, I'm good. You enjoy yourself." He raised his eyebrows, a mischievous glint cutting through the sadness in his rich brown eyes. "Should I give you and the pancakes some alone time? Because with the noises you're making . . ."

"Shut up," I said, laughing as I threw a pillow at him.

Garth dodged it, then moved closer to sit on the edge of the bed beside me, his hip touching my knee. "You died," he said, taking my left hand in both of his. His thumb rubbed the back of my hand. A hand that, I was glad to see, was no longer misshapen. Looked like someone had taken care of re-breaking and setting the bones while I was out. Sweet.

"You were gone for nearly fifteen minutes," Garth said.

The bite of pancakes became a giant gummy wad too big for me to swallow. Somehow, I managed it anyway. I hadn't known I'd been out for so long. Had Nik really spent fifteen minutes trying to revive me? I had to commend the guy for his refusal to give up. I touched my breastbone, recalling the searing agony, but felt no pain. Good as new.

I cleared my throat once more. "I guess I'm lucky." But, deep down, I knew that wasn't true. Luck had no part of my miraculous return to the living.

Everything between my death and the moment I came back to life felt like a dream. I wasn't sure it had really happened—Isfet, *Duat*, almost getting sucked into *Aaru*. Who's to say it wasn't just some twisted dream my subconscious made up to fill in the long minutes when I'd been unconscious?

Except I hadn't just been unconscious. I'd been dead. Not breathing. No heartbeat. D-E-A-D, dead.

Which meant everything that happened during my second trip

to *Duat* had been real. Isfet had been real. And she'd given me the mother of all missions. As soon as I was out of bed, I had to dedicate all of my energy to fulfilling my promise to Isfet—first and foremost, figuring out how the hell I was supposed to rescue her from *Aaru*.

"Garth, listen, I—"

"Kat, I think we should—"

We started and stopped speaking simultaneously, both cutting off with nervous laughter.

"You talk," I said, then smiled wryly. "I'll eat." I stuffed another bite of pancakes into my mouth.

Garth inhaled and exhaled deeply, that somberness returning. "I did a lot of thinking while you were out, and, well . . . you're the most fascinating person I have ever known, and you're meant for great things." He broke eye contact, lowering his gaze. "But me—us—that's not one of them."

I set down my fork and became very still.

Garth took another deep breath. "I want a small life. A safe, comfortable life." Laughing softly, he shook his head. "I understand now that that will never be enough for you, and that's okay. Much as I'd like to be, I know I'm not your happy ending." Finally, his eyes returned to mine. "I hope you can understand where I'm coming from . . . and that there are no hard feelings. I know people say it all the time without meaning it, but I really would like for us to be friends."

I was quiet for a moment, chewing on my lip. Then, clearing my throat once more, I nodded. "Thank you," I said, reaching out to cup his cheek. A moment later, I lowered my hand.

Garth laughed uncomfortably. "For what?"

I smiled to myself. He'd given me so much. Taught me so much. In just a few days together, he'd broken down walls I'd been building for almost two decades. He'd changed me, making me a better person. "I couldn't explain it if I tried," I told him.

"Oh."

I flashed him another smile. "I don't mean to change the

subject, but, um, I think I'd like to shower," I said, pushing the tray of barely touched breakfast farther down the bed.

"Oh, right," Garth said, standing. "Of course. Do you want help? I can fetch Lex or Aset—"

"No," I said, maybe too quickly. What I wanted was a moment alone to work through everything that had happened while I was dead. "I'll be fine. I just feel . . ." I shimmied my shoulders. "Well, like I haven't showered in eleven days," I said, ending with a laugh. A dull throbbing was starting at the base of my skull, and I reached back to rub my neck.

I picked up a piece of bacon as I stood and faced Garth. "Thanks for the breakfast." I play-punched his shoulder. "You rock, friend."

He stepped closer to me and leaned in, pressing his lips against my forehead. "You are such a weirdo."

"Duh," I said as I leaned into him, hoping it wasn't too obvious that I was multitasking by munching on the strip of bacon while giving him a hug.

"Glad you're back, Kat."

I smiled, then pulled away and turned to the bed. "Me too." I picked up the tray and carried it to the bathroom.

"Are you taking that into the shower with you?" Garth asked, stifling a laugh.

I peeked at him over my shoulder. "Don't judge me. I died."

He laughed and shook his head, then made his way to the door. "You're one of a kind, you know that?"

I frowned. He had no idea.

CHAPTER THIRTY-FIVE

"I've thought long and hard about the best way to fight the Senate and their followers," Heru said, standing behind the chair at the head of the long, mahogany table, his fingers gripping the top of the leather-upholstered chair.

We'd gathered in the former Council chambers located on the second floor of the Bainbridge house, a remnant from back when the Council of Seven was a thing and my people were ruled by an all-powerful patriarchy. Lately it seemed to have become the war room, where all of our side's important decisions were discussed and made.

This was my first time being included in one such discussion, and while I was honored to be there, I was antsy for it to be done. I wanted to check on Robert—or Bobby, as the others had settled on calling him while I was out. The toddler was playing with Reni in her playroom down the hall under Garth's watchful supervision. Since waking a couple hours ago, I'd only been able to spend a few minutes with him before Heru called this meeting. By the time I returned to the playroom, I figured he'd probably have forgotten who I was entirely.

"And it is not with weapons and battles that we shall fight them," Heru continued, "but with knowledge and strategy." He surveyed the faces of all nine Nejerets seated around the table. "Specifically, one very strategic alliance."

"Curious," Dom said. His standing mirror was positioned on my left side. "He's usually in favor of more violent, absolute measures . . ."

I sniffed quietly in response. Speaking out loud would've been plain rude.

Nik sat across from me, his mother on his right and Carlisle, Heru's go-to guy, at his left. Neffe sat opposite Carlisle, at her father's right hand, as always. Mari and Mei sat opposite each other, Mari beside Dom, and Mei beside Aset, and Lex occupied the spot at the far end of the table. The room was sealed within a shell of *At*, ensuring that everything discussed in here would be heard only by the intended ears.

"The Senate's supporters outnumber us four to one," Heru said. "It pains me to say it, but we must accept that severe pride and vehement anti-humanism is too deep-seated in many of our people's hearts for any logic or attempts at persuasion otherwise to fall on anything but deaf ears." His fingers gripped the chairback more tightly, the leather creaking in response. "Our action must be swift and permanent, and above all else, it must take the opposition by absolute surprise."

I exchanged a questioning glance with Nik, who was leaning his chair back, balancing on two legs. He gave a minimal shrug. He had no idea where Heru was going with this either.

"We must forge an alliance," Heru said, his voice hardening. He wasn't asking for permission, and his decision wasn't open for discussion. "We must come out of the shadows." He scanned each of our faces. "We must, once and for all, reveal ourselves to the humans."

My eyes opened wide. Neffe choked on the sip of water she'd just taken, and Nik let his chair fall forward, the front legs making a sharp *knock* on the hardwood floor. But at the end of the table, the tiniest, tight-lipped smile touched Lex's mouth, and she bowed her head in agreement.

"Um . . ." I raised my hand tentatively, and when Heru looked my way, I raised the other in defense. "Not that I'm against this 'strategy' or anything, and I've only been awake for a couple hours so maybe I'm missing something, but how exactly are we supposed to get people to believe us when we tell them"—and I used air quotes—"'an immortal race has been living among you for thousands of years . . . oh, and some of us have superpowers!' I mean, obviously we'd have to tell everyone all over the world all at once for this to be a sneak attack—which alone is a logistics nightmare—but using a video feed leaves us with no way to prove to the humans watching that whatever display of 'magic' we show them to prove we're really what we say we are isn't just special effects." A swift survey of everyone's faces showed considering expressions and a couple frowns, all except for Lex and Heru. "Unless there's something I'm missing . . ."

"Valid points, Kat," Heru said with a slight nod my way. "Luckily, one of Mei's most loyal subjects"—because Mei, like Heru, had been a Senate member before the war with her own territory, specifically the Rocky Mountain region of these ol' United States—"is quite the gifted hacker. I'm certain that taking over the PNS feeds for a few minutes and locking all others out shouldn't be an issue for him." His statement ended with the uptick of a question, and his stare shifted to Mei.

She frowned thoughtfully, then nodded. "It seems easily within Liam's skill set. I don't see why it would be a problem."

Heru nodded his thanks to her, then returned his attention to me. "As for the rest of the world, Tarsi will be streaming a live concert celebrating the recent 'miracle'—it's predicted to have record-breaking viewing numbers—and she has agreed to feature the announcement, live, between her two most popular songs."

I raised my eyebrows, impressed. Must be nice to have the world's most famous and beloved superstar as your daughter.

"And as for the belief issue, well . . ." Heru grinned wolfishly and his golden eyes lit with an assessing intensity that made me feel like he was trying to decide which of my fleshy bits would be tastiest. It was all I could do not to lean away from him. "That's what you're here for."

"I . . ." I shook my head slowly. "Yeah, you totally lost me there."

Heru's grin shrank to a smug smile, and he picked up a tiny remote and pressed a button. The huge screen on the wall directly behind him turned on, showing a still shot of a PNS news story. The headline on the red bar below the anchorwoman read: *GODDESS UPDATE.*

Heru pressed another button on the remote, and the video started to play.

In the wake of the social media flood of sketches and paintings of the mysterious woman who appeared to nearly every person who recovered from the Cascade Virus, experts from the FBI and CIA have used the influx of information to create official renderings of the woman we've all come to know as "the Goddess." The images have been released, and we're pleased to have the exclusive reveal.

An incredibly realistic image filled the screen. It was a digital painting of a kneeling woman, her arms outstretched and her head thrown back, her long, dark hair floating wildly around her head. She was wearing jeans and a black leather coat, and her skin glowed with a multicolored luminescence. Though her face wasn't visible, there was little doubt in my mind who she was supposed to be.

As someone who was personally affected by the Cascade Virus, I can personally attest to the striking accuracy of these renderings.

Another image filled the screen. A face, glowing with that ethereal light. *My* face.

My mouth was suddenly a desert. I licked my lips, but my tongue was so dry that it did no good. Swallowing was equally as useless.

For those of us who experienced the miraculous cure, there's no doubt in our minds that it was anything other than an act of divine intervention. And to the Goddess, if you are listening, we thank you.

Tears welled in my eyes, and I clenched my teeth to keep my chin from quivering.

"In related news," the anchorwoman continued, but Heru paused the video.

I was breathing hard, overwhelmed by a bevy of emotions I wasn't used to feeling. I turned to Dom's mirror and cleared my throat. "Did you know?"

He blinked at me with those dark, silvered eyes. But he didn't say no.

My nostrils flared, and my skin started to glow with a faint rainbow luminescence. The air around me crackled with charged energy, making my hair float. "You did," I said breathily, feeling utterly betrayed. I'd been feeling it so often these days I figured it should start to feel normal at some point. I hadn't reached that point yet.

I pushed my chair backward and stood. I needed to move, to dispel the magical energy building up around me. "A heads-up would've been swell," I said to nobody in particular as I paced the length of the room. "Now everybody on the fucking planet thinks I'm some kind of—of—of savior."

"Aren't you?" Nik said, voice bland.

I froze behind my chair and looked at him.

He, too, stood, his hands planted on the table. "Correct me if I'm wrong here, Kitty Kat, but didn't you sacrifice yourself to save humanity?" He leaned in. "In what way are you *not* their savior?"

"I didn't want—" I rubbed my hand across my forehead. "I didn't do it for that—for them to *know*." I stared up at the ceiling, shaking my head. "I'm nobody's savior." My shoulders slumped. "I just did what had to be done."

Seconds of silence filled the room.

"The Senate may still be recouping from this loss," Heru finally said, "but do not, for one second, allow yourself to believe that this will be their final attempt to wipe humanity off the earth and claim it as their own." He inhaled deeply, then held the breath. "Humanity needs you to protect them once more." Slowly, he made his way toward me. "Show them your face. Let them believe." He placed a hand on my shoulder. "They need you, Kat. *We* need you. Please."

I bowed my head, honored, humbled, and outright stunned by the fact that Heru—high and mighty king of us all, Heru—had said please. To me.

I closed my eyes and took a deep breath. "Alright," I said, raising my head and meeting Heru's hawkish stare. "I'll do it."

CASSIE

"Cassie! Hurry up!" Melanie dragged Cassie through the crowd toward the stairs that led to the section where their seats were. The stadium was absolutely packed, with thousands of extra seats arranged down on the field where the Seahawks and Sounders usually played.

It wasn't that Cassie didn't want to be there. Like, for reals, what sane teenage girl wouldn't die to go to *the* concert of the century? None, that's who. Not even a tomboy like Cassie.

The Tarsi Tiff Survivors Tour was almost impossible to get tickets to—the fact that tickets were only open to CV survivors hardly made a dent in demand—and this *was* the kickoff concert . . . but Cassie was tired. Keeping the biggest secret in the history of pretty much everything was downright exhausting.

She wished, desperately, that she didn't have to hide that she knew exactly who the "Goddess" was, and that she was way cooler and amazing-er and more badass than anybody even knew. Not telling even her best friend, Melanie, was brutal.

"Hurry up, you goober," Melanie shouted over her shoulder. "I don't want to miss the opening song, and ohmygod did you look at the map online? Our seats are *killer*!"

Cassie rolled her eyes. She knew exactly how good their seats were. She got the tickets from her brother, who was good friends with the "Goddess"—a.k.a. Kat—and had an in with the one and only Tarsi Tiff through that mind-blowing connection. He was *also* Cassie and Melanie's escort and chaperone for the night. He'd dropped them off to park the car, with promises to join them at their seats soon enough.

"I have no idea how you scored these, but seriously—front row!" Melanie squealed. "I will be your slave for the rest of forever for sharing this *a*-mazing experience with me!"

Cassie laughed, unable to not be affected by Melanie's infectious joy.

Melanie guided Cassie onto the field and showed their tickets to the attendant.

The hulk of a dude raised his eyebrows and whistled. "Down to the front," he said, pointing toward the stage. "Your seats are in the front row, near the center."

"Eeeeeee!" Melanie squealed, hopping up and down on both feet. And then she was back to the dragging thing.

Once they were finally in their seats, Cassie started to get into the excitement. It was all around her; the place practically thrummed with it. And when Tarsi Tiff came out on stage, the crowd exploded, Cassie included.

"I'd like to welcome you all to the inaugural Survivors Concert!" Tarsi said as she took center stage, her voice booming all around Cassie.

The roar of the cheering crowd grew louder.

Tarsi held her mic up, and the sound of the crowd reverberated through the gazillions of speakers. It was so loud that Cassie had to cover her ears.

"Alright!" Tarsi yelled into the mic. "Alright, let's bring it down a notch . . . or ten!"

The crowd quieted, and after a few seconds, music kicked on, and Tarsi launched into her first song of the evening: "Girl of Stone." It was Cassie's all-time favorite song, and she lost herself to it, singing and swaying and crying. It was literally the best moment of her life. *Literally*.

Cassie's older brother, Garth, must've showed up at some point during the song, because he was sitting in the seat beside Cassie's when she finally came out of the song's spell.

Cassie threw her arms around her brother. "Thankyouthankyouthankyou!"

Garth's laugh was lost to the roar of the crowd, but she could feel him shake with it.

"Let's hear it for all of you *survivors*!" Tarsi said, and once again, the crowd went wild. After a few seconds, she made a quiet-down gesture with her hand, and the noise cut in half. "We've got an amazing show planned for tonight," she said, "but first, there's a very special person I'd like you all to meet." The enormous screen behind Tarsi showed a close-up of her face, but Cassie didn't need to look at the screen to see Tarsi's sassy wink—one that Cassie was pretty sure was aimed at her.

Cassie totally died a little bit in that moment.

"She's my aunt, sort of . . . or my cousin?" Tarsi laughed, and the crowd laughed with her. "Relationships are confusing in my family. Anyway, how about a big round of applause for our special guest!"

Of course, the crowd obeyed, clapping wildly, Cassie included.

The woman who walked out of the shadows and onto the stage was wearing jeans, combat boots, and a black leather jacket over a sweatshirt, the hood pulled up and her head bowed to hide her face.

The hush that fell over the crowd was almost instantaneous. There was no denying the resemblance of this woman's outfit to that of the Goddess, and everyone there knew it.

"Now this is *super* important," Tarsi said. "I need you all to stay in your seats. *Do not* rush the stage. This is for the safety of all of you. You've all survived so much, it would be tragic for anyone to get injured here tonight. I hate to play bad cop, but if you leave your seat, you'll be thrown out. Got it?"

There were *yes*es shouted and people nodding and murmurs of assent all around.

Cassie looked at Garth, her mouth hanging open. Was it really *her*?

"You're about to see history in the making, munchkin," he said, wrapping his arm around Cassie's shoulder and hugging her to his side. "Enjoy the ride."

Eyes opened wide, Cassie returned her attention to the stage. She wouldn't blink. She couldn't. She was too afraid of missing *any single thing*.

"I'd say I'd like you all to meet my Aunt Kat," Tarsi said, "but I think most of you have already met her."

The woman standing beside Tarsi raised her head and pushed her hood back, and the roar of the gasps that filled the stadium was almost as loud as the cheering had been. And then, once again, there was silence.

It was her—Kat. Her face filled the big screen behind her, and nobody who'd been visited by the Goddess during the miracle would be able to deny that this was her, standing on the stage before them. That she was *real*.

Cassie didn't think the crowd could be any more stunned. In a stadium full of thousands upon thousands of people, it was pin-drop silent.

Until Kat—the Goddess—started to glow.

People all around Cassie sat down. Many started crying, or reaching their hands out, like they might be able to touch Kat from their seats. Melanie took a step forward but stopped when Cassie grabbed her arm.

"Stay at your seat," Cassie whispered. "Remember?"

Melanie blinked, seeming to wake from a daze, then nodded.

Cassie had to remind herself that not everyone knew what she knew. That almost *nobody* knew what she knew.

"My name is Katarina Dubois," Kat said, walking closer to the edge of the stage, "and I am not a goddess." She stopped and scanned the crowd. "But I'm not human, either. I'm a member of an ancient species of immortals who have been living among you for thousands and thousands of years.

"We are called Nejerets."

The end

Thanks for reading! You've reached the end of *Underground*, the third book in the Kat Dubois Chronicles and the last book in this bundle. But don't worry! Kat's adventures continue in the second bundle, including *Soul Eater, Judgement,* and *Afterlife*.

Sign up for Lindsey Fairleigh's Newsletter to stay apprised of new releases and receive previews and other book-related announcements in your inbox.
www.lindseyfairleigh.com/join-newsletter

CAN'T GET ENOUGH?

Join Lindsey's mailing list to stay up to date on releases AND to get a FREE copy of *Sacrifice of the Sinners.*
www.lindseyfairleigh.com/sacrifice

www.lindseyfairleigh.com

Facebook: www.facebook.com/lindsey.fairleigh
Instagram: @authorlindseyfairleigh
Pinterest: www.pinterest.com/lindsfairleigh
Patreon: https://www.patreon.com/lindseyfairleigh

LOVE THE KAT DUBOIS CHRONICLES?

Reviews are always appreciated. They help readers find indie authors like me, which enables me to continue writing. Great places to post reviews:

Amazon
Goodreads

ALSO BY LINDSEY FAIRLEIGH

ECHO TRILOGY

Echo in Time

Resonance

Time Anomaly

Dissonance

Ricochet Through Time

KAT DUBOIS CHRONICLES

Ink Witch

Outcast

Underground

Soul Eater

Judgement

Afterlife

THE ENDING SERIES

The Ending Series Origin Stories

After The Ending

Into The Fire

Out Of The Ashes

Before The Dawn

World Before: A Collection of Stories

ATLANTIS LEGACY

Sacrifice of the Sinners

Legacy of the Lost

Fate of the Fallen

Dreams of the Damned

For more information on Lindsey and her books:

www.lindseyfairleigh.com

To read Lindsey's books as she writes them, check her out on Patreon:

https://www.patreon.com/lindseyfairleigh

Join Lindsey's mailing list to stay up to date on releases

AND to get a FREE copy of *Sacrifice of the Sinners.*

www.lindseyfairleigh.com/sacrifice

ABOUT THE AUTHOR

Lindsey Fairleigh is a bestselling Science Fiction and Fantasy author who lives her life with one foot in a book--as long as that book transports her to a magical world or bends the rules of science. Her novels, from Post-apocalyptic to Time Travel Romance, always offer up a hearty dose of unreality, along with plenty of history, mystery, adventure, and romance. When she's not working on her next novel, Lindsey spends her time walking around the foothills surrounding her home with her dogs, playing video games, and trying out new recipes on her husband. She lives in the Pacific Northwest with her family and their small pack of dogs and cats.

www.lindseyfairleigh.com
Facebook: www.facebook.com/lindsey.fairleigh
Instagram: @authorlindseyfairleigh
Pinterest: www.pinterest.com/lindsfairleigh
Newsletter: www.lindseyfairleigh.com/join-newsletter
Patreon: https://www.patreon.com/lindseyfairleigh

Printed in Great Britain
by Amazon

56032491R00359